Joss Wood loves books and traveling—especially to the wild places of Southern Africa and, well, anywhere. She's a wife, a mum to two teenagers and slave ... wo cats. After a career in local ... ...ow ... es full-time. Joss is a member of ... ... Writers of ...erica and Romance Writers of South Africa.

Sarah M. Anderson is happiest when writing. Her book *A Man of Privilege* won the 2012 RT Reviewers' Choice Best Book Award. *The Nanny Plan* won the 2016 RITA® Award for Contemporary Romance: Short.

Find out more about Sarah's conversations with imaginary cowboys and billionaires at sarahmanderson.com, and sign up for the new-release newsletter at eepurl.com/nv39b.

LONE STAR REUNION

JOSS WOOD

SEDUCTION ON HIS TERMS

SARAH M. ANDERSON

MILLS & BOON

First Published in Great Britain 2019
by Mills & Boon, an imprint of HarperCollinsPublishers,
1 London Bridge Street, London, SE1 9GF

Lone Star Reunion © 2019 Harlequin Books S.A.
Seduction on His Terms © 2019 Sarah M. Anderson

Special thanks and acknowledgement are given to Joss Wood for her contribution to the Texas Cattleman's Club: Bachelor Auction series.

ISBN: 978-0-263-27170-6

0219

MIX
Paper from
responsible sources
FSC™ C007454
FSC
www.fsc.org

This book is produced from independently certified FSC™ paper to ensure responsible forest management.

For more information visit: www.harpercollins.co.uk/green

Printed and bound in Spain
by CPI, Barcelona

LONE STAR REUNION

JOSS WOOD

Prologue

Over the decades many wedding receptions had been held at the Texas Cattleman's Club, and there had been a fair amount of scandals, for sure. Alexis Slade remembered talk of a groom being caught in a compromising position with the matron of honor, and a father of the groom passing out under a lavishly decorated bridal party table after streaking across the dance floor, wearing nothing more than a very lacy pink thong. There had been tearful brides, drunk brides, regretful brides and emotional brides, but Shelby Arthur was the first bride who hadn't made it to the altar.

The Goodman-Arthur wedding, or nonwedding, would undoubtedly be talked about for weeks on end. Alex looked across the still-crowded reception room and saw Reginald Goodman, father of the groom, with a tumbler of whiskey in his hand, looking pale but composed. Her eyes tracked left and there was the mother of the bride, a handkerchief clutched in her fist. Alex snorted at her wobbling lower lip, her crocodile tears. Daphne Goodman was a designer-dress-wearing barracuda who'd made no secret of the fact that she despised her son's fiancée and was totally against their marriage. Having been an object of Jared's affections in high school, Alex believed Shelby came to her senses just in time.

Marrying the spineless groom meant marrying his awful family—Brooke Goodman, Jared's sweet-natured sister, was the exception—and really, no woman deserved that. Marriage was tough enough without any added pressure from the in-laws. Jared and Shelby's marriage would've been a marriage of three, with Daphne Goodman calling the shots.

Alex turned when the door next to her right elbow opened and Rose Clayton walked into the reception area via the side entrance. Cool gray assessing eyes met hers and Alex reminded herself that she wasn't eighteen anymore, so the unofficial queen of the Texas Cattleman's Club should no longer intimidate her.

But she did.

Over that long summer ten years ago, Rose waged a war to separate her and Daniel, Rose's beloved grandson and heir. Gus, her own grandfather, had done the same. Because God and every Texan knew, family loyalty and a decades-old feud between Gus Slade and Rose Clayton trumped first love. At the time, she and Daniel had been the Romeo and Juliet of Royal, minus the death by poisoning.

Losing Daniel had felt like another death—she'd missed and mourned him that much. Alex remembered her tears, the desperation and loss she'd endured when Daniel refused to leave Royal with her so she could attend school out of state.

Daniel had said he belonged at The Silver C, but she disagreed, proclaiming they belonged together. They'd yelled; she'd cried. Daniel's stubbornness and intransigence, his unwillingness to choose her—*them*—ultimately killed their relationship.

Yes, they'd been young but, in his own unique way, he'd abandoned her. Unlike her parents, her childhood friend Gemma and, just last year, her beloved grandmother Sarah, Daniel had left her life through choice and not death.

And that somehow hurt more.

Rose approached her and a part of her still wanted to curl up in a ball when faced with Daniel's imperial grandmother. Annoyed with herself, Alex straightened her spine and managed a jerky nod. "Miss Rose."

"Alexis Slade."

Alex rolled her eyes when Rose turned her back on her and glided away, five foot something of sheer haughtiness and holier-than-thou poise. If not for their volatile history, she might even admire the woman for her steely self-assurance, her ability to carve out her rightful place in a world filled with take-charge alpha men.

But Rose was a Clayton and, as such, a sworn Slade enemy. Alex and her brother knew the basics of the Slade-Clayton feud: a half century ago, Gus, her grandfather, left Royal to make his fortune on the rodeo circuit, believing that Rose Clayton would wait for his return. He saved enough to buy a small spread next to the Clayton ranch and went to propose to Rose, excited to start his life with the woman he desperately loved. But Rose had married Ed the year before.

In doing so, Rose fired the first shot and war was declared.

Gus's marrying Rose's best friend—Alex's beloved grandmother Sarah—just escalated the conflict. And her grandfather buying up more portions of the once-mighty Clayton ranch was a nuclear strike. Families took their feuds seriously in Texas, and although sides were most certainly chosen, the Texas Cattleman's Club remained the demilitarized zone.

The Slades and Claytons, both old and young, were all members, and here within these walls, they had to play nice. Or when that wasn't feasible, they opted to ignore each other as much as possible. Just like Gus was ignoring Rose, and Alexis was ignoring Daniel, which was, annoyingly, very damn hard to do.

What woman with a pulse could? Surrendering to temptation, Alex looked toward the bar…and at the devastatingly handsome man who she'd once considered to be the love of her life. She drank in every inch of him. The black curls he hated—but she loved—and those mysterious dark brown eyes he'd inherited—everyone presumed—from his father, because his mother was light skinned with blue eyes. Boring brown, Daniel had once called them, but Alex vehemently disagreed. They could be as rich as expensive coffee, as deep as the night. However, they could also turn as hard as ship-destroying rocks on a jagged, inhospitable coastline.

So much had changed over the years, Alex mused with a wistful sigh. Her once-gangly boyfriend was now taller, broader, every inch a man. He was still lean but with hard muscles and a harder streak. Strong stubble covered his jaw and he looked as good in a tuxedo as he did in worn jeans, but neither was his sexiest look.

A naked Daniel Clayton, as she'd discovered when she was younger, could easily be classified as one of the wonders of the world.

In the past decade, her ex had done quite well for himself. He'd acquired degrees in both agriculture and business, and all the hard work he put into The Silver C had, judging by his designer tuxedo and the German sports car he occasionally drove, paid off. He was smart, wealthy and good-looking, and that trifecta made him one of the most sought-after bachelors in the area. Hell, possibly even the state. Although he hadn't brought a date to this wedding, Daniel Clayton was never, so she'd heard, short of a female companion.

In bed or out of it.

A hand on her arm pulled her eyes off her former lover and she smiled at Rachel Kincaid, her closest friend. Alex didn't make friends easily, but Rachel was someone who'd sneaked under her defenses.

"Why are you standing here by yourself?" her friend asked, handing her a glass of champagne.

"Trying to avoid another conversation about Shelby or what I think of the new president of the TCC," Alex admitted, taking the glass with a grateful smile.

"James Harris is a great guy."

Alex nodded. "I like him, too." She glanced at the tall African American man standing next to the right of them, talking to Rose Clayton. "And, oh my God, he's seriously hot."

In fact, there were many drop-dead gorgeous men in this room, most of them members of the TCC. She knew why she was single—chronic commitment and abandonment issues—but that didn't mean she had to be celibate. Yet she was.

"You keep looking at Daniel Clayton," Rachel remarked. "Not that I blame you. I swear he was birthed by an angel."

An unfortunate choice of words, Alex thought wryly, since Daniel's mom was reputed to be anything but celestial. Daniel never spoke about Stephanie but there were enough gossips in Royal to ascertain a little of what his life with his tempestuous and unstable mother had been like. According to the grapevine, Rose had been the only responsible adult in his life. His loyalty to his grandmother was rock-solid and unshakable.

Their romance had been doomed from the start. Because, as it turned out, Alex had never been able to compete with Rose and Daniel's fierce allegiance to The Silver C ranch.

"Matt Galloway is just as good-looking," Alex commented, partly to be perverse but also to distract Rachel from linking her and Daniel together. There was no "her and Daniel," and there hadn't been in a long, long time. And she wasn't lying, Matt Galloway was a young Clooney: as good-looking, as rich and charming, and as much of a reputed playboy as George used to be.

"He is—was—Billy's best friend." Alex wasn't sure what Matt's looks had to do with him being Rachel's dead husband's friend, but she was familiar with the don't-go-there look on Rachel's face, since it was an expression she often used. Alex liked her own privacy, so she didn't push Rachel.

Rachel wound her arm around Alex's waist and squeezed. "Have I said thank you lately for letting me stay with you at the Lone Wolf Ranch?"

"We love having you and baby Ellie there," Alex responded.

"And I don't take it personally that you frequently run away to Sarah's tree house."

"That's more to avoid Gus's lectures about finding a husband and giving him a great-grandchild than avoiding you, as you well know. Gus is determined to get me bound and breeding. I, on the other hand, need to think about getting back to Houston, to my life there. I came home to be with Grandma Sarah in her last days, but I'm still here, a year after her death. Royal was only meant to be a stopgap. My life isn't here."

"Sure looks like it is," Rachel commented. "As a digital-media strategist, you can work anywhere in the world, and you love the ranch, spending time with Gus."

Of course she did, but being with Gus and working part-time as the Lone Wolf's business manager didn't stop her from missing her grandmother with an intensity that still threatened to drop her to her knees. It didn't stop her from wallowing in the past, from remembering how happy she and Daniel had once been before she learned that love didn't conquer all.

Alex sucked in her breath when his eyes slammed into hers and, as always, she felt caressed by the light of a million stars. Electric tingles skittered across her skin, tightened her nipples, sent heat to that place between her legs. This was just red-hot, carnal lust, and nothing, she silently insisted, like what they'd experienced so long ago.

Back then, they'd been constantly drunk. On love, on each other. They'd hurtled headfirst into love and sex and passion, blithely thinking they could handle the thousand-degree fire they'd created, stoked and fed. Pfft. She'd emerged with third-degree burns. But the worst part? Alex still found Daniel physically intoxicating. And judging by the unbanked desire flashing in his eyes, she made him feel equally off balance.

Good. He deserved nothing less.

Rachel accepted a dance from Gus, old flirt that he was, and Alex, wanting fresh air, slipped out the side door. She inhaled the cool, fragrant night air and wrapped her arms around her waist as she walked toward the gardens surrounding the TCC. In daylight it was immediately apparent that the surrounding grounds, flower beds and paths that meandered through the once-glorious garden needed some updating and attention. But at night the gardens were mysterious and welcoming, an old friend. She remembered playing hide-and-seek in these gardens with her brother and her friends, sneaking down to the small pond to steal a kiss from Daniel Clayton, away from their eagle-eyed grandparents.

Fun times, Alex thought with a bittersweet pang.

She heard the crunch of boots on the gravel path, and then a jacket covered her bare shoulders. She inhaled his familiar scent—sandalwood and leather, wood and wildness. Big, manly hands settled on her shoulders and she instinctively leaned back, her head resting against his collarbone, his warm breath on her ear.

Suddenly she was eighteen again. Daniel had his hands on her…and all was right with her world.

"Lexi." Daniel's deep voice rumbled over her skin, as deep and dark as the night.

Alex knew that she should run away. But she was so tired of tamping down her fantasies of what it would be like to have Daniel naked and in her bed. Of dreaming how he would make love. Teenage Daniel had been hesitant, cautious, but adult Daniel would possess her the same way he did everything else, with confidence and raw virility.

And she wanted him. God, how she wanted him!

Alex sighed as his hand brazenly moved over her shoulder, down her chest, to slide under the lapel of his jacket and cup her breast. His thumb swiped her nipple as he pulled her earlobe between his teeth, gently nibbling.

"Still so sexy, Lexi. Love what you are wearing."

She couldn't remember what she'd put on so she glanced down... Right, a loose, off-the-shoulder black top with a full, flower-patterned pale pink skirt.

Alex knew she should push him away, but instead of being sensible, she placed her hand behind her back, her fingers seeking out his erection. There it was, hard and long and thick, and she heard his low, guttural moan as his cock jerked beneath her touch. Then she was making whimpering sounds of her own as his hand pushed aside the fabric of her top so that he could feel her naked flesh and pull her tight nipple between his fingers.

She lifted her head up and to the side, and then his mouth was on hers. Parting her lips to receive his tongue, she moaned her frustration when he smiled against her mouth, silently telling her that he enjoyed teasing her, making her wait. He'd always been more patient, more interested in drawing out every moment of their pleasure.

Daniel's chaste kisses were in direct contrast to his roaming hands. He bunched the fabric of her skirt and pulled it up her legs, and his fingers trailed up her thighs, played with the tiny V shape of her panties. Alex felt him shudder when he discovered her panties were only comprised of one triangle and a few thin cords.

"Naughty underwear, Miss Slade," Daniel growled against her mouth.

"Shut up and touch me, Clayton," Alex demanded, spinning around and slapping her hands on his cotton-covered chest. Ignoring his loose tie and open collar, she gripped his shirt and yanked it from his pants, desperate to find hot, sexy, olive-toned skin. Her fingers danced across a set of impressive washboard abs, and she pushed her fingers between that hard stomach and the band of his pants, seeking and finding the tip of his erection. Daniel released a low hiss, sucked in his stomach and suddenly she had more of him against her fingers, hot and oh-so potent.

"I want you, Lex," Daniel muttered, smacking her bare butt cheek and pulling her into him, squashing her hand between her body and his erection. Needing more, needing everything—she'd missed him, missed this so much—Alex lifted her thigh and wrapped it over his hip, grateful to yoga for making her supple. Then nothing but fabric separated her core from his shaft, and she rocked her hips and lifted her mouth up to his to be kissed.

This time he didn't hold back and his tongue swept between her parted lips, branding, rediscovering, wiping away any doubts that reliving the past was foolish and dangerous.

There was only Daniel, his taste and heat and power, the adult version of the boy she'd known so long ago. Standing in his arms, panting and with soaked panties, her only thoughts were of how much she'd missed his touch, missed his kisses. In this moment they didn't have feuding grandparents, unforgivable betrayals or hurt and pain between them. There was only desire— hot, potent and demanding.

Daniel wrenched his mouth off hers, and in the moonlight his eyes, normally so shuttered, were as deep and dark as a desert night. "Come home with me, Lex."

She had to be rational…and she couldn't be, not when she had her hand in his pants. She couldn't think, breathe. Alex pulled her hand from between their bodies and tried to step back, but Daniel's hands on her hips kept her up close and very personal. "Dan, don't ask me that."

"Why? Because you are scared you're going to say yes?"

It was a typical no-frills Daniel response. He never beat around the bush, and although he was the strong and silent type, when he did speak, people listened. Her ex just had a way of cutting through BS to get to the heart of the matter, and as per usual, he was right. She was terrified that she was going to say yes, but even more scared that she was going to force herself to say no.

"I've been watching you all evening and you've been watching me, too," Daniel murmured, lifting his hand to trace patterns on her jaw. "We've both been wondering what it would feel like to be together again. Especially now that we're older, more experienced…confident in how to satisfy one another in bed."

She was sexually confident? Oh, she was anything but. She might be older and wiser, but she was still more girl next door than femme fatale.

"Come home with me, Lex. Let me peel that ridiculously sexy dress from your gorgeous body and replace it with my lips and hands. I'll make it good for you, I promise."

He'd make it *too* good, and yeah, that worried her. "Daniel, this is *madness*."

"So let's be mad, just for a night. In the morning we can go back to being a Clayton and a Slade, opposing forces in this long, futile war that we never started."

Alex closed her eyes and shook her head. She wanted him but she didn't like wanting him, found herself wishing instead that she could put him in the past, where he belonged. Maybe she *did* need to sleep with him again to flush him out of her system. After all, reality was never as good as fantasy, and then they could both finally move on.

"So, yes or no?"

Alex thought she saw apprehension in his eyes, the fear that she'd reject him, but the emotions flashed across his features too quickly for her to be sure. "Yeah, I'm coming with you."

Daniel stared down at her, his handsome face serious. "Your place or mine?"

Alex thought about their options, knowing that the ranch house at the Lone Wolf was out of the question and, as she'd heard, Daniel had converted an old barn on The Silver C. While his house was a better option than Gus's mansion—Daniel might be met with the working end of her grandpa's shotgun if they were caught—their chances of discovery were still too high.

Which left only one other place available to them…

"Sarah's tree house."

Daniel's hand tightened on her hip and she knew that he was remembering, just as she was.

A long time ago, the tree house had been a boys' fort and a girls' secret club. It had held sleep outs and camping trips and overnight sleepovers. Much later it had been the place where Daniel took her virginity, where they'd spent stolen afternoons and blissful starry nights.

"You remember where it is, right?"

Daniel rubbed his jaw. "Of course I can find it. I just haven't been there since…"

You left, Alex filled in the words for him. The tree house was deep in Slade land and Daniel had no reason or wish to be on Slade land. Land that had once been part of The Silver C spread.

The river-fronted land was one of the first parcels of land Gus bought from Rose when times had got tough, and Alex knew that Daniel mourned the loss of the property. The Silver C had once been the largest spread in four counties, but it was now on par with the Lone Wolf in acreage, a bit of a comedown for the once-mighty Claytons.

"I'll meet you at the tree house," Daniel said, his voice clipped. He lifted his wrist to look at his expensive watch. "In half an hour?" He rubbed his hand over his jaw and shook his head. "I can't believe that I am risking getting splinters in my butt to have you again. Nobody but you, Alex Slade, would tempt me to do this…"

His words shouldn't make her smile but they did. She opened her mouth to explain that the tree house wasn't as bad as it had been… No, she'd let it be a surprise.

"Are you going to walk there?" Daniel asked.

In moonlight or bright sunshine, she always walked to the tree house. "Yes."

"I'm going to go home, pick up my dirt bike and I'll be there as soon as I can," Daniel told her, his eyes steady on her face.

Good, that gave her some time to think about what she was doing, to talk herself out of this madness.

Daniel narrowed his gaze. "Do *not* stand me up, Alexis."

Although it unnerved her how he'd been able to read her thoughts, she couldn't suppress the shiver of excitement that tap-danced up and down her spine. He was gorgeous and determined and he wanted her.

No, she wouldn't stand him up. She couldn't; she wanted this, wanted *him*. "I'll be there."

Daniel nodded, swiped his mouth across hers in a brief but molten-lava-hot kiss. "See that you are."

One

Mid-November

Daniel Clayton released a low curse and buried his head in the soft pillow, cursing his early-morning alarm. Unfortunately, neither cattle nor his ranch hands cared that he'd spent most of the night making love, that he'd had minimal sleep. The Silver C Ranch and his grandmother demanded a daily pound of flesh and since he didn't tolerate excuses or less than 100 percent effort, he knew he should haul his ass out of bed and get to it. He rolled over and pressed his chest to Lexi's back, filling his hand with her perfect, perfect breast. Daniel skimmed his thumb across her nipple and buried his nose in her fragrant hair. Best way to wake up, bar none. His rock-hard erection pushed into her bottom and he skated his hand down her torso, across her stomach, and his fingers flirted with the V shape below. There was nothing like sleepy, lazy sex… His cell phone alarm screeched again.

"Dammit, Clayton," Lex muttered, reaching across him to grab his phone. Mercifully, the strident alarm ceased, and despite wanting Lexi again, Daniel found himself drifting back to sleep. Then Alex's sharp elbow dug into his ribs and he rolled over, frowning.

"What was that for?"

"Sun's up in forty-five minutes, and we both have to leave," Alex told him, whipping off the covers and exposing his naked body to the chilly morning air.

The tree house was heated by a woodstove, which they didn't bother to light because a stream of smoke from the chimney would raise questions—questions neither of them wanted to answer. As it was, he'd already endured a few lectures from Rose, demanding to know the status of his love life. He'd blown her off, as usual, but then she'd upped the ante by expressing her fervent hope that he'd meet a lovely girl through the upcoming bachelor auction—as if!—and that she would be bitterly disappointed if she found out that he was carrying on with "that Slade girl."

Since that Slade girl was currently standing naked by the window, long blond hair tumbling down her oh-so-sexy back, he didn't give a rat's ass what his grandmother or anyone else thought. They'd been hooking up for six weeks—maybe a week or so more—and he'd enjoyed every second he'd spent with Alex. But what they shared was sex and desire and heat and want and nothing his grandmother needed to worry about.

He loved his grandmother—he did—but he just wished she'd stay out of his damn business. Alex, what they had together, was separate from The Silver C— one didn't impact the other. For a decade his entire focus had been on the family spread, trying to restore the somewhat tarnished reputation of the Clayton clan. While Rose held the respect of the residents of the town of Royal and the counties of Maverick and Colonial, his late grandfather, Ed, and his mother, Stephanie, did not. One was a bastard and the other was irresponsible, wild and borderline psycho. Despite his dubious parentage, he'd worked hard to command a little of the respect his grandmother did.

And he thought he was getting there.

While not nearly as big as it had been in its heyday, The Silver C was now regarded as being one of the best-managed spreads in the country, lauded for its breeding program and producing award-winning bulls. He had a waiting list as long as his arm for buyers wanting to purchase his quarter horses, and he ran the entire ranching operation with the utmost professionalism and integrity. And by doing so, he'd recently been inducted as a member of the Texas Cattleman's Club.

Daniel sat up, rested his forearms on his thighs and shoved his hands through his hair before running his palm over his stubble-covered jaw. He watched as Alex picked up a sweatshirt—one of his—and frowned when the voluminous fabric covered her to midthigh. She then pulled her hair out from under the band of the garment and gathered it into a messy knot on top of her head, and he thought that he'd never seen anyone so naturally beautiful, so effortlessly sexy.

"I'm going to make coffee. Do you have time for a cup?"

Daniel glanced at his watch and nodded. "Yeah, I do. Thanks."

He watched Alex leave the room, her hips swaying seductively as she did so. She'd been pretty as a teenager but she was spectacular as a grown woman. Blue eyes the color of the summer sky, high cheekbones and that luscious, made-to-kiss mouth. Yards and yards of fragrant, wavy hair. And… God, that body…lean and slender, finely boned but with curves and dips and flares that made his mouth water.

At eighteen he'd thought he'd loved her, but now, ten years later, he knew that he'd been blinded by lust, had confused love with desire. He didn't believe in romantic love and Daniel sometimes wondered if he ever, deep down, really had. God knew he hadn't been exposed to any marital, or even family, harmony growing up.

He was the unwanted son of Rose's daughter, who had also been raised in a tense household. There had been little love between Rose and his maternal grandfather, and his mother, Stephanie, wasn't able to love anyone but herself. He'd been the unwanted result of one of Stephanie's many bad decisions when it came to men.

Daniel had no idea who his father was and one of Stephanie's favorite games had been to play "Who's Your Daddy?" She'd thrown out names to tease, later telling him that she'd made up names and occupations to amuse herself. It was cold comfort that Stephanie had also played Rose like a fiddle, using him as her bow.

Thanks to his dysfunctional childhood, he was cynical about love. But he did believe in family, in loyalty, in hard work and respect—Rose had shown him the value of those traits, in both word and deed. She'd never lied to him, not even during those worst times, when Stephanie was crazier than a wet hen.

So when his grandmother expressed her reservations about his teenage romance with Alex, calmly pointing out that he'd be throwing away his future at the ranch to follow a girl he *thought* he might love, he'd eventually listened to her advice. And why wouldn't he? She was the one stable adult in his life, the only person he'd ever felt was looking after his best interests.

And yeah, after emotionally and physically divorcing himself from his mother, he vowed that he'd never let anyone emotionally blackmail him again.

Shaking off his disturbing thoughts, Daniel stood up, strode to the small bathroom next to the only bedroom and used the facilities. He returned to the master suite, smiling as he remembered how surprised he'd been when he'd first laid eyes on this renovated tree house.

Gone was the rickety structure from before. Now a sleek, beautifully designed house rested in the massive cypress trees overlooking the river that meandered its way through both The Silver C and the Lone Wolf ranches. Instead of a one-room platform, the tree house consisted of a master bedroom, a sleeping loft above the main living space, this tiny bathroom and a small kitchenette. The abundance of windows and a sliding glass wall allowed for amazing views of the river and Lone Wolf land. He wished he could lie on the sprawling deck, beer in his hand, Stetson over his face, soaking up some winter rays. But there was work to do, and the needs of The Silver C Ranch always came first.

Hearing Alex walking up the stairs to the bedroom, he stepped into his jeans and pulled on his shirt, then his fleece-lined leather jacket. Sitting down on the edge of the bed, he reached for his socks and boots, lifting his head as Alex appeared in the doorway. He took the cup of coffee she held out—hot and black—and sipped gratefully. Another three of these and he might feel vaguely human.

She sat down on the bed next to him, scooted backward and crossed her legs. "Dan…"

There was something odd in the way she said his name, so he whipped his head around to look at her, his eyes narrowing at the frown pulling her arched eyebrows together. "Yeah?"

Alex cradled her mug in both hands and he saw the tremble in her fingers, the way the rim of the cup vibrated. Oh crap, this wasn't good. He removed the cup from her fingers, placed it on the wooden bedside table and turned back to face her. "What's wrong, Lex?"

"Has Rose been giving you grief about me?"

He really didn't want to have this conversation now, didn't have the time for it. "Yeah. She asked me whether we were seeing each other, told me that she wouldn't be happy if I was."

Alex sighed. "I got a similar lecture from Gus, telling me how it would break his heart if he found out we were together." Alex looked miserable and Daniel could relate. Neither of them liked disappointing their grandparents.

"Gus is trying to set me up with guys who are taking part in the bachelor auction."

"That damned auction," Daniel growled, the thought of being sold like a steer raising his blood pressure. Then, to add insult to injury, he would have to pay for the date with the woman who'd paid to spend time with him. Why couldn't he just write a check to cover the costs of the date? Hell, he'd double, even triple, the amount if he could get out of going on a stupid date with someone not of his choosing.

"That *damned* auction is going to raise an awesome amount of money for the Pancreatic Cancer Foundation." Daniel saw the blue fire in Alex's eyes and reminded himself that the charity auction was her pet project. Her beloved grandmother Sarah had died from the disease, and as it was a cause that was near and dear to her heart, Lex had committed herself to raising funds to find a cure.

"I'll be glad when it's over," Alex said. "A few more sleeps and counting. Roll on Saturday and then Gus can stop throwing me into the arms of any man with a pulse."

The thought of Alexis being in another man's arms was enough to have him grinding his teeth together. Daniel reminded himself that he had no right to feel jealous, but the enamel still flew off his teeth. Reaching across him to pick up her cup of coffee, her hair brushed his face and he inhaled her lavender-and-wild-flower scent. He immediately felt himself grow hard, and as much as it pained him, he told himself to stand down.

"If I don't leave soon, Lex, I'm going to be late. What's on your mind?"

Alex sipped, sighed and sipped again, before finally getting to the point. "I…um…think we should put this on hold, at least for a while."

"*This* meaning us?"

Alex nodded. "I've got a lot on my mind, so much to do, and while this has been fun, it's taking time and energy I don't currently have."

Daniel felt the prick—hell, stab!—of dismay and pushed the pain away. Sure, he hadn't expected this to last forever, but damn, he and Lex were good together. They enjoyed each other, knew exactly how to make each other writhe and squirm and scream. It would be a good long while, Daniel admitted, before he could even *think* about sleeping with someone else.

Because Alexis—warm and wonderful—was truly one of a kind.

Alex looked like she was waiting for an answer, so he shrugged and uttered the only word he could wrap his tongue around. "Okay."

Disappointment flashed in her eyes. At his one-syllable answer or because he wasn't arguing for them to carry on?

"I'd also like to tell our grandparents that we are wise to them trying to set us up with other people, that they can't interfere in our love lives," Alex stated, her voice determined.

"You want to tackle them together? In the same room?" Daniel heard the skepticism in his voice. "Would Royal survive the fallout?"

"I think it would have more impact," Alex stubbornly replied.

"They've avoided each other for five decades, Lex. You're not going to get them in the same room, at the same time." This feud was exhausting but it wasn't theirs to fight. Gus and Rose had decades of tumultuous history to work through, and Daniel wasn't fool enough to get sucked up in that craziness.

Besides, he had bigger things to deal with, like Alex cutting him off. He didn't want this to end… "You sure this is what you want to do, Lex?"

Alex lifted her shoulders, dropped them and released a long-suffering sigh. "I'm tired of the lectures, the disapproving looks from Gus. I'm tired of sneaking around. I need more sleep and I have a couple of personal decisions I need to make. You're a…complication."

A complication, huh? "It's just sex, Alex."

Was that reminder directed at her or himself?

Annoyance glimmered in Lexi's gorgeous blue

eyes. "Of course it is, but since it's sapping my time and energy, it needs to stop." She looked away from him, shrugged before dragging her eyes back to his. "Maybe once the auction is over, after the holidays, if I'm around, we could maybe pick things up again."

So many maybes, Daniel thought, pulling on his boot. *Wait, what did she say?* "You said, *if* you're around? Are you thinking of leaving?"

Another thought to cool his head. He definitely wasn't getting enough sleep!

"I've had a job offer that might take me back to Houston," Alex said. "I've stayed in Royal longer than I thought I would. My plan was always to return there."

"What's the offer?" Daniel asked, standing up and tucking his shirt into his jeans.

"Managing partner in a social media strategy firm. It's a good offer. I've always wanted to be my own boss."

He quirked a brow. "Isn't that what you are here on the ranch?"

"Gus is still the boss, Dan," she reminded him. "And while I can run the finances, I'm not a rancher. In Royal, everything has a memory associated with it. My parents, Sarah…"

He heard her unsaid *you* and could almost taste the emotion in her voice. They'd both had hard childhoods, had been knocked around by life, but he knew that losing her parents as a little girl had rocked her world. And then to lose Sarah, on top of all that, had truly devastated her. "I am sorry, Lex. Sorry for you, for Gus."

Alex managed a wobbly smile. "Thanks, I appreciate it." Standing up, she placed her hand on his chest, and Daniel felt his heart rate kick up, his throat tightening. Alex just had to touch him and the thoughts of stripping their clothes off and taking her again were front and center. He forcibly held himself still as Alex stood up on her pretty painted toes to kiss the side of his mouth. "Thanks for this, Dan. It was fun. And maybe it exorcised some ghosts."

Yeah, but maybe it also, Daniel couldn't help thinking, *created a whole bunch more.*

She'd said goodbye to him as a teenager but watching him walk away as an adult was surprisingly a great deal harder than she'd imagined it would be. She'd been madly in love with him then, but she wasn't in love with him now, so... Why on earth was she so upset?

You have to let him go. There is no other option. This is not a situation where you can have the cowboy and ride him, as well.

But she still couldn't keep her eyes off him as he strode toward his dirt bike. Sighing appreciatively, she watched as he threw a long, muscular leg over the saddle and gripped the handlebars, dark curls shining in the early-morning light. Man, he was gorgeous, a perfect combination of Anglo and Hispanic. Olive skin, black hair, those smoldering brown eyes and that lean, powerful physique.

Alex leaned her forearms on the railing of the deck and watched her lover—no, her *ex-lover*—ride away, ignoring her wildly beating heart. There was no denying that this man had the ability to liquefy her insides, to shut down her thought processes, to invade her thoughts. But he'd also broken her heart, and she'd never give him the power to do that again.

She'd noticed that Daniel was starting to sneak under her skin, that her thoughts went to him at inopportune times—like every ten seconds—and this morning, while making coffee, she'd thought about asking him whether he wanted to attend a country music concert in Joplin with her the following week. They could stay in a bed-and-breakfast, try out that new restaurant she'd heard was fabulous...

Shocked at her thoughts, she'd given herself a mental slap. Daniel wasn't someone to make plans around, to date, to spend time with. If she was starting to think of him as a potential partner and not just as a fun, sexy hookup, then it was time to cut him loose.

So she did.

When the sound of Dan's bike faded away, Alex walked back into the bedroom and sat on the edge of the bed, staring at the expensive Persian carpet beneath her feet. *Only in Texas would you find an exquisite Persian carpet on the floor of a very upscale tree house*, Alex thought. Only her grandmother Sarah would put it there. Damn, she still missed her. But Sarah, like her parents, was gone, and Alex couldn't help feeling that the people who loved her the most tended to leave her...

Intellectually, Alex understood that death was a part of life, that people died and hearts got broken. Tough times came along to make one stronger, that everything was a lesson...blah, blah, blah.

But losing her parents and her beloved grandmother long before they were supposed to go was just damn unfair. It was like some bored god was using her heart as a football.

Daniel had left her, too, but his desertion had strangely hurt the most. It was his choice to leave her and it was obvious, even so many years later, that she'd loved Daniel so much more than he loved her...

Alex flopped back onto the bed and placed her arm over her eyes. And that was why she'd cut him loose today: she couldn't—wouldn't—put herself in the position of being left brokenhearted again.

Wanting to stop wallowing, she started to make a mental list of everything she had to do today. Getting together with Rachel to plan Tessa's makeover was high on her list. As the only bachelorette up for auction, they were going to make her the star of the show. Not that Tess needed much help—the girl was stunningly beautiful, both inside and out.

And as the master of the ceremonies, she had to plan her introductions, find some funny jokes to keep the audience entertained. She also had to psych herself into selling Daniel, the only man she'd seen naked in the longest time, to some woman with a healthy bank account. That was going to be so much fun.

Not.

Alex felt nausea climb up her throat. Really, she was being ridiculous, having a physical reaction to auctioning off Daniel. Yes, sure, the idea of sending her former flame off on a date with another woman wasn't a pleasant prospect, but they'd just shared their bodies, not their hearts and souls. She had no hold on him—she didn't *want* a damned hold on him, and that was why she'd severed their connection! She was being utterly asinine by allowing her emotions to rule her head, and this behavior was unworthy of a Slade.

But still, the nausea wouldn't subside and Alex cursed herself as she bolted for the bathroom and made her acquaintance with the toilet bowl.

Two

Late November

Alex stared down at the long list attached to her clip-board, wondering if she would survive this crazy day. And what had she been thinking, agreeing to be the emcee for The Great Royal Bachelor Auction? It was one thing being the master—mistress?—of ceremonies at friends' weddings and birthday parties, but this auction was a major social event.

What she'd thought would be a small local fund-raiser had morphed into something a great deal bigger and was attracting press attention from media outlets in both Austin and Dallas. The tickets to the function had sold out within a day or two, but the loud demands from wealthy single women from the two cities and the neighboring town of Joplin forced her and Rachel to upscale the event, adding another five tables to the already crowded TCC function room.

Who would've thought that this small-town auction for their eligible bachelors would've generated so much buzz? Alex flicked through the program, looking at the faces of her bachelors and lone bachelorette. Who was she kidding? If was the perfect opportunity for wealthy singles with money to burn to buy themselves a hot date. Good, because she intended to make them pay mightily for the privilege.

Alex glanced at her watch, saw that it was just past four and looked down at her messy list. The tables were set, and the flower arrangements had arrived and looked superb. The band was doing a sound check and she heard the haunting sounds of a saxophone drifting from the ballroom to this anteroom that would host the bachelors as they were waiting for their turns to be auctioned. Alex walked over to the fridge, yanked open the door and was relieved to see the bottles of beer that would be needed to calm nervous dispositions. She smiled. Her bachelors were successful businessmen, alpha men every one of them, but every time they were reminded that they'd have to stand in the spotlight and be auctioned off like prize bulls, they all looked terrified.

Hearing the door to the greenroom open, she shut the fridge door and turned to see waiters from the Royal Diner entering the room, carrying platters of food. As she well knew, nothing short of a nuclear holocaust would stop her cowboys from eating.

"Hey, guys." Alex indicated the table where she wanted the platters to be placed. "Those look amazing. What did Amanda send over?"

"The Royal Diner's famous ribs, sliders, quiches. Doughnut and choc chip cookies for dessert."

"Please thank Amanda again for her generous donation. The guys and Tessa will appreciate it." Alex dug in her pocket to pull out a tip. She waved away their thanks, and when she was alone, she placed her clipboard between two of the platters and ran through her list again.

Flowers. Check.

Band. Check.

Food. Check.

Test sound system. That was currently happening.

Tessa's makeover. Alex checked her watch again. She'd allocated forty-five minutes for her and Rachel to give Tessa a makeover. Well, to be honest, to hold Tess's hand while the professionals she and Rachel hired did Tess's hair and makeup. Tess was going to rock the house tonight. Alex smiled. Girl power was a marvelous thing.

Tess reminded Alex of Gemma—she was as humble, as sweet and unaware of her good looks as Gemma had been. Alex pushed her fist into her sternum, thinking of her redheaded, emerald-eyed friend, a band of freckles across her nose. Sixteen years had passed since Gemma's death, but there were times, just like today, when she felt that Gemma was just waiting for her to call, like she was around the corner, about to stride back into her life.

She still missed her best friend; sometimes it felt like she'd lost her a few weeks back instead of so long ago. But grief, as she learned, had no respect for time. She'd lost her parents at ten, her best friend at twelve and Sarah just a year ago. She remembered her parents as well as she did Sarah. And Gemma as well as she remembered Sarah.

She'd heard that memories fade, that lost ones become indistinct. It had yet to happen to her. She could be doing something mundane and she'd hear Gemma's laugh, Sarah's voice or smell her mom's scent, and grief would slam into her, stopping her in her tracks.

When the pain subsided, just a little, she was left feeling abandoned, so damn alone. She was able to wrangle grief back into its cage, but those other feelings always lingered, casually snacking on her soul.

Could anyone blame her for pushing people away? She loved hard and she loved deep, giving all that she had. Sometime in the future, hopefully a long time from now, she'd have to face losing her grandfather Gus. Losing him, she hoped, would be easier than losing her parents, Gemma and Sarah. They'd all died way before their times, but hopefully her healthy and fit grandfather would live until he was a hundred and slip off in his sleep after a life well lived. She could live with that—it was the circle of life—and unlike before, she wouldn't feel abandoned.

Alex flipped the program over and traced Daniel's gorgeous face with the tip of her finger. Although she was right to put some distance between them, she still ached for him for him with every fiber of her being. Warmth pooled through her as she remembered the way he kissed her, the way his clever hands would stroke her body, the rasp of his stubble, the play of hard muscles under her hands.

The growl of his voice against her mouth, painting her skin with sinfully sexy words…

Tonight is all about making you weep as I pleasure you…

Just feeling your eyes on me makes me so hard.

You're going to pass out from satisfaction…

Daniel was a master of the art of talking dirty, using words and phrases that upped the sexy factor by 1000 percent. Then he lived up to his words with his skillful touch and used his mouth like a Jedi Master.

She missed him…

No, her body missed him. Her body missed him a whole bunch…

But stepping away from Daniel had been a wise move and one she'd make again. Her self-protection instinct had been carefully, meticulously honed and was now scalpel sharp. Nobody would slice and dice her again.

Alex shoved the program under the rest of her papers and straightened. Returning to her list, she lifted the plastic cover off the nearest platter and reached for a doughnut. She groaned as the treat touched her tongue, sighing at the prefect combination of fat and sugar.

God, so good. Alex chewed, swallowed and chewed again, polishing off the doughnut in three bites. She reached for another and it was halfway to her mouth when she heard a horrified gasp from the doorway.

"What the hell are you doing, Slade?" Rachel demanded, hands on her slim hips, brown eyes narrowed.

Alex pulled off a piece and chewed. Swallowing, she lifted her eyebrows at the astonished look on Rachel's face. What was her problem? "Um, eating a doughnut? Freshly made, courtesy of Amanda Battle."

"Actually, Jillian from the pie shop made them, but that's neither here nor there." Rachel stepped into the room and closed the door behind her. "Why are you eating them?"

Was that a trick question? "Because they are good?"

Rachel scratched her forehead, still looking confused. "Alex, I haven't seen you eat sugar in four years. You don't eat junk food, *ever.*"

Alex looked at the doughnut in her hand, puzzled.

Rachel was right, she never ate junk food and very infrequently ate carbs. So why on earth was she eating one now? And, knowing that, why was she unable to throw it in the trash?

Alex popped the last of the doughnut into her mouth and contemplated her actions. Was she finally losing it? Was the stress of organizing the bachelor auction, breaking up with Daniel and trying to work through the job offer she'd had from Houston finally getting to her?

"Alex, are you okay?"

"It's just a doughnut, Rach. Okay, two little doughnuts," Alex retorted. Then she reached for a paper napkin and wiped the powdered sugar off her fingers. "My sugar levels are probably low. I just needed a boost."

"I'd believe that if I didn't see the way you refused coffee this morning, wrinkling your nose at the smell. And last night you drank some chamomile tea."

"I had indigestion."

"You loathe chamomile tea," Rachel pointed out.

Was her best friend trying to make a point? Because if she was, she was taking a hell of a long time to get to it. "You've obviously got something to say, Rachel, so why don't you spit it out so I can get back to work?"

"Ooh, grumpy," Rachel quipped, stepping forward to grip Alex's biceps with her hands. "Honey, I think you are pregnant."

Alex had never thought it possible that she could feel like she was burning up from the inside, as well as feeling soul-deep cold. "Okay, that's simply not funny."

"Am I laughing?" Rachel asked, her expression serious. "Alex, having been through this myself, I can spot a pregnancy at fifty paces. You, my friend, are pregnant."

"Stop saying that!" Alex hissed, panic closing her throat. "I can't be! I had my period…"

Rachel lifted her eyebrows, patiently waiting for an answer.

"Give me a sec, dammit! I have to think!" Alex pulled her phone from the back pocket of her jeans and clicked on her calendar app. She always kept a record of her cycle and she'd show Rachel that she was talking out of her hat. Alex flipped through dates, didn't see anything and flipped back a month. Oh man, there was no denying it. She was late.

"Apart from eating junk food, has anything else changed? Have you felt nauseous, tired?"

"I threw up a couple of weeks back, felt nauseous once last week and I'm tired because I've been organizing this damn function. I can't be pregnant... Maybe I have a bug! It's far too early for me to have any symptoms of pregnancy anyway."

That was the answer, she had a bug, had picked up a virus. Phew!

"It's not a disease, Alex," Rachel patiently replied. "And everyone is different."

"Oh God. Oh God."

Rachel's grip on her arms tightened. "Breathe, honey. Let's think about this logically. Did Daniel use condoms? Are you on birth control?"

"You know I've been seeing Daniel?" Alex demanded. "Who else knows? Does Gus? Oh crap!"

"It was a guess, which you just confirmed," Rachel replied, her voice low and smooth. "So, condoms?"

"Yes, dammit. We are responsible adults who don't make juvenile errors." Alex bent over, covered her face with her hands and dropped to her haunches. "But there was one time...he pulled out and then put on a condom. God! No! I can't be pregnant, Rach. I can't!"

"I think there's a good possibility that you are."

Rachel ran a gentle hand over Alex's hair. "Alex, just breathe. In and out. Good girl."

Alex sucked in air, using every bit of self-control she had to push away the breath-stealing panic that threatened to engulf her. Still on her haunches, she placed her hand on the floor to steady herself. This couldn't be happening to her. *Why* was this happening to her? She'd had a hot, passionate fling with a man she'd always been attracted to. They'd used protection… She wasn't supposed to end up pregnant! This wasn't how her life was supposed to go.

And in a couple of hours, she had to go onstage, act charming and auction off the father of the baby that might be growing in her womb. *Noooo…*

Rachel pulled her up to standing position and cupped her face, her eyes radiating support and sympathy. "Alex, there's nothing you can do about it now. In the morning, we'll go and buy you a pregnancy test and I'll hold your hand while you do it. For now, try to set it aside. We have a function to host, an evening to orchestrate."

Alex heard a couple of unladylike curses leave her lips. "I won't be able to concentrate until I know, Rach."

"You won't be able to concentrate if you do," Rachel pointed out.

"No, it'll be better if I know. I far prefer to deal with reality than what-ifs." Alex sucked her bottom lip between her teeth and felt the sting of tears. "I have to know, Rach."

Rachel wrinkled her nose. "We need you here, Alex."

Alex pushed her shoulders back and blinked away her tears. "And I will be, Rachel. I promise you, I won't let you down. I'll run to the superstore just out of town and I'll use the facilities there to do the test. I'll be back in thirty minutes, forty at max."

Too many people had let her down, pregnant or not, so she wouldn't do that to her best friend. She'd made a commitment to this evening and she'd honor it, baby or not. But she had to know. It was a burning compulsion, a primal need.

Rachel shrugged. "Okay."

Alex gave her a brief hug, pulling away before she completely lost it and started to ugly cry. She handed Rachel the clipboard, and then she all but ran to the door, yanked it open and slammed into a hard wall.

Another set of hands held her biceps; this time they were far bigger and rougher than Rachel's but oh-so familiar. Alex inhaled Daniel's distinctive scent and lifted her eyes to his chiseled face, sweeping them over his sensual lips and meeting his dark, brooding eyes.

Then, to her mortification, she heard a suppressed sob escape and felt the trickle of tears down her cheeks. Daniel's grip tightened on her biceps as she rested her forehead against his chest. God, she couldn't do this, she couldn't be pregnant.

"Lex, what's wrong?" For a moment, she wished she could lay her fears on him, allow him to enfold her into his strong arms, trust him to hold her up, have her back. But that was foolishness—she couldn't trust anyone. There was only one person she could rely on and that was herself. After all, she couldn't lose herself.

"I… It's nothing for you to worry about."

He remained silent as he lifted one hand to gently stroke her hair,

And, man, even though she knew she should pull away, she couldn't bring herself to. Not yet. Just once, it would be nice not to have to stand alone and be strong, to allow someone else to carry some of her burden.

But that wasn't the way she operated.

Even so, Alex relished the feel of Daniel's hand on the back of her head, his lips against her temple. "Lex, I need to know what's upsetting you."

He almost sounded like he cared. But that was a lie. He loved her body, loved making love to her, but he didn't care enough. Not to stick by her when things got tough, when she asked him to choose her. She'd made the mistake of relying on him when she was a teenager, and she knew not to do that again.

Alex shoved away from Daniel, swiped annoyed fingers across her eyes to wipe away the tears blurring her vision and sent him a hard smile. "I've got to go."

"Wait! What's wrong with you?" Daniel demanded. "Why are you crying? Dammit, Alexis, talk to me!"

She sent him a quick brittle smile. "Talking wasn't part of the deal when we were lovers, Daniel, even less so now. If this turns out to be something you need to know, I'll tell you, but for now, butt out! Okay?"

Alex moved away from Daniel, but she clearly heard the words he threw at her back. "You're crying, Lex! How am I supposed to let you just walk away?"

Alex turned, walked backward and spread out her hands. "It's not like it's the first time we've done this, Daniel. Ten years ago, I walked away from you in tears and you let me go. Let's repeat history, okay?"

Daniel watched Alex stride away from him, bunching his fists as he fought the urge to go after her, to shake her until she spilled her secrets. But, God, she was right. They weren't lovers anymore and even when they were—a handful of hookups over the past two months—they hadn't spent their time talking. That wasn't what they'd wanted from each other…

They'd wanted sex, hot and fast and furious. They'd wanted deep kisses and gliding hands, bone-melting pleasure and mindless nights, an escape from the day-to-day world that they lived here in Royal. They'd always, even when they were kids, had the ability to separate themselves from reality, to pretend that the outside world didn't exist. And they'd done that again, using sex as an escape, as a way to divorce themselves from their lives.

When they were entangled in one another's arms, he wasn't a Clayton and she wasn't a Slade. They were just Dan and Alex, two people who'd once loved each other with all the force and fury that was only possible when you were a teenager, before life showed you the million shades of gray between black and white. He shook his head at his youthful folly; he'd been such a sap for her.

But his days of being a sap for anyone were long over.

"Are you just going to stand there, staring into space?"

Daniel looked into the room that he'd been told was where the bachelors and Tessa were supposed to wait and saw Rachel standing by the refreshment table, her arms crossed and her eyes narrowed.

"Can you tell me what that was about?" he asked. Rachel was Alex's best friend and the two were said to be close. But how close? Like him, Alex had never been one to wear her heart on her sleeve and they rarely, if ever, had deep and meaningful conversations. Did she have those types of conversations with Rachel? Had she had them with another lover?

And why did that thought feel like the tip of a burning cigarette incinerating his stomach? He had no claim

on Alex. There was nothing between them but one blissful summer long ago and some recent hot sex.

He had no claim on her. He didn't want to have a
claim on anyone and most definitely didn't want someone to have a claim on him. With attachments came
pain and he was happy with his own company, to live
his life alone.

People, and their expectations and emotions, drained
him.

"Is there anything you can tell me?" Daniel demanded, shoving his hands into the front pocket of his
battered jeans. In an hour or two he would swap his
jeans and flannel shirt for a designer tuxedo, but for
now he was comfortable. With what he was wearing,
at least.

"Nope," Rachel replied, shaking her head. She lifted
her clipboard. "I have a ton of work to do."

"And that is why I'm really surprised Alex bolted out
of here like her tail was on fire. With her work ethic,
normally you'd have to pry her away with a crowbar."

"I don't know what you want me to say, Daniel."

Tell me what's going on! Tell me why Alex was crying. Tell me something, anything to help me understand.
Daniel rubbed his hands over his face, before turning to head out the door. He needed a whiskey, possibly two. Anything to help him numb his worry about
Alex, his annoyance that he'd agreed to be part of this
dumb auction. Not to mention the vague apprehension
that no one would bid on him, the bastard son of Royal's wildest child.

God, now he sounded like a loser wallowing in self-
pity. He'd brought The Silver C back from the brink of
ruin, was regarded as one of the most talented young
ranchers in the state. He was rich, respected. Who the

hell cared that his mother was a crazy narcissist who was incapable of love and that his father had walked out on them before he was born?

"Daniel."

He was about to step through the door when he heard Rachel speak his name. He turned around slowly and saw the anxiety in her eyes. Oh crap, this was bad. "Yeah?"

Rachel hesitated and blew air into her cheeks. "Nothing. Ignore me."

Daniel growled his frustration and threw up his hands. "For God's sake, Rachel! What?"

Rachel's hands were white against her clipboard. "Tonight, later, when you run into her, just be gentle, okay?"

And what, in the name of all that was holy, did that mean?

Three

Daniel loved his grandmother—he did—but right now, he didn't like her. Not even one little bit. It was her fault that he was dressed in this stupid suit with a noose around his neck. She'd nagged him until he agreed to take part in this auction, and he'd finally relented, thinking that it was easier to say yes than listen to her harangue him. It was because of her that he'd have to go and stand on that stupid stage while his old ex-girlfriend and his recent ex-lover auctioned him off like a piece of meat.

And his grandmother's latest little surprise? Well, as one of the most eligible bachelors in the area, and one of the wealthiest, she'd informed him about meeting with a lifestyle reporter who was covering the auction. She and the journalist had discussed the possibility of Daniel giving an interview on whether his hopes and expectations of this evening lived up to the reality…

He had only one hope—that he managed to keep control of his seldom-seen-but-explosive temper—and exactly zero expectations.

And his grandmother was doomed to be disappointed. He had no intention of doing any damn interviews.

"Hi, Daniel."

Daniel whipped his head up and saw Tessa Noble standing by the refreshment table, her hand holding a quiche. Judging by the comments his grandmother had recently sent his way, he knew that she hoped that he and Tessa would finally connect, but unfortunately he only had eyes for an annoying blue-eyed blonde. But... *hot damn.* Tessa had always been attractive but tonight she was smokin' hot.

"Tessa? God, you look...incredible." Daniel shoved a hand in the pocket of his pants. "What are you doing here?" As soon as he asked the question, he had his answer. "Wait... Are you the surprise?"

Of course she was. It was classic Alex, when the crowd was expecting one thing, to do the exact opposite. And Tessa, looking like five million dollars, was a hell of a surprise.

"Guilty." Tessa blushed.

"Everyone will definitely be surprised," Daniel said. *Oh, smooth, Clayton. Just tell the woman that her normal look is subpar.* Which it so wasn't. "Not that you don't look good normally."

"It's okay, Daniel. I get it," she mumbled around a mouth full of quiche. "It was quite a surprise to me, too."

Distracted, Daniel leaned his shoulder into the wall, darting a quick look toward the door, hoping to see Alex. He'd sent her a couple of text messages, asking if she was okay, but she'd yet to respond. He needed to know whether, at the very least, she'd stopped crying. If she hadn't, she'd not only go onstage with red eyes, but he might be compelled to kick someone's ass. If she ever deigned to tell him whose ass needed kicking.

Daniel turned his attention back to Tessa. "You must be tired of people telling you how different you look. How did Tripp and Ryan react?"

There was something between her and Ryan, something more than the best friends they professed to be. Any idiot could see it and maybe that was why he'd never asked Tessa out on a date. Subconsciously, he supposed he always felt that if he asked Tessa out, he would be violating the bro code. And since Ryan was a good friend, that wasn't happening.

"Neither of them has seen me yet. I'm a little nervous about their reaction."

She had a right to be. Ryan would take one look at her and, if he was as smart as Daniel knew him to be, would take her to bed and keep her there.

"Don't be. I can't imagine a man alive could find fault with the way you look tonight." Oh crap, that had come out wrong. "Or any night...of course."

Tessa laughed and Daniel smiled at her, feeling at ease in her company.

Tessa walked toward him and laid a hand on his arm. "You know why I feel like a fish out of water. But are you okay? You look out of sorts."

He really had to try to look like he was enjoying this evening, like he was looking forward to meeting his date. He wasn't, but as a Clayton he had a duty to his community and to the event. He wanted Alex to succeed, he wanted this evening to be a resounding success. He just didn't want to stand there, wanting one woman while being auctioned off to another...

Damn you, Gran.

Normally Daniel would deflect the question, change the subject, so he was surprised to find himself giving Tessa an honest answer. He sighed heavily, the frown returning to his face. "For one thing, I'd rather not be in the lineup. I'm doing this at my grandmother's insistence."

"She seems like a perfectly reasonable woman to me." Ha! When his grandmother wanted something, she was as subtle as a combine harvester, or as an F5 tornado. "And she loves you like crazy. I'm pretty sure if you'd turned her down, she would've got over it pretty quickly."

She really didn't know Rose Clayton. His grandmother would make her displeasure known. Quietly but consistently. He shrugged, feeling the need to explain. Damn, Tessa Noble was easy to talk to. Strange that he could talk to her and not want to rip her clothes off, but with Alex, he wanted to do the exact opposite. "I owe my grandmother so much. I don't know where I would've ended up if it wasn't for her. Makes it hard to say no."

As difficult and demanding as she could be, Daniel would do whatever he could to make his grandmother happy. She'd taken a lost boy of mixed heritage and made him the man he was today. He owed her, well, a hell of a lot. Everything.

Daniel thought the subject was closed, but then Tessa spoke again. "You said 'for one thing.' What's the other reason you didn't want to do this?"

Oh damn. The last thing he wanted to do was to get all touchy-feely here. But, God's honest truth, the thought of making small talk with another woman, listening to her flirt, feigning interest in her life while the woman he really wanted to be with wanted nothing to do with him, made him want to put his fist through a door. Or a wall.

As easy to talk to as Tessa was, there were some things he'd never discuss. With anybody. He'd especially never admit to his ongoing, long-term obsession with the girl next door.

"Okay, bachelors and bachelorette."

Daniel heard Alex's command and forced himself to turn around. When he did, he noticed that not only had she entered the room but so had the rest of the bachelors who were up for auction. But his attention was completely captured by Alex. He started at her face, looking for signs of tears, and yep, her eyes were red. But her face was composed, and she had her emotions under control. Daniel released the breath he'd been holding and allowed his eyes to rove. Her hair was pinned up into a sexy knot, and her makeup was expertly yet subtly applied. His eyes widened as he took in the plunging high-slit silver dress she wore like a second skin. It was obvious that she wasn't wearing a bra and he had to wonder whether she'd forgone panties, as well.

Daniel licked his lips.

She looked magnificent, sexy, ravishing, so damn doable. He wanted to go caveman on her by tossing her over his shoulder and taking her straight to bed. Or following her down to the nearest flat surface. Hell, even a door or a wall—he wasn't picky.

Dammit. He'd seen lots of beautiful woman before, and had bedded several of them. But Alex was beyond beautiful. She was… God, what was that word? *Alluring? Captivating? Entrancing?* All three and more?

He wanted her. The thought that he always would terrified him.

"The proceedings will begin in about ten minutes, out in the gardens—which, you have to admit, look amazing. It looks like a real winter wonderland!" Alex said with a wide smile. "So, finish eating, take a quick bathroom break, whatever you need to do so you'll be ready to go on when your number is called."

Alex was in tough-girl mode, and damn, that prissy, bossy voice coming from that sexy mouth sent all his blood rushing south. Daniel resisted the impulse to bang his forehead against the nearest wall and settled for biting the inside of his lip until he tasted blood.

Act like the adult you are, Clayton.

Alex issued another set of instructions, none of which he listened to, his eyes too full of her to take in anything she was saying. How hard could it be? Walk on, try not to scowl, get sold, walk off.

At the end of her lecture, Alex smiled again, and Daniel immediately recognized that fake-as-hell, I'm-trying-to-act-normal expression. The other men in the room might have had all their brains fried by the combination of Tessa Noble looking super hot and Alex Slade looking super sexy, but in the small part of his brain that was still functional, he knew that something was up with Alex. Something life changing, crazy making, worry inducing. He could see the tension in her shoulders, the tight cords of her neck. And that blinding smile didn't come anywhere near her sky blue eyes.

Daniel started to go to her but then her gaze clashed with his and he easily read her request not to approach her, her guarded expression telling him that she couldn't deal with him. Daniel lifted one eyebrow, a silent appeal, asking her what the hell was going on, and she gave him the tiniest shake of her head.

Daniel tapped his shirt pocket, where the outline of his cell phone was clearly visible, hoping she'd understand that he needed to know, even if it was only by text message.

A tiny nod, but Daniel didn't fool himself into believing that his phone would soon buzz with an incoming message. Alex had only acknowledged his request, not agreed to do what he asked. The woman had her own mind and, God, he liked her that way.

Frankly, he liked her any damn way he could get her.

"Six thousand dollars, ladies, for Lloyd Richardson. Who has seven?"

I'm pregnant.

Alex acknowledged a bid from Gail, Tessa's friend, and that bid was quickly topped by Steena Goodman. Alex briefly wondered what these women saw in Lloyd to make them go that high. Gail, looking sulky but determined to have her date with Lloyd, raised her paddle again. Well, she'd have to pony up because Steena had deep pockets and her wealthy now-dead husband's money to spend.

She was pregnant with Daniel's baby.

It was like two halves of her brain were operating independently. One half was playing the role of the merry, if slightly manic, auctioneer, while in the other half, she was curled up in a fetal position, battling for breath.

Grandpa's first great-grandchild is going to carry Clayton blood.

"Eight thousand dollars, Gail? Wow, that's super generous." *Too generous*, Alex thought, alarm bells ringing in her head. Gail didn't look like she had that sort of money lying around. "Oh, a new bidder at nine thousand dollars! Marvelous."

She had to tell Daniel…and Gus. Daniel would have to tell Rose and, God, what fun that was going to be.

"Fifty thousand dollars."

Alex blinked at Steena's outrageous offer. She couldn't possibly have heard her right. Alex looked at Rachel, who was standing to her right, and judging by Rachel's shocked expression, she knew that her hearing wasn't faulty. Steena Goodman had just bid fifty thousand dollars for a date with Lloyd. Was she out of her ever-lovin' mind?

But knowing her money was good—those weren't fake diamonds hanging from her ears and decorating her fingers—Alex gripped the gavel, preparing to sell Lloyd to the woman before she came to her senses. She flashed a smile at Rachel and lifted her gavel.

"One hundred thousand dollars."

Oh no. Oh hell. Oh crap. Alex widened her eyes at Gail's ridiculous offer, waiting for her to wave the offer away, to tell her it was a joke. But Gail just kept her eyes on Lloyd, one hand on her hip. A low buzz swept through the room as the drama unfolded. Alex knew that she should sell the date, that nobody—not even Steena—would top Gail's ludicrous bid. She also knew that there was no way that the charity would see a hundred thousand dollars from Gail.

Call it a hunch.

Alex looked toward James Harris, the new TCC president, and he lifted his hands in a what-can-you-do gesture. Maybe she was judging a book by its cover; maybe Gail did have a hundred grand to spare. This was, after all, Texas, where anyone could be a billionaire. It had happened before.

Alex dropped the gavel, hiding her trepidation. "Lloyd Richardson has been sold to Gail Walker."

Gail clapped her hands like a little girl getting an award and skipped up to the stage to fling her arms around Lloyd's neck. He responded by laying a hot kiss on her. Gail kicked up her foot and Alex immediately noticed the scuff mark on the back of the heel of her shoe. Oh boy, this wasn't going to end well.

Alex felt a little dizzy as she watched Lloyd and Gail leave the stage. She was exhausted and overwhelmed. Two more to go and then she could go home and collapse.

Tessa wouldn't be a problem; she'd just have to watch the bids roll in. But Daniel? Well, hell, crap and damn. How was she going to sell her baby's father to another woman?

Alex, after spending thirty excruciating minutes accepting congratulations on the success of the evening, slipped out of the festively decorated gardens and headed toward the TCC clubhouse.

She needed some time alone to get her racing heart under control, to reflect on this crazy day, to think, dammit!

Wrapping her arms around her waist, she stepped inside the clubhouse and headed for the small office James had allocated for auction-related business. After closing the door behind her, she flipped on a desk lamp and half sat, half leaned on the wide wooden desk.

Selling a date with Tessa had been a dream, as she'd barely been able to keep up with the flurry of bids for her gorgeous friend. Tessa had looked surprised at the attention she garnered and then relieved when Ryan topped all the other bids with a whopper offer. She'd caught Tessa's pleading look and quickly closed the bidding, accepting Ryan's overly generous bid with a quick snap of her gravel. Maybe there had been a man in the audience who could top Ryan's bid, but Tessa had been a good sport and she deserved a date with Ryan. And maybe, finally, the two of them would figure out what the rest of the community already knew: that they should only date each other. Permanently.

Selling a date with Daniel hadn't been as easy. Rachel, bless her, had offered to take over as auctioneer but that would've caused speculation they could ill afford. So she'd gritted her teeth, pasted on a bright smile and, after fifteen excruciating minutes, she sold Daniel to an oil baron's daughter from Houston: a tall, cool brunette with a predatory look in her eyes.

She'd wish him luck—everyone knew Iona Duckworth had a thing for cowboys. And cowboys who also owned and operated one of the most iconic ranches in the state? Jackpot!

Alex dropped her head, finally able to devote her full attention to the problem at hand. She was pregnant.

With Daniel's baby.

God.

Alex stared down at the exotic wooden floor. How did this happen? Why was life punishing her like this? She wasn't ready to be someone's mom, and couldn't imagine being fully responsible for another life. Moreover, she knew nothing about babies—except how they were made, and apparently she didn't know enough about that! How on earth was she going to raise a child, accept Mike's amazing offer to be a partner in his new start-up and… God!

Through this child growing inside her, she was now connected to Daniel forever. Well, at least until their child became an adult, but that was long enough. Once she told Daniel about the baby, he'd be a permanent and constant part of her life, exactly what she'd been trying to avoid when she told him that they had to stop sleeping together. She didn't want Daniel in her life— she couldn't cope with all the emotions he pulled to the surface, all the memories, the resurgence of the hopes and dreams she'd had as a stupid-with-love teenager.

Being close to Daniel, even if it was just a physical thing, was dangerous enough. But this child, their baby, would require them to find a way to interact, emotionally. Emotional interaction led to attachments and she didn't do attachment.

Though, apparently and according to the three pregnancy tests she'd done earlier, she had no choice but to become attached. That was what happened with moms and babies, wasn't it?

Oh God, she was going to be a mommy.

Alex heard the door to the office open and then she felt Daniel's arms around her. Her bones liquefied, and she fell into him, utterly exhausted and emotionally winded. She didn't think she could take much more tonight.

"Lex. God, honey, what the hell is going on with you?" Daniel demanded, lifting her up and pulling her into his body.

Should she tell him now or later? What was the point of delaying? This news wouldn't be any easier to hear tomorrow or a month from now.

Daniel held her head with one hand and for a moment she felt safe, not so very alone. If she told him now, he'd push her away from him and she'd lose this closeness, this support. Should she tell him? How could she not?

"Lex, you're scaring me," Daniel said with concern

in his voice. "You're as white as a sheet and you're trembling. I'm starting to freak out here."

He was freaking out? And he hadn't even heard the life-altering news yet.

Alex wound her arms around his waist and rested her forehead on his chest. Once she told him, she'd have to build another wall between them, reinforce her barriers. It would be so easy to allow Daniel to take control—he was a take-charge and do-what-I-say type of guy. He was an alpha male, supremely comfortable with making quick decisions, plotting a course and following it.

And she was so tired, feeling so utterly overwhelmed that it was tempting to let him take control, to follow his lead. But at some point, she'd start to rebel and argue. Or worse, she might—although, given her contrary nature, this wasn't likely—start to like him taking charge. No, she was the captain of her own ship.

Even if her ship was currently a leaky rowboat with a broken oar.

Alex gathered her courage and stepped out of Daniel's arms. Pushing her hair off her face, she met those deep, dark worried eyes.

"Dan, I have something to tell you. You're not going to like it."

He lifted one eyebrow. "What can be worse than having to spend *any* time with the cowboy-obsessed Iona Duckworth?"

Oh, she could easily top that. "I have a date for you that's going to last the rest of your life."

Surprise and shock skittered across Daniel's face. Then panic set in. He lifted up his hands and took a step back. "Lex, it was just an affair. We haven't spent enough time together to make those sorts of pronouncements. You don't know me anymore."

If her heart wasn't threatening to jump out of her chest, she might've laughed at his erroneous assumption. "I'm not talking about you and me, Daniel!"

Relief replaced panic and Alex ignored the flare of disappointment. He'd once spent hours with her, painting their future, but now the thought was abhorrent. Yes, they'd grown up, they were adults now, and she'd packed up dreams of her and Daniel a long time ago.

It shouldn't hurt but it did. Far too much.

This, *this*, was why she had to keep her emotional distance, why she had to spend as little time with Daniel as possible. With him, foolish thoughts, remembered dreams and unwelcome emotions crept in and threatened her unattached heart. She'd planned on walking away from him and Royal—leaving all these pesky emotions behind. But if she left now, she'd be taking a part of Daniel with her...

"Seriously, I'm about to shake your news out of you," Daniel muttered.

"I'm pregnant, Daniel."

His guttural bark was short on amusement and long on disbelief. "That's not funny, Alex."

"I know. It really isn't. And I really am pregnant."

Alex walked around her desk, pulled her bag out from the bottom drawer and shoved her hand inside. She pulled out the three pregnancy tests and threw them across the desk. Daniel picked up each one in turn, saw the positive indications and Alex watched a muscle jump in his tight jaw. His sensual mouth was now a slash in his face and his olive skin turned pasty. The news was finally starting to sink in...

"It's mine?"

What the hell? How dare he ask that? She dramatically slapped her hand against her forehead. "Oh, wait, *no*! It could be one of the many other men I was sleeping with at the same time I was sneaking around with you!"

Daniel shoved his hand through his hair, pushing an errant curl off his forehead. He sent her a sour look. "Still as sarcastic as ever."

"It's my default response to stupid comments," Alex shot back. She walked out from behind her desk, sat on the corner and crossed her legs. "I'm newly pregnant, just a few weeks."

Daniel released a couple of f-bombs and followed those with a string of creative curses. When he was done, he stopped pacing, stood in front of her and curled his big hands around her bare upper arms. The heat of his hands burned into her skin as lust burned through her. Her desire for him surprised her; she'd thought that the news of her pregnancy would've killed any thoughts of sex.

But no. She wanted him as much as ever.

"What do you want to do, Alex?"

She lifted one shoulder. "What can I do? It's here."

"You're not considering an—getting rid of it?" Daniel asked, obviously worried.

"You wouldn't want that?"

He shook his head and she noticed his bleak eyes, the desperation. "This sucks. It's not what either of us wanted, but...it's a consequence of the choice we made. We have to deal."

We. Not *you.* On hearing that one small word, Alex relaxed a fraction. She wasn't in this alone...not entirely.

Daniel rested his forehead against hers, released another swear word and sighed. "I'm sorry, Alex. Jesus, this wasn't supposed to happen."

Alex heard the buzz of her phone and looked down at the desk. She frowned at the message that popped up on her screen. It was an SOS from James Harris, of all people. The auction was done and some of the guests had already drifted away. What on earth could've happened that warranted three SOS texts and a terse "We have a major situation"?

She also noticed two missed calls from James and four from Rachel.

"I need to go."

"Uh, *no*. We need to discuss this, Alex!"

"Something has happened—"

"Damn right something's happened. You're pregnant with my child. I want to discuss this, find a way forward."

Yep, alpha male. Alex remembered her grandmother's words, heard Sarah's voice in her head. *Start as you mean to go on, honey. And don't take any horse crap.*

Alex pulled away from his strong grip. "The baby will still be here tomorrow, Daniel, and the next day. We have time." She could see that her answer irritated him, but she didn't much care. Daniel liked having all his ducks in a row, knowing where they were going and how to get there. He'd once confided in her—a moment that was both random and rare—that living with his mom was like standing in a bucket on a raging river, not sure when or how he'd be tossed into the rapids or over the waterfall. He liked planning his own route, being in control of his destination.

She understood that, and they would sit down and have a decent conversation, but right now the bachelor auction had hit a snag and she was needed.

Daniel threw up his hands. "I cannot believe you are walking out on me. You've just told me that we are having a baby, Alex!"

Alex drilled her index finger into his chest. "*I* am

having a baby, Clayton, not *we*. Do not think that you can stomp into my life with your size thirteens and take over. That's not going to happen." She huffed out a breath. "When I am ready to deal with you, with the situation, I will give you a call."

Daniel's eyes widened at her strong statement. Good. The sooner he realized she wasn't a pushover, the better off they'd both be. *This is what happens when you spend your time together making love and not talking*, Alex realized. Assumptions were made.

And babies, too.

She picked up her cell phone, walked toward the door and slipped into the hallway. Pushing away thoughts of that big gorgeous, confused man she'd left behind inside, she walked down the hallway to James's office.

Another fire to extinguish. Hopefully this would be the smallest, as well as the last, of the evening.

Four

In the parking lot of the TCC, Daniel glanced at his watch and grimaced. It was after 1:00 a.m., and he was exhausted. Tired and worried and, yeah, completely freaked out.

He was going to be a dad. Holy crap. He'd never had a father, or even a proper male role model, and as a result he knew next to nothing about being a good father. He was going to be responsible for a tiny human life… a terrifying prospect for someone who didn't have the smallest idea about what to do or how to be a dad. Fatherhood, a state he'd thought he'd only consider far into the future, was a nebulous concept, something as inexplicable as black holes or the binary code.

There was nothing Daniel hated more than the fear of the unknown.

Thanks to his erratic and unsettling childhood, he found security in planning his life, breaking down his future into five-, ten-, fifteen-, twenty-year goals. But to be honest, those plans were all ranch and business related, he hadn't spent a lot of time planning his personal life.

Or any at all.

Leaning back against Alex's sports car, he linked his hands behind his neck and stared up at the vast Texas sky. All his energy—every drop of sweat and blood—went into making The Silver C Ranch the best it could be. He knew and loved every inch of his land and he knew that the ranch was his place, his corner on earth. People came and went, but his grandmother and The Silver C kept him stable as a child and anchored as an adult.

According to Alex's earth-tilting news, the first of the next generation of Claytons was baking inside of her, and what did that mean? For Rose and for the future of The Silver C? And what did it, *should it*, mean to him?

Having children wasn't something he'd thought much about, and when he did, it was only in terms of who would inherit the ranch sometime in the very distant future. Honestly, at this point in his life, he didn't want to be a dad and he had no interest in being tied down—he was perfectly content with brief affairs and one-night stands, keeping emotionally distant. But Alex… Dammit. Well, she'd recently managed to narrow that distance, to pull him closer. She tempted him to unbend a little and to open up a fraction, probably because he subconsciously wanted a way to recapture some of the magic and joy of that heady summer so long ago.

It had been the happiest three months of his life, so why wouldn't he want to experience it again? But she'd been right to call it off, to make them move on. What he hadn't expected was that they'd be left with a lifetime memento of their fling.

They'd made a child. God. He was utterly determined to be a better parent, and the exact opposite of his mother—and to be a stable, responsible and hands-on dad.

His child would know that he loved him, or her, that he would be a constant and consistent part of his child's life. That was nonnegotiable. His child would know his, or her, father's love. *His* love...

He wanted to be there for the big and small things, and that meant having his baby's mother in his life. But Alex... Being with Alex made him feel alive, uncontrolled, impulsive. The way she made him feel terrified him. But he'd just have to deal, find a way to keep her at arm's length, because he planned on being a vital part of his child's upbringing. He wanted to change diapers, do the midnight feedings, pace the floors while he tried to put his child to sleep. He'd do whatever was needed, but in order to be a part of his child's life, he had to be *in* that life. That meant marriage—*God!*—or at the very least, him and Alex living together.

Where could they live? Since Alex lived in the main house at the Lone Wolf Ranch, his house was the most reasonable option. Or they could build a new place, something that suited them both. And they'd have to tell their grandparents—that was going to be a barrel of laughs...

First things first, Clayton. Talk to Alex, offer to marry her, secure his child's future. As for the way Alex made him feel, well, he'd simply have to get over that. He would not allow her to cause him to lose control or focus. They could marry and within that union they'd be friends, even lovers, but he'd always keep himself emotionally detached. It was safer that way.

Daniel heard footsteps and lifted his head to see Alex

walking toward her car and him. Cold air caught in his throat as the rest of his body heated, then sizzled. Man, she looked amazing, so damn sexy. When she noticed him leaning against her car, she released a long sigh. She was past exhausted, he realized, and a wave of protectiveness swept over him. He was right to feel protective over her, he rationalized, because she was the mother of his child. By protecting her, he protected his son. Or daughter.

When Alex reached him, he lifted his hand and ran his knuckles over her pale cheek. "You look done in, honey," he said, his voice gruff.

"It's been a hell of a night," Alex replied, surprising him by resting her butt on the side of her car. She'd pulled a jacket over that sexy dress, but her shapely thigh slid out from under the high slit in the skirt. He wanted to pull the slippery material up and find out for sure whether she was wearing panties or not.

Like that was important! Daniel mentally slapped himself as he moved to stand in front of her. They had a future to discuss, plans to make.

Alex held up a hand and he saw that her eyes were red-rimmed and that she now sported blue stripes under her eyes that her makeup could no longer conceal. "Not tonight, Daniel. I can't take anymore."

He curbed his impulse to push and tipped his head to the side. "What was the great bachelor-auction emergency?"

"Ah, that. Well, that hundred-thousand-dollar bid Gail made for Lloyd was a fake bid—neither have that type of money. To distract a reporter from reporting on that juicy piece of gossip and totally ruining the success of the evening, we've offered the reporter complete access to Ryan and Tessa's super romantic date.

And to distract him further—" Alex's eyes narrowed in the moonlight "—you are, according to Rose, giving an interview to the same reporter on what it feels like to auction yourself off and how it feels to be one of Texas's most eligible bachelors."

Daniel waited for Alex to laugh, to give him any indication that she was joking, but she just sent him a steady look with no hint of amusement. So, ah, this interview was going to happen whether he was on board or not.

Crap.

Daniel closed his eyes and gripped the bridge of his nose. "My damn interfering grandmother."

"Tonight, I am grateful for her interference. The two stories will be a welcome distraction from the fake bid."

"I swear, my grandmother only hears what she wants to! I'm going to kill her. I swear I am!"

"She'll just come back and haunt you," Alex said behind a yawn. "Look, Mr. Most Eligible, I am exhausted, as it's been a hell of a day. I'm going home."

But they hadn't talked about the baby or come up with any concrete solutions. Daniel started to argue but then he saw the sheen of tears in her eyes, noticed that her hands were trembling. *Stop being an ass and think about her for one sec, Clayton. She's been on her feet for fourteen hours, she's just found out she's pregnant and, after hearing that news, she still managed to stand in front of a huge crowd and pull off a super successful event.* Alex had grit and courage in spades—he had to give her that.

Making a quick decision, he took her bag off her shoulder and shoved his hand inside, looking for her car keys. Ignoring her protest, he wound his arm around her waist and lifted her up to walk her around the car, pulling open the passenger door.

"What the hell are you doing?" she demanded as he bundled her into the seat.

"Taking you home."

"I can drive," Alex protested.

Daniel crouched down between the car door and its frame and placed his hand on her slim thigh. "Lex, let me do this for you. You are played out and I don't want you making the drive back to the Lone Wolf exhausted and emotional."

Alex licked her lips and sighed. "I was going to go to the tree house, spend the night there. I need some space, to be alone."

"I'll take you anywhere you want to go, honey. I just want to make sure you get there in one piece," Daniel said, keeping his tone noncombative.

"What about your car?"

Daniel shrugged. "It'll be safe enough here." He moved his thumb to stroke her bare thigh. "Let me take you home, Lex."

Alex dropped her head back against the headrest and gave a quick nod. Daniel gathered the rest of her dress, put it inside the car and slammed her door shut. In the five minutes he took to adjust her seat to his longer legs, back out of her space and reach the TCC gates, she was sound asleep.

"No, I'm not going to marry you, and I'm not going to move in with you, either."

With her battered cowboy boots propped onto the railing of Sarah's tree house, Alex held Daniel's hot stare and shook her head to emphasize her point. However, Daniel, dressed in faded, formfitting denims and a green-and-black flannel shirt worn over a black T-shirt, tried to scowl her into submission. But she'd been raised by Gus and had learned at an early age to stand her ground or get run over.

When he started to argue his point—again!—Alex rushed in, "Daniel, we are not living in the 1800s. My honor, your honor, is not at stake. Sure, Rose and my grandpa are probably going to blow a gasket, but they will just have to deal. I am not jumping into a marriage with you or into sharing a house just because I'm pregnant. That's a terrible reason to be together!"

"I want to see my child, Alex." Daniel pushed the words out from between clenched teeth.

"He or she will arrive in only seven months' time. How will us moving in together or getting married help you with that right now?"

Daniel opened his mouth to issue what she knew would be a hot retort only to have the words die on his tongue. Ha! He didn't have an answer to that argument! And there wasn't a reasonable answer because he was being an idiot!

She dropped her feet to the ground and rested her forearms on her thighs. "Daniel, I have no intention of denying you access to our child, but this idea you have of you being a full-time dad—that's not going to happen." Alex caught the flash of pain in his eyes, knew that her words were harsh but it was better to clear this up now before expectations were created that could not be fulfilled.

She was not eighteen anymore and dreaming of this man, fat babies, horses and a life on the ranch, filled with laughter and love. Dreams were for children, for the naive, and she far preferred cold reality. "We're not going to be a couple and we are not going to live together. I've had a business offer. I'm probably going to take it. It's lucrative and it's in my, and the baby's, best interest for me to accept it since my bills are going to quadruple."

Daniel's eyes turned cold. Oh damn. Now she'd properly insulted him.

"I am fully capable and prepared to pay for everything you or the baby need."

Of course he was, the guy was a millionaire fifty times over. That wasn't the point! "And I am an independent, successful woman who can earn her own money and support her own child," Alex stated, her voice dropping ten degrees. Standing up so that she did not feel like Daniel was looming over her, she slapped her hands onto her hips and handed him her most ferocious scowl. He didn't look remotely intimidated, dammit.

"I do not need you, or any other man, to pay my way."

"Goddammit, woman, you are so contrary!"

"Pot. Kettle. Black." Alex threw his words back in his face.

Daniel threw his hands up in the air, whipped around as if to leave and, before she could blink, he'd spun back and he was in her space, his fingers tunneling through her hair and his mouth falling toward hers. Alex knew that she should stop him but instead of pushing him away, she stood on her toes so that she could feel his lips against hers a second sooner. Waiting even a moment longer than she needed to was torture. She wanted him, of course she did, always had. Probably always would.

He drove her nuts. Nobody had the power to annoy her as intensely as Daniel could but, God, when he kissed her, he morphed from Irritant Number One to Sex God to Have-to-Get-Him-Naked-Immediately.

Those amazing lips moved over hers and his hand

on her butt pulled her into him. Denim rubbed against denim and underneath the fabric she could feel the evidence of his desire. They might not know how to be friends and had even less idea of how to co-parent. But, God, this? This they knew how to do.

Daniel's tongue slid into her mouth to tangle with hers, and she groaned deep in her throat. She should stop this; it wasn't sensible. This would just further complicate a crazy situation, but instead of pushing him away, her hand skated up under his T-shirt to find hot, hard skin. Daniel had the same idea, since his hand was down the back of her loose jeans, cupping her bare backside with his big calloused hand.

He yanked his mouth off hers to speak. "I've got to know, were you wearing panties last night? Under that sexy dress?"

It took Alex a moment to make sense of his words. She'd worn the tiniest thong she had and really, she still didn't know why she bothered. But she wasn't about to admit that to Daniel. He wanted to hear that she'd worn nothing more than that silver slip dress. "No."

Alex felt him tighten and harden, saw the fire in his eyes and knew that there was no going back. They were headed for the bedroom, or the sitting room. Hell, they might not even make it inside.

Daniel pulled her long-sleeve T-shirt up and over her head, looking down at the sheer lacy bra she wore. She was in the early stage of her pregnancy, and she'd yet to feel different, but Daniel was looking at her like she was made of spun glass, of delicate platinum strands. His index finger gently traced the outline of her nipple and she sucked in her breath, watching his dark hand against her lighter skin. Even in winter he looked tanned, courtesy of his Hispanic heritage. So sexy, Alex thought as he pushed the lace away to touch her, skin on skin. Daniel bent his knees, wrapped his big, powerful arms around her thighs and lifted her so that her nipple was in line with his mouth. Holding her easily, muscles bunching but not straining, he tongued her, pulling her nipple into his mouth, nibbling her with his teeth. She ran her fingers through the loose curls he hated, tracing the shell of his ear, the strong cords of his neck.

"I want you, Lex. I know I shouldn't but, God, I do," Daniel muttered, pulling away from her to look up, his eyes blazing with lust.

"Dan…"

He rested his forehead between her breasts, still holding her, and she felt his ragged breath against her skin. She knew that he expected her to ask him to let her go, to step away, but she couldn't. She didn't know how to be a mommy, to have Daniel in her life, how to navigate her suddenly complicated future, but she knew how to make love to this sexy, infuriating man.

She loved being naked with him.

"Take me inside, Dan. Love me until I can't think anymore," Alex whispered, brushing her fingers across his lips, his jaw.

Daniel flashed her a grin that was sexy enough to melt glass, and then he carried her inside. Allowing her to slide down his body so that their mouths could meet, he kissed her as he navigated his way to the bedroom at the back of the tree house. With long hot slides of his tongue, and hands possessively skimming her skin, he silently demanded that she match his passion. Alex held on to him as he lowered her to the bed and sighed when he settled into the V shape between her legs. Right place, far too many clothes.

Her shirt was gone, so Alex pulled his over his head

and tossed it to the floor. She sighed when his naked chest touched hers and lifted her head so that she could tongue his flat, masculine nipple. A good start but not enough.

"Please, Dan, I don't want to wait. It's been too long."

Daniel heard her pleas and pulled back to yank her boots off her feet and tug her jeans down over her hips. His eyes moved down, stopping on her breasts before moving over her still-flat stomach to her relatively modest bikini panties.

His eyes widened and he released a low chuckle. God, he had a great smile. It crinkled his eyes, revealed his straight white teeth and hinted at the tiniest dimple in his right cheek. But as much as she liked seeing his smile, she couldn't understand why he was laughing.

Alex pushed herself up to rest her weight on her bent elbows.

Daniel arched an eyebrow. "I'm game if you are."

Ah…what was he talking about? They'd had great sex but nothing weird or kinky, so where was he going with this?

Daniel gestured to her panties and Alex tried to read the slogan upside down. Okay, but Afterward We Get Pizza?

She groaned. She was *not* wearing her sexiest lingerie. "They were a gag gift from Rachel," she explained, blushing. "I haven't had a chance to do laundry."

"Silk or cotton, I can pretty much guarantee that anything you wear will always end up on the floor."

Daniel slowly peeled the panties down her legs, his smile still tugging at the edges of his gorgeous mouth. He dropped the panties to the floor and stood up to undress. Lifting his feet, he pulled his boots off, then pushed his jeans over his hips, taking his underwear with him. Embarrassment forgotten, Alex stared at him and Daniel stood there, allowing her to look her fill. Broad shoulders, muscled arms, that wide chest. He had sexy abs, but she also adored those long hip muscles, his lean, powerful thighs, the arch of his surprisingly elegant feet.

Daniel was a curious combination of masculine grace and rugged good looks, but beneath it all, he was a man of honor. By marrying her, he wanted to do what was right, what he thought was best for their baby. She respected that, respected *him*. But she couldn't marry him or move in with him; she shouldn't even be making love to him.

But this…thing…between them ran too deep and she couldn't resist him. She would always, as long as she breathed, want him but she wouldn't let herself love him. She couldn't afford to do that, to let him hurt her again.

Daniel placed his hands on the bed on either side of her face and placed his mouth on hers, sipping, tasting, exploring. They'd had slow sex, hot sex and crazy sex up against a door, but his kisses seemed different tonight, intense with a hint of gentleness. Alex slipped her tongue into his mouth and tried to dial up the passion. Hot and fast she could deal with, but she didn't know how to handle slow and sexy and profound.

She lifted her hips to make contact with his shaft, wanting to get out of her head and fully into the physicality of the act. Daniel didn't take the hint so she ran her thumb up his dick and when she stroked his tip, he jerked and then groaned.

"Need you, Dan, now." And she did. She needed him to remind her that this was all sex, that she couldn't have the ranch and the horses and the hot baby daddy in her life. Dreams like those put her heart at risk…so she'd just take the sex.

It was simpler that way.

Daniel nudged her legs farther apart with his knee before stroking her secret folds with his fingers. "You're so wet, Lex."

"Because I need you, Dan. I need sex." Alex heard the desperation in her voice and didn't know whether she was trying to convince herself or him.

He pushed inside her and Alex wrapped her legs around his back, pulling him closer. Heat, warmth, completion. The rest of her life was crazy confusion but, as Daniel started to move, Alex realized that this made sense. It was the only thing that did.

As he pushed her higher and higher, the needs of her body stilled her whirling thoughts and all she wanted was more of him. Her hands skated over his back, his butt, down the backs of his thighs. A strand of hair landed in her mouth and she thrashed her head from side to side as he kissed her neck, pulled her earlobe between his teeth. She was so close, teetering on the edge of pleasure, when she heard Daniel's demand to let go, his reassurance that he would catch her.

She wanted to stay here, just for another minute, bathed in that silver light of anticipation. "Dammit, Lex, I can't hold on," Daniel muttered.

Placing his hand between their bodies, he found her clit and stroked it, just once with his thumb. It was the sexual equivalent of a hard hand shoving her between her shoulders and she plunged over the cliff… Falling, falling, shattering. But he fell with her, his body shaking as he came.

Daniel collapsed on her and Alex didn't mind that her breath was shallow, that his body weight pushed her into the soft mattress. When they were lying like this, intimately connected, they were at peace. It was only when they started to talk that things went wrong.

Alex pushed her nose into his neck, kissed his skin and ran her hand down his spine. Beautiful but stubborn. Gorgeous but flawed.

Just as she was, contrary and imperfect.

Daniel pulled himself up and gazed down at her, holding his body weight on one hand as he pulled the strand of hair from her mouth and tucked it behind her ear. Alex saw her confusion reflected in his eyes. Then determination replaced confusion and she knew that he was looking for the right words to use to convince her to come around to his way of thinking.

Okay, she might be stubborn but he was relentless. "I'm not marrying or moving in with you, Clayton. No matter how good you are in the sack."

"Dammit." Daniel slipped out of her, stood up and stalked to the small bathroom attached to the bedroom. "You are a stubborn pain in the ass!"

Sure she was but that didn't make her wrong!

Five

The end of January

Gus heard the door to his study open and looked up to see his still-beautiful Rose, and his heart, old and jaded, thumped against his rib cage. He'd waited for fifty-plus years to see that soft smile on her face, for her to walk into the room and into his arms.

Man, he was riding the gravy train with biscuit wheels.

Rose placed her hands on his chest and her mouth drifted across his.

"Mornin', husband."

He was her husband. And how freakin' great was that? He smiled, allowed his hand to drift down over her ass and grinned. "Mornin', *wife*."

After a little canoodling—the best way to start a morning—Rose rested her head on his chest and sighed. "Have you had any more thoughts on what to do about our grandchildren?"

During their wedding reception last night, Rose dropped the bombshell news that Alex was pregnant and that Daniel was the baby's father. Strangely, instead of feeling angry, he'd felt content. Like this news was right, simply meant to be. He'd initially thought that he was so very relaxed because he'd been floating on a cloud of wedding-induced happiness, but upon waking this morning, it still felt right, like it was preordained.

He wasn't, however, happy that Alex and Daniel were going to try to raise their great-grandchild separately and not as husband and wife. That wasn't acceptable. Not because he cared about convention or how it would look, but because, dammit, those two were meant to be together.

They'd meant to be together ten years ago—shame on him and Rose for making their grandchildren casualties in their stupid, long-held feud—and they were meant to be together now.

"My Alex is 'more stubborn-hard than hammered iron.'"

Rose pulled back and smiled her appreciation. "Shakespeare, Gus Slade? I'm impressed."

Gus felt his ears heat at her admiration and then shrugged it off. They had more important things to worry about. "So, about these darned kids…"

He refused to allow them to repeat his and Rose's foolishness and waste so much time. They had to reunite Alex and Daniel and, after showing his wife exactly how much he loved and wanted her, he'd spent a good part of the night working out how to do just that. "I have a plan, but it might involve a sacrifice on our part."

"Okay. How big a sacrifice?"

Oh man, she wasn't going to like this. "Our honeymoon. I'm sorry, sweetheart. I want to spend some time with you alone and I know you want that, too—"

Rose stepped away from him, pulled a chair from the dining table, sat down and crossed her legs. She didn't look mad but, since they'd been married for less than a minute, what did he know? "Gus Slade, I have waited fifty-two years to be your wife and I don't care about going away for our honeymoon." A soft radiant smile lit up her lovely face. How could she possibly be more beautiful today than she was half a century ago? Yet she was. "Being with you—whether it's here in Royal or at Galloway Cove or on the damned moon—is where I want to be."

"Such language, darlin'." Gus tsk-tsked.

Rose rolled her eyes. "I'm not a fragile flower, Gus. Neither am I sixteen anymore. And I can swear if I *damn* well want to."

Gus hid his smile with his hand. But before he could investigate this saucy new side of his wife—man, that word just slayed him, every single time—he saw the speculation in her eyes.

"Tell me what you have in mind, and I'll gladly sacrifice our week on Matt's island to get those two to see daylight."

Gus outlined his plan and watched as Rose stared out the window at the east paddock, where his old paint horse, Jezebel, was keeping company with his prized Arabians and Daisy, the airheaded goat.

"Do you think it can work?" Rose asked him, worry in her eyes. She no longer wore her mask of aloofness and he was clearly able to read her concern for both Daniel and Alex. He could see her deep desire to see them happy. Rose didn't wear her heart on her sleeve, but that didn't mean she didn't feel things deeply, sometimes too deeply.

Gus sighed. They'd wasted so much time being angry

with each other, but he couldn't regret loving Sarah—they'd had a good marriage. Losing his son so early had been horrible but raising his grandkids had given both him and Sarah a second lease on life.

Rose's life hadn't been so easy. Her daddy had been a hard man and Ed, her husband, had been as cuddly as a hornet and had made her life hell. They'd made so many mistakes, but he was damned if he'd watch Alex and Daniel repeat their history. They might argue like crazy but the room crackled with electricity when the two of them were together. They owed it to themselves and their baby to make it work.

"Gus? Will your plan work?"

He shrugged and, needing to touch her, held the back of her neck. "I hope so, honey."

Rose nodded and leaned her head against his side. "If it doesn't, we'll lock them in the barn until they come to their senses."

Gus laughed, thinking she was joking. When she remained silent, he looked down at her. "You're joking, right?"

Rose stood up and wound her arms around his waist. "We're giving them the chance to come to their senses in a nice way. After all, it's the least we can do after everything we pulled to keep them apart. But if it doesn't work, we'll do it the hard way." He saw her stubborn expression and grinned. His wife was fierce. And he loved her that way.

He loved her, period. Always had.

The first week of February

Alex sat on the leather seat of the private plane Gus hired to fly his bride to Galloway Cove for their honeymoon and wished that she could ask the pilot to close the doors and whisk her away to Matt's stunning private Caribbean island. She couldn't think of anything she'd rather do more than stretch out on white sand beneath a blue sky, read a book and just be.

But no, before he left, her grandfather wanted to give her one last lecture and that was the only reason why he would've asked her to meet him and Rose on the plane. He'd leave her with a reprimand about doing the right thing, raising her baby with its father and not as a single mom in Houston.

She was depriving Daniel of being a full-time dad, depriving Gus and Rose of having quick and easy access to the baby, making life ten times harder for herself without having the support of Daniel, as well as her family and friends.

Yada yada.

She knew that—how could she not? Being on her own in Houston, trying to run a company as a single mom, was going to be the hardest challenge of her life! But Gus didn't understand—she doubted anyone would—that was less scary than remaining in Royal, utterly in lust and half in love with her baby's father. The best chance she had to stop thinking about Daniel Clayton and the life she could never have was for her to move back to Houston. She had a far better chance of pushing him out of her mind there than here in Royal.

If she stayed here, she might just do something crazy.

"Grandpa, Daniel and I had our chance."

"That doesn't mean that you can't have a second one," Gus replied.

It was like talking to a brick wall. In an effort to get through to him, Alex pulled out the big guns. "One of the reasons we missed our chance was because you and your new bride were vehemently opposed to us being together."

Gus hesitated before replying. "We might not have been completely correct in that assumption."

Okay, that was as close to an apology as she was going to get from her taciturn grandfather.

"But in our defense, you were also very young."

"Daniel," Alex reminded him, "chose The Silver C over me. His loyalty to Rose and to the ranch has always been stronger than any love he had for me."

She hadn't been able to explain further, unable to admit to Gus that she couldn't trust that Daniel would be there for her and her baby when life got tough, couldn't tolerate the thought of being second or third on his list of priorities.

"I think you are making a mistake, Alexis," Gus quietly told her.

"But, Grandpa, it's my life and my mistake to make," Alex insisted.

"Except it's not—you have a baby to think of," Gus replied before ending the call.

Why couldn't he understand that she'd lost so much? If she and Daniel lived together, raised their child together, there was a good chance that she would fall in love with him again; of that she had no doubt. Wasn't that the reason she'd broken up with him recently, because she could feel herself sliding downhill into love?

Alex had lost Daniel's love once, and she'd mourned him for years. Their breakup had been another type of death, and she was done with death, of all types.

She wouldn't survive another loss. Her shattered heart would crumble into pieces too fine to be patched back together again. And while she had no intention of denying him access to his child, she needed to start getting used to being on her own, to a life that didn't have Daniel in it. He was her baby's father, not her lover and definitely not her friend.

It was better, safer, this way. Gus might've found love after a half century—and she was truly happy for him—but his path wasn't hers. She didn't want love in her life, it hurt too damn much when it left.

If only she could get Gus, and by extension Rose, to understand that.

Alex heard footsteps and turned to look down the aisle, expecting to see the happy couple. Oh crap. Daniel. Maybe she wasn't in for a lecture; maybe Gus and Rose simply wanted a glass of champagne with their two favorite people before jetting off for a week of sun and sand and sex—*ooh, can't go there*. Sun and sand was descriptive enough.

Daniel took the seat opposite her and looked at the open bottle of champagne sitting in an ice bucket. "We're here for a dressing-down, aren't we? This time they are going to tackle us together?"

Alex wanted to think otherwise but she nodded. "Probably."

Daniel placed his boot on his ankle and Alex noticed that his denims, soft from washing, had a rip at the left knee and that the hems were frayed. She pulled in a deep breath and her womb throbbed at the intoxicating scent of soap, sun and ranch life mixed with pure, primal alpha male. She'd missed him so much. Keeping her distance was torture but so very necessary.

"Thanks for answering my fifty million calls," Daniel bit out, pulling his designer shades off his face and hooking them onto the neck band of his T-shirt.

"Don't exaggerate," Alex retorted.

"Stop evading the subject. You've been avoiding me

for weeks and I don't like it." She had. Leaving Royal for Houston for a couple of weeks helped. She'd needed to meet with Mike, discuss their partnership agreement and get a feel for his business, but the fact that she was half a state away from Daniel had helped with her evasion tactics.

"I saw you at the wedding," Alex pointed out.

"Where you refused to discuss anything to do with the future and the baby. We have plans to make, Alex! We need to know where we are going!"

"Do we really have to go through all this again?" Alex threw up her hands and leaned forward. "I am going back to Houston. I am taking a partnership in a start-up company, and you are staying here. In five months I will give birth."

"What about visitation rights? A nanny to help you? Child support?" Daniel bellowed.

"We can sort that out later when—" Alex broke off when she noticed the attendant approaching them. The young woman stopped, stood in the aisle alongside them and tossed them an easy smile.

"Sorry to interrupt but we've just had word that Mr. and Mrs. Slade are running a little late. But we need to move the plane so that the next aircraft can take our slot."

Alex looked at Daniel and they both shrugged. "Okay?"

That bright, mischievous smile flashed again and Alex saw that her name tag read Michelle. "Safety regulations state that we can't taxi without you both wearing a seat belt. Regulations, you know?"

"For God's sake!" Daniel muttered, reaching for his seat belt and pulling it over his waist. "Do you have an idea when they might be here? I need to get back to the ranch. I have a meeting in an hour." He frowned at Michelle, as if it were her fault their grandparents were late.

Michelle watched Alex buckle up before turning her attention back to Daniel. "They should be here soon, Mr. Clayton."

Alex felt the aircraft move forward as the pilot guided the plane to its new position. The attendant walked away and Alex reached for the bottle of champagne and a crystal glass. Now, this was the way to fly. And if Gus had meant this champagne to be for Rose, then he should've been prompt. Besides, any sane woman needed alcohol while dealing with Daniel Clayton. It was deeply unfair that that much sexy covered a whole bunch of annoying.

Before she could tip the bottle to her glass, the champagne was whisked from her hand and the bottle dropped back into the ice bucket. "Not happening."

Alex glared at Daniel. "When did they make you the no-champagne-for-breakfast police? Last time I checked, I'm an adult and I can have—"

"Cut it out, Alex. I'm the dad who's telling his baby's mom that she can't have alcohol while she's pregnant."

Alex wanted to lash out at him, tell him that he had no right to tell her what to do, but dammit, on this point he was right. She couldn't drink alcohol while she was pregnant. Gah! What had she been *thinking*? Probably that she needed the soothing power of the fermented grape, especially if she had to deal with Mr. Impossible.

Alex risked looking at Daniel and saw the smug smile of his face at winning that minor battle. Annoyed, she kicked out and smiled when the toe of her right boot connected with his shin.

"Ow, dammit!" Daniel howled before bending down to rub his injury.

"Don't be a baby, Clayton." Alex looked out the window, saw that the plane was whizzing past the trees bordering the airport and frowned. "Aren't we going a bit fast?"

"Don't kick me again," Daniel warned and followed her gaze to the window. He released a low curse. "We're not taxiing."

Alex gripped the arms of her seat. "Daniel, what's going on?"

"If I'm not mistaken, we're about to take off." Daniel looked around, saw an electronic panel and jabbed at the button labeled Attendant.

"This is Michelle. What can I do for you, Mr. Clayton? Miss Slade?" Michelle's melodious voice drifted over them.

Daniel didn't waste time looking for explanations. "Stop this plane right now or I'm going to have you all arrested for kidnapping." Alex shivered at the I'm-going-to-kill-someone note in his voice. She'd only heard that voice once, maybe twice, before and she knew that you didn't disobey Daniel Clayton when he used it.

"Sorry, sir, but we can't do that. Besides, Mr. and Mrs. Slade promised to pay all our legal fees if you decide to sue us. Plus a hefty retainer."

"What the hell are you talking about?" Daniel asked, his eyes widening.

Alex immediately understood why. They'd left the ground and they were literally jetting off to God knew where.

"There is an iPad in the side pocket of your seat," the airline attendant continued, and Daniel kept his eyes locked onto Alex's face as he dropped his hand to the side of his seat.

"Switch it on and there's a video clip on the home screen. It should answer all of your questions," Michelle stated, and Alex heard the click as she disconnected the intercom.

Daniel booted up the iPad, glared down at the screen and impatiently jabbed the screen. He leaned forward so that she could see the screen and there, looking far too pleased with themselves, were their respective grandparents.

"Yes, we've kidnapped you. Yes, we are bad people," Gus said, sounding utterly unrepentant.

Rose jabbed him with his elbow and stared into the camera. "Alexis and Daniel, we are sorry for being so intransigent a decade ago. We should not have pulled you into our little dustup and we apologize."

Only in Texas could people call a fifty-year feud a dustup.

Gus leaned forward, his blue eyes serious. "That being said, it must be noted that you two are the most stubborn creatures imaginable and unable to see what's in front of your faces. To help you with your lack of vision, we are sending you to Galloway Cove in our place. Matt's house is the only one on the island, and it is fully stocked with everything you might need. We packed a suitcase for each of you, which Michelle will give to you when you land."

Daniel hit the pause button, looked at Alex and shook his head. "I'm adding breaking and entering to the charges I'm laying against her."

Alex rolled her eyes and tapped the play button so that the video could continue. Gus picked up the conversational train wreck. "The plane will return in a week and, by then, we want a proper, thought-out, reasonable plan on how you two intend to raise this child together. And by together we mean in the same house, preferably the same bedroom."

"Just to be clear, marriage is our first choice," Rose added.

"When hell freezes over," Alex muttered. On-screen, Rose smiled, oblivious to their anger. Which was exactly why they recorded this message and didn't video call them. Alex snorted. Cowards.

"And don't try to bribe the pilot and his crew to turn around. We already told them we'd double whatever you offer." Rose, looking pretty and content, blew them a kiss. "One day you'll thank us for this!"

"Not damn likely," Daniel muttered.

The video faded to black and Daniel tossed the iPad onto the seat next to him. He groaned and covered his eyes with his hand. Alex opened her mouth to speak but no words emerged. She tried again—nothing—and shook her head. Had Rose and Gus lost it completely? "They can't do this," she whispered.

"They just did," Daniel shot back, pulling his phone out from his back pocket. He hit a button, dialed a number and waited impatiently for it to ring. "Voice mail."

"Gran, I am not happy! What the hell gives you the right to meddle in our lives? We're adults and your actions are reprehensible and unacceptable. Have you completely lost your mind?"

Knowing that Gus rarely carried his phone and that when he did he was prone to ignoring it, Alex called her younger brother, Jason. He answered on a rolling laugh.

"Not funny, Jason! I'm on a plane because Grandpa has arranged for us to be kidnapped. Tell him to turn this plane around. Better yet, just let me talk to him."

"He's not here, sis. Or if he is, he's keeping a very low profile, if you get my drift. He is, after all, on his honeymoon."

Ew. The words *Gus* and *honeymoon* did not sit well next to each other. "I don't care what you have to do but find him and tell him to turn this damned plane around!"

Another chuckle. God, when she saw Jace, she was going to throttle him. "Grandpa told me to tell you, if you made contact, to pull on your big-girl panties and suck it up."

"*Find. Him.* Tell him that this isn't funny, that we want to come home!"

"Are you mad? You've been sent off to stay in a luxurious house on a private island in the Caribbean. It's windy, wet and cold here in Texas, and our grandfather is getting more action than I am. My heart bleeds for you! As I said, big-girl panties—"

Screw big-girl panties, she was going to take off her thong and strangle him with it! "Find Grandpa," she muttered, death in her voice. "Tell him what I said."

Alex disconnected the call and rubbed her forehead with her fingertips. "It looks like we're going to Matt's island."

"Looks like?" Daniel snapped back, his expression blank but his body radiating tension.

Alex sent a wistful look at the champagne bottle. "Don't you think this warrants a little champagne? For medicinal use only?"

"No, you're pregnant. No alcohol."

Daniel narrowed his eyes at her, pushed the intercom and ordered a whiskey, straight up. He looked at Alex and his small smile was just shy of evil. "But, as you said, this situation warrants alcohol."

Alex responded to his smirk with one of her own and deliberately, swiftly kicked him again.

After playing Daniel's voice message to Gus, Rose lifted her eyes to meet his. His body, like hers, was older and they didn't have the energy they once had. But his eyes were still those of a young man's, with the power to stop her in her tracks. And underneath the layer of mischief, she saw his grit and determination, his rock-steady calm. Gus did what he needed to do and always stayed the course.

"He is not a happy camper," Gus commented.

"I've seen him lose his temper and it's not pretty," Rose admitted, pushing her phone away. She picked up her coffee and took a sip.

Gus was silent for a good twenty seconds. "Would he hurt her?"

"Hurt Alex?" Rose demanded, horrified. "Good God, no!" When Gus still looked skeptical, she placed her hand on his arm. "No, honey, he would never hurt her. He witnessed his mom being slapped around, beaten up, and he'd never hurt a woman or a child."

Gus's eyes softened with sympathy. "His rough childhood must have done a number on him."

Rose nodded, not bothering to hide her sadness from her man. They were married, so she could share any-thing, and everything, with him. "Stephanie... God, Gus, she was so wild. I couldn't tell her a damn thing—never could. She hit thirteen and entered self-destruct mode."

"I don't know whether she's alive or dead. When she lost custody of Daniel, she refused to have any contact with us."

"And that happened when he was twelve?"

Rose released a quavering breath. "He spent the summer of that year with me, and when Stephanie came to fetch him, he told her that he wasn't going back with her. Neither would he let me pay her to let him stay."

Rose knew that her chin was wobbling. "He told her that he was staying with me, that he was going to go to school in Royal. That if she made trouble for him or me, he'd go to the police and detail every drug deal he saw, finger every dealer she had, tell the police about every 'uncle' who lifted a hand to him." She released another breath. "She had a choice—she could leave him with me without a fuss or he'd make life very, very difficult for her. Stephanie chose to leave him with me."

"And he never spoke to her again after that?"

Rose shook her head. "Neither of us have."

She ran her finger around the rim of her cup. "I can't help thinking that if I'd done some of this and not that, loved her more, disciplined her more, gave her more time and energy, she would've turned out better."

"Sometimes there is no better, Rosie."

"She's her daddy's daughter—she's Ed through and through. Mean, aggressive, malicious." She saw the concern on his face and quickly shook her head. "Daniel isn't like that. He's a good man, Gus. You'll see that eventually."

Her husband pondered her words. "The TCC members seem to think so. The younger members trust him implicitly and they say he has integrity." Gus smiled at her. "I'm looking forward to knowing him, darlin'. It's time to put the past to bed, and young Daniel has done nothing to me."

"Except get your granddaughter pregnant," Rose replied.

Gus shrugged. "The way those two look and act

around each other, I'm just grateful it didn't happen when they were teenagers."

"He's the best thing—apart from you, recently— that's ever happened to me. I can't lose him, Gus."

Gus took her hands is his and waited until her eyes met his. Then he squeezed her hands. "You're not going to lose him, Rosie. I promise you that."

"He's so mad…"

Gus shrugged. "Let him be mad—he'll get over it. In a little less than an hour, he'll be on a deserted island with a beautiful girl he's crazy about. Trust me, he'll be thanking you soon."

"I doubt it," Rose retorted. "They just might kill each other. Or maybe they'll wait to do that until after they've killed us." She frowned at him. "Why are you looking so chipper? Didn't you get a nasty voice mail?"

Gus's cocky smile belonged to the young man she knew so long ago. "Prob'ly did. Don't carry my phone. No doubt that Alex has sent Jason an annoyed message to give to me."

Rose shook her head in exasperation. "You've got to start carrying a phone, Gus. What if I need to get a hold of you?"

"Not a factor." Gus lifted her knuckles to kiss her fingertips. "I don't plan on being a couple of feet from you anytime soon." His mouth curved as she moved her hand to his cheek. "But I am thinking of getting another phone, one that only you have the number to."

"That would make me feel so much better," Rose told him. "I don't want to be that woman who constantly keeps track of her man, but you know…in case of an emergency."

Gus's smile turned wicked. "To hell with an emergency. I'm only getting it in the hope that you'll call me up for a—what do the kids call it—booty call?"

Rose's shocked laughter bounced off the walls. "Augustus Slade!"

Gus looked at her, his face full of love. Then he waggled his eyebrows to make her laugh. "Anytime you have the urge, I'm your guy."

He really was her guy. And damn if she didn't have one of those urges now. Rose looked out the window and saw that it was ten o'clock on a cold, wet winter morning in February, not the time a woman of a certain age should be slinking upstairs. But to hell with that; this was supposed to be her honeymoon. Rose took his hand, grinned and stood up.

"Come upstairs and rock my world, handsome."

It was Gus's turn to look utterly poleaxed, but that didn't stop him from leaping to his feet with all the energy of a twenty-year-old.

Six

Upon landing at Galloway Cove, Michelle lowered the steps to the private jet, stowed their suitcases in the back of the golf cart parked to the side of the landing strip and tossed them a jovial smile. "Have fun." With that, she ran back up the steps to the plane. Minutes later the jet was in the air and headed back to Houston.

Alex climbed into the golf cart and sat down next to Daniel, her thigh brushing his. Leaning forward, he pulled off his flannel shirt and threw it into the back of the cart, before placing his hand on the wheel and cranking the small engine.

Tired of their silence, Alex darted him a look. "Any idea where we are?"

"West of the Bahamas."

Alex wrinkled her nose at his brief reply. "Can you tell me anything about where we are going, what to expect?"

"Matt is one of the wealthiest guys in Texas. All I

know is that the house is completely secluded, has its own private beach and reef. It will be jaw-droppingly amazing." He gritted his teeth. "The other thing I know is that I need to get the hell off this island. I've got a ranch to run. I can't just take off on a Monday morning with no warning!"

"You've said that before, numerous times," Alex told him testily. "Look, you might as well accept that we are stranded here until that plane returns." She gestured to the awesome view of a flat turquoise-colored sea. Below them, nestled against the cliff and partially covered by the natural vegetation, they could see the tiled roof of what she assumed to be Matt's beach house. She gestured to the well-used track in front of them. "The sun is shining. The sea looks amazing. So, on the bright side—"

"There *is* no bright side," Daniel muttered, and Alex gripped the frame of the cart as he accelerated forward.

"I can't think of anything better than lying on the beach for a week. I'm exhausted and it will give me time to think. We don't even have to talk to each other. Actually, it would be better if we didn't."

Clenching his jaw, Daniel steered the car along the track, and Alex heard the cry of a seagull and the sound of a rushing creek above the cart's rumble. Daniel kept moving his head from the path to look at her and back again. Annoyed, she half turned in her seat and glared at him. "What? Why do you keep looking at me like that?"

"What about sex?"

"Where did that out-of-left-field question come from?" Alex lifted her hands in confusion.

Daniel's dry look suggested she get with the program. "We're together. Alone. On an island. We might be as frustrated as hell with each other and the situation, but you cannot be that naive to think that, with our sexual chemistry, we're not going to end up in bed."

She wanted to deny his words, but she knew she would come across as being disingenuous if she brushed off his comment. Alex lifted her thigh up onto the bench seat, her knee brushing his hard thigh. After marshaling her thoughts, she picked out her words. "Daniel, we've known each other for a long time but we don't *know* each other."

"What do you mean?"

She'd been thinking about this a lot lately. She and Daniel communicated with their bodies, not with their minds. They were both guarded people and they both struggled to let people in. They knew each other's bodies intimately, knew exactly how to behave naked. But fully clothed? They were like drunken cowboys stumbling around in the dark. As her baby's father, Daniel was going to be in her life for a long time, so didn't she owe it to herself and their child to get to know his mind a fraction as well as she knew his body?

"Let's be honest here, we've always been sexually attracted to one another, and even as teenagers, we far preferred to make out than to talk—"

"And it's still my first choice."

Although tempted, Alex ignored his interruption. "That trend continued when we hooked up. I don't know you—not really—and you certainly don't know me."

Daniel sent her an exasperated look. "Of course I do."

Alex snorted. "Rubbish. Let's test that theory, shall we?"

Daniel released a frustrated sigh. "If you're going to ask me a dumb-ass question like what is your favorite color, then I won't know."

Alex thought for a minute. "No, let me start with an easy one. Do I prefer to shower in the morning or at night?"

Daniel hesitated before guessing. "At night."

It was a good guess. "What do I like on my pizza?"

He hesitated and she pounced. "You don't know. Neither do you know whether I have allergies and I don't know if you vote."

"Of course I vote!" Daniel retorted.

Alex ignored him. "Do you believe in God? What are you currently reading? What is your favorite season? Are you on social media? What is your favorite meal? Who is your closest friend?"

"Yes, sort of. A Corben novel. Fall. Hell, no, I don't have time to post crap no one cares about on Facebook. Beef stew. And yes, I have friends… Matt. Ryan. I talk to James Harris pretty often, too."

She'd said *closest* friend, not friends in general, but she'd still found out more about him in thirty seconds than she had in ten years. How much more would she find out about him if they actually conversed instead of kissed?

"We're going to be raising a kid together, separately but together. Should we not use this time to get to know each other better?"

Daniel steered the cart around a corner and Alex was momentarily distracted by the magnificent house in front of them. It hugged the side of a cliff, and trees and natural vegetation cradled the house like a mother holding her child. A massive wooden door broke up the sprawling white expanse and Daniel parked the cart to the right of it. Leaving the cart, she turned to take her bag but noticed that Daniel already had it in his grasp, as well as his own duffel bag.

She smiled her thanks and watched as he walked up to the front door. Alex took a moment to appreciate his long-legged, easy grace, the way his big biceps strained the bands of his T-shirt, the width of his shoulders. It was brutally unfair that he was the walking definition of sex on feet. Alex sighed and watched as Daniel placed his hand on the door. It swung open from a central pivot and he stepped back to motion her inside.

Alex stood in the doorway, unwilling to go inside until she had an answer from Daniel. "So, are we going to try and get to know each other a little better?"

"We can try," Daniel replied. He shrugged and looked down at her with those deep, compelling eyes. "But I guarantee you that, thanks to the combination of sand, sea and you in a tiny bikini, you're going to be under me sooner rather than later."

Arrogant jerk, Alex thought, walking into the beach house. How dare he think that he could just click his fingers and she would lie down, roll over and let him scratch her tummy. Sure their attraction was explosive, but she wasn't so weak that she'd just fall into bed with him—

Oh my God, this place is fantastic.

Alex stopped in her tracks as she drank in their luxurious surroundings. It was open plan, as all beach houses should be, with high vaulted ceilings displaying intricate beams. As soon as they stepped out of the hall and into the living space, the eye was pulled toward the massive floor-to-ceiling windows, across the infinity pool to the view beyond. Alex was momentarily unsure where the pool ended and the sea began. Stepping forward, she spared a glance at the sleek kitchen, the wooden dining table and the chairs that were the same blue as the sea. Under comfortable sofas, an expensive rug covered the floors, but it was the view that captured her attention: it was the only piece of art the room needed. The white beaches, the aqua sea, the lush emerald of an island in the distance.

"Holy crap."

Alex turned to look at Daniel but he was equally entranced by the house and the view. Dropping their bags to the floor, he strode over to the windows and looked at the frame. Within seconds, the windows turned into sliding doors, and warm, fragrant air rushed into the room. Alex walked out onto the covered deck and looked left and then right. "It looks like the deck runs the length of the house. I imagine all the bedrooms open up onto it. We can sleep with the doors open and listen to the sound of the sea."

Daniel looked down at the tranquil sea and lifted an eyebrow. "It's as calm as a lake—I doubt we're going to hear the sound of crashing waves."

"Don't be pedantic—" Alex's eyes widened when she saw Daniel bend over to pull off his boot. When his feet were bare, he pulled off his T-shirt before attacking his belt buckle and ripping open his fly. "What the hell are you doing?" she demanded.

He gave her a wicked smile and gestured to the pool. "Going for a swim."

His hands slipped under the fabric of his jeans and Alex squeaked when she saw that he was stripping them off. "You're swimming naked?"

Daniel shrugged as his clothes pooled at his feet. "We're totally alone and you've seen it all before."

She had and every inch of him was absolutely glorious. "You're not going to help our cause of not sleeping together if you're going to parade around buck naked, Clayton."

Daniel's smile broadened. "That's your cause, Slade, not mine. I intend to get to know you and sleep with you. I also plan to spend a great deal of time trying to convince you not to go to Houston. If you won't marry or move in with me, then I want you as close as I can possibly have you."

"I—you—argh!" Alex, annoyed by his cocky smile and his self-assurance, threw up her hands. She did, however, watch that magnificent body dive into the pool.

After his swim, Daniel pulled on his wet clothes and padded barefoot into the house. Not seeing Alex in the living area, he picked up his bag and walked down the hall, opening doors as he went along. Study-cum-library, gym—nice—and a sauna. He entered the first bedroom he came to and threw his bag onto the massive double bed, taking a minute to appreciate the view. Like he suspected, the floor-to-ceiling windows were in fact another set of doors, and he immediately opened them, welcoming fresh air into the room. This room was super nice but he wouldn't bother to unpack; he would end up sharing whatever bedroom Alex chose.

Which, if he knew her, would definitely be the master suite.

Daniel pulled his phone out of his pocket and checked for a signal, of which there was none. Cursing, he tossed it onto the bed and left the room to head for the study. If he was going to stay on this godforsaken island, he would have to send some emails, leaving instructions for his foreman, his PA and his business manager. And he would drop his grandmother another message, reminding her how out of line she was.

Daniel sat behind Matt's desk, pulled out the first

drawer, and yep, as he thought, inside the drawer rested a state-of-the-art laptop. If Matt had a laptop, then he'd have an internet connection, which was exactly what he needed. Daniel leaned back in his chair as he waited for the laptop to boot, thinking that he could, with a couple of keystrokes, have another plane on the runway in a couple of hours.

He could hire a private plane as easily as Gus had, and this farce could come to a quick end. Except that maybe he didn't want it to...

Daniel stared out at the tranquil ocean. He was here, Alex was here and they were nowhere near Royal. They could escape their grandparents' machinations, the Royal gossips, the crazy normal that was their day-to-day lives. They could both take this week to find a way forward, to have some heart-to-heart conversations, to plot a course.

He still wanted to marry Alex—that was the plan that still made the most sense to him. The Clayton-Slade feud had been buried with Gus and Rose's marriage—something that Royal was still talking about—and after their nuptials, his and Alex's nuptials would barely raise a brow or two. He wanted to raise his child in a conventional family, one with a father and mother close at hand. He'd spent the first twelve years of his life with an unstable mother, constantly wishing he had a father he could run to, live with, a bigger, stronger man he could look to for protection and comfort. He never ever wanted his child to think—not for a second—that he wasn't there for him, that he was anything but a shout away. He wanted to teach his son to ride, shoot, fish. Hell, if he had a bunch of daughters, he'd teach them the same thing. He wanted them to have the run of the farm. And if his kids were Alex's, then they'd have the

Slade ranch as an additional playground. He wanted them outside, on horses and bikes, in the stables, swimming in the river or in the pond. He wanted his kids to have the early childhood he never had, with two involved, loving parents.

For the sake of their kids, he and Alex could make a marriage work. They were super compatible together sexually, and they could, if he took her suggestion to learn more about each other, become friends. Friends who had hot sex—wasn't that a good marriage right there? Love? No. Love—having it, losing it, using it as a carrot or a club—just complicated the hell out of everything.

Marriage was a rational, sensible decision. He just had to convince Alex that this was the best option available to them both. Hell, even if she balked at getting married—and he had no doubt that she would—she could still move into his place. Gus and Rose wouldn't be happy at their nontraditional living arrangements, but it was better than nothing.

Right, he had a plan. He liked having a plan; it made him feel in control.

Alex leaned back against a sun-warmed rock and watched the sky change. Blue morphed into a deep purple, and then an invisible brush painted the sky with streaks of pink and orange. This Caribbean sunset was possibly one of the prettiest she'd ever witnessed, and she couldn't help but sigh her appreciation.

Alex felt warm, strong fingers graze her shoulder and she turned to look up at Dan, who held out a bottle of water. She smiled her thanks, shifted up a bit, and when he sat down next to her, she noticed the bottle of beer in his hand. He'd changed into a pair of swimming shorts and wore a pale yellow T-shirt. She wore a sleeveless tank over her bikini and her hair was a tangled mass of still-damp curls.

"Thanks."

Daniel's bare shoulder nudged hers and Alex ignored the flash of desire that ricocheted down her spine. Taking a sip from the bottle he'd thoughtfully opened for her, she gestured to the sunset. "I wondered if you were watching the sunset."

"It's stunning," Daniel murmured.

She hadn't seen him since before lunch and she wondered what he'd been up to. "So, what have you been doing?"

Daniel took a moment to answer her. "Hanging out, chilling. Seeing if I could find signal for my phone."

"Did you find one?"

"Nope."

She also had no cell phone signal, and it was a problem. She needed to talk to Mike, ask him for some more time to think about his offer, to work out the logistics of moving to Houston. "I need to send my grandpa an irate email, telling him how much I resent his interference and machinations. He doesn't carry a phone but he does read his emails."

Daniel's chest lifted as he pulled in some air. "You can."

"I can what?" Alex asked, digging her toes into the sand.

"Send an email," Daniel admitted. "I found a computer in Matt's study. I should've realized that the guy, with all his business interests, would have to have some contact with the outside world. On further examination, there's also a satellite phone for emergencies."

Alex flew to her feet. "Why didn't you tell me sooner?

Why are we here? Why aren't we at the airfield, waiting for a plane?"

She could go home, confront Gus, talk to her clients, Mike. She could put some distance between her and Daniel, start her life without him. At the thought, her heart stuttered, then stumbled. She had to; she had no choice. She and Daniel didn't have a future, not as anything more than co-parents.

She wasn't marrying him or moving in with him; both options were impossible.

Daniel pulled his legs up and rested his forearms on his knees as he squinted up at her. "You're missing the sunset, Lex."

"We can go home, Daniel! We need to go home."

He gently took her wrist and pulled her back down so that she sat with her back to the sunset. The pink-and-yellow light danced across his face. Daniel's thumb stroked the sensitive flesh on the inside of her wrist.

"Let's not, Lex."

"Let's not what?"

"Go home," Daniel said, and she sent him a shocked look. He'd been furious about leaving, about being manipulated into taking this time away and now he wanted to stay?

"I don't understand," Alex said, pulling her hand out of his grasp. She couldn't talk to him and touch him—she wasn't that strong.

"As loath as I am to give those two meddlers any credit, I think that they are right. We need to work some stuff out, and we can do it here," Daniel suggested. "You're exhausted. Organizing the auction was hard work, and I haven't taken a break for nearly a year. We both can do with some downtime. And while we relax, maybe we can plot a way forward."

"You and your plans, Daniel!" Alex muttered. "You can't plan for every eventuality. Some things you have to allow to evolve, to work themselves out."

"Work themselves out? God!" Daniel released a harsh laugh. "That's such a stupid thing to say. Things very rarely work out, Alexis!"

Wow, that was quite the reaction to an innocent comment. Instead of jumping on him, Alex tipped her head to the side and waited for him to speak.

Daniel picked up a handful of sand, clenched his fist and allowed the particles to slide down the tunnel his hand created. She'd never seen such sad eyes, she decided. Sad and angry and distraught.

"Do you know what it's like to live a life lurching from crisis to crisis? Do you know how unsettling it is not to know where you are going to be, what bed you're going to be sleeping in? Whether your mother will be there when you wake up? It sucks, Alex!"

She stared at him, shocked at his outburst but even more surprised that he'd revealed that much about his childhood to her. When they were younger, she'd pried, tried to get him to open up about his life with the infamous Stephanie, but he'd never so much as mentioned his mother and what his life was like before he came to live at The Silver C. From the pain she saw in his eyes, Alex knew that it was way worse than she'd ever imagined.

"I'm sorry—"

Daniel immediately cut her off. "Forget it. Ignore what I said. My point is that I like to plan. I always will."

Because it made him feel secure, like he was in control. Alex understood that now. She picked up a handful of fine sand and allowed it to trickle through her fingers. Knowing that Daniel had said everything he intended to for now, she contemplated whether to stay on the island or to leave. She could call for a plane and within hours they'd be winging their way back to Royal and nothing, not one damn thing, would be settled between them.

But on the other hand... With a couple of emails, she could clear her schedule, take this time they both desperately needed. Didn't she owe it to herself, to Daniel and her child, to stop, to breathe? To think?

To plan? Dammit.

Alex made herself meet his eyes and reluctantly nodded. "Okay, we can stay here."

His eyes turned smoky and Alex immediately recognized that look. She held up her hand. "Hold on, cowboy. If we do this, then there are going to be some ground rules."

Daniel released a low curse, and a frown pulled those black brows together. It wasn't a surprise to see that Clayton didn't like anyone else calling the shots. Tough—it was something he was going to have to deal with. She wasn't eighteen anymore and so desperately eager to please.

"I'll only do this if we can start fresh."

"What the hell does that mean?" Daniel demanded, grumpy again.

"I am not hopping back into bed with you." Alex drew a heart in the sand and quickly erased it, hoping he hadn't noticed. "As I said, I want us to do something different, be different!"

"Lex..." Daniel muttered.

"Dan, we're having a baby together! We're not going to get married, or even live together, but if we are going to be in each other's lives, see each other every weekend, then there has got be something more between us than some hot sex."

"I'm not good at talking, Lex."

Neither was she. But they had to make an effort. "I know, Dan, and neither am I. We're not good at opening up, at sharing, but, God, the next eighteen years are going to be sheer misery if we don't start to communicate."

Daniel stared past her shoulder and Alex picked up the tension in his body, saw his hard jaw, his thin lips. She needed this, she suddenly realized. She needed to dig beneath the surface to find out what made this amazing man tick, and not only for her baby. She needed to know him. Because even if they couldn't be lovers, they could be friends, and being friends with Dan was infinitely better than being lovers and casual acquaintances. He had fabulous mattress skills but between that gruff exterior was, she suspected, a lonely guy who needed a friend. And to be honest, so did she.

Daniel's cheeks puffed and then he expelled the breath he'd been holding. When he turned to look at her, his expression turned rueful. "I can't promise you anything, but I can try, Lex. That's all I can give you."

"I still want to sleep with you, though," Dan added, being brutally honest.

"I know." Alex picked up her water bottle from the sand and dusted it off. "But we can either have one or the other, not both."

"I vote for sex."

She rolled her eyes. "You're a guy—I wouldn't expect anything else. But no, that's not going to happen. I think we need to be friends."

"Not half as much fun," Daniel grumbled.

Alex smiled at his sulky face. "Man up, Clayton."

Although his expression remained sober, she caught the amusement in his eyes. He leaned toward her, his amazing eyes on her mouth and his mouth hovered over hers. She should pull back—she *would* pull back…but how much could one little kiss hurt?

Alex frowned when she saw his lips twitch and then he resumed his position against the rock.

Oh, that was just mean.

"Jerk."

That twitch widened into a sexy, full smile. "You're easily distracted, Lex. I like it."

She nailed him with a don't-push-it glare.

Daniel's expression turned serious. "You've changed. You're not half as biddable as you used to be."

"Yeah, I grew up." Alex half turned, put her hands behind her and leaned back, stretching out her legs. She looked at the sunset—the light was slowly fading and the colors were deepening in intensity. She turned her head to look up at the house and noticed that it was fully lit. There were also lights along the entire length of the path running from the beach to the house. It looked like a totally different structure, mysterious and sexy.

Just like the man lounging next to her.

Daniel followed her eyes and whistled in appreciation. "Wow. Matt Galloway is one lucky bastard to own this place." He turned his head to look at her. "So, did you choose a room?"

"Yeah, I couldn't resist the master bedroom. When the doors are open, it's like you are sleeping outside, and it has this amazing shower enclosure. It's three walls of glass and utterly breathtaking."

Daniel's mouth twitched with amusement. "That would give anyone on the beach an eyeful."

"I thought the same thing," Alex said with a smile.

"But when I walked down to the beach, I checked. It's made of that fancy glass where you can see out but not in."

Standing up, Daniel held out his hand. Alex put her hand in his and he hauled her to her feet. "I'm starving. Let's go see what's in the fridge. I think I saw some no-alcohol beers if you're interested."

"I'd far prefer a glass of wine," Alex said as she headed to the path with Daniel behind her.

"Well, I'd prefer to be sharing your bed. But apparently we can't always have what we want."

Seven

The next day, Daniel looked up and saw Alex standing in the doorway of the study. He leaned back in his chair and indulged himself by giving her a top-to-toe look. A red-and-white blousy shirt was tied at her still-slim waist and flirted with the band of the sexiest, most flattering pair of cutoff jeans he'd ever seen. Her feet were bare, as was her face, and she'd pulled her thick blond mane into a loose bundle on top of her head. She'd never looked more beautiful, and he desperately wanted to take her to bed.

Friends. They were trying to be friends.

Worst idea ever.

Daniel glanced at his watch and then grinned. It was past nine and that meant that she'd had a solid night's sleep. Good. She'd needed it. He was happy to see that the blue smudges were gone from beneath her eyes.

"Hey, sleepyhead. I'm not going to ask you if you slept well, because you obviously did."

Alex walked into the room and hopped up onto the corner of the desk, facing him. "I did. And for your information, I did wake up during the night and I did hear the sea. The tide must've been in."

Alex liked being right and he couldn't blame her because he liked it, too. He smelled the mint on her breath and forced himself not to lean forward and have a taste. Man, this week was going to be a drag if he couldn't touch or taste her.

Daniel leaned back and linked his hands across his stomach. If he kept them there, maybe he wouldn't give in to the urge to scoop her up, haul her outside and lower her to the sun bed on the porch. Excitement pooled in his groin at the thought of stripping her down until only the sun, his fingers and his mouth were touching her soft, fragrant skin…

Pull your head out of the bedroom, Clayton.

"How are you feeling?" he asked. He darted a look at the small strip of bare flesh he could see above the band of her jeans. Nobody would ever suspect that she was pregnant.

"Fine, actually. I haven't had any morning sickness or cravings for weird food." She smiled as she answered him, banging the heel of her foot against the leg of the desk. "And… Yay… I still fit into all my clothes, which is a definite plus."

Alex picked up a glass paperweight from the desk, turned it over and lifted her eyebrows. She carefully replaced it and when she looked at him again, her eyes were bright with astonishment. "That's Baccarat crystal and super expensive."

Daniel didn't care if it was a solid-gold nugget. He wanted to talk about her and the baby growing inside her. "Have you seen a doctor?"

Alex nodded. "I visited the clinic and had a blood test to confirm I was pregnant. I was prescribed some vitamins, given a handful of pamphlets to read through and was recommended a couple of books. I need to visit an ob-gyn when I get back and have an ultrasound scan. That way the doctor will get a better idea of my due date. It's also to check that the baby is growing as it should."

Daniel leaned forward, opened his online calendar and sent her an expectant look. "When is the appointment?"

"Do you want to come with me?"

She sounded surprised. "When are you going to realize that you're not alone, Lex? That we are in this together?"

Alex rattled off the date and time and Daniel tapped the it into his calendar. He was determined to be the exact opposite of his father—and his mother—who'd missed every milestone of his life, from his birth to football games to graduation.

Alex sent him a grateful look. "Thanks. Knowing you will be there will make me feel less—" she hesitated before completing her sentence "—alone. I've never missed my mom more than I have in the past few weeks and I dare not even think about Sarah. If I do, I won't stop crying."

Daniel placed his hand on her knee, his skin several shades darker than hers. He started to stroke back and forth, and then reminded himself that he was touching her in comfort, not for pleasure. "Your mom and dad died when you were pretty young. Do you remember them?"

Alex wrinkled her nose. "A little. But I'm not sure if my memories are my own or because I heard so many stories about them. I can't tell what's real or what's been planted."

"Does it matter, if they are good memories?" He didn't have any good memories of his mom, of his early life. He'd been so damn busy trying to survive, to get through the day, the week, until he could next visit The Silver C and his grandmother. On the ranch, under that big blue Texas sky, riding and exploring, he could let go, find a little peace.

Alex touched her stomach with her fingertips. "I just wish she was here."

Daniel squeezed her knee, choosing to express his sympathy through touch rather than words. Then he removed his hand because there was only so much temptation he could take.

"Have you eaten? There's a fruit salad in the fridge. Or I can make you pancakes. And bacon."

Alex's eyes widened in disbelief. "You cook?"

"Yes, smarty-pants, I can cook. In fact, I intend to catch and then cook our lunch."

Alex gestured to the ocean beyond the open windows. "I'm impressed. Maybe you should get to it, because the fish might not be in a cooperative mood. I haven't seen any fishing rods lying around."

"They are in the storage shed, along with fins, goggles and a Jet Ski. And a spear gun, which I'm going to use."

"Marvelous idea." Alex looked deeply skeptical at his abilities to provide her with food. She smirked. "If you come back empty-handed, I suppose we can always have peanut-butter-and-jelly sandwiches."

"Oh, you of little faith." Daniel heard the ping indicating that he had a new email and leaned forward to check the screen. He read the subject line and released an annoyed groan.

"Problem? Can I peek?" she asked. He nodded, her legs tangling with his bare ones as she leaned forward to look at the screen. He smiled at her squint.

"Do you need glasses to read, Lex?"

"Bite me." Lex cheerfully responded before frowning. "'Please date me.'" She read out the subject line for an email. There were more, some more direct than others. "'I'm your soul mate. I think I may be in love with you. I have really big…'" Alex's laughing eyes met his. "Did you register for a dating site or something? Or place an ad for a date on some skanky message board?"

Daniel glared at her. "No, that's the response from that article Grandmother made me do to promote the auction, and what it's like being one of the state's most eligible bachelors."

Alex giggled. "Oh my. This one says she's a bit of a nymphomaniac. How on earth did they get your email address?"

"They printed the ranch's website address. The public can email the ranch through the website. As they did." He gestured to the screen and grimaced. "Repeatedly."

Alex peered at the screen again. "Hey, this one is from a guy. The subject line mentions that the two of you have a mutual acquaintance."

"Not interested." Daniel leaned forward, highlighted all the offending emails and deleted them in one swift move. There was only one woman he wanted, and she was sitting next to him, driving him insane.

Daniel closed the lid of the laptop and stood up. Putting his hands on Alex's hips, he gently lifted her off the desk. But after placing her on her feet, he didn't—couldn't—let her go. How could he? She smelled like expensive soap and sunscreen, and her upturned mouth looked soft and inviting. Too much temptation—he had to kiss her, taste her. It had been so damn long.

Daniel threaded his fingers through her soft, upswept hair and held the back of her head as he covered her lips with his, keeping his kiss gentle, exploratory. It would be so easy to fall into heat and passion, but he didn't want to scare her. He just wanted to kiss her in the sunlight, skim her body with his fingers, be with her in this moment with only the blue sea and the hot sun as witnesses.

She tasted like coffee and spearmint and sexy woman, a combination that made his head swim. Daniel skimmed her rib cage, brushed his knuckles over her waist and laid his palm possessively over her stomach, his hand almost covering her from hip to hip. Pulling his head back, he looked down and emotion tightened his throat.

He pushed the words out. "Somewhere in there is my baby."

Alex's big smile was a kick to his heart. She lifted her hand and pushed back that annoying curl that always fell down his forehead. "I hope our baby has your beautiful eyes."

"I hope he has yours," Daniel whispered back. "You are so lovely, Lex."

"You're not too bad yourself, cowboy," Alex murmured, her lips moving against his. Daniel sucked in his breath as her breasts pushed into his chest. Then Alex pulled away and Daniel felt her arms tightening around his neck as her nose burrowed into the side of his throat. He barely heard her words, but somehow they still lodged in his soul. "Having a baby is scary, Dan."

"I know, sweetheart. But I'm here with you, for you."

Alex pulled back and he noticed the brilliant sheen

in her eyes. He cradled her face and tipped his head to the side. "Why the tears, Lex?"

"If you are going to leave me, Dan, do it now. Before it hurts too much."

Leave her? His child? No chance. "I'm not going anywhere, Lex. I promise."

Alex forced a laugh before stepping back to wipe her eyes with the heels of her hands. She sent him a smile that was part embarrassment, part fear. "Ignore me. That's just hormones."

He nodded to give her an out, to allow her to walk away with her pride intact, but he knew that outburst had nothing to do with pregnancy hormones and everything to do with her fear of him disappointing her. Again.

Didn't she know that he would give her everything he was able to? His time, his support, his money, all his effort. Except his heart. He wouldn't give her that roughed-up organ. He liked it right where it was, thank you very much.

Daniel was either a very competent fisherman or the lady fish simply flung themselves onto his spear, thrilled to be caught by such a luscious merman. Alex was convinced the latter was true because they'd been eating from the ocean a lot lately, including tonight's dinner of a lobster salad. She could easily imagine the below-the-waves conversation:

Yes, Daniel, of course I will sacrifice myself for your eating pleasure.

No, take me.

He's mine to die for.

"What are you smiling about?" Daniel asked.

"I'm imagining a lady lobster's last words," Alex

confessed, sitting down in the chair he pulled out for her. She was a modern girl, living a modern life, but she never tired of being the recipient of his gentlemanly manners.

"You are very weird," Daniel commented as he took his seat to the right of her. He reached for the bottle of white wine in the middle of the table and twisted the bottle to show her the label. "I found this in the cellar. It's nonalcoholic. Would you like some?"

"Drinking nonalcoholic wine is like drinking coffee with no caffeine," Alex grumbled.

Ignoring her, Daniel merely lifted a brow. Alex pushed her crystal wine goblet toward him. "Oh okay, then."

His mouth twitched as he poured the wine. Or, more accurately, grape juice. Alex gestured to the food. "Thank you for preparing dinner again. You're spoiling me. It's going to be difficult going back to Houston and having to look after myself. I've been living in the lap of luxury at the Lone Wolf and now here, with you. Real life is going to be a bit of a shock."

Daniel handed her a glass of wine and lifted his beer bottle in a silent toast. Alex sipped her wine—not too shabby, as it tasted like a decent chardonnay—and watched him in the low light, courtesy of the single candle between them and the firepits dotted around the pool. She sighed. How could she *not* look at him? They were on a private island in the Caribbean, her surroundings were absolutely exquisite, but still they paled in comparison to Daniel.

Graceful but masculine, mysterious and sexy with a thick layer of smart. His body was a masterpiece, and she could literally gaze at that face forever. She craved to hear his laughter fill the air, his lips drawing patterns on her skin. She wanted him. She would for the rest of her life.

And that was why she'd mentioned Houston, spoke about life after Galloway Cove. Because she needed a reminder that having Daniel in her life on a full-time basis was impossible. Deep down she knew this, and she couldn't allow herself to be seduced by a hot man who cooked for her.

She wasn't that weak.

Okay, she *was*, but wasn't identifying the problem the first step to finding the solution?

Daniel, bless him, helped her pull herself together by changing the topic to one she expected. "Tell me about your job offer."

She could talk about work—it was a nice, neutral topic of conversation. "Mike and I joined the company I still work for shortly after we left college. He left about six months ago to start his own business. He's asked me to join him—"

"This is in PR?"

Alex wrinkled her nose. "We don't handle public relations in a traditional sense. I specialize in creating social media strategies that best display and promote a brand or a company's image in the digital space."

Daniel grimaced. "Sounds like hell."

She flashed him a quick smile. "It would to someone who has absolutely no social media presence."

Daniel smiled at her and her stomach flipped over. "You stalking me, Slade?"

She'd never admit that in a thousand years. "I cy-berstalk lots of people. But you should be embarrassed that your grandmother is very active on social media and you are not."

"Yet I'm not embarrassed." Daniel reached for the

lobster salad and the serving utensil. He spooned food onto the plate in front of Alex before dishing up his own food.

"And this guy, Mike, wants to give you a partnership," Daniel asked, returning to the subject at hand. "Why would he do that?"

Alex forked up some lobster and groaned when the creamy sweetness hit her taste buds. Midchew, a thought hit her and she gripped Daniel's arm, her nails digging into the exposed muscle beneath his rolled up shirt sleeve.

"Problem?"

"I don't know if I should be eating shellfish," Alex said, pulling a face. "I think I read something about it not being safe for pregnant women."

Surely that was an old wives' tale. How could she be expected to walk away from all that bright, tasty, luscious salad? Resisting Daniel was hard enough, and now life was throwing another temptation in her way? Two words.

So unfair.

"I checked and it's safe to eat during pregnancy as long as its fresh and properly cooked. I caught and cooked it, and it's fine." Daniel waved his fork at her plate. "Eat."

Alex felt touched that he'd checked. It had been a long time since she felt protected, cosseted, fussed over. It was a nice feeling but dangerous. She couldn't allow herself to get used to being the center of any man's attention. Especially since that attention, along with love and respect and commitment, had the tendency to vaporize.

"You were telling me about Houston," Daniel prompted, leaning back and picking up his bottle of beer.

"Mike loves dealing with the clients—he's a born salesman but he's not so fond of overseeing the staff or paperwork. And the financial aspects of running a business. He's offered me a full partnership if I take over that side of the business."

Daniel looked out into the inky darkness. Alex followed his gaze and could just make out the boulders on the beach, the white bubbles of waves hitting the shoreline. "And you have to be in Houston to do that?"

Initially, Mike had suggested that she could spend the bulk of her time in Royal, commuting to Houston only a few days a month. Theirs was a web-based business and there was little that couldn't be managed over email and by video calling. It was Alex who'd pushed to move to Houston, who'd felt the need to get away from Royal and a certain sexy cowboy.

Yeah, that plan had worked out so well.

"I think I should be in Houston," Alex said, keeping her voice low.

Daniel took a few more bites of his dinner before pushing his food away. He used his thumb to trace the lines of the bamboo place mat. "What the hell happened to us, Lex?"

"We had sex and I got pregnant."

Daniel ignored the sarcastic retort. "I mean…back then."

To her, it was simple. He'd chosen The Silver C and Rose over her. What was there to discuss?

Daniel's eyes met hers and she almost whimpered at the pain she saw in his depths. "I asked for a long-distance relationship when you went off to college. You told me that it had to be all or nothing. Why? Why did you insist that my leaving was the only way I could prove that I loved you?"

"Because I needed you—I needed *someone*—to choose me, to make being with me the most important thing they could do."

Daniel sat up and linked his hands behind his head. "I needed to stay on The Silver C. I couldn't leave, Lex."

"No, you *wouldn't* leave. Rose said no, and you just did her bidding. You didn't fight for me, Daniel."

Alex pushed back her chair and stood up, taking her nonalcoholic wine over to the edge of the pool. She sat down and dipped her bare feet into the sun-warmed water and stared out to sea. The rising moon was the silver blue of a fish scale, the flash of an angel's wing. It was a night meant for passion, for making love in the sweet, fragrant air. It felt wrong to be opening old wounds under the light of a benevolent moon.

She heard Daniel crack open another bottle of beer and then he was sitting next to her, thigh to thigh, leg to leg, feet touching in the tepid water of the pool.

"I'm sorry I hurt you, Lex," Daniel said in a raspy voice, and Alex heard the sincerity in it.

"I just wanted you to come to college with me, Dan. To be somewhere else with me, away from our grandparents and their disapproval and their stupid feud. I wanted to see who we could be when we didn't have all of that hanging over us."

"I couldn't and wouldn't leave, Alex. And it wasn't because I didn't want to."

Alex pulled her thigh up onto the stone rim of the pool and pushed her hair off her forehead. Half facing him, she ran her hand down his arm until she found his fingers. His spread open in welcome and her hand was quickly enveloped by his. She took a breath, knowing that she shouldn't ask a question she wasn't completely sure she wanted the answer to. But she was going to anyway.

"Explain it to me, Dan, because I still can't work it out."

Daniel pulled her hand from his and leaned back, his hands behind him. He tipped his head up to look at the stars, and Alex knew that he was looking for his words. Instead of answering her question, he turned his head and swiped his lips across hers, his tongue sliding into her mouth. Alex instantly ignited, and she wound her arms around his neck, falling into his touch. How could he fire her up with just his mouth on hers, his big hand holding the back of her head, anchoring her to him?

God, he was a magnificent kisser...

He was also, she dimly realized, brilliant at avoiding the subject. Reluctantly, Alex pulled back and scooted a few inches from him. "Nope, I'm not going to be distracted, Clayton. Talk to me."

"I always envied you, you know," Daniel quietly stated. "I know that you lost your parents when you were really young but, God, you had this family that was pretty damn awesome."

"How would you know that? I mean, thanks to the feud, it's not like we saw much of each other growing up."

"Before I came to live with Grandmother full-time, I saw you when I was visiting. At church, at the town parade, the cookout at the community center." A small smile touched Daniel's face. "And maybe I saw more of you than I should've..."

"Meaning?" Alex demanded.

Daniel lifted one powerful shoulder. "I used to sneak onto Slade land, head for the tree house and watch you and your brother." He grimaced. "I'm sorry, that sounds creepy as hell, but I was young and, I suppose, lonely. After I moved to The Silver C, I started at school and life became busy and I stopped sneaking onto Slade land."

"Until the day you came across me in the high meadow. You were trespassing."

Daniel's mouth twitched. "I was on Clayton land."

"You wish you were," Alex retorted, her voice holding no heat, because how could it? Memories washed over her, as sweet as that summer's day. They'd started arguing about who was trespassing and before they knew it, they were inching closer and then Daniel grabbed her hips and she his biceps, and their lips touched.

"And then you kissed me."

"You kissed me," Alex replied because she was expected to. Soft laughter followed their familiar argument and Alex dropped her forehead to rest it on Daniel's muscled shoulder. "We loved each other so much, Dan, but it vaporized. I don't understand how that happened."

Daniel moved his head so that he could kiss her hair. "You asked me to do the one thing I could not do. You told me that leaving was the only way I could prove my love and that you would only carry on loving me if I did what you asked."

Alex frowned. "I don't remember saying that."

"Trust me, I heard it. And then you made me choose, Alex."

"And you chose The Silver C."

"I did."

His easy agreement hurt, but for the first time since she was eighteen, Alex felt the need to push aside the pain and understand. Daniel wasn't a guy who was careless with people's feelings, and she wanted to know and understand what drove him back then.

And now.

She was having a child with the man, so she had the right to try to understand him.

"I have no idea who my father is. He left before I was born, or so my mother said. She also said that he left after I was born, so who the hell knows what's true? I was raised in apartments, in trailers, in rented rooms and, for one memorable month, a women's shelter."

Dan ran his hand through his thick hair, then over his face. This wasn't easy for him and Alex respected him for opening up.

"Life with my mother was a matter of measuring the depth of the trouble and debt we were in—sometimes it was nose-deep and we were about to drown, and sometimes it was only ankle-deep. But it was always there… and she created most of it."

Alex kept her eyes on his face, scared to move in case he had second thoughts and stopped talking. She schooled her features because she knew that sympathy would make him clam up as quickly as inane platitudes would.

Stay still, don't breathe and just listen, Slade.

"When Stephanie tired of me or couldn't cope, she'd send me to Grandmother at The Silver C. Or my grandmother would ask to have me. Either way, she had to pay to have me at The Silver C. I once tried to work out how much she paid my mom and I stopped counting after fifty thousand dollars."

A low whistle escaped.

"Yeah, my mom was a piece of work," Daniel said, his voice steady and unemotional. But Alex could see the pain in his eyes and noticed the tiniest tremble in his bottom lip. His mother's lack of maternal instinct and his father's lack of interest still had the power to hurt him, Alex realized.

"So yeah, I watched you and seeing you with your family, with Sarah, I was envious of how much you were loved. How secure you felt." Daniel placed his hand on her thigh and skimmed the tips of his fingers across her knee. "That summer, I know that you argued with Gus, with Sarah—you were angry with them so often."

Of course she'd been angry with them, as well as with Daniel. She loved him, he loved her, they wanted to be together and they were being kept apart because of a stupid feud. At eighteen, it had been all about her and what she wanted, and to hell with anyone else.

Ashamed of herself, Alex lifted her hand and gently touched Daniel's jaw. "Why did you let me leave, Dan? Why did you let me go?"

"You needed to go and I needed to stay." Daniel lifted his hand to rub the back of his neck. "Grandmother wanted me to stay, to learn about The Silver C. It was going to be mine someday and I needed to learn the ropes. I assumed that leaving with you meant risking the land, my job, my inheritance."

Alex jerked back, angry. "She said that?"

"No, you're not listening. I said I *assumed* that. The truth was, I didn't want to leave Royal. I felt safe there—welcomed, protected."

"And I asked you to leave it, to risk it."

"In hindsight, I know that I used my assumption of my grandmother disinheriting me and her displeasure as an excuse, but I couldn't tell you that I—"

"That you loved The Silver C more than you loved me." Daniel started to deny her words but then stopped talking and shook his head. "I don't know, Lex. Maybe. All I know for sure was that I didn't want to leave. But neither did I want to let you go. I was so hurt, confused, unable to tell you what I was feeling."

"And I wanted you to make the grand gesture, to prove that you loved me," Alex admitted hoarsely.

"Stephanie did that, all the time. If I did *x*, I loved her. If I did *y*, I didn't. As a child I was constantly re-assuring her of how much I loved her, tying myself up in a knot trying to please her. After I went to live with Grandmother, I swore I'd never allow anyone to use love as a weapon against me again."

And by linking his love to his actions, she'd done precisely that. Ironically, the one thing she needed was the very thing her couldn't give her. What a mess.

Alex closed her eyes, trying to keep the tears away. "We were so young, Dan, dealing with feelings far beyond our comfort zone."

"And a raging attraction. It was like God gave the keys to a Formula 1 car to an eight-year-old. We were bound to crash and burn."

Alex touched her stomach and gave him a wry grin. "And it's happening again."

Daniel pushed his hand under hers so that his palm lay across her stomach. He placed his lips against her temple before drawing back. "The one thing I know we can handle is our attraction to each other. We can be friends and lovers, Lex. Trust me on this."

He sounded so sure, but Alex was still convinced that that toxic combination had the potential to blow up and rip them apart. Alex made the mistake of looking into those eyes—more umber than chocolate tonight—and saw need and desire swirling within those dark depths.

She felt herself yielding, relinquishing her grip on common sense.

I'm exposing myself—I know that I am—but Daniel needs me.

And God knew, Alex needed him. Because here, right now, Daniel was silently telling her that he chose her, that he wanted her in his arms, in his bed.

No, he more than wanted her—he craved her.

As she did him.

Alex leaned forward and stroked the pad of her thumb over his lower lip. "Take me to bed, Dan."

She heard his sigh of relief and then his body tensed again. "Are you sure? You said this wasn't a good idea."

She lifted her shoulders and let them drop. "It isn't. We haven't found a long-term solution, and we should do that, but not tonight, not right now."

Daniel followed her to her feet and loosely held her hips. "What do you want us to do tonight, Lex?"

"I want you to love me, Dan. As only you can."

Eight

Instead of entering the house, Daniel led Alex down the deck and into the master bedroom, through the open sliding doors.

At the foot of the bed, he stopped and cupped her face in his hands, his thumbs tenderly stroking her cheekbones. In this dark room containing shadows and secrets, Daniel realized that right here, right now, for as long as it may last, they were about to reignite their love affair.

There had never been anyone else like her, no one who captured his imagination as thoroughly as Alexis Slade did. Whether she was lying in a meadow, hair in two plaits, or standing on a stage, raising money for a worthwhile cause, or lying on his bed, she entranced him.

He wished he could say otherwise but that was what Alex did. Entranced and ensnared. How was he ever going to let her go?

But that was the problem for Royal. Here, he wasn't a Clayton with commitment issues and she wasn't a scared Slade. They were Dan and Lex, lovers.

"God, you are so beautiful, Alexis."

Alex smiled at the use of her full name; she knew he only used it when he was overcome by strong emotion. Unable to wait another moment to taste her, Dan dropped his head and, not trusting himself to go caveman on her, gently touched his lips to the corner of her mouth. *Such sexy lips*, he thought. He wanted them on his, moving over his skin, wrapped around his—

No, if he went there now, before he'd even started, he'd lose it. No, tonight was about Alex and how best he could show her how much he lov—*adored* her.

Alex released a long sigh. "Daniel. The way you make me feel…"

Daniel dropped his hands to caress her neck and sighed when her tongue traced the seam of his lips, asking for entrance. His small release of air allowed her to slip inside to touch his tongue, and he was lost—control was vanquished. Daniel released a deep groan and he placed his hands on her hips and boosted her up, grateful when her legs locked around his hips, bringing her hot core against his harder, desperate dick. Wrenching his mouth off hers, he sucked in a breath, telling himself to calm down, that they had all night, that this wasn't a onetime deal. He had time tonight, tomorrow and the day after next.

Would it be enough?

Would forever be enough?

And why was he thinking of forever if this was just flash-in-the-pan lust?

"Lean back, Lex," Daniel growled. Frustrated with himself, he pulled her shirt up her body.

"Let me help." Alex whipped her shirt off and un-snapped the front clasp of her bra, allowing the lacy garment to drop to the floor and his mouth to close around one watermelon-pink nipple. Laving it with his tongue, he pulled back to blow on the puckered bud, smiling as he noticed her tan line, the darker and white flesh. Alex groaned and pushed his head toward her other breast, and he was happy to lavish attention on that bud, as well. It gave him time to lecture his dick, to remind it to go slow, to take it easy.

This was about Lex; it would only ever be about Lex.

Daniel lowered Alex to the bed and bent over her to tug her jeans apart, to pull the battered fabric down her hips and over her pretty toes. Running a hand down her long thigh and shapely calf, he blew on her aqua-lace-covered mound, pleased at her aroused scent—sex and sea and sun. Two cords held the triangle in place and Daniel's impatience had his thumbs and fingers gripping the cord and twisting, easily snapping the thin fabric. He pulled the fabric away from her and stared down at her.

"You're pretty and perfect. And mine, Lexi. Right now, tonight, you're mine."

He saw her gasp of surprise, caught the flash of pleasure in her eyes.

Standing up, Daniel whipped his shirt off, pushed down his board shorts and looked down at his lover, the mother of his child, the woman who'd slid under his skin at eighteen and whom he'd never been able to dislodge.

Mine. Only mine.

Daniel looked at her face, expecting her attention to be on him, and he frowned when he noticed that she was looking past him. If she'd changed her mind, he'd punch a hole through that expensive wooden screen that separated the bedroom from the bathroom. Replacing it would cost him an arm and leg, but it would be worth it.

Daniel pressed his forehead against hers. "Lex? Do you want to stop?"

Instead of replying to his question, Lexi placed her hand on her heart and sat up. When she finally looked at him, Daniel realized that he could see the moon in her eyes.

Literally. The moon was in her eyes.

He turned slowly and his mouth dropped in astonishment. The moon was as wide as the sky and he thought that if he leaned off the deck, he could run his hand across its silvery surface.

It was blue and aqua and silver and white…and absolutely magnificent.

"Daniel, it's so lovely."

He looked back at Lexi and slowly shook his head. The moon couldn't hold a candle to her. She was more radiant, more entrancing than any Caribbean moon hanging outside their bedroom window.

He ran his hand over her shoulder, his finger burning when it met her sun-touched skin. "I need you, Lex."

Lexi smiled and his heart spun in his chest like a damn prima ballerina. "Can I have you and the moon?" she asked, her eyes darting from him to the view outside.

He touched her nipple and rolled it between his fingers, his erection swelling when her eyes clouded with desire. Then Lexi's hand encircled him and the world stopped turning. He felt a tremor shoot him and told himself that he couldn't plunge… He had to hold still.

Lexi's voice was soft but sure. "I want you and the moon, Dan."

Since his brain didn't operate without blood, which

was plunging south, Daniel shook his head to indicate his confusion.

Lexi kneeled and sent him a sultry smile. "Come behind me, Daniel. I want you to hold me, cover me, envelop me, make me scream. And I want to watch the moon while we do that. It's going to be a memory I'll always treasure."

Daniel moved to kneel behind her, his hands stroking the length of her back before placing his hand on her stomach to pull her back, to tilt her hips up. Wrapping his arms around her, he slowly entered her, his eyes burning at the sheer perfection of this moment. His completing her completed him.

He moved, slow, sexy movements that raised them up and up, closer to that silver orb hanging in the sky. His every sense was amplified: he heard the wind in the trees and the waves hitting the sand. Lexi's smallest whimper, her sighs of pleasure, were loud in his ears. Her scent filled his nose and when she turned her neck to find his mouth, he caught her eyes and they were an intense shade of touched-with-moonlight blue.

Lodged deep inside her, Daniel felt the rush of warmth, felt her contract and allowed himself to caress the moon and grab the stars.

In the Royal Diner, Gus looked up from his biscuits and gravy and into Amanda Battle's lovely face. The owner of the diner was one of his favorite people and he stood up to drop a kiss onto her cheek. "Good morning, beautiful."

Amanda laughed. "Should you be flirting with me now that you are married, Gus Slade?"

"Just stating a fact, ma'am." Gus took his seat again and sent a grinning Rose a wink. How wonderful it was to see his wife relaxed and smiling, happy in her skin. He'd done that, Gus thought, feeling proud. He'd made her glow from the inside out.

Amanda turned to Rose and bussed his wife's cheek with her own. "It's so nice to see you, Miss Rose. Congratulations on your wedding. I'm so happy for you."

Rose thanked Amanda for her kind words and for refilling her coffee cup. Amanda passed the carafe of coffee on to a passing waitress and tipped her head to the side. "So, the latest gossip is that you two sent your grandkids off on a honeymoon in your place? Are you crazy? Do you know how beautiful Galloway Cove is?"

Rose poured some cream into her coffee. "Those two are like two mules fighting over a turnip."

Amanda laughed at Rose's pithy saying. "Have you heard from them?"

"They managed to find a computer and have been in contact." Gus finished his breakfast and wiped his lips with his napkin. "They both sent us polite, gentle thank-you notes—"

Amanda swatted his shoulder. "They did not!"

"No, they didn't," Gus admitted. "But neither have they, after three days, called to be picked up or, as far as we know, killed each other."

"They might kill us when they get back, though," Rose said, wrinkling her nose.

"They'll work it out," Amanda assured her. "Or at the very least, they might be mad for a while, but they'll come around. You're family and they love you."

Amanda turned at the sound of her chime and Gus followed her gaze to the front door. Amanda frowned at the tall, well-built man entering the diner, his sharp business suit at odds with the rest of the customers' more casual attire. Amanda turned her back on him and looked at Rose. "Miss Rose? That man—do you know him?"

Rose leaned to the side to look at the Latino man and Gus saw the flare of appreciation in her eyes. Yeah, yeah, he was good-looking, but she wore his ring now.

"Rosie…" he warned.

Rose flashed him an impudent grin and turned her attention back to Amanda. "He looks a bit familiar, but no, I don't know him. Why?"

"He was in here the other day, looking for you. I think someone gave him directions to The Silver C."

"Since the wedding, I've been staying with Gus at the Lone Wolf," Rose said, blushing.

They really had to work out where they were going to live on a permanent basis, Gus thought. Strangely, Rose seemed more at home in his house than she did in hers. He'd been on tenterhooks, waiting for Rose to suggest that he move into Ed's house and still didn't know how to respond—he didn't think an "over my cold dead body" would go down well—but Rose had yet to make the request. That being said, they needed a house that was theirs, one neither of them had to share with the ghosts of the past.

"I should go to The Silver C, check up on the work."

"Daniel's foreman is a good man and no doubt Daniel is issuing his orders from Galloway Cove." Gus stroked the inside of her wrist to reassure her. He tipped his head back in a subtle gesture to the stranger. "Do you want to see what he wants?"

Rose shrugged and then nodded. "I'm here. He's here. Might as well." Rose looked at Amanda and smiled. "Would you mind sending him our way, Amanda, honey?"

Amanda nodded and glided, graceful as ever, away.

Gus turned in his seat as dark, flashing eyes snapped to them. Gus looked at him, instantly recognized those eyes—funny that Rose didn't—and sighed. Oh hell, this could be either very good or very bad. The man slid off his chair at the counter and walked over to him.

The man stopped by their table and Gus could feel the tension rolling off him. He primed himself, ready to jump up and defend his woman. He might be old, but his reflexes were still sharp. Nobody would ever be allowed to hurt his Rosie again.

"Ms. Clayton—"

"That's Mrs. Slade to you, son," Gus growled.

"My apologies." The man held out his hand to Rose, and Gus felt his temperature rise, when instead of shaking it like a good Texan would do, he lifted Rose's knuckles to his lips. "My name is Hector Lamb and I believe I am—"

"Daniel's father." Rose snatched her hand out of his grip, leaned back and sliced and diced him with her laser-sharp eyes.

"Where the hell have you been and why are you only showing up now?"

At the top of the trail, Daniel stopped, turned and looked at her as if he were surprised to see her on his heels. "Are you sure you're pregnant?" he demanded, hands on his hips, his eyes shaded by the brim of a well-worn ball cap.

"What makes you say that?" Alex removed her own cap and wiped her forearm across her forehead before resettling the cap on her head. They were deep into the mini jungle that covered most of the island, and it was humid as hell on a rainy day. She couldn't wait to get to the swimming hole that was reputed to be at the end of this long trail.

"You aren't experiencing morning sickness, you haven't had any weird cravings, you haven't been moody," Daniel replied. "And you're still as slim as you always were…"

Admittedly, it was taking some time for her to show, but there were signs. "The band of these shorts is tight and my boobs are definitely bigger."

Daniel sent her a steady look but she caught the devilry in his eyes. He lifted his hands and placed them on her bikini-top-covered breasts. "I don't believe you. I have to check."

His thumbs immediately found her nipples and Alex tipped her head up to receive his kiss. Oh, she liked this Daniel, this relaxed, funny, thoughtful man. For the first time since she'd moved back to Royal, they were connected on both a mental and physical level, and yeah, they gelled.

Whenever they weren't making love—which seemed to happen morning, noon and night—they talked and laughed. They had their differences, but their value systems were the same, their priorities were in sync. Respect and independence of action and thought were important to them and family always came first.

Family came first. But by moving to Houston, striking out on her own, she was deliberately putting time and space between not only the baby and Daniel, but the baby and its grandparents, uncle and her friends. Was she making life harder for herself in her effort to protect herself?

Daniel broke the kiss, took her hand and they continued walking alongside each other until the path narrowed and she was forced to fall into step behind him.

She didn't *have* to move to Houston; it wasn't a condition of the partnership.

Alex bit her lip and stared at the back of Daniel's head, her eyes tracing his broad shoulders, muscles rippling under the red T-shirt he wore. She'd traced those muscles with her tongue...

Wrenching her eyes off Daniel, she pulled her thoughts back. The point was, she had options. Or, deep breath now, she could also move in with Daniel and give this—whatever *this* was—a shot. They could be a couple, raise their child together, day in and day out. Alex sucked in her breath and placed her hand on her sternum as she waited for the wave of unease to pass through her. When it didn't, she tipped her head, surprised. Huh. So moving in with Daniel didn't scare her as much as it did a week ago.

Her heart skipped a beat. They didn't need to get married but they could make this work. They had fantastic sex, enjoyed each other's company, had the same priorities...

Of course she knew the risks involved. Back in Royal, they would have to deal with real life, two careers, a baby on the way, their grandparents and...stuff. The mundane and the boring and the tedious. And there was always the chance that Daniel would one day decide that this wasn't the life for him and, well, leave.

Could she cope with that? Would she be able to watch him walk away without her world falling apart? Yeah, it would hurt when—if—he left, but he might not.

Could she do this? Dare she take a chance on Daniel, on the life he was offering?

Alex could feel her heart racing, and a fine sheen of perspiration covered her forehead. Feeling her courage well up inside her, she started to speak, but no words came out.

How was she supposed to tell him she'd come to a decision without saying the words?

"Here we are."

Alex pulled her attention from her thoughts and looked around, her mouth falling open at the tall waterfall plunging into a pool below their feet. Flat boulders dotted the natural swimming hole, providing a perfectly flat surface to stretch out on, to soak up the sun's rays after a chilly dip in the pool.

"Awesome." Daniel walked down the path to the first boulder, dropped his backpack to the rock and kicked off his trainers. Whipping off his shirt, he dropped it at his feet and then shimmied out of his shorts. What was it with this man and his need to swim naked? Not that she was complaining but...

Daniel sent her a wicked smile. "Secluded. No one else here. No one to see me and you've—"

"Seen it all before," Alex said, completing his sentence.

"Strip and join me," Daniel suggested, waggling his eyebrows. Yeah, she could live with Daniel looking at her like he'd been waiting his whole life to make love to her in a pool at the bottom of a pretty waterfall. Heat and warmth rushed to that special place between her legs and her nipples pebbled with expectation.

Alex felt beautiful, desired and wanton. Daniel stood in front of her, utterly unselfconscious, the sun touching his tanned skin. The wind ruffled his jet-black curls, and as her eyes traveled over his impressive physique, his erection jerked as he hardened before her eyes.

Having such a masculine, focused man want her

made Alex feel intensely feminine, immensely power-ful. She was life, she carried life, a goddess of the glen.

Alex quickly stripped down and stood in front of her man, sighing when the sun's warm rays caressed her bare back and buttocks. She pushed her breasts into his chest before dragging her nipples across his skin, her hand lifting to encircle him, her thumb brushing the tip of his cock. Daniel groaned and pushed into her hand.

"Make love to me, Dan. Here, in the sun, on this rock. On our secluded island."

Daniel nodded and she had a moment's warning when his eyes glinted and his mouth twitched. Strong arms wrapped around her and then she was flying off the rock, hitting the freezing cold water with a heavy splash.

Alex spluttered, shivered and kicked her way to the surface to see Dan's wicked smile and laughing eyes.

"You are such a child," Alex told him, launching a wave of water into his face.

Daniel ducked, grabbed her and she instinctively wound her legs around his waist only to find out that cold water had absolutely no effect on his erection at all.

Well then. It seemed like a shame to waste it.

Nine

After making love, they swam some more until they realized it was past lunchtime and they were hungry. They dressed, Alex in her fuchsia bikini and Dan in his board shorts, and then they ate the sandwiches Alex had prepared earlier and polished off the apples they had also brought along.

Feeling relaxed, Daniel replaced the cap on his water bottle and, after rolling up his towel, lay on his back and tucked the towel beneath his head. Enjoying the sun, he opened one eye to look at Alex. "Come lie down with me."

Alex curled into his side, her head tucked under his chin. The gentle breeze blew a strand of hair across his mouth. He picked up her hair and tucked it behind her ear.

"Best forced holiday ever," Alex murmured, her fingers idly drawing patterns above his heart.

"Best holiday ever," Daniel corrected her. "I love spending time with you, honey. I always did."

Alex opened her mouth to speak but closed it again. She had something on her mind—he knew that she was toying with a decision. Did he dare to dream that she'd reconsidered her living arrangements, that their forced week away—yeah, yeah, thanks old-timers—had worked?

"What's going on in that beautiful head of yours, Lex?"

Alex took a while to answer. "That job I was offered… I could actually stay in Royal and still take the partnership."

Daniel forced himself to stay still, but inside he was leaping to his feet, punching his fist in the air. "Are you thinking of doing that?" he asked carefully.

"Maybe. I sort of allowed you to believe that I had to move to Houston to take the partnership. I could stay in Royal and work remotely, traveling a couple of times a month."

He wanted to sit up, to whoop with delight, but he knew he had to tread softly because Alex was like a skittish colt that needed careful handling. Which was okay—he could tiptoe with the best of them. As long as he got what he wanted in the end, he didn't care how he got there. And he wanted Alex. In his arms, his bed.

And in his life.

"I'm scared of starting something, because I'm terrified I could lose it."

Daniel turned her words over in his head, trying to make sense of her out-of-the-blue statement. Pulling his head back, he looked at her but her eyes remained closed. He ran his hand up her spine, keeping his touch light and comforting.

"Care to explain that, Lex?"

Alex sat up, crossed her legs and he pulled himself up, bending his knees and allowing his hand to dangle between them.

"I don't like being left, Daniel. It's happened too often, and I don't think I can do it again."

He thought he knew where she was going with this but asked her to explain anyway.

"As we discussed earlier, losing my parents when I was young was a sad time, but Gus and Sarah stepped in and I was okay. However, when I was twelve, I lost my best friend Gemma, too. I don't know if you remember her—she was a redhead?"

He had a vague memory of seeing the two girls together, but he remembered the town's grief at Gemma's death more than he remembered the child herself.

"I was devastated. I thought my world ended." Alex pushed her hair back over her shoulder. "I had friends at school but nobody I was close to. I didn't want another friend who could die on me. So I kept my thoughts and feelings to myself and Sarah became my best friend. Then, in a meadow, I met and kissed you and I felt my heart opening up, expanding, and it became so full of you. That summer, you were my everything and I thought I was your world."

Alex touched the tip of her tongue to her top lip and when she looked at him, Daniel noticed the tears in her eyes. "I know it sounds dramatic but losing you felt like losing Gemma again. But somehow it was worse because you weren't only my best friend but my lover. All I wanted you to do was to choose me, to stick with me."

He suddenly understood. "You were angry that your parents and Gemma and, later, Sarah left you. You felt abandoned."

He got it.

"But I'm not allowed to be angry with them because they didn't have a choice to stay or to go."

"But I had a choice and I didn't choose you."

Alex nodded and scratched her head above her ear. "Being all grown-up, I thought I could handle having a fling with you. I thought I would sleep with you and keep it light and fluffy. And I was okay when I called it quits. I mean, I missed you but I knew that I could live without you. I think it helped that we didn't make an emotional connection, that it was all about sex."

They didn't make that connection because they'd both been too damn scared to go there. They still were. "Anyway, as for our current predicament... It makes sense for us to be together, to live together, to raise our child together," Alex quietly stated.

Thank the baby Jesus...

"But it also doesn't."

Crap.

Daniel looked at her and waited for her to continue, conscious of his heart thudding in his chest. Where was she going with this? "Carry on, Lex. Tell me what you are thinking."

"I'm scared of moving in with you, falling for you and then having to deal with you leaving, whether that's by death or a woman or whatever life might throw my way."

She was worried that he might leave her for someone else? Yeah, that wasn't going to happen. Not now, not ever. Alex pulled her bottom lip between her teeth. "I'm scared, Dan. I'm scared to try this, terrified that it won't work. I'm scared that you will become the center of my world again and when the day comes for you to make a choice, it won't be me."

She was a lot stronger than she gave herself credit for. They were both strong people; they'd both, in their different ways, survived so much. They could handle this.

He had to touch her, so he used the tip of his index finger to stroke the inside of her wrist. "I know you're scared, sweetheart. But there's something more frightening than fear and that's regret."

Alex released a heavy sigh and lifted her shoulders in a tired shrug. He could see that she was feeling overwhelmed and out of her depth. So was he but his childhood of rolling with the punches had taught him to not make decisions when he was emotional, that it was always beneficial to step back and look at a situation with some distance.

As much as he wanted to install Alex in his house as soon as he got back to Royal, he needed to give her time to find her way back to him. It was going to be hard, when his instinct was to take control, but if he wanted a family—this family—he had to take it slow.

"Can you see yourself staying in Royal? Is that something you can do?"

Alex stared at the pool below them and it took all of Dan's patience to remain silent. Eventually she nodded her head. "Yeah, I think that's a decision I am comfortable making."

Thank God. Do not punch the air, Clayton. You are not a child. Daniel held himself still. *You still have work to do but, God, that was a massive hurdle overcome.* "Okay then. Good."

He put his hands on her knees and waited for her troubled eyes to meet his. "Lex, you don't need to make any more decisions today. Take some time, think it through."

Alex bit her bottom lip. "What if I'd decided to move to Houston?"

He pushed his hand through his hair and met her eyes. "I don't know, Alex. It would've been more complicated, financially and logistically. But I like to think that we would've made it work."

Daniel prayed that she wouldn't pursue this line of questioning, that she wouldn't ask whether he would've moved to Houston and left The Silver C. Maybe. Possibly. Yes. But admitting that was a step too far. He was opening the door to his heart a bit too wide. Alex needed time and so did he.

"Rose and Grandpa are going to pressure us to get married," Alex said, directing her words to the pond and refusing to meet his eyes.

The last time he asked, she almost drew blood, her reply had been so cutting. "Do you want to get married?"

Alex shook her head. "I'm still coming to terms with my decision to stay in Royal. I can't think much beyond that. But, Lord, the gossip!"

"You speak as if the Claytons and the Slades haven't been gossiped about before," Daniel said, his tone wry. "Let them talk, Alex. We're working on our timeline, no one else's. We only have to answer to each other, nobody else."

Alex lifted her eyebrows. "Have you met our grandparents?"

He smiled at her quip but shook his head. "We don't have to be in a rush to figure this out. Let's take it step by step, day by day. Today you decided to stay in Royal—let that be enough for now."

Alex looked down at her hands before her deep blue eyes met his. "Okay. But I have one request."

Didn't she realize that he'd give her anything he could. "What, sweetheart?"

"I don't do well when there's no communication, when I think I am drifting on the wind. I need to be able to talk to you and you to talk to me. I feel better when we talk, when we have these conversations. I might not have the answers, but I don't feel so alone."

Touched beyond measure, Daniel clasped her neck with his hand and leaned forward to kiss her forehead. He'd watched her as a child, kissed her as a girl but this woman next to him? She was phenomenal.

"Do you know how many boys named Daniel were born in the greater Dallas area in '91?"

Rose looked from her kitchen at The Silver C to the informal dining table in the open-plan entertainment area and caught Gus's eye. How handsome he looked, she thought. How lucky she was to be married to him.

"How many?" Gus asked Hector Lamb, pushing the bottle of red wine in his direction. The red wine came from Ed's cellar. He'd collected the expensive wines because he thought it a classy thing to do but never drank the stuff. He'd never allowed anyone else to drink his collection, either. In the years since his death, Rose had sold the more collectible bottles and given away other bottles as gifts. She intended to drink the rest.

Rose pulled the cheesecake out of the fridge and looked around her immaculate kitchen. It was large and spacious and far too big for her and Gus. On the fridge was a magnet Ed had brought back from New York City, inside that drawer were his steak knives. She kept the flour in the same canister his mother did, the sugar in another. The windows were too small, the storage space badly designed.

Rose yanked open the second drawer and cursed when it became stuck before it was fully out. She was sick of sticky drawers and old furniture and poky rooms. She hated this house and was finally in a place where she could admit to it.

"Five thousand six hundred and sixty-two little boys were born during September and October of that year," Hector replied. "I knew the dates when Stephanie and I slept together—it happened over a week, so I gave Stephanie a little leeway in case the baby decided to be late."

Daniel was, in fact, early. "Hold on, boys, I want to hear how you tracked Daniel down," Rose told them, expertly slicing even portions of cheesecake. She scowled down at the half-cut dessert. When had she become so pedantic, so perfectionistic, so boring?

Rose defiantly cut the cake up into oddly shaped, differently sized pieces and wrinkled her nose. That didn't make her feel any better. She knew exactly what would…

After picking up the cake and three side plates, she walked over to the table and banged the cake down in the center of the table. She darted a quick glance at Hector before dropping an openmouthed kiss on Gus's lips.

Gus looked at her, shocked. No wonder. Regal Rose never ever engaged in public displays of affection.

"Are you okay, darlin'?" Gus drawled, surprise quickly turning to concern.

Rose nodded. "I hate this house."

Gus leaned back in his chair, rested his hands across his still-flat stomach and lifted his heavy gray eyebrows. "Do you now?"

"I don't want to live here anymore."

Hector cleared his throat and pushed his chair back. "Excuse me, please. I need to visit your bathroom."

Rose smiled, grateful to be able to speak to Gus alone. "Hurry back, Hector. This won't take long."

Hector nodded and walked away from them to the powder room just off the hall. Rose sat down next to him and placed her chin in the palm of her hand.

Gus smiled at her, a sweet, slow smile that was part devil, all charm. "Now, where are you wanting to live, Rosie? With me? My wife might have something to say about that."

She knew he was teasing but she was too nervous to smile. He'd adored Sarah. How was he going to react to her suggestion?

"You can tell me anything, Rose."

"I want to move into Sarah's house. I feel at home there, like she would be happy I was there, happy that I made you happy."

Gus's hands covered hers. "She missed you so much, Rose."

"I know. I missed her, too." Gus's wife, Sarah, had been her closest friend and Rose didn't know if she'd ever forgive herself for walking away from Gus and her best friend, the two people who knew and loved her best. How stupid young people could be! And that was why she felt no compunction in meddling in Daniel's and Alex's lives. If they couldn't see the wood for the trees, she'd damn well provide them with glasses and a chainsaw.

She had more to say and she might as well get it all out there. "I'd like Alex and her brother to choose what pieces of Sarah's furniture they'd like, and if there's anything special of hers you'd like to keep, I'd understand but—"

"But?" Gus asked gently.

"But I'd like a house of my own. I inherited most of everything that's in this home from my parents and great-grandparents and Ed didn't see the point of buying new when old worked as well as new." She was being silly but maybe Gus would understand. "I want my own stuff, Gus, new stuff. *Our* stuff."

Gus nodded once. "Then that's what we shall do, darlin'. And maybe Daniel and Alex can move in here. Alex will want to renovate and redecorate, do all that stuff new wives want to do but old wives don't let happen."

Rose grinned. Hearing Hector approaching her, she turned her attention back to him and smiled. "I am so sorry. We've been so rude. Tell us how you tracked down Daniel. And why did it take you so long?"

Alex looked out of the window of the private jet and saw the familiar landscape of Texas thousands of feet below her. In a half hour they'd be on the ground, and she and Daniel would be hurtled back into real life.

Dammit.

Real life meant deadlines and doctor's appointments, conversations with Gus and Rose, meetings with Mike. Real life wasn't lazy mornings, waking up tangled in Daniel's arms, listening to the sound of gently lapping waves and a gentle, fragrant breeze blowing across her skin. Real life wasn't fresh fish caught straight from the ocean, skinny-dipping in the cove or in the pool, making love in the outdoor shower.

Real life was grown-up life and she wasn't ready for it. On the island it seemed a lot easier to imagine staying in Royal, commuting to Houston for work, creating a life with Daniel. Now, a half hour out from that life, Alex once again questioned whether staying in Royal was the right option for her and her child. Was she taking too big a risk believing that she and Daniel could make this work?

Had she been seduced by spectacular sex on a sun-kissed island?

Alex drummed her fingers on the leather-covered armrest of her seat and gnawed her bottom lip, wishing that Daniel would look up, see her nervousness and say something, anything, to reassure her. But ten minutes after leaving Galloway Cove, he'd connected his cell phone to the in-flight Wi-Fi and hadn't stopped working since.

"Dammit to hell and back," Daniel muttered.

At least he was talking to her. Sort of. "Problem?"

Daniel lifted his head and grimaced. "More responses to that interview I did on being one of the state's most eligible bachelors. I have a thousand emails asking for a date."

"A thousand, really?" Alex asked, skeptical. He was a hot, sexy guy and there were a lot of desperate, lonely women out there, but that had to be an exaggeration.

Daniel turned the phone toward her and she saw the stream of emails on his screen. Okay, there were a *lot* of emails. "I thought you were picking up emails on the island, so why didn't you see these then?"

Daniel looked down at the screen again. It took him a while to answer as his finger flew over the small keyboard. "After deleting that first batch, I only checked my private email account on the island. This one is more of a general and PR account." He flashed her a quick grin. "I've opened a few emails and a couple of women did make a contribution to your charity to bribe me to date them."

Sex sold and, dammit, Daniel was sex on a stick.

Alex tipped her head to the side and looked at him, dressed in his white button-down shirt and khaki pants, designer sunglasses hanging off his shirt pocket. If he ever became sick of being a cowboy/businessman, he could find another career as a male model. She could easily see him diving off a cliff, into a blue sea, swimming up to a boat and crawling all over a sexy, skinny model...

Modeling... Hmm...maybe next year she could do a skin calendar featuring Daniel and all the sexy, sexy men of the Texas Cattleman's Club. God knew there were a bunch of them.

Daniel narrowed his eyes at her. "No. Whatever you are thinking, just no."

Alex just smiled and didn't bother to argue. When the time came, she'd have him posing naked, maybe against a tractor or one of his fantastic quarterback horses, his Stetson covering his essential bits.

"Forget it, Slade," Daniel muttered, now looking nervous.

Alex handed him a coy smile and glanced at her watch. "So, what are your plans for today?"

Daniel tapped his index finger against his thigh. "I need to catch up with my foreman, get my PA to re-schedule some meetings I missed, return calls. You?"

"Pretty much the same. Except that I am scheduling some time to kill my grandpa."

Daniel laughed. "Come on, honey, I thought we'd partially forgiven them. After all, we are back together."

What did that mean? Was she now his girlfriend, his partner, his lover? Alex looked out of the window as the plane started to descend. They'd only spoken in general terms about her staying in Royal... Did he still want her to move in? Was she supposed to look for a house to rent in Royal itself? What did they tell Gus and Rose?

Where, exactly, did they stand?

All she knew for sure was that she'd agreed to stay in Royal. Was she sure that was the right thing to do? For her and the baby...?

The baby. Alex frowned. "What's the date today?"

Daniel tossed out the date and she slapped her hand against her forehead. "Dammit, I nearly forgot that I have an appointment with the ob-gyn this afternoon."

"This afternoon?" Daniel demanded. "Didn't I put that into my calendar?" he glanced at his cell phone and nodded. "Yeah, here it is, five thirty."

Alex nodded. "She's fitting me in as her last patient of the day."

He sighed, ran a hand across his face and glanced down at his phone. He quietly cursed. "Can you re-schedule? I've got a crazy day."

"I don't think I should. I should've seen her already and I won't be able to get an appointment for another two weeks if I miss this one," Alex told him. She lifted her hands and lied. "I can go on my own—it's not that big a deal."

"It's a very big deal and I told you I want to be there," Daniel retorted. "Today is just not a good day."

"I can't help that," Alex pushed back, becoming an-noyed herself. "When I made this appointment, I didn't know we were going to be kidnapped and out of touch for a week."

Daniel scrubbed his hand over his face before speak-ing again. "Okay, let's calm down. You said the appoint-ment is at five thirty? Where?"

Alex gave him the doctor's address before adding,

"I'll understand if you can't make it, Daniel." Well, she'd try to understand.

Daniel leaned forward and covered her hand with his. "I said that I'd make you and the baby a priority, Lex, and I mean it. It would help if I could meet you there."

Alex linked her fingers in his and squeezed. She felt the warmth his words created and instantly relaxed. This was going to be okay; *they* were going to be okay. "Sure, we can do that."

Daniel leaned forward, brushed his mouth against hers and smiled. "Ready to go home?"

Alex smiled against his mouth. "No."

"Me neither. And please don't kill Gus. Prison orange is not your color."

Ten

Much later that day, Daniel gripped the bridge of his nose and closed his eyes. A headache pounded at the back of his skull and his shoulders were flirting with his ears.

It felt like he'd been back in Royal eight months instead of eight hours and he didn't know if he could fight another fire. He had cattle missing, he'd had to call the vet for a sick mare and one of his best men—who also happened to be one of his most experienced hands—had suddenly decided to retire.

On top of all of that, his PA had a stack of messages he needed to return, he had a pile of checks to sign and his accountant needed to speak with him urgently. Damn. He needed another vacation. But more than that, he needed Alex. Needed to see her smile, hear her voice.

Daniel looked at his watch. It was four twenty, which mean he'd need to leave the ranch by five to be on time for Alex's doctor's appointment. An image of Lex, rounded and beautiful, carrying his baby, flashed through his mind. He smiled. His woman was staying in Royal and in a few months' time, he'd meet the first of what he hoped would be a few children they'd make together.

Daniel heard the knock on his office door, jarring him from his thoughts, and looked up to see his grandmother's face between the frame and the door itself. He forced himself to keep his face blank, refusing to allow her the satisfaction of knowing her plan had worked out. Sort of.

"Can I come in?"

Daniel folded his arms as Rose stepped into the room. She looked good, he thought, and content. He liked seeing her happy but dammit, he wasn't going to smile at her...yet. "I'm not happy with you."

Rose didn't look even a little intimidated. "I don't care. I did what I needed to do."

Daniel spread his arms open. "Do I look like a little boy who needed your help?"

"You looked like a man who was going to allow the best thing in your life walk away from you." Rose walked over to his desk and placed her hands on the back of a visitor's chair. "I was not going to let her and that baby walk out of your life. And ours."

He couldn't help the smile that lifted the corners of his lips. "Be honest, you just want to dote on the baby."

Rose's smile made her look fifteen years younger. "I *so* do." She bit her lip and looked up at him, her eyes luminous. "So how did it go?"

Daniel smiled. "Do you use that look on Gus? Does he just fall at your feet and agree to anything you ask?"

"Of course he does," Rose replied. Daniel laughed

and Rose surprised him by walking around the desk and winding her arms around his waist. He knew Rose loved him, but she wasn't given to spontaneous bursts of affection. Closing his eyes, Daniel gathered his grandmother close, resting his chin in her hair. This woman had been his rock and his safety net, his moral compass and his true north. He might not have had a father or much of a mother, but she'd filled the gaps with her no-nonsense attitude and her integrity. And her love. She wasn't a hugger but he'd always known that he was loved.

But yeah, he was going to hug the hell out of his kid.

Daniel dropped a kiss on Rose's head and started to step away. He frowned when his grandmother's arms tightened to keep him in place. "Gran? Everything okay?"

Rose stepped back and he was shocked to see tears on her face. Bending so that he could see into her eyes, he gently held her biceps. "Are you okay? Is Gus okay? Did something happen? Crap, something has happened! Alex, is she okay?"

"Alex is fine, darling." Rose smiled and waved her hands in front of her face. "Do you have a handkerchief?"

Who used those anymore? Daniel cast an eye over his desk, saw a marginally clean bandanna and scooped it up. He found the cleanest corner and gently wiped away Rose's tears. "What's going on, Gran?"

Rose held his hand and led him to the leather couch that stood against the far wall. Daniel waited for her to sit before taking the seat next to her. Rose immediately took his hand in both of hers.

A million butterflies in his stomach started to beat their wings. What the hell was going on? "Okay, you are starting to scare me."

Rose stared down at his hands before releasing a sigh. "Have you checked your emails lately?"

Weird question. "I've been keeping up-to-date, mostly on my private email account. I glanced at the emails on the general account and now know that there are a lot of desperate women in Texas. Who sends an email asking a perfect stranger out on a date just because they read an article about him in a magazine?"

"Lonely girls who want to marry a good-looking, rich cowboy. You're a real-life fantasy."

Daniel snorted his disagreement. The only person he wanted to fantasize about him was Alex. The thought of Alex reminded him that he had to get this conversation moving or he'd be late. "What's your point, Gran?"

"You might have missed it but there have been a couple of messages to you from a Hector Lamb."

Hector Lamb? He recognized that name. "Did he send me a message on the ranch account, saying he wanted to meet me to discuss a mutual acquaintance?" The butterflies started to take flight. "I presume he is talking about Stephanie."

Rose nodded.

Daniel ran a hand across the back of his neck. "What does he want? Does he know that we haven't had any contact with her since I was a kid?"

This wasn't the first time one of Stephanie's marks showed up at their door, demanding restitution. When he was younger, it had been a common enough occurrence—money frequently changed hands to keep Stephanie out of jail—but even after she broke off communications, there had been a few men who tried their luck trying to extort money from them.

"He doesn't want anything," Rose replied. "No, that's not true. He wants to meet you."

"Me? Why?"

Rose's eyes brimmed with tears again. "Hector was in Austin for business. He met your mom. They had a weeklong affair. He left and when he returned five months later, it was obvious that she was pregnant. Your mom told him that the baby was a boy, that it was his and that she was going to name him Daniel."

Daniel felt the room tilt, his vision go blurry. He forced himself to concentrate on Rose's words, to make some sort of sense of what she was saying.

"Stephanie was still married to her loser ex and she was using his name. Hector offered to look after her and his baby, and he returned to Houston to rent her a flat, to buy furniture and a car. She was supposed to arrive in Houston two weeks later but—"

"She never arrived."

"Because, you know, Stephanie could never make life easy for herself. She went back to using the name Clayton and Hector couldn't find her. More important, he couldn't find you."

Daniel forced the words out from between clenched teeth and dry lips. "He looked for me?"

"He never stopped." Rose's smile was gentle. "He saw that picture of you in that magazine article and just recognized you. He knew you were his."

"How?" Daniel croaked the word.

"You look just like him, darling. You couldn't be anyone else's child." Rose placed her hand on his shoulder. "Honey, you're trembling. I know it's a shock, but he wants to meet you, wants to know you."

Daniel scrubbed his hands over his face, his heart banging inside his chest. He took a couple of deep breaths before he remembered that parental attention and love always came with a price. Why was his father here? What did he want? What was in it for him?

And, crucially, how much was he prepared to pay to have his father in his life?

Rose's hand drew big circles on his back. "Do you want to meet him?"

He'd have to meet him to discover why he was here, what he wanted. "Yeah, I guess."

Rose's smile was pure delight. "Excellent!" She jumped to her feet and clapped her hands. "Because he's waiting at the main house with Gus. He wants to meet you, too."

Today? Now? Jesus...

Alex left the doctor's room, clutching a black-and-white picture of her baby, who looked—admittedly—more like a peanut than a baby. But the heart was beating strong, and everything, as the doctor had informed her, was progressing normally. She was as healthy as a horse and the baby was thriving. Could she come back in two months, and would the baby's father be joining her at future appointments?

Well, no. Because she was going to Houston, to start a new life there.

Alex looked up and down the street and glanced at her watch. Daniel had missed the appointment and was nearly two hours late. Obviously, she and the baby were not the priority he'd promised her they would be.

It was better, Alex told herself as she slid behind the wheel of her car, that she found out now and not later. She could still leave, she could wrench herself away from Daniel and Royal, and start afresh in Houston.

He didn't love her, and he would never put her first. They'd landed ten hours ago, and Daniel had already forgotten about her, forgotten that he'd promised to accompany her to this appointment. He'd looked her in the eye and told her that she and the baby were his top priority, that he'd put them first. It only took him ten hours to forget that promise, to put his work and The Silver C in front of her.

Alex felt the tears slipping down her face as she stared at the picture of their baby. Her heart cramped and she felt the familiar wave of uncertainty. Since breaking up with Daniel a decade ago, and reinforced by Sarah's death, she'd avoided emotional entanglements and this was why. Because she couldn't handle the disappointment, the fear and the uncertainty. Relationships made her needy, vulnerable and so very insecure. She'd spent so many years running away from those weak emotions, and by sleeping with Daniel, she'd opened herself up to them again. What a fool she'd been to think that they could raise this child together and that, maybe one day, she could trust him enough to build a future with him.

She couldn't even trust him to keep a damned appointment, so how could she trust him with her love, her feelings, her very scarred heart? No, it was better that she return to Houston, and in a few months, she'd contact him and make arrangements for him to be part of the baby's life. Hopefully by then, she'd be stronger and mentally together.

Her passenger door opened and a gust of cool, wet wind accompanied Daniel into the car. He slammed the door shut and fiddled under his seat for the lever to push the seat back. Leaning back, he stretched out his long legs as far as they would go before turning to face her, looking weary. "Hi. Sorry I'm so late."

Daniel rubbed his hands over his face as if to wake

himself up before looking at her again. "How did it go? Are you okay? Is the baby okay?"

He was asking the right questions, but he sounded distracted, like he had more pressing problems on his mind. "God, it's cold out there."

Wow. He was talking about the weather. Could he not see that she was upset, that his missing the appointment had rocked her world? While Alex tried to make sense of his preoccupation—was he so oblivious that he couldn't see that she'd been crying?—Daniel reached for the sonograph. "Is this him? Her? Did they know what sex the baby is?" Okay, she now heard a little more interest in his voice. He cared about his child, that was obvious, but he hadn't cared to keep his commitment to her. She hadn't meant for it to be, but today turned out to be a test.

And he'd failed.

Daniel looked at her and frowned. "Are you okay?"

Well, no. "Do I look okay?" Alex asked, her voice soaked with emotion.

Daniel lifted his hand to touch her face and his expression hardened as she pulled back. "Look, I'm sorry I was late."

"You're not late, Daniel. You missed the entire appointment!"

"I know but—"

Alex banged her hand on the steering wheel. "No, no *buts*, Clayton! I asked you to be there, and you said you would."

"Something happened, Lex. If you'd just let me explain—"

She doubted that he could say anything that would make a difference. The fact of the matter was, once again, his precious ranch was more important to him than she was. "You believe that actions speak louder than words, Daniel. You told me this morning that I was your number one priority, that you would be here. Your actions disprove that."

Alex heard the frost in her voice, a direct contrast to the heat of Daniel's curse. She had to walk away—she couldn't do this for the rest of her life. She couldn't love him and not have him love her back. Great sex wasn't a good enough reason to stick around.

"Alex, for God's sake, let me explain."

She couldn't risk being persuaded to trust him, this would just happen again and again. Their time on the island had been a holiday romance, something that couldn't be replicated in real life. Real life wasn't sun and good sex and sparkling water; it was a chilly overcast day in Texas and two people who couldn't give each other what they needed. No, she had to end this today. *Now.* "I'm going back to Houston. That was my first instinct and I think it's the correct one."

"You're leaving Royal? Again? What the hell?"

Alex stared at the still-busy street, her eyes clear of tears. She was too hurt to cry, too empty to fight. She was in survival mode, simply doing what she could to emotionally survive.

"You're leaving because I missed one damn appointment?" Daniel's loud words reverberated through the interior of her car. "Are you completely insane?"

"No, I'm leaving because you can't keep your word! I'm leaving because I'm not a priority in your life and I can't trust you to be there for me!"

Daniel scrubbed his hand over his face. Looking up, he frowned at her, his dark eyes as cold as wind-battered boulders on an Arctic beach. "Jesus, Slade."

Alex gritted her teeth, leaned across him and opened his door. "Get out!"

Daniel pulled the door shut, leaned against the door and looked at her, his face now expressionless. She hated that blank look, the shutters in his eyes. Alex wanted to squirm under his penetrating gaze and forced herself to stay still, to lock stares with him. Daniel broke the heavy anger-charged silence. "You were just looking for a reason to run, weren't you?"

That wasn't fair. He was the one who'd let her down, who hadn't stuck to his word. Alex tapped the picture of the peanut. "Funny, I didn't see you there when I listened to our child's heartbeat. I didn't hear you asking questions."

"If I made it today, then something else, soon, would've made you run," Daniel gritted out.

"That's not fair."

"Oh, it so is. When you get scared, you run as fast and as hard as you can."

His words were as sharp and as bitter as the tip of a poison dart.

"I'm not scared," Alex protested.

"You acted out of fear when, ten years ago, you ran instead of trying to find a way to still go to school and see me. We started sleeping together last year and as soon as we started laughing together, talking, you broke it off."

"Our grandparents—"

Daniel leaned forward, his face harsh. "Don't! Don't you dare blame this on them! This is about you and me and the fact that whenever you find yourself in deep water, emotionally speaking, you swim back to shore!"

That was because she didn't want to drown. She knew what it felt like to lose air, to feel like you were dying without the people you loved in your life.

Daniel shoved both hands into his hair and tugged his curls in frustration. "We could have such an amazing life, Lex, but you value protecting yourself above loving me, loving us." Daniel dropped his hands and, in his eyes, Alex saw the devastation she'd put there.

"I can't keep trying to prove my worth to you, Alexis. I did that constantly as a child and I refuse to do it as an adult. You either want us—me—or you don't. I'm not going to continuously try to prove myself to you." Daniel picked up the photograph of their baby and looked at it for a long time. "I'm tired of fighting for us on my own, Lex. I want you. I want my family, but I need you to want it, too. And I'm not going to sit here and beg you for that chance. Go back to Houston, live in your safe cave."

She heard the words, thought that was what she wanted, so why did it feel like he was ripping her soul in two? Daniel opened the door, swung his long legs out of her small car and looked at her over his shoulder. "I'll contact you in a few weeks to check up on my kid."

Daniel left those parting words behind as he exited her vehicle. To check up on his child, not her. She'd pushed him, and she'd got what she wanted. A Daniel-free life. Alex ran the tips of her fingers over her forehead, utterly confused. She felt like she'd placed the last piece into a giant puzzle only to find that the focal piece of the picture was missing. What had she missed?

Acting on instinct, she flew out of the car and saw him walking away, his shoulders hunched and his head bent. "Daniel!"

He stopped at her shout, hesitated and finally turned to face her, lifting a dark eyebrow. "What?"

Hold me. Take me in your arms and soothe my fears.

Tell me that you'll never let me down. Never leave me. Love me, please.

"Why were you late?" she asked.

A small smile touched his mouth but didn't reach his eyes. "Oh, that little thing?" He hesitated, drawing the moment out. "A half hour before I was supposed to meet you, my father walked back into my life."

Eleven

The next morning, Daniel rested his forearms on the whitewashed pole fence and watched as one of his stable hands led Rufus, his prize stallion, from the barn to spend the day in the paddock behind his house.

Rufus had it made, Daniel thought. He and Rose and every other hand petted and pampered him and treated him like the king he was. Rufus got fed and brushed and stroked, and he could frolic and mate with a variety of mares.

Lucky Rufus. His life had certain parallels with his favorite horse. He thought he could go through life running his ranch, socializing with his friends and falling into the arms and bed of any available woman who caught his fancy. He thought that was living, but as it turned out, he hadn't had a clue.

Truth was, he wanted what he couldn't have. He wanted Alex, he wanted his child, he wanted a life together. Early-morning coffee in bed, long trail rides over the Clayton and Slade ranches, alone or with their child safe between his arms and knees. He wanted to walk into his house and see her there, watch her grow rounder and bigger, kiss her mouth when she brought their child into the world. He wanted to make dinner with her, listen to her read stories to their children, snuggle with her at night.

He wanted to love her body and nurture her soul.

He simply wanted the opportunity to love her.

Daniel scratched his forehead, his head pounding from sadness, stress and the half bottle of whiskey he'd consumed when he got home last night. He'd missed one appointment—and had a damn good reason for doing so—and she'd written him off as being untrustworthy, inconsiderate. She should've allowed him to explain and then decided, not jumped the gun. If he spoke to another woman, would she think he was having an affair? If he was a minute late, would he be in for a night of receiving the cold shoulder? He wasn't perfect; no man was, and Alex didn't seem to allow any room for him to maneuver.

He couldn't love someone who only loved you back when you proved your worth, who was only happy when you did what she wanted you to do. He loved Alex but he wanted a wife and a partner, not a shadow. He wanted a friend and a lover, not a prosecutor, cross-examining him on his every move.

Sighing, Daniel stared at the empty paddock. Maybe she was right, maybe they were better off apart. Maybe they'd been living in a fool's paradise while they were on vacation at Galloway Cove, allowing the fresh tropical breezes and the island's sultry allure to sway them into believing that they could have the impossible.

How many times were they supposed to try? Shouldn't he just accept that he and Alex were not meant to be?

"Morning."

Daniel turned to see Hector approaching him, dressed in an Italian suit. He looked down at his jeans and worn denim jacket over a flannel shirt and thought that while he and his father looked so alike, he didn't have Hector's taste in clothes.

"Hey."

Daniel hadn't had the chance to have a private moment with Hector, to take him aside and find out what he really wanted. The meeting at Rose and Gus's had carried on and on, and his grandmother had been less than pleased when he insisted that he had to go because he had a prior commitment that couldn't wait. Hoping to catch the tail end of Alex's appointment, he'd floored it to Royal, but he'd been too late.

And because he was late, his world had fallen apart.

"We didn't have time to have a one-on-one conversation last night," Hector said, coming to stand next to Daniel. "Your grandparents are extremely hospitable, and they love you very much."

"Rose is my grandmother. Gus is a new addition to the family," Daniel replied. Tired, upset and not wanting to indulge in small talk, he looked Hector in the eye. "What do you want?"

Shock passed over Hector's face before he schooled his features. "What do you mean?"

"Money? An introduction? A new sports car? A loan?"

Hector cocked his head to the side and instead of anger or annoyance or shame, Daniel saw sympathy in his eyes. "None of those."

"Well, what?" Daniel demanded, his voice ragged.

Because there had to be a reason he was here, back in his life.

"I have more than enough money, and I don't need your connections. I own six sports cars and I am excessively liquid." Humor touched Hector's mouth. "But thank you for offering."

Daniel pushed a hand through his hair. "Then why are you here?"

Hector placed his hand on his shoulder and squeezed. "I am here because you are my son. I have three daughters with a lovely woman who has been my life for more than twenty-five years, but you are my firstborn, my son. I am here because I need to know that you are happy, healthy, okay. I also wanted you to know that I never stopped thinking about you, that I was always looking for you. There's no price to pay, Daniel."

Daniel stared at him, shocked. "What did you say?"

Hector sent him a soft smile. "I didn't spend much time with Stephanie, but it didn't take me long to work out that life was a series of exchanges with that one. Do this for me and I'll do this for you. Pay me this and I'll do that. Pay me more and I'll pretend to love you.

"Why do you think I was so determined to find you? Apart from the fact that you were mine, I didn't want your life being a series of transactions."

Oh God, that was exactly what life with Stephanie had been like.

Daniel felt like he needed to say something, anything. "I've always thought that was what love was. Up to now, it's all I've known. My grandmother married Ed to make sure her mother was cared for… Stephanie only allowed Gran to have me if she paid for the privilege." A muscle ticked in his jaw. "And then, of course, there's Alex. She dumped me ten years ago when I refused to leave The Silver C with her."

"She was a teenager and, as such, stupid," Hector said, his voice mild. "I'm sure you hurt her, as well."

He had. By refusing to leave The Silver C, choosing the ranch over her, he made her feel abandoned. To a girl who'd been left by so many people, she felt any loss more keenly than most people did. She'd been scared and was still scared...

So was he. When there was so much to lose, love was goddamn terrifying.

Earlier, instead of explaining, instead of reassuring her, he'd turned the tables on her, accusing her of wanting to run. Guilt coursed through him. Rather than trying to see things from her perspective, he'd cast blame, got angry. He'd been confused and upset about Hector dropping back into his life, worried that the man he instinctively liked would disappoint him by putting a price on fatherhood.

Driving to Royal, he remembered thinking that his life had been so much less complicated last year: he'd had affairs that had the emotional depth of a puddle, his grandmother wasn't in love with her oldest enemy and Alexis Slade was a girl he saw around town, whom he was determined to keep at arm's length.

His life had been safe. But, God, so boring.

He didn't want that. He wanted to watch his grandmother fuss over her new husband, and he wanted to get to know this man who'd looked for him for the better part of three decades. He wanted his woman, his child, the two most important things in his life.

Because while he loved this land, loved The Silver C, the *love of his life* was probably packing up her car and heading south.

Daniel looked at Hector and lifted his shoulders and his hands. "I'm running out on you again but it's not because I want to, but…"

Hector smiled. "But there's a girl leaving, and you want to stop her."

Rose and her big mouth. Daniel smiled. "I intend to make that girl your daughter-in-law."

Hector grinned. "Sounds good to me." He pulled a card out of the top pocket of his suit and handed it to Daniel. "When you are ready, come to Houston, bring Alexis, meet my family. Or come alone, whatever…"

Daniel took the card and nodded once before scuffing his boot over the short dry grass. He cleared his throat, pushing down the emotion that threatened to strangle his words. "Thanks for looking for me."

Hector squeezed his shoulder again. "It's what fathers do. Go get your girl, son."

Son. Daniel heard the word and closed his eyes. He was finally someone's son. It felt good, wonderful. But it would be freakin' fantastic to be Alex's husband and the peanut's dad.

Alex recognized the sound of Gus's ancient ATV and wondered how much longer he'd continue to nurse that ancient beast. It sputtered and belched smoke and was in the shop for repairs more often than it was on the road. Gus had access to three brand-new ATVs a couple of steps from his front door but his loyalty to that old, paint-deprived quad bike remained constant.

Her grandfather was the most loyal of creatures. He'd loved Sarah—of that she had no doubt—and he'd treated her like a queen, but when he was with Rose, he glowed. Her hard, tough, frank-as-hell grandfather was putty in Miss Rose's hands. He loved her to the depths of his soul, beyond time, for eternity.

Rose, she was surprised to find, seemed to love him just as much. Rose was now Gus's world and Alex was happy for him. Happy that he'd spend the rest of his life loving and being loved.

She couldn't help feeling a little envious, but she shrugged it away, thinking that love like that perhaps now only existed for people of a certain age, a particular generation. She and Daniel were modern people, living in a modern world, and they'd been conditioned to be selfish, to be self-obsessed. How could true love flourish in a society that was so materialistic, self-loving and narcissistic? It was all about them, only about them. She was a classic example because she'd been so caught up in her own drama, in thinking how badly Daniel had treated her in failing to make the doctor's appointment, that she'd brushed aside his explanations. *Her* feelings, *her* heartache had been all she'd been worried about.

Daniel meeting his dad had been a damn good excuse to miss her doctor's appointment, and if she hadn't reacted so selfishly, she might not be sitting in the chair on Sarah's deck, her car fueled and packed, ready to make the journey to Houston and a new life.

She was thoroughly ashamed of herself. And now, more than anything, she wanted to know how he was dealing with his father's reappearance. What did Daniel think of his dad? Was the reality of meeting him as an adult as good as the dream he'd had of him as a boy? But no, because she'd acted like a selfish brat, he was dealing with this all alone.

Alex sighed as she heard Gus's footsteps on the wooden stairs that led to the tree house. Her grandfather's shadow fell over her and she lifted her head and greeted him. Gus nodded, dropped into the Adirondack chair next to her and propped his old boots on the railing. His pushed his ancient but favorite Stetson back with one finger like she'd seen him do a million times before. Old ATV, old boots, old Stetson, Rose.

The man never gave up on the things he loved. Alex bit her lip as the thought struck home. Gus didn't give up; few Slades ever did. So why was she?

Gus cleared his throat and Alex turned her head to look at his profile. "Do you remember when Gemma died?"

Alex jerked her head back, surprised at his question. That was the very last thing she expected him to say. "Sure. I remember getting the news. I thought my world had stopped."

"Do you remember the funeral?"

Alex shook her head. "Not so much, actually. I remember the coffin, the flowers, Sarah holding my hand."

Gus stared at the barren winter landscape beyond the river. "We woke early that morning, the day of the funeral. Sarah looked into your room but you weren't there, and we couldn't find you. We looked everywhere. You never took your hound with you that day. You two were never apart and that scared me."

Olly had died in her arms only a few months later after being kicked by a horse. It had been another loss in a string of losses. "I eventually saddled a horse and told your dog to find you. We went for miles and I eventually found you in the top paddock, the one that borders the Clayton land."

The one where she first kissed Daniel. Yeah, she knew it well. "It was the farthest point you could go without crossing onto Clayton land, and you were standing right on the boundary line."

Alex tried to remember but nothing came back. "I don't remember any of this."

Gus rubbed the back of his neck. "You told me that you were running away, that you couldn't go back. That going back would make it too real."

That sounded like her.

Gus slid down the seat, rested his head on the back of the chair and closed his eyes. Alex waited for him to continue but he just sat there, soaking up the winter sun. She flicked his thigh and he cranked open one eye. "What?"

"Aren't you going to tell me that I run away from stuff I don't want to have to deal with? That I did it ten years ago when I left Daniel—"

"In fairness, I did encourage you to do that," Gus said, his eyes still closed.

"So why aren't you pointing out that running away is what I do, that it's the way I deal with life when things get hard? That I push people away when I think they can hurt me? Why aren't you telling me that?"

"You seem to be doing a right fine job working this out on your own, sweetheart. Seems to me that you don't need my input."

Alex glared at him before dropping her gaze to her hands, which were dangling between her thighs. Running, hiding, staying away—emotionally, as well as physically—was what she did. She dipped her toe in and yanked it out when the water got deeper, the current stronger. As Daniel suggested, she played in the shallows, too scared to take a chance.

"I'm so scared, Grandpa," Alex whispered, her voice so low, she wasn't sure he had heard her small admission.

"So?" Alex looked at him and he shrugged. "Be scared. Be whatever you need to be, but instead of running, be scared while you stand in one place, while you try something new." Gus stood up and pinned her to her chair with his don't-BS-me blue eyes. "I loved your grandmother, Alex. I really did. But a part of me always regretted walking away from Rose, for missing out on fifty years with her. Regret is a cold hard companion I don't want you to live with. Daniel is a good boy—"

Alex couldn't help putting her hand on her heart and feigning shock at his praise of a Clayton.

Gus blushed and waved her mockery away. "Yeah, yeah. But he is a good man—he's loyal and hardworking, and God knows you two burn hot enough to start a wildfire."

Alex grimaced. That wasn't something she wanted Gus noticing. Gus bent down to kiss her cheek. "Don't run this time, Lexi. Stay still and see what happens. Gotta go. Need to check on the calves in the stable paddock."

He had hands and Jason to do that for him, but Gus would ride back on the wheels-on-death because he wanted to. No, because he *needed* to. Alex watched the best man she knew walk away, his back still strong, his gait still steady. He was hard and tough and frank, but her grandfather had an enormous capacity for love. For his family, both present and past, for his land and for his beloved Rose. He'd lived and loved and cried on this land. He tended it and it repaid him by providing a good livelihood for his kids and grandkids. His beloved wife and children and pets were buried in the family graveyard, and every inch held a memory. The land was an intrinsic part of him, just as Clayton land was a part of Daniel.

And they belonged here. Both of them, on this land. Together.

It was time, Alex thought as she stood up, to put this latest, most stupid Clayton-Slade feud to bed.

Her car was filled to the brim and Alex knew that if anyone saw her driving it, they would immediately assume she was leaving Royal and the gossip would fly around town. She and Daniel had created enough gossip lately, so she decided to quickly unpack her vehicle before tracking down Daniel.

She wouldn't take all her worldly possessions back up to her room, as that would take far too long, so Alex decided to dump them in Gus's spacious hall until she returned. She parked her car as close as she could get to the front door of her childhood home, exited her car and walked around to the other side. She had a heavy box of books in her arms when she heard the low rumble of a powerful pickup. Turning, she squinted into the sun and saw the dusty white truck with The Silver C's logo on the side panel.

Alex held the box, conscious that her mouth was as dry, as Gus would say, as the heart of a haystack. Watching as the truck stopped next to hers, Alex stared wide-eyed as Daniel flew out of the car, his face radiating determination and a healthy dose of kick-ass. He was at her side in two seconds and then the heavy box was yanked out of her hands and tossed, with very little effort at all, into the back of his truck. The corner of the box hit a fence post and the box split open, spilling books over the bed of the truck.

Before she could protest, Daniel grabbed her biceps and slammed his mouth against hers in a hard kiss, but as Alex started to sink into the kiss, he whipped his mouth away. Holding her arms, he easily lifted her away from her spot by the door and grabbed a suitcase and a toiletry bag, tossing both into the bed of his pickup.

Since that was exactly where she wanted her stuff, Alex watched him, her shoulder pressed into the side of the car as he emptied her car in a matter of minutes. She wished he'd taken a little more care in moving her potted plants, but she was sure they'd be okay.

When her car was completely empty—Daniel had even chucked her bag and phone onto his passenger seat—he stormed back to her and placed his hands on his hips, his chest heaving.

"You are not going to Houston," he stated, his voice gruff.

She'd gathered that already. Alex just resisted throwing herself into his arms and it took everything she had to lift an insouciant eyebrow. "You kidnapping my stuff, Clayton?"

"I couldn't give a damn about your stuff," Daniel muttered. He jerked his head toward the pickup. "Get in."

There was something wonderful in seeing her man slightly unhinged, Alex thought. She was quite curious to see what he'd do if she dissented. "And if I don't?"

Alex expected him to toss her over his shoulder, to bundle her into his car, and she was turned on thinking about Daniel going caveman on her. But instead of utilizing his physical strength, he lifted his hand to gently touch her face. "I need you, Lex. Right now, I need you to get into my truck because I have things to say…"

"Like?"

Daniel rested his forehead on hers. "I want to tell you that I need you, period. In my bed, my house, my damned life. Nothing makes sense without you."

Alex turned her cheek into his hand, refusing to

drop her eyes from his. This was Daniel, naked and exposed in a way she'd never seen him before. "We make sense, Alexis. We made sense ten years ago, but we were too young and dumb to know it. We made sense three months ago, but we were too scared to acknowledge it. You and I, we're two puzzle pieces that interlock. You're…"

Alex felt the moisture on her face, saw the sheen of emotion in his eyes. "What am I, Dan?"

Daniel held her face within both of his hands as her heart slowly slid from her chest to his. "You're everything, Lex. You're both my future and my past, my baby's mother and the beat of my heart. Please don't go to Houston. Stay here with me."

"Okay."

Daniel yanked his head back, a smile hitting his eyes with all the force of a meteor strike. "Are you being serious?"

Alex nodded. "When you roared up, driving like a crazy man, I was actually unpacking, not packing. I was coming to look for you."

Daniel's thumb skated over her cheek. "Why?"

Alex gripped his shirt, bunching the fabric in her hands. Preparing to jump, she gathered her courage. "I want to stay. I want to be here with you. Raising our children together."

More shock. Daniel looked down at her stomach and jerked his head up. "We're having twins?"

Alex laughed. "Not this time. I was talking about the future, the future I see with you."

"Damn. Twins would've been fun." He brushed her hair off her forehead, his expression tender. "How do you see our future, Lex?"

"Pretty much as you said earlier. I know that I have

some issues, Dan, but I don't want to live my life fearing something that may not happen. I'd rather have any time I can have with you than no time at all. I'm not saying that I'm not going to be insecure, to worry. I probably will but I'll try not to be ridiculous about it."

"And instead of getting frustrated, I'll just hold you tighter and tell you that I'm never going to let you go."

He was gruff and bossy and powerful and sometimes annoying, but he was also perfect. She tipped her head back. "I love you, Daniel. I'm crazy in love with you."

Daniel's smile was pure tenderness. "I love you, too, sweetheart."

Alex's mouth lifted to meet his and she tasted love on his lips, relief in his touch, happiness dancing across his skin. She was feeling pretty damn amazing herself. The kiss deepened, became heated and Daniel pulled her into his hard body, chest to chest, groin to groin. Tongues tangled as love and belonging and desire merged into a sweet, messy ball. This was the start of a new chapter and Alex couldn't wait for the rest of the book.

Daniel's hand came up to cover her breast and it took all her willpower to pull away from his touch. She gestured to the busy stables to the left of the house, blushing when she saw Gus and Jason leaning against the wall, unabashedly watching them.

"Jerks," she muttered.

"On the plus side, I didn't get my head blown off," Daniel murmured, laughter coating his words.

"Actually, Grandpa quite likes you," Alex told him. "He'd like you more if you married me."

Daniel jerked back, frowned and then released a strangled laugh. "I'm not sure what to say to that." He rubbed his jaw. "How do you feel about that?"

"Getting married?" Alex cocked her head to the side, pretending to think. "I think that sounds like a fine idea." She grinned at his astonishment and held up her hand to keep him from grabbing her again. "Slow down, cowboy, I'm not getting engaged with tear tracks on my cheeks and blue rings around my eyes and with my male relatives watching us like hawks. But do feel free to propose in the high meadow, preferably with a lovely ring and a bottle of champagne."

Daniel pretended to consider her statement. "Hmm, the ring I can do. But it'll have to be nonalcoholic champagne, and whose land will it be on?" He smiled and Alex's heart flipped over.

"Ours," Alex said, the words catching in her throat. "Yours, mine, ours."

Daniel nodded, raw, unbridled emotion in his eyes and on his face and in his touch. Alex watched his eyes as he bent to kiss her, silently saying a heartfelt thank-you to whatever force had brought them to this point. They were going to have a hell of a life and she couldn't wait for it to start.

"Hey, you two, what's the status?" Alex jumped, startled, and she turned to see her Gus a few feet from them, waving his phone in the air. Since when did he carry a phone? Alex wondered. "Rosie wants to know."

Daniel gently banged his forehead on her collarbone. "God."

"Everything is sorted," Alex told Gus, making a shooing movement with her hand.

"Rosie, let's hallelujah the county! Call everyone—we're going to paint the house. And the porch." Gus flipped his phone closed—so old-she was surprised it still worked—caught Daniel's eye and gestured to the truck. "Well, come on, then. This stuff isn't going to move itself. Take it into the house and we can have a chat about what comes next."

The last thing she wanted to do was to talk to Gus, or anyone. What she really wanted to do was to divest Daniel of his clothes and make love to him as his future wife.

Daniel looked from her to his truck, adjusted his ball cap and shook his head. "As much as I appreciate the offer, sir, I'm going to stick to my original plan."

"And that was?" Alex asked as his hand enveloped hers.

"To kidnap you and your stuff." He flashed a grin at Gus as he wrapped an arm around her waist and easily carried her to his truck. He bundled her into the passenger seat and saluted Gus. "I try to learn from my elders, sir."

Epilogue

At six months pregnant, Alex required a wedding dress with an empire waistline but, catching a glance at her reflection in the gleaming glass door as she stepped out of the TCC function room, she saw that she still looked pretty amazing. The dress's bodice gathered into a knot behind her breasts and the chiffon overskirt, which was dotted with embroidered roses, flowed to the floor. She was, as everyone kept telling her, glowing. Alex knew that had as much to do with her husband of two hours as it did her pregnancy.

She was married. Alex looked down at the band of diamonds Dan had put on her ring finger earlier, a companion piece to her sapphire-and-diamond engagement ring, and took a moment to count her many blessings. Her partnership with Mike was smooth sailing, and while commuting was a pain, so far it was working. She was living in Dan's house and they were deciding how to completely renovate Rose's old house together. In Rose she found both a mentor, a friend and an ally. And in getting to know Sarah's oldest friend, she felt like she had a piece of her grandmother back.

Best of all, she woke up with Dan and fell asleep with him, secure that her heart was safe in his hands.

"Have I told you how stunning you look?"

Alex turned at her husband's voice and smiled. He didn't look too shabby himself, looking almost as hot in a tuxedo as he did in worn jeans and a T-shirt. But Daniel naked? Couldn't get sexier...

Daniel approached her, held the back of her head and tipped her chin up to brush her lips. "We haven't had a moment to ourselves since we walked into that church."

Their friends and family—including Daniel's father, his wife and his three half sisters and their spouses and many children—all wanted some time with the new bridal couple. While Alex appreciated their well wishes, her cheeks were sore from smiling, her feet ached and she just wanted to step into Daniel's arms for a cuddle.

"You doing okay?" Daniel asked, placing his hand on her round stomach.

"A little tired." Alex looped one arm around his neck and rested her cheek on his chest. "I'm so thrilled that we are going back to Galloway Cove for our honeymoon, Dan. I just want you and the sun and the sea."

"I just want you. Naked," Daniel muttered. He gathered her to him and she felt his erection against her stomach, and felt his hand cupping her butt.

"I missed you last night," Alex told him before pushing up onto her toes and placing her lips against his. Daniel immediately responded, his tongue sliding into her mouth and sending heat to her core.

Alex, as she always did, melted and wondered if anyone would notice if they sneaked away.

"My beautiful, sexy wife. How I love—"

The door behind them banged open and Daniel
cursed at the interruption. Stifling her groan, she turned
to see Rachel in the hallway, Matt Galloway a step behind her. Still leaning against Daniel, she lifted her hand
at her matron of honor.

Rachel rubbed her arm. "Are you okay, Alex? You're
looking a bit flushed."

That was because her husband still had his hand on
her butt.

"Just taking a breather," Alex told her, turning to
look at Matt. "I was just telling Dan that I'm so excited
to be going back to Galloway Cove for our honeymoon."

Matt nodded. "I was surprised when Dan asked me.
I thought that since you were basically kidnapped and
tossed off the plane onto my island, it wouldn't be your
first choice for a honeymoon."

Alex shook her head. "No, I loved it!" She loved
making love to Daniel at the waterfall and by the pool
and on the bench, in the outdoor shower…

Rachel lifted her eyebrows at her, Alex lifted hers
back and they both burst out laughing. Yep, she was
pretty sure that Rachel liked the island, too. And not
only because it was a place of immense natural beauty.

The door opened again, and Tessa glided through,
followed by Ryan. "Alex and Rachel, there you are! I've
been looking for both of you."

Alex put her back to Daniel's chest, linking her hand
with the one that now rested on her stomach. Her brides-
maid looked radiant and about to burst with news. Alex
held up her hand as Caleb and Shelby joined their party,
followed by James and Lydia. They were just missing

Brooke and Austin, but Alex had barely finished that thought when they walked into the hallway from the main entrance, Austin carrying a frame covered in brown paper.

"The gang's all here," Ryan commented.

"Alex, I want to run something by you—" James started to speak, only to be interrupted by Tessa.

"Wait, hold on, I need to—"

"Austin, honey, we need Rose and Gus," Brooke said a second later.

Alex laughed and tipped her head up to look at Daniel. He grinned down at her before lifting his fingers to his mouth to let out a shrill whistle. Their friends immediately quieted down. "We need to get back to our guests, so make it snappy." Daniel pointed to Tessa. "Tess, you're up."

"Alex, would you and Rachel both be my matrons of honor?"

Alex jumped up and down and Rachel squealed with excitement. Alex wanted to hug Tessa but Daniel held her tight. "Fantastic," he said. "Not meaning to be rude, but we need to hurry this along. I want to cut the cake, have a first dance with my bride and get to the fun part of the night."

Daniel pointed his finger at Caleb. "Go."

Shelby rested her temple on Caleb's arm. "We're having twins."

Alex let out a whoop, tore away from Daniel's hold to hug Shelby. As everyone else congratulated the happy pair, Alex took the chance to hug Tessa and then, because she was overflowing with happiness, to hug Rachel, as well.

Daniel gently hooked his finger into the back of her dress and tugged her back into her previous position. "We really do need to get back inside."

Alex nodded. "I know. Rose is going to have a fit if she finds us hanging out in the hallway with our friends."

Daniel grinned and jerked his head at James. "What's up?"

"Nothing that can't wait. I was just thinking that maybe Alex could do another fund-raising function next year."

Alex nodded enthusiastically, her mischievous side surfacing. "Absolutely. I was thinking about a skin cal-endar, tentatively called 'The Rogues of Royal.' I'd need you all to model. I hope you are comfortable stripping down in front of a camera."

The five male faces in front of her paled in unison. Alex looked up at her husband, who was laughing. "You know that I have no problem stripping down," he mur-mured before looking back at the group. "To be dis-cussed later. Much, much later. Brooke, what have you got there, honey?"

Yet again the door opened, and Alex winced when she saw Rose's unamused face. "Ladies and gentle-men, the party is inside, not out here." This time, twelve grown men and women shuffled their feet at the dis-pleasure in Regal Rose's voice.

Alex opened her mouth to apologize, but then her grandfather slipped past Rose, his eyes on the package in Brooke's hand. "Rosie! It's here!"

Rose clasped her hands in delight and joined Gus at Brooke's side. Alex stepped away from Daniel and wondered what was going on. "What is it?" she asked.

Rose beckoned her to come closer. The group made a circle behind them and Daniel dropped to his haunches, his hand on the frame. Alex heard movement behind Ryan and glanced over to see Hector joining the group, his eyes not moving from Daniel's face.

Gus nodded, and Daniel ripped the paper away. Alex took a moment to absorb the significance of Brooke's painting. A wolf rested in the first of three circles—one each for her, Daniel and Jason—and beneath it, Brooke had carefully painted the words *The Silver Wolf Ranch*.

Daniel turned to look at her and she saw love and adoration in his eyes. He stood up and took her hand and raised her knuckles to his lips. "Equal partners, Slade?"

"Equal partners, Clayton," she murmured.

Daniel kept her hand in his as he led her back to their wedding reception and their guests. "One dance, the cake cutting and then I'm hauling you out of here, Lex."

Alex grinned at him. "As you already know, I'm always up for a good kidnapping, my darling."

* * * * *

SEDUCTION ON HIS TERMS

SARAH M. ANDERSON

To the Quincy Public Library and the lovely librarians
and staff, especially Katie, Farrah and Jeraca,
who feed my book addiction!
Thank you for helping make my son a reader
and for making literature a part of so many lives!

One

"Good evening, Dr. Wyatt," Jeannie Kaufman said as the man slid into his usual seat at the end of the bar. It was a busy Friday night, and he sat as far away as he could get from the other patrons at Trenton's.

"Jeannie," he said in his usual brusque tone.

But this time she heard something tight in his voice.

Dr. Robert Wyatt was an unusual man, to say the least. His family owned Wyatt Medical Industries, and Dr. Wyatt had been named to the "Top Five Chicago Billionaire Bachelors" list last year, which probably had just as much to do with his family fortune as it did with the fact that he was a solid six feet tall, broad chested and sporting a luxurious mane of inky black hair that made the ice-cold blue of his eyes more striking.

And as if being richer than sin and even better looking wasn't tempting enough, the man had to be a pediatric surgeon, as well. He performed delicate heart surgeries on babies and kids. He single-handedly saved lives—and she'd

read that for some families who couldn't afford the astro-
nomical costs, he'd quietly covered their bills.

Really, the man was too good to be true.

She kept waiting for a sign that, underneath all that perfection, he was a villain. She'd had plenty of rich, handsome and talented customers who were complete assholes.

Dr. Wyatt…wasn't.

Yes, he was distant, precise and, as far as she could tell,
completely fearless. All qualities that made him a great surgeon. But if he had an ego, she'd never seen it. He came into
the bar five nights a week at precisely eight, sat in the same
spot, ordered the same drink and left her the same tip—a
hundred dollars on a twenty-dollar tab. In cash. He never
made a pass at anyone, staff or guest, and bluntly rebuffed
any flirtation from women or men.

He was her favorite customer.

Before he'd had the chance to straighten his cuffs—
something he did almost obsessively—Jeannie set his Manhattan down in front of him.

She'd been making his drink for almost three years now.
His Manhattan contained the second-most expensive rye
bourbon on the market, because Dr. Wyatt preferred the
taste over the most expensive one; a vermouth that she ordered from Italy exclusively for him; and bitters that cost
over a hundred bucks a bottle. It was all precisely blended
and aged in an American white oak cask for sixty days and
served in a chilled martini glass with a lemon twist. It'd
taken almost eight months of experimenting with brands
and blends and aging to get the drink right.

But it'd been worth it.

Every time he lifted the glass to his lips, like he was
doing now, Jeannie held her breath. Watching this man
drink was practically an orgasmic experience. As he swallowed, she watched in fascination as the muscles in his

throat moved. He didn't show emotion, didn't pretend to be nice. But when he lowered the glass back to the bar?

He *smiled*.

It barely qualified as one, and a casual observer would've missed it entirely. His mouth hardly even moved. But she knew him well enough to know that the slight curve of his lips and the warming of his icy gaze was the same as anyone else shouting for joy.

He held her gaze and murmured, "Perfect."

It was the only compliment she'd ever heard him give.

Her body tightened as desire licked down her back and spread throughout her midsection. As a rule, Jeannie did not serve up sex along with drinks. But if she were ever going to break that rule, it'd be for him.

Sadly, he was only here for the drink.

Jeannie loved a good romance novel and for three years, she'd imagined Robert as some duke thrust into the role that didn't fit him, nobility that hated the crush of ballrooms and cut directs and doing the pretty around the ton and all those dukely things when all he really wanted to do was practice medicine and tend to his estates and generally be left alone. In those stories, there was always a housekeeper or pickpocket or even a tavern wench who thawed his heart and taught him to love.

Jeannie shook off her fantasies. She topped off the scotch for the salesman at the other end of the bar and poured the wine for table eleven, but her attention was focused on Wyatt. She had to break the bad news to him—she'd be gone next week to help her sister, Nicole, with the baby girl that was due any minute.

This baby was the key to Jeannie and her sister being a family again. Any family Jeannie had ever had, she'd lost. She'd never met her father—he'd left before she'd been born. Mom had died when Jeannie had been ten and Nicole...

It didn't matter what had gone wrong between the sisters in the past. What mattered was that they were going to grab this chance to be a family again now. Melissa—that was what they were going to call the baby—would be the tie that bound them together. Jeannie would do her part by being there for her sister, just like Nicole had been there for Jeannie when Mom had died and left the sisters all alone in the world.

In an attempt to demonstrate her commitment, Jeannie had even offered to move back into their childhood home with Nicole. It would've been a disaster but Jeannie had still offered because that was what family did—they made sacrifices and stuck together through the rough times. Only now that she was twenty-six was Jeannie aware how much Nicole had sacrificed for her. The least Jeannie could do was return the favor.

Nicole had told Jeannie that, while a thoughtful offer, it was absolutely *not* necessary for them to share a house again. Thank God, because living together probably would've destroyed their still-fragile peace. Instead, Jeannie would keep working nights at Trenton's—and taking care of Dr. Wyatt—and then she'd get to the house around ten every morning to help Nicole with the cooking or cleaning or playing with the baby.

Jeannie might not be the best sister in the world but by God, she was going to be the best aunt.

That was the plan, anyway.

The only hiccup was sitting in front of her.

Wyatt didn't do well with change, as she'd learned maybe six months into their *partnership*, as Jeannie thought of it. She'd gotten a cold and stayed home. He'd been more than a little upset that someone else had made him a subpar Manhattan that night. Julian, the owner of Trenton's, said Tony, the bartender who'd subbed for her that night, had gotten a job elsewhere right after that. Jeannie knew that wasn't a coincidence.

Maybe half the time Dr. Wyatt sat at her bar, he didn't say anything. Which was fine. But when he did talk? It wasn't inane chitchat or stale pickup lines. When he spoke, every single word either made her fall further in love with him or broke her heart.

"So," he started and Jeannie knew he was about to break her heart again.

She waited patiently, rearranging the stemware that hung below the bar in front of him. He'd talk when he wanted and not a moment before.

Had he lost a patient? That she knew of, he'd only had two or three kids die and those times had been…awful. All he'd ever said was that he'd failed. That was it. But the way he'd sipped his drink…

The last time it'd happened, she'd sobbed in the ladies' room after he'd left. Below his icy surface, a sea of emotion churned. And when he lost a patient, that sea raged.

After three years of listening to Dr. Wyatt pour out his heart in cold, clipped tones, Jeannie knew all too well how things could go wrong with babies. That was what made Jeannie nervous about Nicole and Melissa.

"I heard something today," he went on after long moments that had her on pins and needles.

She studied him as she finished the lemons and moved on to the limes. He straightened his cuffs and then took a drink.

She fought the urge to check her phone again. Nicole would text if anything happened and there'd been no buzzing at her hip. But tonight was the night. Jeannie could feel it.

Wyatt cleared his throat. "I was informed that my father is considering a run for governor."

Jeannie froze, the knife buried inside a lime. Had she ever heard Dr. Wyatt talk about his parents? She might've assumed that they'd died and left the bulk of the Wyatt Medical fortune to their son.

And who the heck had *informed* him of this? What an odd way to phrase it. "Is that so?"

"Yes," Dr. Wyatt replied quickly. That, coupled with the unmistakable bitterness in his voice, meant only one thing.

This was extremely *bad* news.

Jeannie had been working in a bar since the day she'd turned eighteen, three whole years before she was legally allowed to serve alcohol. She'd been desperate to get away from Nicole, who hadn't wanted Jeannie to get a job and certainly not as a bartender. She'd wanted Jeannie to go to college, become a teacher, like Nicole. Wanting to own her own bar was out of the question. Nicole wouldn't allow it.

After *that* fight, Jeannie had moved out, lied about her age and learned on the job. While pouring wine, countless men and women poured their hearts out to her. In the years she'd been at this high-priced chophouse, she'd learned a hell of a lot about how the one percent lived.

But she'd never had a customer like Robert Wyatt before.

Wyatt finished his drink in two long swallows. "The thing is," he said, setting his glass down with enough force that Jeannie was surprised the delicate stem didn't shatter, "if he runs, he'll expect us to stand next to him as if we're one big happy family."

Wiping her hands, she gave up the pretense of working and leaned against the bar. "Sounds like that's a problem."

"You have no idea," he muttered, which was even more disturbing because when did precise, careful Dr. Robert Wyatt *mutter*?

His charcoal-gray three-piece suit fit him perfectly, as did the shirt with cuff links that tonight looked like sapphires—he favored blues when he dressed. The blue-and-orange-striped tie matched the square artfully arranged in his pocket. It was September and Chicago still clung to the last of the summer's heat, but the way Dr. Robert Wyatt dressed announced that he'd never stoop to *sweating*.

She could see where the tie had been loosened slightly as if he'd yanked on it in frustration. His hair wasn't carefully brushed back, but rumpled. He made it look good because everything looked good on him, but still. His shoulders drooped and instead of his usual ramrod-straight posture, his head hung forward, just a bit. When he glanced up at her, she saw the worry lines cut deep across his forehead. He looked like the weight of the world was about to crush him flat.

It hurt to see him like this.

If it were any other man, any other customer, she'd honestly offer him a hug because Lord, he looked like he needed one. But she'd seen how Wyatt flinched when someone touched him.

"So don't do it," she said, keeping her voice low and calm.

"I have to." Unsurprisingly, he straightened his cuffs. "I won't have a choice."

At that, she gave him a look. "Why not?" He glared but she kept going. "For God's sake, you have nothing *but* choices. If you wanted to buy half of Chicago to raise wildebeests, you could. If you opened your own hospital and told everyone they had to wear blue wigs to enter the building, there'd be a run on clown hair. You can go anywhere, do anything, be *anyone* you want because you're Dr. Robert *freaking* Wyatt."

All because he had looks, money and power.

All things Jeannie would never have.

His mouth opened but unexpectedly, he slammed it shut. Then he was pushing away from the bar, glaring at her as he threw some bills down and turned to go.

"Dr. Wyatt? Wait!" When he kept going, she yelled, "Robert!"

That got his attention.

When he spun, she flinched because he was *furious*. It

wasn't buried under layers of icy calm—it was right there on the surface, plain as day.

Was he mad she'd used his given name? Or that she'd questioned his judgment? It didn't matter. She wasn't going to buckle in the face of his fury.

She squared her shoulders and said, "I have a family thing next week and I'm taking some vacation time."

Confusion replaced his anger and he was back at the bar in seconds, staring down at her with something that looked like worry clouding his eyes. "How long?"

She swallowed. She was taller than average, but looking up into his eyes, only a few inches away… He made her feel small at the same time she felt like the only person in his universe.

He'd always leave her unsettled, wouldn't he?

"Just the week. I'll be back Monday after next. Promise."

The look on his face—like he wouldn't be able to function if she wasn't there to serve the perfect Manhattan to the perfect man—was the kind of look that made her fall a little bit more in love with him while it broke her heart at the same time.

"Will you be okay?" she asked.

Something warm brushed over the top of her hand, sending a jolt of electricity up her arm. Had he *touched* her? By the time she looked down, Robert was straightening his cuffs. "Of course," he said dismissively, as if it was impossible for him to be anything *but* perfectly fine. "I'm a Wyatt."

Then he was gone.

Jeannie stared after him. This was bad. Before she could decide how worried about him she was going to be, her phone buzzed.

It's time! read Nicole's message.

"It's time!" Jeannie shouted. The waiters cheered.

Dr. Wyatt would have to wait. Jeannie's new niece came first.

Two

Jeannie was back tonight.

Robert hadn't gone to Trenton's, knowing she wouldn't be there, and he felt the loss of their routine deeply. Instead, he'd spent a lot more time in the office, reviewing cases and getting caught up on paperwork and not thinking about Landon Wyatt or political campaigns.

But finally, it was Monday and Jeannie would be waiting for him. On some level he found his desire to see her again worrisome. She was just a bartender who'd perfected a Manhattan. Anyone could mix a drink.

But that was a lie and he knew it.

He never should have touched her. But she'd stood there staring at him with her huge brown eyes, asking if he was going to be okay, like she cared. Not because he was the billionaire Dr. Robert Wyatt, but because he was Robert.

That was what he'd missed this week. Just being… Robert.

Lost in thought, he didn't look at the screen of his phone before he answered it. "This is Wyatt."

"Bobby?"

Robert froze, his hand on the elevator buttons. It couldn't be…

But no one else called him Bobby. *"Mom?"*

"Hi, honey." Cybil Wyatt's voice sounded weak. It hit him like a punch to the solar plexus. "How have you been?"

Almost three years had passed since he'd talked to his mother.

He quickly retreated to his office. "Can you talk? Are you on speakerphone?"

"Honey," she went on, an extra waver in her voice. "You heard from Alexander, right?"

That was a *no*, she couldn't talk freely.

Alexander was Landon's assistant, always happy to do the older man's bidding. "Yes. He said Landon wanted to run for governor." A terrible idea on both a state level and a personal level.

Robert knew the only reason Landon Wyatt wanted to be governor was because he'd discovered a way to personally enrich himself. He wasn't content having politicians and lobbyists in his pocket. He always wanted more.

"Your father wants you by his side." The way she cleared her throat made Robert want to throw something. "*We* want you by *our* sides," she corrected because the fiction that they were all one big happy family was a lie that had to be maintained at all costs, no matter what.

"Are you on speaker?"

She laughed lightly, a fake sound. "Of course not. All is forgiven, honey. We both know you didn't mean it."

Hmm. If she wasn't on speaker, she was probably sitting in Landon's opulent office, where he was watching her through those cold, slitted eyes of his—the same eyes Robert saw in the mirror every damn morning—making sure

Mom stuck to the script. "Let me help you, Mom. I can get you away from him."

"We're having a gala to launch his campaign in two weeks." Her voice cracked but she didn't stop. "It's at the Winston art gallery, right off the Magnificent Mile."

"I know it."

"It'd mean a lot to your father and me to see you there."

Robert didn't doubt that his mother wanted to see him. But to Landon, this was nothing more than another way to exert control over Robert and he'd vowed never to give Landon that much power again—even if it cost him his relationship with his mother.

"Tell me what I can do to help you, Mom."

There was a brief pause. "We've missed you, too."

Dammit. He didn't want to pretend to be a happy family, not in private and most certainly not in public. But he knew Landon well enough to know that if he didn't show, Mom would pay the price.

Just like she always did.

Robert couldn't let that happen. Of all the things Landon Wyatt had done and would continue to do, dangling Cybil as bait to ensure Robert cooperated was one of the meanest.

He had to fix this. "Think about what I said, okay? We'll talk at the gallery."

She exhaled. "That's wonderful, dear. It starts at seven but we'd like you to get there earlier. Your father wants to make sure we're all on the same page."

Robert almost growled. *Getting on the same page* meant threats. Lots of them. "I'll try. I have to make my rounds. But if I can get you away, will you come with me?" Because after what had happened last time…

"Thank you, Bobby," she said and he hoped like hell that was a *yes*. "I—*we* can't wait to see you again."

"Me, too, Mom. Love you."

She didn't say it back. The line went dead.

Robert stared at nothing for a long time.

This was exactly what he'd been afraid of. Landon was going to force Robert to do this—be this...this *lie*. He was going to make Robert stand next to him before crowds and cameras. He was going to expect Robert to give speeches of his own, no doubt full of bold-faced lies about Landon's character and compassion. And if Robert didn't...

Would he ever see his mother again?

Landon would do whatever he wanted, if Robert didn't stop him. There had to be a way.

You can do anything you want because you're Dr. Robert freaking *Wyatt*, he heard Jeannie say.

Maybe she was right.

Now more than ever, he needed a drink.

"Well?" he said in that silky voice of his.

Once, Cybil had thought Landon Wyatt's voice was the most seductive voice she'd ever heard.

That had been a long time ago. So long ago that all she could remember was the pain of realizing she'd been seduced, all right. She could barely remember the time when she'd been a naive coed right out of college, swept away by the charming billionaire fifteen years her senior.

She'd been paying for that mistake ever since. "He's coming."

Landon notched an eyebrow—a warning.

Cybil smiled graciously. "He'll try to get there early, but he has rounds," she went on, hoping Landon would dismiss her. Hearing Bobby's voice again, the anger when he'd promised he could get her away from her husband of thirty-five years...

God, she'd missed her son. Maybe this time would be different. Bobby had grown into a fine man, a brilliant surgeon. Landon hated that both because Bobby worked for a living and, Cybil suspected, because Landon knew Bobby was far smarter.

If anyone could outthink Landon Wyatt, it'd be his own son.

Something warm and light bloomed in her chest. With a start, she realized it was hope.

What if there really was a way?

But Landon would never let her go.

A fact he reinforced when he stood and stroked a hand over her hair. Years of practice kept her from flinching at his touch. "I know you've missed him," he murmured as if he hadn't been the one keeping her from her son. His hand settled on the back of her neck and he began to squeeze. "So I know you'll make sure he does what's expected. Otherwise…"

"Of course," Cybil agreed, struggling as his grip tightened.

Like she did every day, she thanked God Bobby had gotten away. If he were still trapped in this hell with her, she didn't know how she'd bear it. But the knowledge that he was out there, saving children and living far from *this*—that kept her going. As long as her son was safe, she could endure.

She looked up at the man she'd married and smiled because he expected her to act as if she enjoyed being with him. Maybe… Maybe she wouldn't have to endure much longer.

"Mr. Wyatt?" The sound of Alexander's reedy voice cut through the office. "My apologies, but the campaign chairman is on line one."

"Now what?" he growled, abruptly letting her go.

Cybil did not exhale in relief because he'd already forgotten she was here. She merely escaped while she could.

She didn't want Bobby to be drawn back into his father's world, and the fact that Landon was using her to get their son to fall into line sickened her. But Bobby's anger, his willingness to stand up to his father...

No, maybe she wouldn't have to endure this marriage much longer at all.

She needed to be ready.

Would Robert convince his mother to leave Landon?

The last time, it'd gone...poorly.

He needed a better plan this time.

More than just hiding Cybil Wyatt, Robert needed to make sure Landon wouldn't ever be in a position to track her down.

His heart beat at a highly irregular pace. Last time he'd merely tried to hide his mother, in his own home, no less. He hadn't had a contingency plan in place and without that plan, the whole rescue had been doomed to fail.

This time would be different.

Wyatts didn't fail. They succeeded.

He entered Trenton's at five past eight. Thank God Jeannie was back tonight. She might not be able to offer assistance but she could at least tell him if New Zealand was a good idea or not. She might be the only person he knew who'd tell him the truth. Now all he had to do was find a way to ask.

A soft, feminine voice purred, "Good evening, Dr. Wyatt. What can I get you?"

His head snapped up at the unfamiliar voice, the hair on the back of his neck standing up. The bar at Trenton's was dimly lit, so it took a few moments for Robert to identify the speaker.

The woman behind the bar was *not* Jeannie. This woman was shorter, with long light-colored hair piled on top of her head. Jeannie was almost tall enough that she could look Robert in the eye, with dark hair cropped close.

"Where's Jeannie?" he growled.

It was Monday. She was supposed to be *here*.

The woman behind the bar batted her eyes. "I'm Miranda. Jeannie's on vacation. I'm more than happy to take care of you while she's gone…"

Robert glared at her. Dammit, Jeannie had said one week. She'd *promised*. And now he needed her and she wasn't here.

The pressure in his head was almost blinding. If he didn't see Jeannie tonight—right *now*—he might do something they'd all regret.

"Dr. Wyatt?"

The world began to lose color at the edges, a numb gray washing everything flat.

He needed to leave before he lost control.

But he couldn't because his mother had called him and there had to be a way to save her and he *needed* to see Jeannie.

She was the only one who could bring color back to his world.

"She's not on vacation. Tell me where she is." He leaned forward, struggling to keep his voice level. *"Or else."*

Miranda's teasing pout fell away as she straightened and stepped back. "She's not here," she said, the purr gone from her voice.

He wasn't going to lash out. A Wyatt never lost control.

So instead of giving in to the gray numbness and doing what Landon would do, Robert forced himself to adjust the cuffs on his bespoke suit, which gave him enough time to breathe and attempt to speak calmly.

He studied Miranda. She held his gaze, but he could see her pulse beating at her throat. She was probably telling the truth.

"I'd like to speak with the owner. Please."

The buzzing in his head became two discordant sounds. He could hear Landon snarling, *Wyatts don't ask*, at the same time as he heard Jeannie say, in that husky voice of hers, *There, was that so hard?*

When was the first time Jeannie had said that to him? He didn't remember. All he remembered was that she was the first person who'd ever dared tease him.

When he was sure he had himself back under control, he looked up. Miranda the substitute bartender wasn't moving.

"Now," Robert snarled.

With a jolt, she turned and fled.

It felt wrong to sit in his seat if Jeannie wasn't on the other side of the bar. Like this place wasn't home anymore.

Which was ridiculous because this was a bar where he spent maybe half an hour every night. It wasn't his sprawling Gold Coast townhouse with million-dollar views of Lake Michigan. It wasn't even the monstrosity of a mansion where he'd been raised by a succession of nannies. This was not home. This was just where Jeannie had been when he'd walked into this restaurant two years and ten months ago and sat down at this bar because he'd felt…lost.

It had been thirty-four months since Jeannie had stood in front of him, listening while he struggled to get his thoughts in order because his mother had refused to stay with him and Landon had come for her. Everything in Robert's carefully constructed world had gone gray, which had been good because then Robert didn't have to feel anything. Anything but the overpowering need for the perfect drink.

Sometimes, when Robert allowed himself to look back at that moment, he wondered if maybe Jeannie had been waiting patiently for him.

Where the hell *was* she?

Then it hit him. She'd said she had a family thing. She wasn't here now.

Something had gone wrong.

The realization gave him an odd feeling, one he did not

like. He liked it even less when Miranda the substitute bartender returned with a man that looked vaguely familiar.

"Dr. Wyatt, it's so good to see you, as always," the man said, smiling in a way Robert didn't trust. "I'm sorry there's a problem. How can I correct things?"

Robert was running out of patience. "Who are you?"

"Julian Simmons." He said it in a way that made it clear Robert was supposed to remember who he was. "I own Trenton's. You're one of our most valued customers, so if there's a problem, I'm sure we can—"

Robert cut the man off. "Where's Jeannie?"

Robert couldn't tell in the dim light, but he thought Simmons might have gone a shade whiter. "Jeannie is taking some personal time."

Only a fool would think personal time and vacation time were the same thing. Robert was many things, but foolish wasn't one of them. "Is she all right?"

Simmons didn't answer for another long beat.

Something *had* happened; Robert knew it. Helplessness collided with an ever-increasing anger. He was not going to stand by while another woman was hurt. Not when he had the power to stop it.

"Jeannie is fine," Simmons finally said. "We're hopeful that she will rejoin us in a few weeks. I know she's your personal favorite, but Miranda is more than happy to serve you."

Both Miranda the substitute bartender and Simmons the restaurant owner recoiled before Robert realized he was snarling at them. "Tell me where she is. Now."

"Dr. Wyatt, I'm sorry but—"

Before he was aware of what he was doing, Robert had reached across the bar and took hold of Simmons's tie.

Robert could hear Landon Wyatt shouting, *No one says no to a Wyatt*, in his mind.

Or maybe he hadn't heard the words. Maybe he'd said them out loud because Miranda squeaked in alarm.

"You," he said to the woman, "can *go*."

He didn't have to tell her twice.

"Dr. Wyatt," Simmons said. "This is all a misunderstanding."

Belatedly, he realized he was probably not making the best argument. Abruptly, he released Simmons's tie. Robert realized he had overlooked the path of least resistance. Instead of allowing his temper to get the better of him, he should've started from a different negotiating position.

"How much?"

"What?" Simmons winced.

"How much?" Robert repeated. "I have frightened you and your employees, which wasn't my intent. I like coming here. I would like to return, once Jeannie is back in her position. I would like to…to make amends."

Which was as close as possible to apologizing without actually apologizing because Wyatts did *not* apologize.

Ever.

Simmons stared at him, mouth agape.

"Shall we say…" Robert picked a number out of thin air. "Ten thousand?"

"Dollars?" Simmons gasped.

"Twenty thousand. Dollars," he added for clarity's sake. Everyone had a price, after all.

Jeannie was in trouble and he had to help her. But to do that, he had to know where she was. If Simmons refused to take the bribe, Robert had other ways of tracking her down, but those would take more time. Time was one commodity he couldn't buy.

The buzzing in his head was so loud that it drowned out the hum of the restaurant. He gritted his teeth and blocked it out.

Simmons pulled his pocket square out and dabbed at

his forehead. "Do you realize how many laws you're asking me to break?"

"Do you realize how little I care?" Wyatt shot back.

When it came to things like abuse or murder, Wyatt knew and respected the law. When it came to things like this? Well, he was a Wyatt. Money talked.

Simmons knew it, too. "Do I have your word that you won't hurt her?"

"I won't even touch her." *Not unless she wants me to.*

The thought crossed his mind before he was aware it was there, but he shook it away.

Simmons seemed to deflate. "There was a family emergency."

The longer this man stood around hemming and hawing, the worse things could be for Jeannie. Belatedly, Robert realized he did not have twenty thousand dollars in cash on him. He placed a credit card on the bar. "Run it for whatever you want."

After only a moment's hesitation, Simmons took the card. "Let me get you the address, Dr. Wyatt."

About damn time.

Three

Jeannie all but collapsed onto the concrete step in front of Nicole's house, too numb to even weep.

No, that was wrong. This was her house now.

Nicole was dead.

And since there were no other living family members, Jeannie had inherited what Nicole had owned. Including their childhood home.

Everything left was hers now. The sensible used family sedan. The huge past-due bills to fertility clinics. The cost of burying her sister.

The baby.

It was too much.

Death was bad enough because it had taken Nicole, leaving Jeannie with nothing but wispy memories of a happy family. But who knew dying was so complicated? And expensive? Who knew unraveling a life would involve so much damned *paperwork*?

That didn't even account for Melissa. That baby girl was

days old. It wasn't right that she would never know her mother. It wasn't right that the family Nicole had wanted for so long...

Jeannie scrubbed at her face. It wasn't Melissa's fault that delivery had been complicated or that Nicole had developed a blood clot that had gone undiagnosed until it was too late. Dimly, Jeannie knew she needed to sue the hospital. This wasn't the 1800s. Women weren't supposed to die giving birth. But Jeannie couldn't face the prospect of more paperwork, of more responsibilities. She could barely face the next ten minutes.

She looked up at the sky, hoping to find a star to guide her. One little twinkling bit of hope. But this was Chicago. The city's light pollution was brighter than any star, and all that was left was a blank sky with a reddish haze coloring everything. Including her world.

She was supposed to be at work. She was supposed to be fixing the perfect Manhattan for the perfect Dr. Robert Wyatt, the man whose tipping habits had made her feel financially secure for the first time in her life. A hundred bucks a night, five nights a week, for almost three years— Dr. Robert Wyatt had single-handedly given Jeannie the room to breathe. To dream of her own place, her own rules...

Of course, now that she had an infant to care for and a mortgage and bills to settle, she couldn't breathe. She'd be lucky if her job at Trenton's was still there when she was able to go back. *If* she would be able to go back. Julian might hold her job for another week or so, but Jeannie knew he wouldn't hold it for two months. Because after an initial search of newborn childcare in Chicago, she knew that was what she'd need. Jeannie had found only day care that accepted six-week-old babies, but the price was so far out of reach that all she'd been able to do was laugh and close the browser. If she wanted childcare before Melissa was two months old, she needed a *lot* of money. And that was something she simply didn't have. Even if she sued the hospital, put the house on the market, sold the family sedan—it still wouldn't be enough fast enough.

Even though there were no stars to see, she stared hard at that red sky. This time she caught a flicker of light high overhead. It was probably just an airplane, but she couldn't risk it. She closed her eyes and whispered to herself, "Star light, star bright, grant me the wish I wish tonight."

She couldn't wish Nicole back. She couldn't undo any of the loss or the pain that had marked Jeannie's life so far. Looking back was a trap, one she couldn't get stuck in. She had no choice but to keep moving forward.

"I need help," she whispered.

Financial assistance, baby help, emotional support—you name it, she needed it.

There was a moment of blissful silence—no horns honking in the distance, no neighbors shouting, not even the roar of an airplane overhead.

But if Jeannie was hoping for an answer to her prayers, she didn't get it because that was when the small sound of Melissa starting to cry broke the quiet.

Sucking in a ragged breath, Jeannie dropped her head into her hands. She needed just a few more seconds to think but...

The baby didn't sleep.

Was that because Jeannie wasn't Nicole? Or was Melissa sick? Could Jeannie risk the cost of taking Melissa to the emergency room? Or...there was a pediatrician who'd stopped at the hospital before Melissa was discharged. But it was almost ten at night. If anyone answered the phone, they'd probably tell her to head to the ER.

The only person she knew who knew anything at all about small children was Dr. Wyatt, but it wasn't like she could ask him for advice about a fussy newborn. He was a surgeon, not a baby whisperer.

Jeannie had helped organize a shower for Nicole with some of Nicole's teacher friends and she had picked out some cute onesies. That was the sum total of Jeannie's knowledge about newborns. She wasn't sure she was even doing diapers right.

"Please," she whispered as Melissa's cries grew more agitated, although she knew there would be no salvation. All she could do was what she had always done—one foot in front of the other.

Jeannie couldn't fail that baby girl or her sister. But more than that, she couldn't give up on this family. She and Nicole had just started again. It felt particularly cruel to have that stolen so soon.

A car door slammed close enough that Jeannie glanced up. And looked again. A long black limo was blocking traffic in the middle of the street directly in front of the house. A short man wearing a uniform, complete with a matching hat, was opening the back door. He stood to the side and a man emerged from the back seat.

Not just any man.

Oh, God, Dr. Robert Wyatt was here. Her best, favorite customer. All she could do was gape as his long legs closed the distance between them.

"Are you all right?" he demanded, coming to a halt in front of her.

She had to lean so far back to stare at him that she almost lost her balance. He blocked out the night sky and her whole world narrowed to just him.

Yeah, she was a little unbalanced right now. "What are you doing here?"

Because he couldn't be here. She looked like hell warmed over twice, and the shirt she was wearing had stains that she didn't want to think about and she was a wreck.

He *couldn't* be here.

He was.

He stared at her with an intensity that had taken her months to get used to. "Are you *all right*?"

It wasn't a question. It was an order.

Jeannie scrambled to her feet. Even looking him in the eye, it still felt like he loomed over her. "I'm fine," she lied because what was she supposed to say?

She liked him as a customer. He was a gorgeous man, a great tipper—and he had never made her feel uncomfortable or objectified. Aside from that phantom touch of his hand brushing against hers—which could've been entirely accidental—they'd never done anything together beyond devise the perfect Manhattan. That was *it*.

And now he'd followed her to Nicole's house.

The man standing in front of her looked like he would take on the world if she asked him to.

His brow furrowed. "If everything's fine, why aren't you at work?"

"Is that why you're here?"

"You promised you'd be back today and you weren't. Tell me what's wrong so I can fix it."

She blinked. Had she actually wished upon a star? One with magical wish-granting powers?

"You can't fix this." It didn't matter how brilliant a surgeon he was, he couldn't help Nicole. No one could.

"Yes, I can," he growled.

He growled! At her! Then he climbed the first step. "I need you to be there, Jeannie." He took another step up, another step closer to her. "I need…"

"Robert." Without thinking, she put her hand on his chest because she couldn't let him get any closer.

She felt his muscles tense under her palm. It was a mistake, touching him. That phantom contact a week ago in the bar? The little sparks she'd felt then were nothing compared to the electricity that arced between them now. He was hot to the touch and everything had gone to hell, but he was here.

He'd come for her.

He looked down to where she was touching him and she followed his gaze. He wasn't wearing a tie, which was odd. He always wore one. She stared at the little triangle of skin revealed by his unbuttoned collar.

Then his fingertips were against her cheek and she gasped, a shiver racing down her back. "Jeannie," he whispered, lifting her chin until she had no choice but to look him in the eye. His eyes, normally so icy, were warm and promised wonderful things. His head began to dip. "I need…"

He was going to kiss her. He was going to press his perfect mouth against hers and she was going to let him because she could get lost in this man.

Just as she felt his warmth against her lips, Melissa's cries intruded into the silence that surrounded them.

"Oh! The baby!" Jeannie hurried into the house.

"The *baby*?" he called after her.

How much time had passed since Robert had emerged from the back of that sleek limo? Could have been seconds but it could've just as easily been minutes. Minutes where she'd left Melissa alone.

By the time she got back to the baby's room, Melissa was red in the face, her little body rigid, her arms waving. Was that normal? Or was Melissa in pain? Or…

"I'm sorry, I'm sorry," Jeannie said as she nervously picked the baby up, trying to support her head like the nurse had shown her. She was pretty sure she wasn't doing it right because Melissa cried harder. "Oh, honey, I'm so sorry." Sorry Nicole wasn't here, sorry Jeannie couldn't figure out the problem, much less how to fix it. "What's wrong, sweetie?" As if the baby could tell her.

Melissa howled and Jeannie couldn't stop her own tears. She couldn't bear the thought of losing this last part of her family.

"Here," a deep voice said as the baby was plucked out of Jeannie's arms. "Let me."

She blinked a few times, but in her current state of exhaustion what she saw didn't make a lot of sense.

Dr. Robert Wyatt, one of the Top Five Billionaire Bachelors of Chicago, a man so remote and icy it'd taken Jeannie years to get comfortable with his intense silences—*that* man was laying Melissa out on the changing pad, saying, "What seems to be the problem?" as if the baby could tell him.

"What…" Jeannie blinked again but the image didn't change. "What are you doing?"

Instead of answering, Robert pulled out his cell. "Reginald? Bring my kit in."

"Your kit?"

He didn't explain. "How old is this infant? Eight days?"

She wasn't even surprised he hadn't answered her question, much less come within a day of guessing Melissa's age. "Nine. Nicole, my sister, went into labor right after I last saw you." She tried to say the rest of it but suddenly she couldn't breathe.

Robert made a gentle humming noise. The baby blinked up at him in confusion, a momentary break in her crying. "What was her Apgar score?"

"Her *what*?"

Who the hell was this man? The Dr. Wyatt she knew didn't make gentle humming noises that calmed babies. There was nothing gentle about him!

Robert had Melissa down to her diaper. The poor baby began to wail again. He made a *tsking* noise. "Where is the mother?"

Jeannie choked on a sob. "She's…" No, that wasn't right. Present tense no longer applied to Nicole. "She developed blood clots and…"

Robert's back stiffened. "The father?"

"Sperm donor."

He made that humming noise again. Just then the door-bell rang and Melissa howled all the louder and Jeannie wanted to burrow into Robert's arms and pretend the last week had been a horrible dream. But she didn't get the chance because he said, "My kit—can you bring it to me, please?"

"Sure?" When Jeannie opened the door, the man from the car was there. "Reginald?"

"Miss." He tipped his hat with one hand. With the other, he hefted an absolutely enormous duffel bag. "Shall I bring this to Dr. Wyatt?"

"I'll take it. Thank you."

"Babies cry, miss," he said gently as he handed over the bag. "The good doctor will make sure nothing's wrong. Don't worry—it gets easier."

The kind words from an older man who looked like he might have dealt with crying babies a few times in his life felt like a balm on her soul.

"Thank you," Jeannie said and she meant it.

Reginald tipped his hat.

It took both hands, but she managed to lug the kit back to the baby's room. Melissa was still screaming. Probably because Robert was pinching the skin on her arms. "What are you doing?" Jeannie demanded.

"She's got good skin elasticity and her lungs are in great shape." He sounded calm and reasonable. "Ah, the kit. Come," he said, motioning right next to him. "Tell me everything."

Jeannie did as she was told, putting her hand on Melissa's little belly as Robert dug into the duffel. "She hasn't stopped crying since I brought her home two days ago. Nicole never even left the hospital. I don't know anything about babies."

"Clearly." She couldn't even be insulted by that. "Which hospital? Who were the doctors?" He came up with a stetho-scope and one of those tiny little lights.

Oh. His kit must be an emergency medical bag. "Uh, Covenant. Her OB was some old guy named Preston, I think? I don't remember who the pediatrician is." She realized that, at some point, Robert had shed his suit jacket and had rolled up his sleeves. He still had on his vest but there was something so undone about him right now...

He'd almost kissed her. And she'd almost let him. The man who didn't like to be touched, didn't show emotion—she'd touched him and he'd come within a breath of kissing her.

Even stranger, he was now touching—gently—Melissa.

This just didn't make sense. Robert didn't like touching people. Simple as that.

What exactly had she wished upon? No ordinary star had this kind of power behind it.

Robert listened to Melissa's chest and then peered into her mouth and ears before pressing on her stomach.

With a heartbreaking scream, the baby tooted.

"Oh, my gosh. I'm so sorry," Jeannie blurted out.

"As I expected," Robert said, seemingly unbothered by the small mess left in the diaper that was thankfully still under Melissa's bottom. He listened to her stomach. "Hmm."

"What does that mean?" Dimly, Jeannie was aware that this was the longest conversation she'd ever had with him.

"When was the last time you fed her?"

"Uh, about forty-five minutes ago. She drank about two ounces." That, at least, she could measure. She'd watched a few YouTube videos on how to feed a baby. Thank God for the internet.

Wait—when had she started thinking of him as Robert? Except for that one time, she hadn't allowed herself to use his given name at Trenton's because that implied a level of familiarity they didn't have.

Or at least, a level they hadn't had before he'd shown up

on her doorstep to make an accidental house call. Or before she'd touched his chest and he'd caressed her cheek and who could forget that near-kiss?

Robert it was, apparently.

"What are you feeding her?"

"The hospital sent home some formula…" She couldn't even remember the brand right now.

"Get it."

She hurried to the kitchen and grabbed the can and the bottle she hadn't had the chance to empty and clean yet. By the time she got back to the baby's room, Robert had apparently diapered and dressed the baby and was wrapping her in a blanket so that only her head was visible.

"This is called swaddling," he explained as, almost by magic, Melissa stopped screaming. "Newborns are used to being in the womb—not a lot of room to move, it's warm and they can hear their mother's heartbeat."

Embarrassment swamped her. "I thought… I didn't want her to get too hot."

"You can swaddle her in just a diaper—but keep her wrapped up. She'll be happier." He scooped the baby burrito into his arms and turned to Jeannie, casting a critical eye over her.

"Where did you learn how to do that?"

"Do what?"

She waved in his general direction. "Change a diaper. Swaddle a baby. Where did you learn how to take care of a baby?"

He notched an eyebrow at her and, in response, her cheeks got hot. "It's not complicated. Now, some babies have what we call a fourth trimester—they need another three months of that closeness and warmth before they're comfortable. Hold her on your chest as much as you can right now. She doesn't need to cry it out." His lips curved into that barely there smile. "No matter what the internet says."

She blushed. Hard.

He tucked Melissa against his chest as if it was the easiest thing in the world. He didn't seem the least bit concerned about how to support her head or that he might accidentally drop her or any of the worries that haunted Jeannie. Nor did he seem worried in the slightest about holding a baby in the vicinity of a suit that probably cost a few thousand dollars. He made the whole thing look effortless. Because it wasn't that complicated, apparently.

She wanted to be insulted—and she was—but the sight of Dr. Robert Wyatt *cuddling* a newborn, for lack of a better word, hit Jeannie in the chest so hard she almost stumbled.

"Here," she managed to say, holding the formula out for him.

With a critical eye, he glanced at the brand. Then, without taking it, he pulled out his cell again. "Reginald? Find the closest grocery store and pick up the following items…"

He rattled off a list of baby products that left Jeannie dizzy. When he ended the call, he nodded to the formula. "That brand has soy in it. Her symptoms are in line with a soy sensitivity."

"Crying is a symptom?"

He gave her a look that was almost kind. But not quite. "Her stomach is upset and she's not supposed to be that red. Both are signs she's not tolerating something well. Reginald will bring us several alternatives."

"So…there's nothing wrong with her?"

"No. Of course it could be colic and something more serious…"

All the blood drained from Jeannie's face so fast that she felt ill. *More* serious?

Robert cleared his throat. "I'm reasonably confident it's the formula."

"Oh. Okay. That's…" She managed to make it to the rocker that Nicole's fellow teachers had all pooled their money to buy. The baby just had a sensitive stomach. It wasn't anything Jeannie was doing wrong—the hospital had given her the formula, after all. "That's good." Her voice cracked on the words.

Robert stared at her. "Are you all right?"

Only *this* man would ask that question. She began to giggle and then she was laughing so hard she was sobbing and the words poured out of her. "Of *course* I'm not okay. I buried my sister and there was so much we didn't say and I'm responsible for a newborn but I have no idea what I'm doing and I don't have the money to do any of it and you're here, which is good, but *why* are you here, Robert?"

He stared at her. It would've been intimidating if he hadn't been rubbing tiny circles on the back of a tiny baby, who was making noises that were definitely quieter than all-out wailing. "You weren't at the bar."

"This," she said, waving her hand to encompass everything, "qualifies as an emergency."

"Yes," he agreed, still staring at her with those icy eyes. "When will you be back?"

If it were anyone else in the world, she'd have thrown him out.

Jeannie had made sure Miranda at work knew exactly how Robert liked his drink. Because Jeannie aged it in a cask, Miranda didn't even have to mix it. She just had to pour and serve. Even someone with standards as impossibly high as Robert's could be content with that for a few damn nights while Jeannie tried to keep her life from completely crumbling.

But for all that, she couldn't toss him onto the curb. He'd examined Melissa and calmed the baby down. He had a good, nonterrifying reason for why she kept crying and he had sent Reginald to get different formula. For the first time in a week, Jeannie felt like the situation was almost— *almost*—under control.

But not quite.

"Why do I need to go back to work?" she asked carefully because this was Dr. Robert Wyatt, after all—a man of few words and suspiciously deep emotions.

He looked confused by her question. "Because."

A hell of a lousy answer. "Because *why*?"

His mouth opened, then shut, then opened again. "Because I… I had a bad day." He seemed completely befuddled by this.

"I'm sorry to hear that. I'm currently having a bad life." He didn't smile at her joke. "Look, I don't know what to tell you. I have to put the baby first—you know, the baby you're currently holding? She's the most important thing in my life now and I'm all she's got. So I can't go back to work until I figure out how to take care of an infant, pay for childcare, possibly sue a hospital for negligence, settle my sister's outstanding debts and get a grip on my life. You'll have to find someone else to serve you a Manhattan!"

If he was insulted by her shouting, he didn't show it. "All right."

"All right?" That was almost too easy. "Good. Miranda at the bar knows how to pour… What are you doing?"

He had his cell again. "I don't like Miranda." Before Jeannie could reply to that out-of-the-blue statement, he went on, "Len? Wyatt. I've got a case for you—malpractice. Postpartum mortality. I want your best people on it. Yes. I'll forward the information to you as I get it."

"Robert?" Admittedly, she was having an awful day. But…had he just hired a lawyer for her?

"One moment." He punched up another number, all while still holding Melissa, which was more than Jeannie had been able to accomplish in the past two days. "Kelly? I'm going to need a full-time nanny to care for a newborn. Yes. Have a list for me by eleven tomorrow morning. I'll want to conduct interviews after I'm out of surgery."

Jeannie stared at him. "Wait—what are you doing?"

"My lawyer will handle your lawsuit. It won't get that far—the hospital *will* want to settle, but he'll make sure you get enough to take care of the child."

She heard the threat, loud and clear. His tone was the same as one time when he'd threatened a woman who'd groped him once. This was Robert Wyatt, a powerful, important man. He might be Jeannie's best customer and she might be infatuated with him but he also had the power to bend lawyers and whole hospitals to his will.

This was what she couldn't forget.

If he really wanted to, he'd bend *her* to his will.

She had to keep this from spinning out of control. "Melissa."

"What?"

"Her name is Melissa."

"Fine." But even as he dismissed that observation, he leaned his chin against the top of the baby's head and—there was no mistaking what she was seeing.

Dr. Robert Wyatt *nuzzled* Melissa's downy little head.

Then it only got worse because he did something she absolutely wasn't ready for.

He smiled.

Not a big smile. No, this was his normal smile, the one so subtle that most everyone else wouldn't even notice it. But she did. And it simply devastated her.

She had to be dreaming this whole thing. In no way, shape or form should Dr. Robert Wyatt be standing in what was, essentially, Jeannie's childhood bedroom, soothing a baby and somehow making everything better. Or at least bearable.

"Now," he went on, "I'll have a nanny over here by two tomorrow." He made as if he wanted to adjust his cuffs, then appeared to realize that he'd not only rolled his sleeves up to his elbows but was also still holding an infant who wasn't crying at all. He settled for looking at his watch. "You should be back at work on Wednesday."

Her mouth flopped open. *"What?"*

"You don't know how to care for an infant. I need you to be back at work. I'm hiring a nanny to help you." He glanced around the room. "And a maid."

He was already reaching for his phone when she snapped, "I don't know whether to be offended or grateful."

"Grateful."

Oh, she'd show him grateful, all right. "I'm not going back to work on Wednesday."

He paused with the phone already at his ear. Something hard passed over his eyes, but he said, "I'll also need a maid. Three days a week. Thanks." Then he ended the call. "What do you mean, you won't go back?"

She pushed herself to her feet. Thankfully, her knees held. "Dr. Wyatt—"

He made a noise deep in his throat.

"Robert," she said, trying to keep her voice calm and level because if she didn't at least try, she might start throwing things. "I'm sorry you're having a bad day and I appreciate that you're willing to throw a bunch of money at my problems, but I'm not going back to work this week. Maybe not next week."

"Why not?" His voice was so cold she shivered. "What else could you possibly need?"

She'd been wrong all these years because it turned out that Dr. Robert Wyatt really didn't have a heart. "To grieve for my sister!"

Four

Jeannie was yelling at him. Well. That was…interesting.

As was Robert's response. Very few people shouted at him and from an empirical standpoint, it was curious to note that his body tensed, his spine straightened and his face went completely blank because betraying any response was a provocation.

Rationally, he knew Jeannie was upset because of the circumstances. And he also understood that she wasn't about to attack him.

But damn, his response was hardwired.

He forced himself to relax, to exhale the air he was holding in. There was no need to let his fight-or-flight instincts rule him.

Jeannie was not his father. This was not a dangerous situation.

He would make this better.

In his office, when there was bad news, he had a basic script he followed. He offered general condolences, promised to do his best to make things better and focused on quantitative outcomes—heart valves, ccs of blood pumped, reasonable expectations postsurgery. And on those rare occasions when he lost a patient, either on the table or, more frequently, to a post-op infection, he kept things brief. *I'm sorry for your loss.* No one wanted to talk to him when he'd failed them, anyway.

Then there was the baby—*Melissa*, as Jeannie had insisted. Robert didn't often think of his patients in terms of their names because children were entirely too easy to love, and he couldn't risk loving someone who might not survive the day or the week or even the year.

But Melissa wasn't a patient, was she? Her heart and lung sounds had been clear and strong, with no telltale murmur or stutter to the beat. This was a perfectly healthy infant who simply needed different formula.

Robert couldn't remember the last time he'd held a healthy baby. By the time patients were referred to him at the hospital, they'd already undergone a barrage of tests and examinations by other doctors. The closest he got was seeing patients for their annual postoperation checkup. Most of them did well but there was always an undercurrent of fear to those visits, parents praying that everything was still within the bounds of medically normal.

Aside from general condolences, though, none of his scripts applied here. He'd already done everything obvious to fix the situation and somehow that had upset Jeannie. If he wasn't so concerned about her reaction, he'd be interested in understanding where the disconnect had happened.

But he was concerned. Jeannie wasn't the parent of a patient. She was… Well, he couldn't say she was a friend, either. She existed outside of work or personal relationships. She was simply…

The woman he'd almost kissed.

Because when the car had pulled up in front of her house, it had felt as if she'd been sitting out there, waiting for him.

Thankfully, he hadn't kissed her. Because she didn't look like she'd appreciate any overtures right now. She was a mess, her short hair sticking up in all directions, dark circles under her eyes, her stained, threadbare T-shirt hanging off one shoulder, revealing a blue bra strap.

He tore his gaze away from that bra strap. He normally didn't respond to the exposure of skin but knowing what color her bra was made him…uncomfortable.

Which was not the correct reaction, not when she was sitting there, quietly crying. It hurt him to see her like this, to know that she was in pain and there was a hard limit on what he could do to fix the situation. And, more than anything, he felt like a bastard of the highest order because he wasn't really doing anything for *her*. The lawyers, the nanny, the maid—that was all for his benefit. The sooner he took care of Jeannie, the sooner she could be there for him.

She swiped her hand across her cheeks and looked up at him. The pain in her eyes almost knocked him back a step.

"I'm sorry," she mumbled.

"Excuse me?"

She sniffed and it hurt Robert worse than a punch to the kidneys. How odd. "I didn't mean to yell at you. It's not your fault everything's gone to hell in a handbasket and you're just trying to help." She blinked up at him. "Aren't you?"

Wasn't he?

Say something. Something kind and thoughtful and appropriate. Something that would make things right. Or at least better.

The doorbell rang.

"That'll be Reginald." Although it certainly wasn't the brave thing to do, Robert hurried to the door.

"They had everything but that one brand—Enfamil," his driver said, straining under the weight of the bags.

"Make a note—have some sent over tomorrow." Robert stepped to the side as Reginald nodded and carried the bags into the house. The smell of something delicious hit Robert's nose. Chicken, maybe? "What did you get?"

"I thought the young lady might enjoy dinner," Reginald said, nodding at Jeannie, who was standing in the hallway, a look of utter confusion on her face. "It's hard to cook with a newborn."

"I… That's very kind of you. I'm not sure I've eaten today," she said, her voice shaky.

Robert experienced a flash of irrational jealousy because Reginald was the kind of man who didn't need a script to recite the appropriate platitudes at the appropriate times. He had a wife of almost forty years, four children and had recently become a grandfather. If anyone could help Robert find the right way to express condolences, it'd be Reginald.

But then Landon's voice slithered into Robert's mind, making him cringe. *Wyatts never ask for help.*

Right. Reginald was an employee. Robert paid him well to fill in the gaps, which was all he was doing here. It simply hadn't occurred to Robert that Jeannie might not have eaten recently.

Reginald smiled gently at Jeannie. "Where would you like the groceries?"

"Oh. The kitchen's right through there." She stepped past Robert and Melissa, her gaze averted. "Thank you so much for this."

Robert glanced down. The baby had fallen asleep, which was a good sign. Robert went to the nursery and laid the child on her back in the crib. She startled and then relaxed back into sleep.

He frowned. A blanket and two stuffed animals littered the mattress, both suffocation risks. He pulled them out. Jeannie really didn't know what she was doing, did she?

If he didn't want the chance to personally interview prospective nannies, he'd have one over here tonight. Maybe he should stay instead...

But he shut down that line of thinking. He had surgery tomorrow, which meant he needed to be at the hospital at four in the morning. He'd never needed a lot of sleep but he always made sure to get at least four hours before surgery days. He never took risks when lives were on the line.

He studied Melissa. The sound of murmuring from the kitchen filled the room with a gentle noise and the baby sighed in her sleep. Robert had handled so many babies and children over the course of his career but this infant girl was...different. He wasn't sure why.

"Sleep for her," he whispered to the baby.

By the time he made it back to the living room—really, this house was little more than a shoebox—Reginald was at the front door as Jeannie said, "Thank you so much again. How much do I owe you?"

Reginald shot Robert a slightly alarmed look over Jeannie's shoulder.

"That's all, Reginald."

"Miss, it's been a pleasure." With a tip of his hat, Reginald was out the door before Jeannie could protest.

A moment of tense silence settled over the house. No babies crying, no helpful drivers filling the gaps of conversation. Just Robert and Jeannie and the terrible feeling that instead of making everything better for her, he'd made things worse.

"Robert," Jeannie began and for some reason, she sounded...sad? Or just tired?

He couldn't tell and that bothered him. This was *Jeannie.* He was able to read her better than he could read anyone. "I'd recommend starting the baby—I mean, Melissa—on this formula," he said, picking the organic one. "No soy."

In response, she dropped her head into her hands.

"It'll take a day or two before the other formula is completely out of her system," he went on in a rush, "but if she gets worse at any time, call me."

Her head was still in her hands. "Robert."

"The nanny should be here by two tomorrow at the absolute latest," he went on, because he was afraid of what she might say—or what she might not say. "She'll teach you everything you need to know. Don't put blankets or stuffed animals in the crib."

She raised her head and stared at him as if she'd never seen him before. *"Robert."*

Inexplicably, his heart began to race. And was he sweating? He was. How strange. "Do you need any other financial assistance? Until Len is able to negotiate a settlement with the hospital, that is? Just let me know. I can—"

"Stop." She didn't so much as raise her voice—it certainly wasn't a shout—but he felt her power all the same.

He swallowed. Unfortunately, he was fairly certain it was a nervous swallow. Which was ridiculous because he was not nervous. He was a Wyatt, dammit. Nerves weren't allowed. Ever.

Still, he stopped talking. Which left them standing in another awkward silence.

Jeannie ran her hands through her hair, making it stand straight up as if she'd touched a live wire. She looked at him, then turned on her heel and walked the three steps into the kitchen.

What was happening here? He took a step after her but before his foot hit the ground she was back, hands on her hips. He stumbled as she strode to him.

"Robert," she said softly.

"I put Melissa in her crib," he said as she advanced on him. "She was asleep."

Relief fluttered across Jeannie's face but she didn't slow down. Unbelievably, Robert backed up. He'd learned the hard way that Wyatts didn't retreat and never, ever cowered.

But before her, he retreated. Just a step. Then all his training kicked in and he held his ground. But he felt himself swallow again and damn it all, he knew it was nervously.

Her mouth opened but then it closed and he saw her chest rise with a deep breath. "Why are you doing this, Robert?"

Doing what? But he bit down on those words because they were a useless distraction from the issue.

He knew what *this* was. So did she.

How could he put it into words? He wasn't entirely sure what those words were, other than he needed her. She was having problems that prevented her from being where he needed her to be so he was solving the problems.

But none of that was what came out. Instead, he heard himself say, "You need the help."

Her eyes fluttered closed and she did that long exhale again. "So that's it? You're not going to tell me why you tracked down my address, performed a medical examination on my niece, ordered your staff to hop to it and are now standing in my living room, condescendingly refusing to answer a simple question?"

"I'm not condescending," he shot back before he could think better of it.

"Of course you're not." Was that…sarcasm? "If you can't tell me why, then I have to ask you to leave." Her throat worked. "And not to come back."

A raw kind of panic gripped him. "I need you. At the bar."

She leaned away from him. "Miranda is perfectly capable of making your drink. I showed her how and there's enough blend in the cask to last a few months. Worst case, I can always go mix up more."

"But she's not you."

Jeannie's brow furrowed. "And that's a problem?"

She was too close. He could smell the sour tang of old formula on her shirt and see how very bloodshot her eyes were. But, in this light, he could also see things that he'd missed in the dim bar at Trenton's. Her dark hair had red undertones to it and her eyes were brown but with flecks of both green and gold. If anyone else had him in this position, Robert would either get around them or force the issue. It was always better to go on the offensive than be left in a weakened position.

But that's where he was now. Weakened.

"I…" To admit weakness was to admit failure and failure was not an option. "I can't talk to her. Not like I can to you."

"Robert, we barely talk," she said, her exasperation obvious. He was doing a terrible job of this. "I mean, I get the feeling you just don't talk to anyone. That's how you are."

"But you're different."

She stilled under his touch, which was when he realized he was, in fact, touching her. His hand had somehow come to rest on her cheek, just like it had earlier. Her skin was warm and soft and just felt…right.

"I can't afford to pay you back," she whispered, her hand covering his. But instead of flinging his fingers away from her face, she pressed harder so that his palm cradled her cheek.

Finally, he found the damned words. "That—that right there is why you're different. Anyone else, they'd look at me and you know what they'd say?" She shook her head, but carefully, like she was afraid she might break that singular point of contact. "They'd be calculating how much they could get out of me, what they'd have to do to get it. Your Miranda—"

"She flirts with everyone, Robert," Jeannie said softly. "Bigger compliments mean bigger tips. That's how things work. Everyone does it."

The thought of Jeannie acting like Miranda for money wasn't right. "You don't. Not with me."

She leaned into his touch. "What happened?"

What *hadn't* happened? Without conscious effort, he wrapped his arm around her waist and pulled her into his chest. "I might have made some threats. There may have been bribes exchanged."

She gasped but didn't pull away. She should have. For years now, he'd kept that part of himself on lockdown, refusing to let Landon win. But tonight he'd been a Wyatt through and through. Thank God she hadn't been there to see it.

"Oh, Robert," she said, his name a sigh on her lips. "Just because I wasn't there?"

No. The denial broke free but somehow, he kept it in because it was a damned lie and he'd come this far. Lying to her would be worse than what he'd done at the bar. "Yes."

"Hmm." Her body came flush with his, soft and warm. She felt right in his arms, her breasts pressed against his chest.

How long had he been waiting for this moment?

"You're touching me," she murmured, tucking her chin against his neck.

"That is correct." He felt her lips move against his skin. Was she smiling? He hoped she was smiling.

"You don't like to be touched."

Of course she knew. That was why he'd needed to see her tonight, needed to do whatever it took to get her back behind the bar. Because she understood him. "No."

Of course, if she were back behind the bar, he wouldn't have this moment with her. She sighed into him, her arms around his waist, her chest flush with his and it should've been too much, too close, too dangerous but...

It wasn't.

He gathered her closer in what he belatedly realized was a hug. How strange.

"I'm sorry for your loss." The words felt right so he kept going. "You must've loved her very much."

"I didn't love her nearly enough. It's...it's complicated.

We had a pretty messed up family and we'd gone almost five years without speaking. We were just…" She sniffed. "We were just figuring out how to be a family again," she went on, her voice tight. "And now we'll never get that back. It's gone forever."

An odd sensation built in his chest. "I'm sorry to hear that."

Was it possible to start a family over like that? Obviously, Landon Wyatt would never be a part of a do-over. But if Robert could get his mother away… Could they figure out how to be a family again?

"So I can't come back to work right now. You understand? I have to protect Melissa and make things right and… and honor my sister, imperfect as she was and as I am. I have to honor our family."

Moisture dampened his skin. He leaned back and tilted her chin up. Tears tracked down her cheeks. He wiped those away with his thumbs. "Anything I can do to help, I'll do."

Her smile was shaky at best. "You mean, besides the lawyer, nanny, maid and your chauffeur making grocery runs for me?"

"Yes."

"Can you tell me why you're here?" It wasn't an ultimatum this time, merely a question.

He opened his mouth to tell her because talking to her was the whole reason he was here, wasn't it?

But she'd had the worst day of her life. And although things were not particularly wonderful for him right now, he simply couldn't bear to add his burden to hers. "No. I won't make things harder for you."

Was that disappointment in her eyes? Or just relief? "You understand that I might not be able to go back to work, right? Julian will hold my job for a few weeks but—"

"Your job will be there," Robert interrupted. "If I have to

buy the restaurant from him at triple what it's worth, you'll have a job there."

Her eyes got very wide but she didn't pull away. "You would do that for me?"

"If that's what you need, I'll make it happen." His gaze dropped to her lips, which were parted in surprise or shock or, hell, *horror*, at his autocratic ways for all he knew.

"Why?"

"I told you," he said, his voice gruff. He dragged his gaze away from her mouth and saw what had to be confusion on her face. She was closer than she'd been outside on the front steps, closer than she'd been during that hug.

"Tell me again," she said, her voice barely a breath on his lips.

Close enough to kiss.

"Because I need you," he whispered against her and then he took her mouth with his.

Five

Fact: Robert was kissing her.

Fact: He didn't like to be touched. But seeing as his mouth slanted over hers, his hands cupped her face and angled her head so he could deepen the kiss, it seemed he was okay with this type of touching. But that just led her back to...

Fact: Dr. Robert Wyatt, heir to the Wyatt Medicals fortune, one of the Top Five Billionaire Bachelors in Chicago, was providing her with a lawyer, a nanny, a maid and was also apparently willing to buy a restaurant just so she could serve him a Manhattan.

And, unavoidably, it came back to this fact: *He was kissing her.*

Heat cascaded from where he touched her, shivering sparks of white-hot need that burned through her with a pain that was the sweetest pleasure she'd ever felt.

When was the last time she'd showered?

That thought pushed her into breaking the kiss, which

was really a shame because for all his overbearing, condescending, threatening behaviors, he was a hell of a kisser.

Right man, wrong time.

That was the thought that ran through her mind as she stared at him, her chest heaving. She crossed her arms in front of her to fight off a shiver. Why now?

"That was…" He seemed to shake back to himself. He started to straighten his cuffs and then realized they were still rolled to his elbows so instead he fixed his sleeves. "That was not what I intended."

"Oh, for Pete's sake, Robert." Okay, so she'd kissed *the* Robert Wyatt. Her favorite customer. The man who had fueled more than a few years' worth of hot dreams and needy fantasies. But even if that kiss would keep her going for a few more years, it didn't change anything.

This was still Robert. Small talk was beyond him.

His brow furrowed as he got one cuff fixed. "What?"

"That's not what you say after you kiss a woman."

He paused and then, amazingly, straightened the sleeve he'd just fixed. "It's not?"

"No." She took a deep breath, but that was a bad idea because without the bar to separate them and the tang of wine and whiskey in the air to overpower her senses, she inhaled his scent, a rich cologne that was spicy and warm and still subtle.

So. There was one aspect of him that wasn't designed to dominate. One and counting.

She headed toward the kitchen where the scent of chicken was stronger. Her stomach growled and she knew she needed to eat. The chauffeur hadn't been wrong. She wasn't sure she'd eaten today and if Melissa would just sleep for another few minutes, Jeannie might be able to get both a meal and a shower out of the deal.

That was a huge *if*. That baby hadn't gotten more than thirty minutes of sleep at a time since… Well, in her whole life. Frankly, Jeannie was probably lucky she'd made it through one of the most perfect kisses she'd ever had without interruption.

"What am I supposed to say?"

She almost smiled because the man had *no* clue. "Something that doesn't make it sound like you wish you hadn't just kissed me." She waved this away. "It's not important."

A rumbling noise caught her attention and she spun to realize that not only was Robert growling, he was moving fast, too. With both cuffs fastened. "You're important," he said and if anyone else had said that in that tone of voice, it would've been a threat but for him? His voice was possessive and demanding and needy all at the same time and it wasn't a threat.

It was a promise.

Oh, how she wanted him to keep that promise.

"The kiss was important," he went on, his ice-blue eyes fierce and surprisingly warm. "But I don't want to make you feel like you *owe* me a kiss or your body. That's not what this is. I'm *not* like that."

"Then what is it?" She managed to swallow. "What are you like?"

His mouth opened and then snapped shut and he stepped back. Damned if he didn't adjust his cuffs again.

"Will you be all right tonight? I can have a nanny here for the night."

Part of her was so, *so* thankful that he wasn't going to suggest he should stay because…she might take him up on that.

So yeah, the other part of her was disappointed that Robert had suddenly become Dr. Wyatt again. Super disappointed. Because if that kiss was any indication, *man.* All that precision and control combined with the heat she felt every single time their bodies touched?

He would be *amazing.*

"We'll be okay." She rested her hand on his arm. Even through the fine cotton of his shirt, she could feel the rock-hard muscles in his arm.

Focus, Jeannie.

"Are you sure?"

Frankly, Robert Wyatt was kind of adorable when he was concerned. Perhaps because the look did not come naturally to him. "Positive. I had this kind man teach me about swaddling, get me different formulas and generally be amazing." She squeezed his arm.

He lifted her hand away from his arm and her heart dropped a ridiculous amount because he was back to being Dr. Wyatt and she shouldn't be touching him. But again, he surprised her because he didn't drop her hand. Instead, he brought it to his lips and, with that hint of a smile tugging at the corners of his mouth, kissed her knuckles.

It was an old-fashioned move right out of a romance novel but damn if it didn't work all the same.

He would be *so* amazing.

She had always managed to keep her lustful thoughts about this man safely contained, but nothing was contained right now, not with his lips warming her body.

His eyes shifted to the side. "Ah," he said, finally releasing her and moving to where Nicole had a message board hung up by the coat hooks. He picked up the marker. "This is my personal number. Call or text anytime. I have surgery in the morning so this," he added, writing a second number, "is my assistant."

She started to protest that she could handle things for another twenty-four hours, but that was when Robert added, "I'll stop by tomorrow night, see how the nanny is settling in."

Oh. He was coming back. The thought sent a little thrill through her, even though she knew it shouldn't. She would definitely make sure she'd showered by then. "That's not necessary."

"I disagree."

Of course he did.

"It should be fine."

"I'll expect the pleasure of your company, then."

The air rushed out of her lungs because that was not only a good line, but coming out of Robert's mouth?

A pleasure, indeed.

"Will you tell me what's bothering you, then?"

A shadow crossed over his eyes. She could feel him retreating—emotionally and physically, because he opened the door and walked out of Nicole's house. "No."

"Why not?" she asked his back.

He was halfway down the steps when he turned, with that confused look on his face. "Because."

She rolled her eyes. "That continues to be a terrible answer, you know."

"Because I won't put you in danger," he said.

Then he walked off to where Reginald was waiting, with the car door open.

The chauffeur tipped his cap at Jeannie and then they were gone.

What the ever-loving *hell*?

Melissa was crying when the doorbell rang because of course she was.

"One second!" Jeannie yelled.

No matter how many times she watched the video tutorial, she couldn't get the baby swaddled. At least, not anything like Robert had done. And while Melissa had definitely slept more after drinking the soy-free formula Robert had recommended, Jeannie was still unshowered and exhausted. Getting ninety minutes of sleep at a time was an improvement over forty-five minutes at a time, but not much of one.

Screw it. She picked Melissa up and settled for tucking the blanket around her little body.

The doorbell rang again at almost the exact same moment her phone buzzed. Jeannie grabbed her phone and looked at the text. Of course it was from Robert.

Maja Kowalczyk
Text me immediately if you don't like her.

This was accompanied by a photo of an older woman, her hair in a bun and her face lined with deep laugh lines.

"Miss Kaufman? Are you able to get the door?" an accented voice yelled—politely—over the sounds of Melissa wailing.

That man was lucky she'd been able to check her phone. That was just like him to expect her to drop everything to respond to him when, in reality, texting back was a pipe dream, one that ranked well below showering.

Jeannie shoved the phone in her pocket and gave up on the blanket. Instead, she wrapped her arms around Melissa and held her tight against her chest, like Robert had been doing last night. It helped, a little.

The doorbell rang and this time, it was accompanied by knocking. Her phone buzzed again but she ignored it and managed to make it to the front door.

"I'm here," she snapped, which was not the most polite start to any conversation but seriously, could everyone just give her a second?

"Ah, good." The woman on the stoop matched the woman in the photo. But Jeannie was surprised to see a rolling suitcase next to her. The older woman smiled warmly and said, "It's all right—she's here. Yes, everything is fine. Thank you, Dr. Wyatt."

Which was the point that Jeannie realized that Maja wasn't talking to her but on her cell phone. To Robert.

And to think, Jeannie had once concluded that Nicole was the biggest control freak in the world.

The nanny ended the call and clasped her hands in front of her generous bosom. She was wearing a floral dress, hideous tan shoes and a cardigan, for Pete's sake. It was at least eighty degrees today! "Hello, Miss Kaufman, I'm Maja Kowalczyk."

"Hi. I'm Jeannie."

Maja's eyes crinkled as she went on, "Dr. Wyatt said you needed…" Her voice trailed off as she took a good look at Melissa and Jeannie. Melissa chose that moment to let out a pitiful little wail. "Oh, you poor dears," she clucked. "May I come in?"

"I guess?" Jeannie didn't have much choice. She needed help and, if Robert was still planning on stopping by at some point in the near future, she needed a shower.

Frankly, she wasn't sure she hadn't hallucinated last night. She'd wished upon something that probably wasn't a star and then Robert had shown up, kissed her, thrown a whole bunch of money at her problems and…driven off into the night.

It was the stuff of dreams. And also possibly nightmares. She wasn't sure which.

Because there was definitely something unreal about watching Maja wheel her little suitcase into the house. Jeannie peeked out the front door, but no long black car blocked traffic and no gorgeous billionaire climbed her stairs, hell-bent on upending her world.

Maja gasped at the mess and Jeannie figured if it was a dream, the house would be a whole lot cleaner. It wasn't like she hadn't tried because she *had*. But Melissa was still super fussy and a splotchy red color. Jeannie had not somehow acquired the power to swaddle anything, much less an agitated infant, and housekeeping had never been a priority for her in the first place, which had always driven Nicole nuts.

So yeah, everything was still a disaster.

"Sorry about this," Jeannie began, but Maja just shook her head.

"That nice Dr. Wyatt, he told me what to expect. I am so sorry about your sister."

And that was when Jeannie found herself folded into a hug against Maja's impressive bosom. Tears pricked her eyes but she didn't know this woman and could only hope that Robert knew what he was doing in hiring her.

"There now," Maja said, taking a step back and looking completely unruffled. "I think I will take this *babisui* and get her dressed and you, my dear, will take a shower and lie down, yes?"

If Jeannie stood here much longer, she was going to start crying because a shower and a nap sounded like the best things ever. "Yeah, okay." Maja reached out for Melissa but Jeannie interrupted. "Um, just so we're clear, what are your qualifications?"

Any qualifications were better than what Jeannie had. But if she was going to hand Melissa off to a complete stranger and then fall asleep with said stranger in the house, she wanted reassurances.

Jeannie had full faith that Robert wouldn't just hire some random woman but she needed to be a part of this decision. Robert might be paying the bills because… Well, she was still really unclear on his reasons at this point.

"Ah, yes." Maja nodded firmly as if she approved of Jeannie's caution. "My husband died and there wasn't much left for me in Poland, so I came here twenty-seven years ago, when my son married a nice American girl. I was a nurse in a hospital nursery in Poland and here I cared for my grandchildren when they were small. When they went to school, my daughter-in-law had a friend who was start-ing the nanny business and she took me on. I speak fluent Polish, English and Russian, as well as some German and

French. Not much French, actually," she said with a rue-ful smile.

"I, uh, speak English. And some bad Spanish," Jeannie blurted out, feeling woefully outclassed by this woman. Five languages plus she'd been a nurse? No wonder Robert had hired her.

Maja nodded. "I have cared for small babies my entire life. I have copies of my medical certifications and back-ground checks for you. Dr. Wyatt also has copies. He has instructed me to stay for a week, including overnights, with your approval until you feel more confidence. Then I am to come every day from noon until midnight, unless you have a different schedule in mind?"

Yeah, noon to midnight was Robert gaming the system so she could be back at Trenton's, serving his drink.

Maja was a former nurse. Someone who'd spent a life-time with babies. Someone who would know if something was really wrong and would teach Jeannie how to handle the basics and…and…

Relief hit her so hard her legs began to shake. This was going to work out. Things were going to get better. They *had* to.

She almost smiled to herself. Robert simply wouldn't allow them to get worse, would he?

Melissa fussed and that was when the blanket and diaper fell off. "Uh, sorry about this," Jeannie muttered as Maja gave her a sympathetic smile. "You're hired and I would *love* a shower."

"And a nap, dear." She took the naked, fussing baby from Jeannie's arms. "Go on. The *babisui* and I will get to know each other, won't we?" she cooed at Melissa, who responded by straightening her legs and arms and farting loudly.

Without a diaper.

"Ah, good," Maja said, not horrified in the least even as Jeannie's face shot hot with mortification. If only Melissa could stop doing *that* when someone walked into the house! "The bad milk is working its way out. Better, my little angel? Let's get you cleaned up. Oh, yes, it's very hard to be a *babisui*, isn't it?" Murmuring softly, she carried Melissa back to the nursery as if she'd spent more than ten minutes in this house.

"Nicole," Jeannie whispered, looking up at the ceiling, "I'm doing the best I can. I hope this is okay."

Her phone buzzed. It was, unsurprisingly, Robert. What was surprising was that he was actually calling her. "Yes?"

"Does Maja meet with your approval?"

"And hello to you, too."

He made that noise that was almost a growl again and although Jeannie was exhausted in ways she'd never even imagined possible, a thrill of desire raced through her. "Is she acceptable or do I need to find a replacement?"

"She's lovely, Robert," Jeannie sighed. "Thank you for sending her over."

"Good. I'll be by later." Before she could get any details about that—like a specific time—he ended the call.

That man.

He was only coming to make sure Maja would be able to get Jeannie back to work as soon as possible. His visit likely had nothing to do with the way he'd held her last night and less than nothing to do with the kiss.

She glanced at the clock. It was two-thirty. If she knew Robert…

That man would walk into this house at exactly eight tonight.

She all but ran to the shower. The clock was ticking.

Six

Last night he'd held Jeannie in his arms. She was right; he didn't like to be touched but with her…

"Sir?"

When he'd felt the light movement against the skin of his neck—she'd been smiling, he was just sure of it. Smiling in his arms and it hadn't been wrong. He hadn't had his guard up like normal. But that'd been the problem, hadn't it? If he'd been operating with his usual amount of caution, he wouldn't have kissed her.

Or ruined it by apologizing. Would she have kissed him again if he'd kept his mouth shut?

"Dr. Wyatt?"

Robert dragged his thoughts away from Jeannie and looked at Thomas Kelly, his assistant.

"Will there be anything else, sir?"

"You have the maid lined up?" Jeannie's house was such a disaster it was veering close to being a health hazard for the child.

Melissa, he corrected.

"Yes, sir," the young man said eagerly.

Everything Kelly did was eager. Only twenty-three, he'd been working for Robert since he'd graduated from Loyola, on the recommendation of a professor whose grandson had come through open-heart surgery with flying colors. Thomas Kelly was someone who existed outside the spheres of influence of Landon Wyatt, which made him valuable.

Kelly checked his tablet. "Rona will arrive at the house tomorrow at ten a.m. She's Darna's sister and the background check was clean."

"Ah." Darna was Robert's maid and had, over the past few years, proven to be trustworthy. He would've preferred Darna handling Jeannie's house herself but Darna's sister was the next best option.

If Landon Wyatt knew that Robert had developed a soft spot for a bartender…

Dammit. What was he supposed to do? He couldn't abandon Jeannie to the winds of fate. Nor could he turn a blind eye to that baby girl. Yes, her allergic reaction had been mild and not life-threatening and yes, Robert could turn the case over to a pediatrician but…

Jeannie had kept him going after what had happened the last time he'd seen his parents. God willing, she'd never know how much he owed her, but he wasn't about to let her twist in the wind. Jeannie needed that infant to be well. Robert needed Jeannie.

What was the point of being one of the most powerful men in the country if he didn't use that power to get what he needed?

"Rona signed the nondisclosure agreement?"

"Yes. Copies are on file."

"Good."

Everyone who worked for Robert signed NDAs. Unlike

Landon, who used NDAs to hide his monstrous behavior, Robert used them to keep his employees from talking. To the press, to Landon, to the board of Wyatt Medicals.

Not that NDAs stopped the talk completely. Robert had still been named to that ridiculous list of billionaire bachelors, which had the same effect as painting a big target on his back. And he didn't make his patients sign NDAs, although after the last time a family had gone to the newspapers to tell everyone how Robert had quietly covered their hospital bills, he'd considered it. Sadly, the hospital lawyers had informed him that making patients sign NDAs was not allowed.

Funny how it'd never even occurred to him to have Jeannie sign one. But then again, she existed on a different level. Besides, she wouldn't tell anyone anything. He trusted her.

He eyed Kelly. "You enjoy working for me, don't you?"

"Yes, sir." The young man didn't even hesitate.

"You feel you're adequately compensated for your work?" Kelly was on call twenty-four hours a day.

Kelly smirked. "If I say yes, have I talked myself out of a raise?"

Robert would give anything to discuss this plan with Jeannie. She'd see things from a different angle, spot any holes in his plan. But she had so much to worry about right now that Robert couldn't add to her burdens.

Kelly was his assistant, not his friend. As much as he liked the young man, Robert couldn't risk weakening his position by confiding uncertainty to an employee.

Which meant Robert was on his own here. "I need a plane."

"I can have your jet ready to take off inside of forty-five minutes," Kelly said, already tapping on his tablet.

"No." Robert must've said it more forcefully than he intended because Kelly's head snapped up. "I need a hired plane and an independent flight crew on standby. They're not to know who's paying them and they can't ask questions."

A look crossed Kelly's face. Confusion? Or concern? It didn't matter. "When?"

"Saturday after next." He straightened his cuffs as Reginald turned onto Jeannie's street.

"That's the night of…" Kelly trailed off and Robert realized he was glaring at the man.

"Yes." This idea felt risky, with a high probability of failure. If he got Mom away, Landon would do everything in his prodigious power to punish his wife and Robert.

If Mom didn't agree… Could Robert really leave her to Landon? Could he abandon his own mother a second time?

It wasn't even a question.

"The destination will be Los Angeles," he went on. "From there, I'll need two first-class tickets to Auckland."

"New Zealand?" Kelly's voice jumped an octave.

"Yes. And it goes without saying that, if you mention these arrangements to anyone, I will be *upset*."

"Completely understood, sir." Kelly cleared his throat. "I'll need names for the commercial tickets."

"Cybil Wyatt."

Kelly inhaled sharply. How much did he know about Robert's family? Kelly had to interact with Landon's assistant, Alexander, from time to time. Surely, he at least suspected…

"I cannot guarantee we'll be able to use her passport, so make arrangements for travel documents."

Kelly nodded. "And the second ticket?"

Robert considered adding his name to that second ticket but someone had to stay in Chicago and throw Landon off the trail.

The possible outcomes played out in his mind. If Robert did this right, not only would he get his mother to safety, but he'd also expose Landon's behavior during the aftermath of

Mom's disappearance and single-handedly knock Landon out of politics. Hopefully, for good.

The car stopped in front of Jeannie's house. Robert's heart did an odd little skip at the sight of the small box of a house. It was squat, with a distinctive air of disrepair. He should hire contractors to fix the siding. That roof looked like it was on its last legs. Plus, the yard was a mess…

Jeannie needed help and he couldn't help her from a different hemisphere, could he?

Plus, you can't kiss her from Auckland, a voice whispered in his mind.

Right. Well. It had been a perfect kiss. But it'd be best for all parties if he didn't kiss her again.

"Make sure there's a nurse on board—that's the second ticket," he said. He wanted to be there for his mother because he missed her in ways that it hurt to think about but if she wasn't around Landon, he could talk to her whenever he wanted. "All expenses paid, with generous bonuses. Be sure to run every check on whoever you hire. This situation requires complete secrecy and discretion. They may be required to prevent Cybil from contacting Landon or returning to Chicago before…" *Before it was safe.* "Before it's appropriate."

Because if he got his mother to Los Angeles but she gave in to fear and tried to back out of the plan like she had three years ago, Robert knew Landon wouldn't stop at just cutting off all contact like he had before. No, the man would salt the earth behind him.

Robert dealt in life and death every day. This was another situation where he couldn't risk a loss.

"Arrange housing in New Zealand," he directed Kelly. "Someplace secluded and safe, with an open-ended lease. Make sure it's staffed appropriately. And hire a guard for this house," he added, motioning to Jeannie's house. It didn't even have a fence to slow someone from approaching the front door. Jeannie had been just sitting on the stoop last night, with the door open behind her. "I don't want anyone to realize the house is under surveillance." Just in case Landon started digging and came across Jeannie.

No, Robert couldn't risk losing anything.

It might not be enough to just get his mother away. If Robert left Landon with the means of tracking her down, the bastard would.

Which meant only one thing.

His stomach turned.

"Yes, sir. Anything else?"

"Schedule a meeting tomorrow morning at six a.m. with Len at my office in the hospital. Who do we know in the prosecutor's office? And a private investigator—someone we trust. Oh, I'll expect you to be there, as well."

Robert had to go on rounds at seven and then see patients. But he could get a lot of strategic planning laid out before that. Kelly could make a great many things happen, but if Robert wanted to take on Landon, he'd need more than just an escape plan.

He'd need to be the one to salt the earth behind him.

Kelly didn't even blink at the early hour. "Of course."

Reginald opened Robert's car door at precisely 7:58 p.m. "That will be all for now."

"Yes, sir," Kelly said as Robert climbed out of the car. He called out, "Have a good evening, sir."

Robert didn't bother to respond as Reginald snapped the car door behind him. "See Mr. Kelly home," he told Reginald. "I won't need you for at least an hour."

It would take that long to get a report from Maja and check Melissa over and make sure that everything he'd ordered had been delivered and…

And see Jeannie.

But just to find out how she was doing. Not because he needed her or anything. He was Robert Wyatt. He didn't need anyone, most especially not a bartender. Last night had just been…

One of those things.

"Very good, Dr. Wyatt."

He strode up the stairs to Jeannie's house but before he could knock, the door opened and suddenly all the air rushed out of his lungs because there she was.

"Robert," she said, her voice soft. "You're on time. As usual."

She'd been waiting for him. Again, he had that sense that she'd always been waiting for him.

"Jeannie." She looked better, he realized. She had on a pair of loose-fitting denim shorts and an old-looking Cubs T-shirt and her feet were bare.

She looked good. She'd showered and the dark circles under her eyes were less prominent and she was smiling.

It hit him like a kick to the chest.

He must have been staring because she asked, "Is there something on my shirt?" as color washed her cheeks. "I just put it on…" She held it out from her chest, which made the deep vee of the neck gape even lower.

Her bra was white today. And moments ago she hadn't been wearing that shirt.

He was here to check the baby and make sure Jeannie had the support she needed for the optimum outcome. He was here to confirm that the people he'd hired were doing a satisfactory job. Jeannie was his bartender and he wanted everything to get back to normal. Because the longer he stepped outside of his routine and the more attention he drew to Jeannie, the more dangerous things were for all of them.

None of that careful logic prevented what happened next.

Knowing he was putting her at risk didn't stop him from stepping into her. Understanding that she'd suffered a painful loss didn't prevent him from pulling her hands away from the shirt and settling them around his neck.

"Oh," she breathed, her eyes wide as she stared up at him.

And God help him, he captured her small noise with his lips and then drank deep.

Today she smelled of…oranges, bright and tart and incredibly sweet.

So he was kissing her. Which was not what he'd planned. But it just felt right, her body flush against his, her arms tightening around his neck, her whispering, "Oh, Robert, *yes,*" against his mouth.

He went hard at that. How he wanted her hands on him. His name on her lips, her body moving over his…

"Jeannie," he all but groaned.

"Yes," she whispered back. His hands went to her waist and then he was walking her backward and kicking the door shut and—

Bang.

The sound of the door slamming jolted them apart. And not a moment too soon because the nanny emerged from the baby's room, a perfectly swaddled Melissa in her arms. "Ah, Dr. Wyatt," Maja said, smiling broadly. "We are doing well."

Robert straightened his cuffs to give himself a moment to get his body back under control but then he made the mistake of glancing over at Jeannie. She was bright red and staring at her toes but he thought he saw a smile tugging at the corners of her lips.

Lips swollen with his kiss.

That made him feel oddly proud of himself, as if he'd done something noteworthy instead of making a messy situation even messier.

Damn it all, he'd lost control and that wasn't allowed.

When he was sure he had his responses locked down, he said, "Yes, Mrs. Kowalczyk. What is your report?"

"The organic formula is helping and lovely little Melissa is already less fussy. Miss Jeannie is an excellent student and has already learned how to properly swaddle a *babisui*

and change a diaper." She cast a maternal look at Jeannie.
"I think, however, it would be good for Miss Jeannie to get
out of the house. She has been under a great deal of stress
and we all need a break, don't we?"

"Excellent idea."

He already had his phone out to call Reginald back
as soon as he'd dropped Kelly off at home when Jeannie made a noise of surprise. "Not tonight, Robert! For
Pete's sake!"

"What?" That was how she'd sounded last night after
he'd ruined the kiss. Like there was an expected code of
conduct in situations like this and he wasn't following it.

"I'm not going anywhere tonight," she said, her tone gen-
tler. "Just because I had a nap and a shower doesn't mean
I'm operating on all cylinders today." Her gaze dropped to
his lips and, as he watched, the tip of her tongue darted out
and swiped over her lower lip.

Hmm. That was interesting. Did that mean she was
having second thoughts about that second kiss? All he
knew was that he could still catch the scent of oranges
in the air.

Cautiously, Robert looked at Maja. She nodded in agreement. "Perhaps for lunch tomorrow?" she suggested.

"Lunch." He didn't eat lunch on a regular basis. He was
always at the hospital, making rounds or seeing patients.

"It's a meal? Most people eat it around the noon hour?"
Jeannie was definitely smiling now. Something in his chest
loosened.

She was teasing him, he realized. No one else would
dare, but she did. "Yes, I'm familiar with the concept." Her
smile got even bigger. "I have appointments tomorrow but
we could do lunch on Saturday." He already knew Maja
would be here. He was paying her an exorbitant rate to live
in the first week, but it was worth it to see Jeannie without
that haunted look in her eyes.

Maja was doing her job. Robert had made it clear that the nanny was responsible for making sure both people in this house were cared for.

Maja gave him that approving nod again as Jeannie said, "Okay, but nothing too fancy. And not Trenton's."

"Of course not." He wasn't entirely sure that he was welcome back. Better to wait until Jeannie could return.

Jeannie eyed him warily. "You do eat, don't you? You never order anything but the Manhattan at the bar."

"Of course I eat." Darna made sure there were fresh-cooked meals for him at home. She cooked to his specifications and that was all he needed. He didn't need to try the latest food craze or go out to be seen. He liked his corner at Jeannie's bar and then he liked his peace and quiet.

For a second, he considered just bringing Jeannie to his town house and serving her the cuisine Darna left for him. If he called Darna right now, she'd probably have time to put together something special. Her roast pork was amazing and those little rice cakes wrapped in banana leaves—Jeannie would like them. He could show her his home and...

And...

That was a terrible idea. Yes, he'd kissed Jeannie twice now—but taking her to his home felt dangerous.

So Kelly would find a restaurant. Someplace quiet, but not romantic. Someplace where Jeannie could relax. Someplace where gossip would not reach Landon Wyatt.

Someplace where she could smile at Robert but a table would keep them from touching.

It was safer that way.

"I know the perfect place," he hedged. He would know it by noon tomorrow, anyway. Kelly did good work. "Now," he went on, because Reginald would be back soon enough and Robert had a role to fulfill. He held out his hands and Maja placed the baby in his arms without hesitation. Melissa squirmed at the change in elevation but when he cradled her, she blinked up at him with her bright baby-blue eyes. "Let's see how we're doing."

Forty minutes later Jeannie had demonstrated everything she'd learned today—how to properly change a diaper, how to swaddle an infant securely, even how to hold the bottle so Melissa didn't have to work as hard to drink.

The whole time Robert had watched her with those icy eyes, doing little more than nodding when she apparently passed inspection. Because that was what it felt like. An inspection. One she'd definitely failed yesterday. Today?

He'd kissed her.

He'd walked right up to her and kissed her and she'd kissed him back and everything felt so much better and that much worse at the same time because he was here and that was great but nothing made sense.

Because he'd kissed her.

And now he was standing there, judging her as she burped a baby.

A baby who thankfully fell asleep.

"Maja," Robert said after Jeannie had laid Melissa down in the completely empty crib and they'd all returned to the living room, "you've done well today."

Jeannie glared at him. Maja was a good teacher who obviously knew what she was doing but *come on, Robert.* Jeannie was the one learning everything from scratch on a few hours of sleep. But the man wasn't even looking at her!

"Thank you, Dr. Wyatt," Maja said, her eyes twinkling. "Jeannie is a most capable student."

"Hmm," he murmured as if he wasn't sure he agreed with that assessment. Which made Jeannie glare harder.

But before she could tell him where to shove his humming noises, he said to the nanny, "Take an hour and get dinner."

Wait. Jeannie cut a glance at Maja, who looked mildly surprised at this…well, this *order*. Which was pretty much how Jeannie felt, as well, considering they'd eaten dinner around six. But Maja was obviously used to taking odd orders from her clients, because all she said was, "Of course, Dr. Wyatt. I need to pick up more formula."

"What…" Jeannie started to say as Maja grabbed her purse and was out the door in seconds. She moved awfully quick for a woman easily in her sixties.

"Reginald?" Robert said before the front door had closed behind Maja. Because of course Robert was on the phone. Probably ordering a butler or something. "An hour from now. Yes."

She stared at him as he ended the call. What was Robert even doing here? Besides continuing to completely take over her life.

"I'm not going to work tomorrow," she said. Unfortunately, it came out sounding petulant and immature. "I don't want to and I'm not ready."

"Of course you're not," he said, sounding almost agreeable about it.

"O…kay. So if you're not going to convince me to get back to work, why are you here?"

He adjusted his cuffs. He still had on his jacket today, although she noted he had foregone a vest. Probably because it'd been close to ninety danged degrees today. To the average person, it might not look like he was stalling but she knew this was how Robert played for time.

He cleared his throat. Yeah, totally stalling. "Are you better?"

"I am." God, this felt six kinds of awkward. She wanted… to go back to where they'd been when he'd walked up her front steps like a man on a mission.

Where he'd come because he wanted to see her.

"Will you sit with me?" she asked, holding out her hand.

He looked at her hand like he didn't trust it. Or maybe he didn't trust himself?

"Are you sure?" he asked and she heard the strain in his voice.

He didn't trust himself. At least, not around her. The realization set her back on her heels.

"Yes," she said because she knew he could be terrifying but he'd never once made her feel unsafe. "Are you?"

He hesitated.

"I only want to sit with you," she said. "Come here." It was as close to an order as she'd ever given him.

An emotion rippled across his face, one she couldn't quite identify. She had to wonder—had anyone ever tried to tell him what to do before? Surely, at medical school?

"*Please*, Robert."

Why didn't he trust himself around her?

She didn't think he was going to bridge the divide between them but then he laced his fingers with hers. They moved to the couch, and he sat. Stiffly at first, but when Jeannie sat next to him and tucked her head against his shoulder, she felt a tremor pass through his body and then, bit by bit, he relaxed.

She didn't let go of his hand. Instead, she covered it with her other hand and stroked along the side of his thumb with her own. His hands were strong, with long fingers and impeccably groomed nails.

"Maja was what I needed," she told him, but what she really wanted to say was that *he* was what she needed. "Thank you."

"Good," was all he said, because of course.

Her mind raced even as her body calmed. Like last night when she'd needed a hug, tonight she needed to lay her head on his shoulder and let his warmth seep into her body. If Robert was here, then things were okay. He wouldn't allow it to be otherwise.

She thought of the nanny, the maid that would probably show up in the next few days, the lawyers, the insistence that she go back to work as soon as was humanly possible, hell, even lunch on Saturday—it all pointed back to something big in his life.

To the bad day he'd mentioned when he first showed up.

"Robert?"

"Yes?"

"Are you okay?"

She had the distinct feeling that, if she hadn't been holding on to his hand with both of hers, he would've straightened his damned cuffs. "I won't let any harm come to you. Or Melissa."

She tensed. "Are we in danger?"

"No," he answered too quickly and then, "No," again, but softer.

"You're touching me." He smelled faintly antiseptic today. *Surgery*, she remembered.

"I...don't mind." He swallowed. Was he nervous? Because they were discussing feelings or because they were touching? "Because it's you."

The man might not spout romantic poetry or random compliments but... "That was probably the nicest thing you've ever said to me."

"What a low bar to meet." Was that humor in his voice? He cleared his throat again. "You did well today. I'm impressed at how quickly you picked things up." Her breath caught in her throat and she tilted her head back to find his face less than four inches from hers. "There," he said, sounding almost cocky about it. "How was that?"

"Better," she told him breathlessly. "Much better."

He smiled. Just the corners of his mouth moving upward but it took everything warm and comfortable about him and kicked it right on over to pure, simmering heat.

"Good," he said again.

That did it. Before she could talk herself out of it, she slid into his lap, straddling his powerful legs and bringing her pelvis flush against his. He inhaled sharply and she felt him tense underneath her.

"What are you doing?" he asked in a strangled voice. His arms stretched along the back of the couch, as far from touching her as he could get.

"Listen to me, you silly man," she said, motioning in the narrow space between them. "I'm not afraid of you, Robert. I trust you."

"You shouldn't," he ground out, digging his fingers into the couch cushions.

"Well, it's too late because I do." She cupped his face in her hands and made him look at her. "I've known you for years and *I trust you* so get used to it. I don't understand you, but for the love of everything holy, stop acting like you're a villain in this story."

"Do you have any idea what I'm capable of?" he demanded, glaring.

Now she was getting somewhere. He couldn't hide behind his shirt cuffs or the bar or the Manhattan. He couldn't hide from *her* anymore.

"Yes," she said, touching her forehead to his. "You're capable of single-handedly saving incredibly sick children, you're rescuing me and Melissa and you're the most obnoxious perfectionist I've ever met. By, like, *a lot*."

His chest heaved. "You don't know." As he spoke, his hands came to rest on the curve of her waist. "You just don't understand."

"No, I don't." She wrapped her arms around his neck and buried her face in his shoulder and hugged the man for all he was worth. "But I will because you'll tell me when you're ready," she murmured against his skin.

After a heart-dropping pause, his arms curled around her. "Jeannie."

She knew what he was going to say and she cut him off with a growl. He really was the most infuriating man. "This is not an obligation, dammit."

"But—"

She leaned back. "Robert—did you ever think that I *wanted* to kiss you? That I'd want to do it again?"

Seven

She was sitting in his lap.

His *lap.*

Worse, she wanted to kiss him. *Just* kiss? Perhaps not, what with the way she straddled him, her breasts flush against his chest.

It should be wrong, the way her weight pressed him against the couch cushions. She shouldn't be like this, definitely shouldn't trust him. Not if she knew what was good for her.

"You want to kiss me."

"I do." She sighed, her warm breath stroking over his neck. "I've wanted to kiss you for years. *Years.* You never realized it, did you?"

He opened his mouth to point out the flaw in her logic, realized he had no idea what that flaw might be and snapped it shut again.

"I'll take that for a *no*," she said. Smugly.

People didn't touch him. Yes, he'd shake hands with worried parents and examine their children, but outside of the office? *Never*.

Except for her, apparently. Because not only had he kissed her, but he also...*liked* her touch.

Jeannie molded herself to him. Her body was warm and light against his and it reached inside him, drawing an answering pulse from his blood. Her thighs felt strong and sure as they bracketed his legs and although he most certainly did not want an erection right now, all that pounding blood began to pound in his dick, as well.

Oh, yes—he liked it.

The heat of her core settled against his groin and he almost groaned at the delicious tension because she was sitting *in his lap* and he couldn't remember wanting to be this close to a woman.

Much to his surprise, he realized he was stroking her back and he'd turned his face into her hair so he could inhale her scent.

It was good.

Because it was her.

She was a temptation he couldn't resist.

She really had no idea what he was capable of, did she?

A tremor raced through his body. It wasn't fear. Because Wyatts weren't afraid of anything. He was merely holding himself back.

For her sake. Not his.

She wanted him...but not for his money or his power?

She was right. He didn't understand a damn thing.

"Stop thinking, Robert," she murmured against his neck. "Just *be*. We've both had crappy weeks and this is nice." She sighed into him. "You're a good hugger."

He highly doubted that. When was the last time he'd been hugged?

Suddenly, he was talking without being entirely sure what was coming out of his mouth. "I'm *not* taking you out to lunch. You're coming to my home. We'll have a quiet meal on the terrace and…" He swallowed, trying not to sound desperate because desperation wasn't allowed. "I… I can just *be* there. With you."

What if she said no or demanded a fancy meal at a trendy spot, like he'd promised? The sort of thing that Dr. Robert Wyatt, a Top Five Billionaire Bachelor, should do?

The thought was almost physically painful. Because, he realized with alarm, that wasn't who he was with her.

Say yes, he thought and dammit, there was desperation in those unspoken words.

Say yes to me.

Her lips moved against his skin. His body responded accordingly. He'd made her smile. It felt like a victory.

"Of course," she agreed. She pushed back to look at him, her weight bearing down on him. God, she was perfect. "No obligations, no expectations. Just two people who can *be* together."

All those colors in her eyes played with the light, making her look soft and otherworldly, like a princess who'd disguised herself as a commoner to test the prince.

He might have failed his mother but by God, he wasn't going to fail Jeannie. She didn't know what he was capable of. He prayed she never would.

"I'll pick you up at twelve," he told her, stroking his thumb over her cheek.

She leaned into his touch. "I'll be waiting."

"Are you sure this is okay?" Jeannie asked for the fourth time. Or maybe it was the fortieth.

Her sleeveless sundress was bright yellow, with a happy print of little pink and blue flowers all over it. Rona, the maid who'd arrived promptly at ten this morning, had even ironed the dang thing.

Jeannie had bought the dress for a date some years ago

and then repurposed it with a shawl to attend Easter services with Nicole, who'd been a church regular. It'd been part of their reconciliation.

It was the fanciest dress Jeannie owned. Hopefully, paired with the shawl and her platform brown sandals, it would be nice enough for a private meal with Robert. He always cut such a dashing figure in his custom three-piece suits and gemstone cuff links and she had...a cotton sundress she'd gotten on clearance four years ago.

But what else did one wear to a private meal with the billionaire bachelor next door? Cutoffs seemed like the wrong answer.

This was ridiculous.

She couldn't go to lunch with him. She shouldn't be alone with him. If she was smart, she'd change into her jean shorts, curl up on the couch and let Maja boss her around in a highly educational way.

"Yes, yes," Maja said again, patting Melissa's back. "You look lovely. Very sweet. Rona, doesn't she look lovely?"

"Oh, yes," the tiny Filipino woman called from the kitchen, where the smells of something delicious wafted throughout the house. "Very pretty."

Upon arrival, Rona had promptly taken over everything Maja hadn't. Dishes had been washed, laundry laundered, the bathroom was already immaculate and who could forget the cooking? It was a little bit like living in a hotel.

Jeannie had no idea who would appear next but she had a feeling Robert wasn't done hiring a staff of potentially dozens to take care of her. She was going to draw the line at a butler, though.

The baby let out a tiny little belch—without crying. Seriously, Maja was magic. Jeannie didn't know how much Robert was paying her, but it was worth it.

"Caregivers need breaks," Maja went on, shifting from side to side. Jeannie was sure the older woman didn't even know she was doing it. Would Jeannie ever get that level of comfort handling Melissa? "The *babisui* and I will be fine together—she will sleep, I will help Rona and you will enjoy a break with your handsome doctor."

Jeannie's cheeks heated so she quickly turned back to her room to rifle through her meager jewelry collection. "He's not *my* doctor." No disputing the handsome part, though.

"Mmm," Maja replied. Or maybe she was just talking to the baby.

Trenton's didn't let employees wear more than simple stud earrings, and most of Jeannie's jewelry was like her sundress—cheaply made, purchased on clearance and several years old. And most of it felt…juvenile. From a period of her life that had passed.

She wasn't the same girl who could ironically wear neon-pink plastic hoops, not anymore. She was something very like a mother now. Besides, the neon hoops definitely didn't match this dress. So in the end, she went with her basic fake diamond studs that she wore at the bar every night.

"He's *not* my doctor," Jeannie reminded her reflection.

This was just lunch. With her favorite customer. While wearing her best dress.

And the cutest pair of matching panties and bralette she owned. The set she'd ordered online in a pink that was more dusty than neon and was very lacy.

Very lacy.

She'd tossed and turned all night long, drifting in and out of lust-fueled dreams that left her hot and bothered. She hadn't stopped with just straddling Robert or holding him. She hadn't stopped at all.

The doorbell rang. "He's here," Maja sang.

Although it wasn't ladylike, Jeannie sprinted out of the bedroom, yelling, "I'll get it!"

Which turned out to be pointless because Maja had already opened the door. Jeannie stumbled over her sandals and nearly took a header at the sight of the man waiting for her.

He wasn't wearing a suit.

Had she thought Robert looked undone days ago when he hadn't been wearing a tie? Because the man standing before her was so far from a suit and tie that she barely recognized him.

Except for his eyes. She would never forget the burning intensity of Robert's eyes for as long as she lived.

Especially when they darkened. "You look lovely," he said. A shiver raced down her back at the sound of his voice, deep and raw and—this wasn't about lunch, was it?

"So do you." Instead of that suit, he was wearing a dark blue button-up shirt that had short sleeves and maybe some little pattern on it, all paired with light khaki shorts.

Shorts. That revealed his well-muscled legs. Her pulse began to stutter as she stared at those defined legs. When had calves gotten so damn sexy? Lord.

"I didn't think you owned anything but suits."

"I didn't know you wore anything other than vests before this week," he returned with a smile that melted her.

"Dr. Wyatt," Maja interrupted. Jeannie startled. She'd forgotten the older woman was in the room. "Would you like a report?"

"The thirty-second version," he replied, not taking his eyes off Jeannie. Dear God, she could practically smell the sexual desire coming off him in waves.

"Little Melissa continues to improve, Rona has made an excellent start and Jeannie—"

"Is late for lunch," he said, coming forward to take her by the arm.

When he touched her, electricity raced over her skin, taking everything that had started to melt and tightening it to the point of delicious pain. She fought to keep from gasping as his hand slid down until his fingers laced with hers.

She threw a glance back at Maja, whose expression clearly stated, *your handsome doctor.*

"We'll be back later," Robert announced in that way of his.

"Enjoy yourselves," Maja said with a conspiratorial wink, shooing them out. "We'll be fine here."

Oh, Jeannie would. If she got the chance, she was going to enjoy this with every fiber of her being.

Reginald was waiting at the car for them. "Miss," he said, tipping his hat to her as she approached.

"Hello again." Reginald's expression was remarkably similar to Maja's, like there was a conspiracy to make her and Robert…

Well, not fall in love or anything because that simply wasn't possible. He was a billionaire surgeon whose family owned a huge medical company and his father was maybe going to be the next governor. She was a bartender who'd never finished college and whose grand dream to own her own bar had been completely derailed by becoming the legal guardian to an infant. Their paths could only ever cross at a place like Trenton's.

She would never fit into his world and he would never understand hers.

Jeannie didn't know what to do with her legs. The hem of the sundress was well above her knees and Robert sat across from her. His gaze roamed over her. Was that hunger in his eyes? Or was he noting the shabby dress, the worn leather straps on her sandals, the hundred other little things that marked her as a different class?

She tucked the hem of her dress around her thighs and stared right back. Of course he looked completely at ease sitting there. In shorts. Shorts! She still couldn't get over it, or the way the sight of the dark hair on his legs stirred something deep inside her.

The man was sin in a suit but there was something so

casually masculine about him right now that her clothes felt too tight.

He, at least, had no problem crossing his legs. "So," she began because several quiet moments had passed and Robert showed no sign of breaking the silence. "What's for lunch?"

"Darna—that's Rona's sister—is preparing a traditional Filipino meal of chicken satay, tinola soup and suman for dessert."

She stared. "Did you hire Darna just for today?"

"No, she's worked for me for almost six years. I trust her," he added as an afterthought.

For some reason that made Jeannie happy. He needed people he could trust. She just wished he counted himself on that list.

He didn't say anything else. They were driving toward downtown and, for once, traffic was light. "What else are we doing today?"

She heard him inhale sharply and felt an answering tug in her chest. "Nothing."

She met his gaze. "Pity."

The tension between them sharpened. "Jeannie…"

"Robert," she replied. If he didn't want to sleep with her, that was fine. But she wanted him to say it. She didn't want any misunderstandings. "Aren't we on a date?"

His mouth opened and snapped shut and Jeannie got to appreciate that rare, wonderful thing where Dr. Robert Wyatt was flummoxed.

"Because this seems like a date," she went on. "I'm wearing a dress, you picked me up in a limo and we're going to eat a meal. Pretty standard date stuff, really."

He was doing that fish thing, his mouth opening and closing and opening again. "I don't date."

"You mean, you're not currently seeing anyone? That's good. I'm not involved, either. Which," she added, "is good for the status of our date. I'm not into being anyone's side piece."

"Side... Never mind." He shook his head. "No. I mean, I don't date. Ever."

"Ever?" Because that sounded ominous. She knew he wasn't married—kind of went with the territory when he was named a top bachelor—but...

He had kissed her. Twice now. And he had definitely started it the second time.

"No," he said sharply. Ominously, even.

"Just going out on a limb here, but you're not going to tell me why?"

That got her a hard look.

"Right." She looked out the window again. They were making great time. "So sex is off the table, then?"

He made a choking noise. "Do you have a filter?"

"Yes. In case you've never noticed, I use it all the time—at work. But we're not at Trenton's. I don't know what's going on with you or what's going on between us but..." His face was completely unreadable, so she went on with a sigh. "This is who I am, Robert. I'm a bartender who hasn't completed a college degree and barely passed high school. My big dream is to open my own bar. I left home when I was eighteen and didn't talk to my sister for almost six years. I can be mean and bitter and a huge pain in the ass when I put my mind to it and I am *not* a shy, retiring virgin. I like sex and I'd like to have sex with you." It was hard to tell in the darkened interior of the limo, but she would've bet large sums of his money that he was blushing. "But I'm not going to push you into anything that makes you uncomfortable."

"Well, there's that," he said under his breath. She detected sarcasm.

"But," she went on, "beyond that, I'm a hot mess. I am singularly unqualified to raise a child, not to mention I have no way to pay for what a baby needs." Robert opened his mouth, no doubt to find another way to spend his money on her. "No, I'm not going to take more of your money. She's not your daughter and we're not your responsibility. I'm in this car with you because I like you. I know what I want from you, you confounding, infuriating man. Not your money, not your name—I want you, Robert. I have for a long time. And I know I may not get it and that's okay, too." She leaned forward and put her hand on his knee. "But the question is, do you know what you want from me?"

He stared at her hand, resting on his knee. She could feel him practically vibrating with nervous energy.

But he didn't say anything.

The car came to a stop.

Eight

If there was one thing Robert had learned growing up in Landon Wyatt's house, it was how to control his physical reactions, because showing joy or sorrow or, worst of all, fear, was the quickest way to pain.

Over the years Robert had gotten so good at controlling those giveaways—the increased heart rate, the stomach-wrenching nausea, the shallow, fast breathing—that, for the most part, he'd simply stopped feeling distress. Even when a surgery went wrong, he was able to keep his emotional reactions on lockdown and he'd lost count of the number of times his cool head had prevented disaster or, worse, death.

Which was good. Great, even. No one wanted to go through life afraid. He certainly didn't.

So why did he feel like he was going to vomit as he led Jeannie up the stairs to his house?

He didn't know. Jeannie was many things—including, apparently, a self-described "hot mess"—but one thing she wasn't was a threat.

At least, not the kind Robert was used to.

"This is...*wow*," she marveled as the front door swung open.

"Welcome home, Dr. Wyatt. Miss Kaufman." Darna beamed at Jeannie. She had a crisp white apron over her uniform and a welcoming smile.

Odd. Darna was efficient and did exceptional work for him. But had he ever seen her smile?

"Darna, is it? I was just getting to know Rona. She's your sister, right?" Jeannie took Darna's hand in hers and half shook it, half just held it. "It's such a pleasure to meet you. I hope you didn't go to too much trouble for this."

Darna's eyes danced with what was probably amusement. "No, no—no trouble at all. I hope you enjoy the meal." She retrieved her hand and turned to Robert. "Everything is set up on the terrace, sir. Will there be anything else?"

"No." Jeannie slanted him a hard look. "No...thank you?"

Jeannie beamed at him. For her part, Darna looked as if Robert had just declared his undying love. "My," she all but giggled. "My, my. Yes." She patted Jeannie on the arm and giggled. "Yes," she repeated.

Robert could feel his pulse beginning to speed up, beating wildly out of time. Which was ridiculous because this was not a risky situation.

This was, as Jeannie had pointed out, lunch. Between two people who...liked each other?

All right, fine. He *liked* Jeannie. He needed to see her on a near-daily basis to function, it seemed. And he was doing everything in his power to help her through a difficult time. True, he'd done that for some of his patients, the ones where the bills would've bankrupted the families.

But he hadn't ever wanted to see those people again. And he certainly hadn't ever wanted to kiss any of them. Like he'd kissed Jeannie. Twice.

Kissed her and held her close—so, so close.

His pulse jumped to a new level of erratic.

With a nod, Darna disappeared into the house and Robert was left standing in the foyer with Jeannie. He needed to move but he wasn't sure he could. Every system he'd spent years mastering was in open revolt right now and that was when Jeannie turned to him, a knowing smile on her lips. "I take it you don't bring a lot of people home?"

"No," he replied. There. At least his voice was still under his control. He sounded exactly normal, even if he felt anything but.

A few nights ago she'd straddled him. Today—mere moments ago—she'd boldly announced that she not only liked sex, but she'd also like to have sex with him.

He would not lose control. He would not hurt her and he would not risk destroying this...liking.

She took a few steps away from him, staring at the ornate ceilings. "This place is huge."

"Yes."

She looked back over her shoulder at him. "Is it just you?"

He began to shake. "Yes. I value my privacy."

"I must say," she went on, running her fingers lightly over the hand-painted wall coverings, "this is more...floral than I would've guessed."

"Oh?" His voice cracked a little as she moved into the parlor. Had she always had that sway to her hips?

"I pictured you in a modern, stark condo—all harsh lines, lots of stainless steel and black. This?" She made a little turn in the parlor. "This is *extravagant*. Obnoxiously so."

No one else would tell him his house was obnoxious, but it was true. And Jeannie saw it. The dress swung around her legs, exposing more of the bare skin of her thighs, and Robert had to brace himself against the door frame. "It came like this."

She stopped twirling, the dress falling back around her

legs. "You…bought the house like this and didn't change anything?"

He shook his head because he wasn't sure he could speak, not with her making her way back toward him, that sway in her hips, that smile on her face. Like she'd been waiting for him.

It wasn't alarm knotting up his tongue and making him feel light-headed and dizzy. It wasn't panic sending his pulse screaming in his veins. It wasn't fear that had given him a rock-hard erection, the one he'd been fighting to contain ever since this woman had slid onto his lap. No, that wasn't right. He'd been fighting this ever since she'd opened the front door and announced she'd been waiting for him. Since she'd been waiting on her stoop.

This was desire. Raw, pure, dangerous desire.

Oh, hell.

Somewhere below, he heard the faint sound of the alarm system being engaged and then a door shut. The noise echoed through the house—the sound of Darna leaving. They were well and truly alone, and Jeannie wanted to have sex with him and he was starting to think it'd be a good idea but how could he let her strip him bare without his control snapping?

"Hey," she said softly, coming toward him. He almost flinched when she put her hand on his cheek. "Just *be*, Robert. Nothing has to happen." She notched an eyebrow and instead of sympathy or worse, pity, he saw nothing but a challenge. "Although I reserve the right to make fun of this wallpaper because who wallpapers a ceiling?"

Odd. He was sure he was glaring at her, which normally sent people running for the closest exit. But instead, this woman smiled and absorbed it. Understood it.

Understood him.

"I don't want to hurt you," he got out and dammit, his

voice shook with the force of emotions that tumbled through him. Desire. Fear. Need. Pain. Want.

An emotion shimmered in her eyes and was gone before he could identify it. "Oh, I don't know about that. Those floral drapes are borderline painful," she said with a mischievous grin and oddly, he was able to draw in a breath. "Why haven't you changed them?"

"It was done by someone famous back in the thirties, and my mother..."

Against his will, his eyes shut. But that was a mistake because he could see his mother delicately arranged on the cushioned chair by the fireplace, a blanket tucked around her legs to help hold the ice packs in place. She'd gazed at the obnoxious wallpaper and frenetic drapes and the gold leaf and said, *I love this room. The riot of colors...it's wild but free.* Then she'd smiled at him, her eyes unfocused from the pain or the meds or both, and had said, *Silly, isn't it?*

He wanted Cybil Wyatt to enjoy riotous colors and silliness and freedom. He had to get her away from Landon. The alternatives were unthinkable.

He heard himself say, "My mother liked it."

"Ah," Jeannie said, her tone softening with what he hoped was understanding and not pity. "So you keep it this way for her?"

He nodded. Darna dusted this room—all the rooms done in this overblown style—twice a week. They were kept in a permanent state of readiness, just in case.

But three years ago it hadn't been enough to keep his mother here. *He* hadn't been enough to keep her here.

"Does she visit often?"

Twice. His mother had been in his home exactly twice. The second time he'd had to carry her in because she couldn't climb the steps. She'd stayed only long enough to be able to walk back down on her own power. Robert had stood in the window, watching her get into Landon's black limousine.

Cybil Wyatt hadn't looked back.

Robert had found himself at Trenton's that night. "No," he said shortly, remembering to answer the question.

"I see."

He was afraid she did.

Suddenly, her touch was gone and Robert stumbled forward, his eyes popping open to find Jeannie moving through the room, her happy yellow dress both clashing with the greens and reds and blues of the formal parlor and, somehow, blending in perfectly.

"So if this is for your mom," she said, running a hand over the hand-carved marble fireplace mantel, "where *do* you live?"

This was a mistake. He didn't bring people here for a good reason. He kept to himself because it was better that way—safer, easier. He preferred being alone.

But Jeannie…

He held out his hand to her and she didn't even hesitate. Her fingers wrapped around his and, on impulse, he lifted her hand and let his lips trail over her knuckles. The contact pushed him that much closer to the edge.

She inhaled sharply. Did she feel the same connection he did? Or was she just looking to get lucky?

Did the answer even matter?

It did. God help him, it did.

"Come with me."

Jeannie did the math as Robert led her up one garish flight of stairs—really, this wallpaper was *something*—to another.

She'd spent about an hour with him five nights a week, approximately fifty-one weeks out of the year, for almost three years. That meant…uh…somewhere around eight thousand hours with this man.

She'd never imagined him living like this. High-rent, yes. Opulent? Sure. But…

It was like she'd entered Opposites Land, where up was down, quiet was loud and Robert was surrounded by hideous decorating. The man was so incredibly particular about everything—the precise formulation of his Manhattan, the cuffs on his sleeves, hell, even where his bartender was. How did he live *here*?

Even accounting for the fact that his mother liked it… it just didn't make sense. If she woke up to these walls and marble and what was probably real gold leaf, she'd have a headache every day of the week and two on Sunday. Jeannie had never pegged Robert for being a momma's boy.

Except he'd sounded so raw when he'd said his mother liked it. Like he had the first time he'd ever walked through Trenton's doors.

Was Mrs. Wyatt a good person or not? Jeannie had a feeling that, if she knew where the woman fell on the spectrum between Sainted Angel and Worst Mother in The World, she'd understand Robert's choices better.

But she also understood that he wasn't going to tell her. In that eight thousand some-odd hours she'd spent with him, she'd barely heard mention of his parents until a few weeks ago. The man knew how to hold his cards close.

When they reached the landing on the third floor, things changed. The landing opened up onto a short, wide hallway and at the end, she could see two French doors thrown open. On either side of that hallway was a door.

That wasn't what caught her attention. Instead of gaudy wallpaper, the walls changed to a soft peach color. She wouldn't have chosen this color for Robert but at least it didn't make her eyeballs bleed. Compared to the explosion of pattern downstairs, this was downright calming—and that was including the fact that Robert had art hung on these walls. It looked old and expensive.

She tore her gaze away from the priceless paintings. Robert unlocked the door on the right side of the stairs and stood at the threshold. Jeannie studied the tension in his shoulders, the way he practically vibrated with nervous energy. She was just about to suggest they go straight to the terrace, where their meal had been set up, because it was clear that Robert wasn't exactly jumping at the chance to show her around.

But the moment she opened her mouth, he turned and held his hand out. She couldn't pass up this opportunity to understand a little bit more about what made the man tick.

Not to mention the way he'd kissed the back of her hand earlier.

So she put her trust in him and let him lead her into a…

"This is my study," he said, softly shutting the door behind him.

Jeannie gasped. *Books.* Shelves and shelves of books and not the kind that had been tastefully arranged to look good. Oh, no. These were paperbacks with broken spines that had been crammed into every square inch of available space—which went all the way up to ceilings that had to be at least twelve feet high. The walls were lined with shelves, and the long room appeared to run the entire width of the house. She turned to the closest one and saw at least twenty Tom Clancy books wedged together. The next shelf had John Grisham and after that, Janet Evanovich. And it just went on and on. Was that an entire bookcase of Nora Roberts?

Thousands and thousands of books in this room. So many he even had one of those little ladders to get to the top shelves.

The rest of the room had an almost cozy feel. Skylights kept the room bathed in a warm glow. The exterior wall housed a fireplace, which, unlike the one down in the formal room, looked like it had actually seen a fire in the past year. It was also only one of two places that didn't have shelves. But even that mantel was crowded with books underneath what was probably another priceless work of art. Before that was a leather chair with matching footstool, next to a side table with a lamp and paper, pens—book clutter, basically—next to it. Behind that was a long desk, piled high with even more books and a computer holding on to a corner of the desk.

She spun, breathing in the smell of paper and leather and trying to grasp the sheer number of books here. "You read," was the brilliant observation she came up with.

"Yes." He sounded embarrassed by this admission. "I don't watch much television."

"This is your room?"

"My study, yes. Darna only comes in here once a quarter to dust."

In other words, this was his private sanctuary. And he'd invited Jeannie inside.

Oh, Robert.

Light streamed in from the French doors that led outside. Robert unlocked them and then wrapped his strong fingers around hers and led her outside to the terrace.

Jeannie gasped, "Oh, my *God*." She was sure the space itself was impressive. She was dimly aware of the sweet smell of flowers, of green and orange and space. A lot of space. But beyond that, she couldn't have described the terrace at all.

Because somehow, despite the fact that they were three blocks away from the shore and surrounded by high-rise condos, she had an uninterrupted view of Lake Michigan. The afternoon sun glinted off the water, marking the only difference between the water and the sky. A breeze blew off the lake, bathing them in cool, fresh air.

"You have a view of the lake." She turned to him. "*How* do you have a view of the lake?"

He wasn't looking at the water. He was staring at her with the kind of intensity she should be used to. But that was in the dim interior of Trenton's, with a bar between them. Here, under the bright sunlight, his gaze felt entirely different.

Entirely possessive and demanding and maybe just a little bit needy.

"I bought the buildings blocking my view and had them razed," he said in the same way he might've said *I got whole milk instead of skim*. "They're parks now. I had playground equipment installed. One has a community garden. The kids plant things, I'm told."

Jeannie's mouth dropped open. "You did *what*?"

He shrugged. "I wanted this house, but with a view."

Jeannie looked back out at the water. The buildings surrounding the view were four or five stories tall, prime Gold Coast real estate that had probably housed condos and apartments that sold for a few million dollars. *Each.*

It made her nightly hundred-dollar tip look like a handful of pennies, didn't it? She knew he was rich. Billionaire bachelor and all that crap. But…

In this real estate market, Robert had single-handedly erased maybe a hundred million dollars of potential profits. So he could sit on his terrace and see the lake.

Sweet Jesus.

Really, why was she here? This man could have any woman he wanted. He could have a wife and mistresses and private jets and his own art museum and nannies and chefs and limos and…anything. He could have it all with just a snap of his fingers.

She was just a bartender. Working-class at best, nowhere near owning her own place. She could never exist in his world. She shouldn't have accepted his help, shouldn't have come to lunch and most definitely shouldn't have told this man she would like to have sex with him.

But she had.

She couldn't have him. Not forever. But she could hold him for just a little bit and then let him go. It was definitely a mistake and just might break her heart, but it was better to have loved and lost…or something like that.

He might just be the best mistake she was ever going to make.

"Do you like it?" he asked, his voice deep and riveting. She felt it all the way down to her toes, that voice.

She nodded. Out on the lake, a sailboat drifted by. It was so perfect it was almost unreal. Much like Robert.

She asked, "Can you see the stars from here?" Because Chicago's light pollution blotted out everything for her. But for him?

Only Robert Wyatt could make the stars shine.

His lips moved in that small way that meant he was smiling and her heart began to pound. "On clear nights, if you look right there…" He stepped in behind her and pointed toward a distant section of the horizon.

His body was warm and solid against her back and the lake breeze teased at the hem of her dress. Jeannie didn't know if this was a seduction or not, because this was Robert and who the heck could tell, but she had to admit, she was being seduced. Perfect, rich, gorgeous Dr. Robert Wyatt, who had his own personal section of the night sky.

"I'd love to see that," she said quietly.

One of his hands came to rest on her waist. Then the other followed suit. "I can show them to you," he said right against her ear.

Oh, thank God. Her nipples went hard as his lips brushed ever so lightly over her earlobe. That lightest of touches sent little bursts of electricity racing over her skin. She had to clench her legs together to keep her knees from buckling, but even that small movement spiked the pressure on her sex to almost unbearable levels of need.

Moving slowly, she lifted his hands off her waist and wrapped them around her stomach so she could lean back into him.

All she felt and heard was Robert.

How he'd turned his head and his breath cascaded over her ear as if he'd buried his face in her hair. Of the rise and fall of his chest as he inhaled her scent. Of the way his arms tightened around her, so slowly as to be almost imperceptible, until he had her locked in his grip. Of how he slowly lowered his chin until it came to rest on her shoulder.

Of the way his entire body seemed to surround her as if he was afraid of startling her or worse, driving her away.

Of how she felt safe in his arms because this was a man who would never let anything hurt her. Hadn't he spent the past few days showing her just that, over and over again?

"You're touching me," she said softly as she ran her hands over his exposed forearms. The hair there was dark and soft and intensely male. Her blood pounded harder, demanding satisfaction as it coursed through her body.

She felt him swallow, then felt his lips move against her neck. "I am."

She turned her head toward him, her mouth only centimeters away from his cheek. She could press her lips against his skin if she wanted, but she waited. More than anyone she'd ever been with, she needed to make sure he wanted her to move, to touch, to *take*.

"Do you like touching me?"

He shifted his arms, grabbing her hands and holding them flat against her stomach so she couldn't pet him. "Yes," he growled.

She shivered, wanting to pull him down into her, wanting to unbutton his shirt and strip off his shorts and leave him well and truly bare to her. Just her and no one else. "Then touch me," she breathed against his skin.

"I don't want to hurt you." He sounded like a man begging for salvation.

She rested her head against his shoulder and he automatically supported her weight. "You won't. But if something's not right, I'll say—" she cast about for a word "—*sailboat*," she said as another boat came into view. "If I say that, you'll stop."

He didn't reply for the longest of seconds—so long, in fact, that she began to think he wasn't going to agree, either to the safe word or the sex. *"Sailboat?"* he finally asked, shifting his grip so that he held both her wrists in one hand. The other hand he set low against her stomach.

She arched her back, pushing her torso into his arms. "It's not a word I shout during sex a lot," she said with a smile.

He jolted as if she'd jabbed him with a needle, his grip tightening. She couldn't touch him, couldn't turn into him. All she could do was stand there, watching Lake Michigan shimmer in the summer heat.

"Jeannie." Her name on his lips was like a call to arms because this wasn't going to be some soft-focus, romantic intimacy marked by sweet words and tender touches. Oh, no.

Sex with Robert was going to be a battle.

She'd always loved a good fight.

Then he kissed her like it was a challenge and for the life of her, she couldn't figure out if he was throwing down the gauntlet for her or for himself. Either way, she met him as an equal on the field, kissing him back just as fiercely as he was kissing her. Their mouths met with a savageness that made her legs shake with need.

She nipped at his lower lip and felt the responding tension ripple through his body. Something hard and long and so, *so* hot began to push against her hip.

She began to pant as the tension spiraled in her body. He didn't loosen his grip on her, didn't give her anywhere else to go. And damn him, he didn't touch her anywhere else. He was holding himself back too carefully, so she bit him again. This time he growled and pulled away, burying his face against her neck. She felt his teeth skim over her skin so she angled her head to give him more.

"Yes," she whispered, hoping encouragement would help him get over this whole *don't want to hurt you* hang-up.

He bit her—gently—right at the spot where her shoulder met her neck. *"Yes,"* she hissed again. When was the last time she'd been this turned on? Every part of her body practically begged for his touch. "Oh, yes. Just like that."

"Don't," he growled against her neck. "Don't talk."

Even through the haze of desire, she laughed at the sheer ridiculousness of that order. "Seriously? Come on, Robert. Have you *met* me?"

"Please," he said. "I…need it to be different."

Different from what? She pulled away from him and he let her go. "But I thought you said you didn't…" He didn't have girlfriends or dates or people he brought back here. But he'd made it clear—he wasn't a virgin. He was breathing hard, panting almost, looking like he was being torn in two.

Oh, God—he really was going to break her heart, wasn't he?

"Okay," she told him. "Those are your rules? No touching, no talking?"

"I… Yes. Those are my rules."

Talking was almost half the fun and touching was definitely the other half. But she was getting a clearer picture of Robert all the time and she was beginning to think he hadn't had a normal, happy childhood. Neither had she, but she had to wonder—how much of what was happening here was Robert letting his scars finally show?

"Fine. My rule is that either one of us says *sailboat*, the other person stops immediately."

"That's it?"

"That's it." She nodded toward the other set of glass doors. This pair was behind a table and chairs set for two. "Is that your bedroom?"

"Yes." But he didn't move.

This man. Honestly, what was she going to do with him? "Can we use your bed?"

"Oh. Yes. Of course." This time he didn't hold out his hand and she didn't reach for him.

He unlocked the glass doors and led her into a masculine bedroom. The walls were a deep navy blue paper with a subtle blue-on-blue pattern. A fireplace with another marble mantel stood in the same spot where the one in the study had been, another impressive piece of art hanging over it.

But what really drew her eye was the massive four-poster bed. Truly, it was huge. She'd heard of California king beds but she'd never seen one in person and the bed probably took up more space than Melissa's whole room back home. Which would've been overwhelming enough but that didn't take into consideration the drapes. Around each of the four posts, airy white drapes were overlaid with pale blue damask that made it look almost like a fairy bed.

"I hope this is all right," Robert said, jamming his hands into his pockets.

"It's amazing and you're cute when you're nervous."

"I'm not nervous," he shot back in a way that was 100 percent nervous.

"That's good, because you're not cute, either." She took a step toward him. He didn't move back, but he inhaled sharply. Not nervous, her fanny. Besides the fireplace, she saw one of those wooden butler things men used to set out their suits. Over the shoulder of a royal blue jacket was a red silk tie. "Here," she said, stepping around him. She snatched up the tie, trying not to wince at the label—Armani, of course. She was about to permanently mangle a tie that probably cost a few hundred dollars.

But then again, this was Robert, who'd knocked down some of the most expensive real estate in the world so he could have a lake view. To hell with the tie.

She looped a quick slipknot around one wrist and turned back to him, her arms outstretched. "How about this? You can tie my wrists to make sure I don't grab you."

His mouth dropped open as color rushed to his cheeks and Jeannie took a perverse sort of pleasure in shocking him. He was barely hanging on to his control and after so many thousands of hours of watching him lock down every emotion, practically every response and expression, she was demolishing those walls.

"You— I—" He snapped his mouth shut and tried to straighten cuffs he wasn't wearing. *"No."*

"No?" She loosely wrapped the other end around her wrist and then lifted the tie to her mouth, letting the silk play over her lips. "Not even to keep me quiet?"

He had to grab one of the bedposts to keep upright. She smiled but didn't get any closer to him. Instead, she circled around him, kicking off her sandals. "Unless you wanted me to leave the shoes on?"

He managed to shake his head.

The bed was so damn big there was a little step stool at the foot of it. She climbed up onto the bed and walked to the center of it.

Robert's eyes never left hers. At this angle, he probably had a decent view of her legs and, if she twirled, maybe even her panties. She knelt on the bed and held out her hands. *"Robert.* Come to me."

"No," he said again, more forcefully. "I could hurt—"

"I don't believe that for a second," she interrupted. "You're not a damned monster, Robert, so stop acting like one. You're a man. And not even a cute one. You're the most gorgeous, complicated, outright *kind* man I've ever met and you're learning how to be a good hugger and you take care of babies and kids and I've spent literal actual years dreaming about you, about this moment. Besides, I'm not that breakable. I trust you."

"I don't trust myself," he ground out, clinging to the bedpost. "Don't you see? I…" He set his jaw. "You shouldn't trust me, either."

Oh, Robert. She let the tie drop away from her wrist and undid the slipknot as she pushed back to her feet.

"Fine," she told him. "Give me your hands."

He shot her a look of disbelief. "What?"

"Your hands. Don't talk. Just do it." For a second she didn't think he was going to do it. "You don't trust yourself? *Fine.* I'll tie you to the bedpost and then you won't be able to do anything."

Nine

Robert sucked in air as Jeannie got closer to him. "I'll tie you down and ride you hard. I won't talk and I won't touch you and you won't be able to do anything about it."

"Wyatts don't submit," he got out, sounding like she'd rabbit-punched him.

That sounded like…like something that had been said to him, but she couldn't think about what it meant right now. The look he gave her would've turned a lesser mortal to stone but she knew him far too well to let a well-placed glare put her off.

"Don't make me wait," she pleaded. Because if he said no…

"Would you really wait for me?" His voice was ragged.

She wasn't supposed to touch him—that was the rule. But she couldn't *not* touch him, not when he looked so desperately devastated. She touched the tips of her fingers to his forehead and, when he didn't pull away, she skimmed them down the sides of his face.

"Always," she whispered against his forehead. "I'll always wait for you. But trust me. Trust yourself."

He made a choked noise and pushed her away. She stumbled a little because this bed was so danged plush and yeah, she'd broken the rules and that was that. But when she got her balance back, she saw he'd held out his hands.

He didn't look at her. He kept his eyes down, shoulders back and yep, this was war. But she knew now—he wasn't fighting her.

He was fighting himself.

Oh, Robert.

She looped the silk tie around his wrists and then around the bedpost. Nothing was tight—if he wanted, he could twist his way free. But this wasn't about restraining him for safety, no matter how he tried to frame it like that.

This was about proving he could trust himself. Because he needed that. She was afraid to ask why.

The knot secured—sort of—she scooted off the edge of the bed so she could stand next to him. "Just to help you on the bed," she said softly as she put her hands on his shoulders.

The man was shaking as she turned him around and undid his belt and the fly of his shorts. For all his defensiveness, there was no mistaking that erection. Dear God, even contained behind his boxer briefs, Robert swelled upward, long and rock-hard. There was so much she wanted to say—that he was as impressive as hell, all the ways she'd dreamed of having him, asking him what he liked, telling him how to touch her—if only to break the oppressive silence of the room.

But she didn't because those were the rules. Instead, she focused on the harsh panting sound of his breathing, the way he tensed when her hand brushed along that impressive ridge. But she didn't palm him, didn't slip her hand inside his briefs. Hell, she didn't even push his briefs down. She could do that when she was on the bed.

She could explore quite a bit before he could get free. She could rip open his shirt and finally take what she wanted from him.

She didn't. He'd given her so much—his money, his time, peace of mind when it came to Melissa. But this? Robert was giving her the most precious gift of all.

His trust.

No way in hell was she going to abuse it.

So she guided him down onto the bed and then swung his legs up. "Scoot down," she said, keeping her voice low and calm. "Just—yeah, like that."

She was trembling, too, she realized. This man was broken in ways she was afraid to understand and definitely couldn't fix, but that wasn't the sum total of who he was. He was still Robert—thoughtful in his demands, overbearing in his caring, seductive in his intensity.

She arranged him so his legs pointed to the center of the bed—which left her plenty of room to work with.

"Okay?" she asked, watching him closely as she slid her panties off.

He nodded.

Okay, she thought, climbing back onto the bed and standing over him.

Even tied to the post, his pants undone and his color high, there was something so ethereal, almost otherworldly, about the way his pale eyes stared at her.

"Dress on or off?" she asked, lifting the hem.

His gaze snapped to where she'd exposed her sex and he inhaled sharply. "On."

Yeah, that didn't surprise her. She stepped over him, still holding on to the hem, letting him get a brief glimpse of her body. Heat flooded her sex as he stared at her hungrily, his hands trapped over his head. He made no move to get free.

She had one of the most formidable men in the city,

maybe even the whole country, at her mercy. The power was intoxicating.

She let her hem drop. Robert made a noise of need, in the back of his throat, but she didn't let him look again. Instead, she lowered herself to her knees, sitting on his thighs. "Okay?"

"Yes." His voice was deeper now as he stared at her breasts, and underneath his briefs, his erection jumped.

She pulled his briefs down, gasping as he sprung free. His length was proud, long and ruddy and curving slightly to the right. She wanted to wrap her hand around it and feel the hot skin sliding over his hardness, wanted to suck him deep into her mouth and let her tongue drive him wild until he broke.

But she'd promised, damn it all. So instead of exploring, she just said, "Condoms?"

He jerked his chin to the bedside table. "The drawer." Somehow, his voice was even deeper now. She felt it rumble throughout her body.

Oh, he was going to be so good.

She slid off him and, half sprawled across the massive mattress, got the box of condoms out of the drawer. The box was unopened, but the expiration date was several years off. Had he bought these just for her?

She got one out and opened the packet, then made her way back to Robert. As efficiently as she could, she rolled the condom on—although he kept twitching, which made it a bit of a challenge, she thought with a smile.

Then she scooted forward so his erection was right beneath her. She could feel him pulsing, sending little sparks of desire throughout her sex. She wanted to touch him so badly but because she couldn't, all her attention was focused on where their bodies met.

"Okay?"

He didn't hesitate. "Yes." If anything, he sounded a little surprised by that.

"Good." She began to rock her hips, letting his erection drag over her sensitive flesh without taking him inside. Her whole world narrowed to the way she moved, how she had to be careful with her balance. To the ragged sound of his breathing mingling with hers. To the splash of red around his wrists that stood out in the sea of blue. To the way he couldn't take his eyes off her.

This was the most erotic moment of her life.

She cupped her breasts through her dress, lifting them and tugging on the nipples. The sensation was dulled by the fabric and her bralette, but she didn't care. She tugged harder, her legs clenching around his hips, her weight bearing down on his erection. Robert groaned as she teased herself, his hips thrusting faster, his movements wilder.

Unexpectedly, an orgasm broke over her, showering her with stars. Moaning, her head dropped back. She would've toppled right off him if he hadn't shifted, bringing his knees up and catching her.

The sound of their panting filled the room. He pulsed against her swollen sex, hot and needy and unable to do a damn thing about it. When she could sit up again, she stared down at him with a dreamy smile on her face. "That was wonderful," she said. What she wouldn't give to lower herself to his chest and kiss him because orgasms like that didn't exactly grow on trees.

He growled. Because of course he did.

She *tsked* him as she lifted herself up and felt his erection rise to meet her. Slowly, she took him inside.

There was nothing else in the world but this. The slash of red above his head. The intense pale blue of his eyes. The cords of his neck straining as he filled her, inch by agonizingly wonderful inch. She bit back a cry of need because *oh, God* she'd never felt anything as wonderful as Robert inside her.

She sucked two of her fingers into her mouth and then lifted the hem of her dress just enough so she could press her slick digits against herself. Robert groaned again, trying to roll his hips, trying to thrust up into her, but she used all her weight to pin him to the mattress.

"Wait," she said, letting her fingers move in slow circles, brushing against where he was joined with her, adjusting to the fullness of him. "Just *be*, Robert. Be with me."

He nodded, a small movement. Maybe it was all he was capable of.

She kept her word. She didn't touch him, except where he was buried deep inside, except where her hips rested on his. She didn't moan or scream his name, didn't tell him what she wanted. She waited until his breathing had started to even out, just a little—until she was sure he had himself back under control and could focus on this intimacy between them.

She tightened her inner muscles around him, pleasure spiking hard and fast as he inhaled sharply. Even that small movement from him—she felt it travel up his length, felt her own body responding. She rubbed herself as she began to shift her hips, rising and falling on him at a languorous pace.

With her free hand, she went back to her breast. She pulled the neckline of the dress down, shoved the pink lace of the bralette aside and, after licking her thumb, began to tease her own nipple.

Robert's eyes were almost black now and he shifted underneath her, using his feet so he could thrust. But that wasn't it. As Jeannie stared down at him, she saw that he reached for the tie.

She froze, just managing to keep her balance. But instead of jerking at the knots, Robert gripped the loose ends of the tie and held on tighter. "Don't…stop, Jeannie." He swallowed. "Please."

Relief broke over her almost as potent as another climax. "There," she said, tugging at her nipple, pulling the hard tip until the most pleasurable pain rocketed through her. "Was that so hard?"

She felt him jolt deep inside her. Then, miracle of miracles, he smiled. Just that small movement of his lips, so tiny no one else would notice it. Just for her.

He was just for her.

This time, when he thrust up into her, she met him as his equal, taking his thrusts and setting her own slow rhythm. She kept rubbing herself, pulling at her nipple, feeling him straining for his release, refusing to make it easy for him. If she wanted to, she knew she could get him off in a matter of minutes. Seconds.

She had no idea if she'd ever get to have him like this again and she wasn't going to waste a single moment of their time together. This moment might have to last her the rest of her life.

She moved over him, fighting for control when all she wanted to do was fall upon him. The noises of sex filled their room, the slap of her flesh against his, their mingled breathing, the squeaking of the mattress.

The red of the tie, the dark desire of his eyes, the pressure on her sex, the way he moved inside her—perfect and strong and right. So, so right.

Oh, God. She gave first, pitching forward. She managed not to plant her hands on his chest, but it was a close thing. Instead, she braced her hands on the mattress and drove her hips down onto him faster and faster.

"Robert," she got out, her climax spiraling but not breaking—building, pushing her faster, slamming onto him harder and harder. "Oh, God."

"Jeannie."

She came apart at the need in his voice and then she kissed him as her orgasm robbed her of thought, of the ability to hold herself apart from him. She kissed him in victory and in defeat, for love and for loss.

She kissed *him*.

He groaned into her mouth, a noise of satisfaction, of completion. He groaned and pistoned his hips up into her before holding and straining and she took him in, all of him. Everything he had, she took—and it all pushed her orgasm even higher. She couldn't help it when she tore herself away from him, throwing back her head as she peaked.

Then she collapsed onto his chest, struggling to get enough air. She barely had the energy to pull herself free of him. "Oh, Robert," she sighed, snuggling down into his chest.

She felt the sharp intake of his breath, felt his hands on her arms as he moved her off his body. He didn't follow her, didn't cover her with his weight.

All she saw was Robert's back as the door slammed shut. He was gone.

Ten

Robert stood at the top of the stairs. He needed to go to Jeannie. Maybe apologize. Maybe wrap his arms around her and kiss her again.

Probably both.

He couldn't move.

He saw a shadow cross the terrace. Ah. She'd gone outside. Pulled by the lake, no doubt. He was glad she liked his view. He hoped she approved of him buying the land and donating the cleared spaces to the city.

Would she be here long enough to see the stars?

He slipped into his room and grabbed new clothes. Aside from the faint scent of oranges, there was no trace of her in the room. The tie had been returned to its starting place. The bed sheets had been straightened; the condom wrapper gone. Even her shoes had been removed.

Strangely, he found himself longing for her to leave her mark.

Silently, he got cleaned up and changed and then stood, watching her through the open doors.

She'd opened the wine. Hadn't needed his help at all. Of course she didn't—she was a bartender. And she'd found the kitchenette, where Darna had undoubtedly had all the food arranged in containers that kept it warm.

Robert wasn't sure how long he stood there, watching Jeannie through the doorway. She looked…the same. Beautiful, but the same.

He envied her that.

It wasn't until she went to refill her wineglass that he moved. He stepped out onto the terrace. "Here," he said, his voice gruff but unable to do anything about it.

She didn't seem surprised when he appeared, nor when he pulled the bottle out of her hand. "I know how to pour wine," she scolded, but at least there was no acid in her voice. He dared to hope she sounded amused.

"You've served me for years," he replied, pleased to see that his hands weren't shaking. Surgeon's hands should always be steady. "It's my turn to serve you."

He saw her smile, but she didn't look at him. Instead, she kept her gaze fixed on the lake.

Robert topped up her glass and then poured a healthy glass for himself because he could use a drink, he realized. Then he put a little chicken on a dish. He wasn't hungry. He rarely ate lunch. But moving around the terrace gave him something to do.

Normally, Robert was fine with silence. He worked in silence. He read at night with nothing but the faint sounds of the city wafting through his terrace doors. He was old friends with quiet.

But at this exact moment, the fact that Jeannie wasn't talking bothered him.

He pushed his food around his plate. She ate silently. They both drank their wine.

"You can talk now," he finally blurted out, feeling ridiculous.

"No," she said slowly, "I've already said my piece. It's your turn."

He forced himself to breathe slowly, to keep his pulse from running away. He was just…overwhelmed by the new sensations, that was all. He'd never dined with company on the terrace. Never shared his view with anyone. Never brought someone to his bed. Never let his arms be tied.

It was a lot to take in. That was all.

Then he was talking. Words flowed out of his mouth as easily as wine flowed from the bottle. "Something changed when I was fourteen," he was horrified to hear himself say. But it was too late. The bottle had been smashed and he couldn't contain the spill. Not around her. Not anymore. "I grew, I guess. *He* called me into his office. It was never good, being called down. Always bad."

Out of the corner of his eye, he saw her grip tighten on her glass. But all she said was, "Oh?" And strangely, that made it easier to keep going because that was what she would've said if they'd been at the bar, shielded by the dim lights.

It was bright out, but the small table stood between them.

"This time there was a woman there. She…" He swallowed, but kept going. "She wasn't wearing much. She was pretty."

Shame burned through him as he remembered his confusion. He'd been braced for threats, for pain. But not for a woman in a slip and nothing else.

"He said—" Robert drained his glass "—I was a man now. I needed to know how to treat a woman, how to dominate."

Jeannie inhaled sharply. She didn't say anything, though. And for once, Robert hated the silence.

"He made me touch her. Kiss her. He wanted me to…"

He took a breath, trying to find the words without remembering all the terrible details. "And when I couldn't…"

Unexpectedly, Jeannie stood. Before Robert could process what she was doing, she'd plucked his plate and glass from his hand. Wine dripped from his fingertips. He hadn't realized his hands were shaking.

She sat sideways in his lap, burying her face against his neck, and it should've been awful because he didn't like to be touched and *never* talked about why but she was touching him and he was talking.

He couldn't stop.

"He pulled me off the woman and told me to watch. Then he showed me what he wanted me to do."

Jeannie's arms tightened around his neck and he realized he was gathering her closer, holding her like he was afraid she would rip herself away from him.

He didn't allow himself to think of that day. He was very good at controlling his reactions, and those memories weren't allowed.

But now?

He remembered everything. The woman's muffled screams. The way his father had smiled. The familiar guilt that, if he'd only done what Landon had wanted, he might've protected her. The realization that he couldn't protect any woman.

Only the knowledge that he would've been beaten senseless for displaying weakness had kept him from leaving the room.

"Breathe," Jeannie whispered against his skin. "It's okay. I'm here. Just breathe."

He wasn't sure his lungs would ever properly draw in air again. "I told my mother what'd happened. I shouldn't have because it wasn't safe. If you were too happy, too sad, too angry—he didn't like it. But I couldn't keep it inside.

I *couldn't*...and she was so mad that she marched into his office, screaming and throwing things and..."

And Landon had exacted his revenge in a thousand small cuts. He'd been exacting that revenge with interest over the past three years, no doubt.

"Did it ever happen again?" Jeannie asked softly.

Out on the lake, a speedboat raced through his view and was gone. "Not right away." His mother's anger had somehow bought Robert a few months of grace.

"Oh, Robert." Something wet and warm ran over his skin as she held him. She didn't push him aside, didn't look at him with disgust. "What did your mom do after the next time?"

"I didn't tell her." Robert hadn't been willing to risk his mother. So he'd buried his disgust and horror and tried to be the man Landon wanted.

He almost laughed. If Landon could've seen him a few short minutes ago, tied to the bed and helpless while Jeannie gave him the gift of her tenderness, her touch—the gift of herself—the old man might just have had a stroke.

Even more so if he heard what Robert was going to say next. "I was overwhelmed when you kissed me. Earlier. I..."

That kiss had been perfect and terrifying. He'd wanted to never let go of her and he hadn't been able to leave fast enough and it had not been his finest moment.

"It's okay," she said softly. "I'm fine. I broke the rule. I'm sorry."

He pulled her in closer because he liked her there. "Me, too."

Oh, how Landon Wyatt would mock him for that apology, even if it barely qualified as such.

He didn't know how long they sat there. The sun glittered off his own personal view of the lake. Finally, he heard himself say, "I haven't seen her in almost three years. My mother, that is."

He had no reason to tell Jeannie any of this. What had happened in his bed earlier...that hadn't come with the obligation that he owed her the truth.

But he couldn't stop himself.

"What happened?" Jeannie asked softly.

The sun began to dip behind the buildings, casting the sky in deeper shades of gold. No matter what happened—who lived, who died or who walked the fine line between the two states—the sun rose and set every day. It kept going. Just like he did.

"She wouldn't stay with me. He'd beaten her badly and I brought her here. But she didn't trust me to keep her safe. She went back to him and..." He swallowed around the rock lodged in his throat.

"When was this?"

"The day I walked into Trenton's."

The day he'd been utterly lost had been the day he'd found Jeannie. It hadn't been an accident. It couldn't have been something as random as a coincidence.

She'd been waiting for him.

She gasped, drawing air across his throat like a caress.

"Will you get to see her again?" Her voice wavered and Robert prayed she wouldn't cry. There was no point to tears. Never had been.

"That's why I have to go to the campaign kickoff. He's using her as bait so I will pretend we're this perfect happy family."

"To lie for him, the asshole." This time she sounded mad. Strangely, her anger made Robert feel better. "What are you going to do?"

"If she'll come, I'll take her away. Send her where he can't get to her."

Jeannie leaned back. He could tell she was staring up at him, but he couldn't look at her, couldn't risk drowning in her brown eyes. He kept staring at the water. "You're not going to bring her *here*, are you? You can't hope that this time she'll walk away just because she has a weak spot for tacky wallpaper."

He almost smiled because he hadn't just spilled his deepest, most shameful secrets. He'd told Jeannie. Somehow, that made things better. "Of course not. I'm sending her to New Zealand." Now he did look down at her. The impact of her watery eyes hit him square in the chest. "That was why I needed to talk to you, the night you weren't there. I had to see you. I needed…" He brushed her short hair away from her eyes. "I needed to know I was doing the right thing."

Because he was technically going to be kidnapping his mother and he didn't doubt that she might hate him, at least a little. Not to mention Landon might punish him and get Cybil back.

The man would try.

But Robert wasn't a kid anymore. Lawyers, accountants, reporters—all were eager to be a part of what had the potential to be the biggest scandal in Chicago since Al Capone had run this town. And Robert was pulling all the strings.

It was time Landon knew what Wyatts were truly capable of.

"You are," Jeannie said simply. "You're absolutely doing the right thing, Robert." She cupped his face in her hands. "What happened before—that was *never* your fault. And you're not like him. He didn't break you, do you understand? You're stronger than he is. You always were. He knows it, too, I think."

Robert's eyes stung, so he closed them. He wanted desperately to believe what Jeannie said. Wanted to feel the truth of it in his bones.

But if he was really that strong, he would've been able to keep Mom safe all these years. And he hadn't.

Jeannie pushed off his lap, pulling him to his feet. Silently, she led him back into his bedroom. For some reason, she stripped him down to his boxers and then pulled her dress over her head. But instead of removing the pretty lingerie she wore, she turned down the sheet and pushed him into bed. He didn't resist. He couldn't. Whatever she was doing, he needed it. He needed her. So he made space for her and she climbed in after him, pulling the sheet over them both.

Then she curled into his side. "I can't stay to see the stars. Not tonight," she murmured, her breath warm against his chest. "I have to get back to Melissa."

His arms tightened around her even as he forced himself to say, "Of course," even though he wanted to argue.

How very odd. He *wanted* her to stay. All the more so when she threw a bare leg over his, tangling their limbs together. It felt…right. Good, even.

"But Robert?"

"Yes?"

Something warm and soft pressed against his chest. A kiss. One of forgiveness, he hoped. "I won't let you face him alone." Before he could process what she could be talking about—because she couldn't *possibly* be suggesting that she would voluntarily place herself anywhere near Landon Wyatt—she leaned up on one elbow and stared down at him with a look he couldn't identify. "I'm coming with you to the kickoff."

Eleven

Jeannie hadn't seen Robert since he'd walked her to her door three nights ago, kissed the back of her hand like an old-fashioned prince and then been driven off by an absolutely beaming Reginald.

She knew he was talking to Maja or Rona or both. Like when Maja said, "Dr. Wyatt wants you to make sure you're getting fresh air, so let me show you how to use this stroller."

Or when Rona said, "Dr. Wyatt asked me to make sure you're enjoying the meals? I can cook other things, as well," as if anyone would turn down real Filipino cooking, which Rona prepared every other day when she came to tidy the already spotless house and do the laundry. Even the next-day leftovers were fabulous. If Jeannie had been on her own, she would've been living on frozen pizza and beer.

But Robert didn't ask *her* how she enjoyed the meals or the walks or the time with Melissa. He didn't talk to her at all and her texts thanking him for a nice time went unanswered. Which was unnerving. Jeannie knew he was busy—

with his practice or Wyatt Medical or making plans for his mother. She refused to think that he was avoiding her because she'd tied him up or kissed him or listened to his secrets. He wasn't a chatty man to begin with. She could see that he simply wouldn't know how to strike up a conversation after what they'd shared.

But after another day of silence passed, she began to wonder if he was trying to keep her from going to the kick-off. And she had no intention of letting him do that.

So instead of small talk, she went to war over text. And it turned out, he was downright chatty.

What time on Saturday?

No.

Yes. I'm coming with you.

You are not. It's not safe for you.

It's not safe for you, either.
Why should you face him alone?
You need backup.

Absolutely not. I won't risk you like that.

Jeannie smiled at that one, pausing to rub Melissa's back. They were snuggled up on the couch and the house was silent. Maja wasn't here. Rona would be back tomorrow. It was just Jeannie and a drowsy infant.

A week ago this situation would've inspired sheer panic, but now? Jeannie let the baby's warmth sink into her chest as Melissa dozed. She still had no idea how she would handle raising a child when Robert stopped paying a small army of people to help her but she was at least no longer panick-

ing at the thought of holding her niece. As long as Melissa
got the right formula and stayed swaddled while she slept,
things were better.

I won't risk you, either.

I'm not taking you.
End of discussion.

Then I'll just crash the party.

No, Jeannie.

She chuckled softly to herself. She could hear his exasperated tone, see him glowering at his phone. He could get
anyone to do anything he wanted with a snap of his fingers
and money—anyone but her.

Yes, she'd talked to Miranda at Trenton's. Robert had
handed over a credit card and rumor had it that Julian had
run that sucker for thirty thousand dollars and Robert hadn't
disputed the charge.

Robert hadn't been back since. Which was fine by Miranda. She didn't care how hot and rich Robert was, she
wasn't dealing with him ever again, she'd said. Miranda
had related the whole thing in breathless, disbelieving tones
but Jeannie believed it all. Thirty thousand was nothing to
Robert.

"He's freaking *terrifying*," Miranda had said.

Jeannie had just laughed. As far as she could tell, no one
at work had any idea that Robert had appointed himself her
guardian angel—or that they'd shared a wonderful, messy
evening together.

I *will* crash.
I've been sneaking into parties and clubs since I was 14.

I'll show up in my yellow dress and be loud and obnoxious.
Trust me I'm good at it.

No.

You can't keep me away so just accept that you're tak-
ing me.
If you take me, you can keep an eye on me.
Who knows what kind of trouble I'll get into otherwise?
Might step on a candidate's toes or splash red wine on
his face.

Jesus.

Whoopsie.

Robert didn't answer that salvo right away but Jeannie
let the space build between them. Melissa grunted in her
sleep, warm and perfect and okay. She was seventeen days
old today. It'd been ten days since Nicole had died, nine
days since Jeannie had brought this baby home and eight
days since Robert had turned out to be the star she'd wished
upon. Today was the first day Maja wasn't living in the
house full-time.

The next time Jeannie was at Robert's house—assuming
he invited her back—she wasn't leaving until she'd seen the
night horizon over the lake.

She could almost see Nicole walking into the small living room, trying her best not to roll her eyes or let fly with
a cutting comment about how this was exactly what Jeannie always did—rushing into something *way* over her head
without thinking.

"You're trouble," Nicole had always said. "And like fol-
lows like."

When Jeannie had been a little girl, Nicole had hissed it

at Jeannie with pure venom, usually seconds before she got Jeannie in trouble. Maybe there'd been a time when Nicole had set Jeannie up—shoving a ruined sweater under Jeannie's bed and then blaming it on Jeannie.

All Jeannie could really remember was deciding that if she was going to get into trouble, she was going to *earn* it.

After their mom had died and it was just Nicole, still only seventeen, and Jeannie, barely ten, Nicole had kept on saying it. But the hatred had changed, deepened. Now Jeannie could look back and see the pure fear Nicole must have been living with, an unwelcome guest who refused to leave. The same fear Jeannie had been stuck in when she'd wished upon a star.

Jeannie had kept right on getting into trouble. Parties, boys, alcohol—driving her sister to the breaking point. They'd both been relieved when Jeannie had packed a bag and left.

Then, when the two of them had finally reconciled, after Nicole had decided she was having a family come hell or high water, Nicole had still said that. Jeannie was still trouble. But now Nicole had said it with almost fondness, and instead of hearing it as an attack, Jeannie heard what Nicole was really saying.

I'm sorry. I'm glad you're here. I love you.

That was how Jeannie chose to remember Nicole. Someone who was complicated, who did the best she could with what she had—a missing dad, a dead mom, a hellion for a sister.

I'm sorry, Jeannie thought. Hopefully, wherever Nicole was, she would know the truth. *I'm glad you were here. I'm doing the best I can. I love you.*

Jeannie's phone chimed again.

I can't allow this.

Oh, wasn't that just like the man? If he were in front of her, she'd be hard-pressed to pick between strangling and hugging him. Hell, maybe she'd just tie him to the bed again and work through some of the frustration he inspired.

He was a very inspiring man.

It'd been three days since their lunch date. Three days since the unreachable, untouchable Dr. Robert Wyatt had let himself be touched. Since he'd held out his hands for her and she'd ridden him in silence. Since he'd shared his darkest secret.

He'd done so much for her and Melissa and all Jeannie had ever done for him was serve him the perfect Manhattan. She might not be able to provide material comfort for the man but by God, she could help him face his demons.

Specifically, one demon.

Like followed like, after all. But this time she promised herself it would be good trouble. The plan was simple. Back up Robert. Help his mom. Hell, protect the good people of Illinois from a damn monster.

Really, it was going to be one hell of a party.

She shifted Melissa so she could text faster.

Robert. I am not your employee.
You don't ALLOW me to do anything.
Let me be there for you.
It's not weakness to accept help.

I can't ask this of you.

You're not asking.

This is not an obligation.

I'm coming. Let me come with you.

Melissa stirred, pushing against her blanket. The little noises she made—Maja had said those were hungry noises. Jeannie glanced at the clock—right on schedule. Who knew babies had schedules? But this baby did, thanks to a stand-in grandmother and by God, Jeannie wasn't going to screw that up. Which meant she couldn't lie around texting much longer.

Robert. Let me come with you. Please.

You can't wear the yellow dress.
This is a formal event.

I don't have anything more formal.
Unless you want me to wear my vest and bow tie?

Lord.
I will send some things over.
If we're going to do this, we're going to do it right.
He can't know who you really are.

I can blend. Promise.

The typing bubble showed for a long time but Jeannie knew she'd won. She absolutely could blend. She'd been serving the upper crust drinks for years now. She knew the mannerisms, the topics the one percent discussed. She could be just as obnoxious and ostentatious as Robert's wallpapered ceilings or as cold and aloof as Robert himself. She could absolutely fake it until she made it, whatever form *it* took.

It couldn't be a small lie because those were obvious and easy to disprove. To pull one over on someone like Landon Wyatt, it'd have to be a grand lie, so bold and ostentatious that no one would dare question her or her place on Robert's arm. She'd have to not just belong there—she'd also have to own the room.

She glanced at the book on her coffee table. *To Dare a Duke.* Hmm.

Of course, it all depended on what she'd be wearing. Heaven only knew what Robert would be sending this time.

Finally, the typing bubble disappeared but instead of a long paragraph of text, all that popped up were two little words that made her grin wildly.

Thank you.

There. Was that so hard?

Saturday at six.

I'll be waiting.

He didn't reply, but then, he didn't need to. He'd said *thank you.* For Robert, that was the equivalent of a regular dude standing outside her bedroom window with a boom box blaring '80s love songs.

Melissa fussed more insistently and Jeannie struggled to her feet. She had to feed the baby and check her diaper and then?

Then she had to get ready for Saturday night.

She had a date with the hottest bachelor in Chicago and she had a feeling that, before it was all over, she was going to see stars.

Twelve

Robert was not nervous because he was a Wyatt and Wyatts didn't get nervous. Anxiety was a symptom of uncertainty, and Wyatts were confident and sure at all times.

So the sense of unease, the sweaty palms, the unsettled stomach—absolutely not nerves. He wasn't concerned about how tonight would go. He had no worries about the traps he'd laid and how it'd all unfold in the public eye. He was confident he could get his mother away and handle Landon.

Robert was positive he could handle himself. Which was why he wasn't nervous at all.

He was excited to see what the stylists had done with Jeannie, that was all. Kelly had sent over a team of three people—hair, makeup and clothes. He anticipated seeing her dressed for his world.

God, he *missed* her.

It'd been a week since he'd brought her into his home. Seven days since he'd allowed her to touch him. Allowed himself to take comfort in another person. All he'd focused on in that time was laying the groundwork to remove the threat that was Landon Wyatt.

Missing her was more familiar now, a sensation he recognized. It was the same feeling that had thrown him off the night she hadn't appeared at the bar. The same longing that had gripped him after he'd brought her home after their date.

Date. Ha. As if that word got anywhere close to accurately describing their afternoon together. Something as simple as lunch didn't leave him a changed man.

And she had changed him, damn her.

The strange thing was…well, he'd missed her. Not just the way she talked to—or texted—him, although he did miss that because no one else dared argue with him. But then, no one else listened like she did, either.

Because of what she'd done—what he'd *let* her do—he had achieved something he'd always assumed to be beyond him.

Sex with Jeannie had been different. So very different, in fact, that he'd been able to keep it separate from his previous experiences. He'd stayed in the moment. Did she have any idea how unusual that was? Of course not. But he'd been lost to the way the silk had bitten into his skin, the way she'd ground down onto him, her weight warm and slick and silent. Perhaps too silent but after all those times marked by fake moans and real screams, it'd been a gift.

She'd given him the gift of something new, something real. He'd watched her take her pleasure, her body drawing his in, tightening around him, and she'd been raw and honest and even now, after a week, it still left him wanting more.

Which was bad.

Wasn't tonight proof? She'd left him in a weakened position, one where he allowed her to convince him to bring her to meet his parents, of all the damn things.

He wasn't entirely sure he wasn't losing his grip. Because Robert Wyatt would've never agreed to this. Introducing her to Landon was not just a bad idea—it carried real risks for Jeannie. For them both.

Reginald parked in front of Jeannie's little house and some of what was definitely not nervousness eased. Well. It was too late to turn back now. The plans had been set into motion. The newspaper photographer and guards were already in place. Kelly, Robert's assistant, had a plane on standby.

And Robert had personally interviewed the nurse, a young single woman with impressive grades, exceptional references, a valid passport and a desire to see the world, in addition to numerous outstanding student loans and a sister who had no means of affording higher education. She had been more than willing to relocate to a foreign country for six to twelve months at the salary and signing bonus Robert was offering.

Perhaps tonight would go well. He would get his mother to leave with him and, ideally, they'd show the world who Landon Wyatt really was.

They'd just need a distraction.

Would Jeannie really throw a glass of wine into Landon's face? Oh, who was he kidding? Of course she would. The better question was, what else would she do?

This was madness.

Reginald opened Robert's door and he stood, surveying the scene before him. Good. The yard had been trimmed and he was fairly certain there were new shrubs around the foundation. The housepainters were due to start after the roofers had finished, which was scheduled for next week.

He almost smiled as he strode up the sidewalk. Jeannie's little house was small and cramped and no one would ever accuse it of conveying wealth or power or even taste but… there was something he liked about climbing those three simple steps, about the way her door swung open before he could ring the bell, about seeing her…

Everything came to a sudden halt. His breathing, his heart, his forward movement—all stopped.

"Robert." She smiled, this goddess, blessing him with her benevolent kindness. "I've been waiting for you."

Oh, dear God. He had to catch himself on the railing to keep from stumbling back. *"Jeannie?"*

The goddess's eyebrow notched up as she grinned at him and then it all snapped back into place and he could see Jeannie underneath the dramatic makeup, the big hair and that *dress*.

"Well?" she said with what sounded like a knowing smirk. He couldn't tell for sure because he was too busy staring at *that dress*. She did a little turn. "What do you think?"

Robert lurched forward, grabbing on to the door frame. A wave of lust, pure and intense, nearly brought him to his knees. He'd seen her body dressed in nothing but those lacy pink underthings. Seen the trimmed swath of dark hair that covered her sex, watched in fascination as her fingers had stroked over it while he strained to be deeper inside her, more a part of her.

But he'd never seen her like *this*.

His bartender was nowhere to be seen. Instead, Jeannie had been completely transformed. Her short hair had been blown out so that it crowned her head, a far cry from the sleek style she normally wore. Her eyes were dark and mysterious, lips two shades darker than the red dress. Diamonds dripped off her ears and an enormous diamond teardrop pendant hung nestled between her breasts, which were barely contained by the vee of her dress that went almost to her waist. The rest of the dress clung to her hips and legs in a way that could only be described as *indecent*.

She was bold and scandalous and, most important, completely unrecognizable.

She was perfect.

"Hmm," she mused, her lips forming a little pout. He noticed, which meant he'd apparently stopped staring at her body. "I do believe I've stunned you speechless. It's quite different from your normal silence." She touched the tip of her tongue to her top lip. Robert had to bite back a groan. "Yes," she practically hummed and he realized he barely recognized her voice. She bit off her vowels differently, held herself taller. Although maybe it was the dress? "*Quite* different."

Maja appeared from the baby's room. "See?" she clucked in that grandmotherly way. "I told you it'd work."

Jeannie beamed and there she was again, *his* Jeannie. "I was afraid the dress was too much—to say nothing of the danged diamonds, Robert," she explained, as if Robert had asked a question when all his brain wanted to do was peel that dress off her and get lost in her body again. And again. And again, until nothing else mattered. "The stylists brought a black one but—"

"But with her coloring—" Maja added. Dimly, Robert realized she was holding the baby "—red was the obvious color," she concluded, sounding triumphant. "The color of luck."

"Yes," he managed to agree. Somehow.

Jeannie turned back to him and she was different again. He couldn't say how, but she was. "And you," she said, her hips swaying indecently as she moved toward him. "That's quite a tuxedo you're filling out there, Robert." She reached out and straightened his tie.

He nodded, which was probably not the correct reaction but it was all he had. What had she texted him?

She could blend. She'd promised.

By God, this was not blending. And he couldn't care less.

"Go on now," Maja said, scooping something off the coffee table and handing it to Jeannie. A handbag, small and black and sparkling. "Enjoy your night. I'll be here the whole time so…"

Her words trailed off and Robert realized the nanny was giving them both permission not to come home.

Well. He did pay her for going above and beyond, didn't he?

He nodded again, this time managing to find his usual imperiousness. Jeannie smoothed his lapels, sending licks of fire over his chest. But then she notched an eyebrow at him again and he saw the challenge in her eyes.

"Thank you," he added. Maja inclined her head in acknowledgment.

Jeannie beamed up at him and it took every last bit of self-restraint he had not to pull her into his arms and mess up her lipstick. This time he wanted to touch her, to see her body bared completely. By candlelight. He wanted to feel her hands on him. He wanted to taste her, every single part, his lips on her skin, inside her body.

To hell with the perfect Manhattan. He would be forever drunk on her.

"We should go," she said softly in that strange voice of hers, giving his lapels a pat.

"Yes," he said, barely recognizing his own voice.

She turned and walked—swayed—back to Maja. "Be good tonight, sweetie," she said, brushing her fingertips over Melissa's head. "Love you."

Robert had to grip the door frame again because this was something new and real and he didn't know how to make sense of it, this display of maternal affection. There was something so right about Jeannie looking down at the baby with such tenderness.

Then she turned back to him, a sultry smile playing across her lips. "Shall we?"

"Yes," he repeated again.

"Have fun!" Maja called out after them.

* * *

Working in silence, Cybil applied the thick foundation liberally, blending it all the way down her neck. Lupe, her maid, spread it over Cybil's back and shoulders, covering the bruises. They hadn't faded yet and if Landon saw any trace of his violence…

It'd be so much easier if she could wear a dress with a jacket, but Landon had chosen a deep blue gown for her to wear tonight and of course it was off the shoulder, with an attached capelet. Elegant and sophisticated—and it left her décolletage and shoulders bare.

Lupe finished with the makeup and began to fix Cybil's hair into an upswept French twist. They worked in silence. In theory, Lupe's English was not very good, which made conversation difficult. In practice, Cybil had learned long ago not to trust a single person on staff.

Tonight she was going to see Bobby again. He was coming, his assistant had assured Landon's assistant, Alexander. He *would* be there. She would see her son with her own eyes, see that he was healthy and whole and, she dared to hope, happy, even. That she'd kept him safe by staying, by keeping Landon away from Bobby.

She dared to hope that Bobby had forgiven her for leaving. That he understood she'd done so to protect him.

She dared to hope…

But she did not allow any of this hope to show. No excitement danced in her eyes as she watched Lupe work in the mirror. She was resigned to her role as hostess for the gala, a role she could perform effortlessly. She was prepared to act the politician's wife, smiling widely as her husband lied through his teeth about how he cared for this state, this city, the millions of people whose lives he could improve—or ruin. She'd had years of practice, after all.

And if Bobby offered her shelter again…

She couldn't go to his home. She couldn't risk him like

that again. But surely, he knew that. Surely, he wouldn't make the same mistake again.

Dear Lord, Cybil prayed, *please don't let me make the same mistake again, either.*

There had to be a way.

"Are you breathing?" Jeannie asked as the car crawled through downtown traffic.

She stroked her thumb over Robert's knuckles. He had a hell of a grip on her hand. She'd explained the persona she was adopting tonight and she could tell he wasn't 100 percent on board. Not that she could blame him.

This was, hands down, the craziest thing she'd ever done.

"Yes," he said after a long moment in which she was pretty sure he hadn't breathed. "I'm fine."

"I doubt it." She saw a quick flash of teeth. "Is there a plan? Because I can wing it but this sort of feels like one of those situations where a plan would be a good idea." After another few seconds, she added, "Sharing it would be an even better idea."

His grip tightened on her hand and she had to work hard not to gasp. "Reginald will be parked by the service entrance in the basement, engine running. There's a service elevator in the back, next to the restrooms. It's down a short hallway." He cleared his throat, sounding painfully nervous. "If I can get her to come with me, we'll leave without a look back."

She thought on that for a moment as she fiddled with the heavy diamond pendant. The rock alone was probably worth more than she made in a year, not to mention the earrings or the dress. A Valentino dress, for God's sake! She was easily wearing thirty, forty thousand dollars' worth of fabric and diamonds. Which was not a huge deal to Robert but, if she let herself think about it too much, it would easily freak her the heck out.

But tonight she wouldn't fret about cost or Robert's

world. Tonight she was going to waltz into that gala party on his arm like she owned the damn room and if it took three stylists, diamonds and a Valentino to do it, so be it. "So I'm to…what, distract your father while you two make a run for the airport?"

"God, no—you stick with me." He pulled his hand free and—shockingly—adjusted his cuffs. "You are not to be alone with him under any circumstances. Ever."

She almost rolled her eyes at his tone. "I can handle myself, Robert. I've been fending off drunks and avoiding wandering hands since I was a teenager. Don't worry."

His head swung around and even in the dark interior of the car, she shivered at his intensity. "You are *not* to be alone with him, Jeannie." His voice was dangerously quiet, all the more menacing for it. *"Ever."*

"O…kay. So how do we know he won't follow us?"

"He won't want to make a scene. The whole point of tonight is to put on a public performance."

She mulled over the options. "What if—and I'm just throwing this out there—what if I can get your mom alone? Like, we go to the ladies' room together. You can stay behind to keep an eye on your father and I can get her to the car." Assuming Mrs. Wyatt would go with Jeannie. A complete stranger.

But it would be easy to get her alone. She needed a drink. One that stained would be best.

Robert's expression reflected doubt. "Reginald knows where to go. Everything else is ready. Take her and leave." He leaned over, his fingertips barely brushing over her cheek. "Just be safe. I… I can't bear the thought of anything happening to you."

Oh, Robert. "Listen to me, you stubborn man. I will be fine. It's you I'm worried about." He was already a mess. The average person wouldn't be able to tell, but she knew. His voice was rough and he was straightening his cuffs *again*. Worst of all, his leg had begun to jump. "If you can get an opening, promise me you'll take it. Send me two texts in a row—so I know you're gone and I'll get away. Trust me, Robert. Don't worry."

"I'm a Wyatt," he said sternly as the car pulled up in front of a building right off the Magnificent Mile, as if that was the cure for the world's ills. "We never worry." But then the hard lines of his face softened and the very corners of his lips curved up in a faint smile. "Ready to crash a party?"

She grinned. "Hell, yes."

Reginald opened the door for them, his normally jovial face a blank mask. Robert handed her out of the car and then tucked her fingers into the crook of his arm. Then he murmured, "Be ready," as they passed and Reginald nodded smartly before closing the door behind them.

A crush of people waited to get through security. The crowd was a sea of black—black tuxedos, black gowns—Jeannie was suddenly glad she'd gone with the red. Her role was to be a distraction and in this dress, she stood out like a siren. Seriously, her boobs in this dress were practically works of art. For how much this dress cost, they damn well better be.

Jeannie squared her shoulders, lifted her chin and tried to look bored as Robert cut through the crowd. A weaselly-looking man with thinning hair stood at the front of the line.

Robert leaned down to whisper in her ear, "Alexander, Landon's loyal assistant."

She nodded, sticking close to Robert's side. Loyal? In other words, this was not a person to be trusted. It was easy to look all icy and disapproving when that was exactly how she felt.

When the weasel caught sight of Robert, he waved them past security, calling, "Dr. Wyatt? This way." Someone in line started to protest, but Robert swung around, daring anyone to complain with a cold glare. Jeannie tried to match his look.

The crowd fell oddly silent in the face of Robert's displeasure. Somewhere nearby, a camera flashed.

Which was good because Jeannie needed to remember that she wasn't here with Robert, a complicated and conflicted man who cared for sick children and infants and who had literally been the answer to her prayers. No, she was here with Dr. Robert Wyatt, of the Chicago Wyatts, a billionaire bachelor and one of the most powerful, dangerous men in the state.

Time to own this room.

She let her gaze slide over the people she passed as if she couldn't be bothered to see them. Alexander led them through the crowd, up a spiral staircase. She was barely able to keep up with Robert's long strides in the strappy black sandals the stylist had put her in to go with this dress.

But even if she didn't acknowledge the other party-goers, she could feel their reactions as she and Robert moved effortlessly through their ranks. People stopped and stared as they passed, but the moment they'd gone by, the loud whispers started.

Hadn't there been rumors of a falling-out between the elder Wyatt and the younger?

How gauche that Wyatt dirtied his hands practicing medicine.

And who was *she*?

Dear God, was Jeannie really doing this? This was more than just crashing a gala. This was pulling a fast one over on the person who could put the fear of God into Robert.

She stiffened her spine. Go big or go home.

"This way," Alexander said. He glanced at Jeannie and she stared down her nose at him, daring him to make a comment about Robert bringing a date.

He didn't. Instead, he led them to where a handsome

man, almost as tall and almost as broad as Robert, was holding court. Landon Wyatt, billionaire gubernatorial candidate and total asshole. Not that anyone else would know it. All the tuxedoed men and glamorous women around him laughed heartily at his jokes, champagne flutes in hand, gems glittering at their necks and wrists and ears.

They sounded like jackals. Maybe they were. Thank God she didn't recognize any of them as customers from Trenton's.

Next to Landon stood an elegant older woman, smiling brightly and occasionally touching her husband on the arm or shoulder as he talked, as if she had to let him know where she was at all times. As Alexander wormed his way through to the inner circle, Robert's mother caught sight of them.

Although the crowd was too loud to hear Cybil Wyatt, Jeannie physically *felt* the woman's sharp inhalation, saw the overwhelming longing in her eyes.

Alexander tugged on Landon Wyatt's sleeve and motioned to Robert with his chin. By the time Landon turned to his wife, her face was carefully blank.

Wyatt's face was how Jeannie might've imagined kings of old looking when a foreign dignitary dared grace his throne room. "Ah, here he is. Robert, my boy, how have you been?"

Jeannie felt the tension in Robert's arm. *Say something,* she mentally ordered him.

"Father," he managed. Then he looked to Cybil. "Mother." He cleared his throat and his arm moved and Jeannie knew that if she hadn't had a hold of him, he would've been straightening his cuffs.

This was exactly why she'd insisted on coming tonight. Robert could be intense and scary—boy, could he—but when faced with his father in front of a crowd, he froze up.

Landon's gaze flicked over her. "What do we have here? I didn't realize you were bringing a date, *son.*"

She gave Robert a whole two seconds to respond but when he didn't she stepped into the gap. "How do you do," she said in her snootiest British accent. She released Robert's arm and extended her hand to Landon, palm down. "Lady Daphne FitzRoy. Charmed."

"*Lady* FitzRoy?" Landon said, his lip curling as if he instinctively knew she was an imposter.

"Of the London FitzRoys?" She sighed heavily and let her gaze narrow dismissively. She hadn't been reading historical romances for the last fifteen years or so for nothing. All those ballroom scenes, with cuts direct and dukes and duchesses—an informal education in the British aristocracy was about to pay off *big time*. "But of course. I forget how you Americans are. Perhaps you've heard of my brother? The Duke of Grafton?"

Because nothing caught the attention of a bully like a good old-fashioned reminder of where he really stood in the food chain.

And it worked like a freaking charm. Landon Wyatt inhaled, his nostrils flaring as his pupils darkened and for a fleeting second, Jeannie understood exactly why Robert was terrified of this man. She felt like a little rabbit who'd just realized the wolf was pouncing.

But she was no meek bunny. She cleared her throat and shot a disdainful look at her extended hand.

Wyatt got the hint. He pressed cold lips to the back of her hand. Jeannie refused to allow her skin to prickle. "I'm not familiar with the FitzRoys of London," he admitted, putting humor into his voice. "But welcome! Any sister of nobility is a friend of mine. And, apparently," he added, cutting a glance to Robert, "a friend of my son's. Well done, Robert."

Had she thought a wolf? That was wrong. He was a snake, one with hypnotizing eyes.

She wouldn't let him charm her. She tugged her hand free and turned to Robert's mother. "You must be Cybil.

Delighted, I'm sure." Jeannie kept her voice bored, determined not to give away her interest in Robert's mother.

"I didn't realize Bobby—Robert—was bringing a guest," Cybil said, her gaze darting between her son and Jeannie. "How…nice to make your acquaintance."

Years of observing customers kicked in and Jeannie noticed Cybil Wyatt wore her makeup too thick and that it went all the way down her neck and across her chest. Hiding bruises, maybe? She held her left shoulder higher than her right and her smile only used half her mouth, as if her jaw on the right side pained her.

Jeannie caught sight of a waiter and impatiently snapped her fingers, mentally apologizing to the dude. People who snapped for attention at the bar got either too much ice in their glasses or a small pour.

He hurried over, looking not the least bit bothered by her rudeness. Jeannie took two glasses from his tray and handed one to Robert. "Is this champagne or that American knockoff you all seem so proud of?" she asked in a voice too loud to be a whisper.

She physically felt people pull back. Good. She'd shocked them—which meant they wouldn't be able to stop looking at her.

With a light laugh, Cybil said, "The champagne is French, I assure you. Sparkling white wine just isn't the same, is it?" Her gaze darted to her husband and then she stepped around him. "It's so good to see you," she said, gripping Robert by the biceps. Jeannie could hear the truth of it in her voice. "I'm so glad you came."

"So am I," he said, staring down at his mother, his concern obvious. Then he seemed to snap out of it. "Daphne was curious how politics work in America."

Right. This was her role. She waved this comment away, slugging back half her glass. She'd need to look drunk in relatively short order. "He exaggerates, of course. Politics and politicians are a complete and utter bore."

The hangers-on actually gasped out loud at this brazen insult but Jeannie refused to cower. She would not cede a bit of her pretend high ground. She was counting on keeping Wyatt's attention by pretending to be beyond his spheres of influence. Instead, she rolled her shoulder in a not-apology.

After a beat too long, Wyatt burst out laughing and quickly, everyone around them joined in. "Ah, that dry British humor," he said out loud, his hand closing around her wrist like a manacle and drawing her by his side. Which was not a safe place to be, but it had the advantage of pushing Cybil and Robert a little farther away. "Tell me about yourself, *Duchess*." This last was said in an openly mocking tone.

"Oh, I'm not a duchess. That's my sister-in-law. You may address me as Lady FitzRoy." She said it pointedly because a true lady would demand respect.

"My lady," Wyatt said, his mouth moving in what might have been a grin. Oh, he was playing along but Jeannie knew he hadn't decided if she was legit or not. "Do tell."

"What is there to say?" She finished her champagne and snapped at the waiter, who hurried to exchange her glass for a full one. "Grafton—my brother—does his part in the House of Lords but he's dreadfully dull, as I said. So responsible." She let her lip curl in distaste but at the same time, she brushed an invisible piece of lint off Wyatt's shoulder and let her fingers linger. "Tell me, why would anyone want to run for office? Especially someone of your *considerable* stature? Public service is just so public. I'd think it'd be beneath a man of your obvious…talents." She cut a dismissive glance at Robert. "Like working. In a hospital, for God's sake," she added in a stage whisper that everyone heard.

Oh, that did the trick. Wyatt threw back his head with a brutal laugh—real humor at the expense of his son. A shiver of terror went down her back, but she smiled and notched an eyebrow at him, playing along. She saw the answer in Wyatt's eyes when he looked at her—he was drunk on power and like any addict, he needed more.

But like a good politician, he said, "As you know, we Wyatts are quite well-off."

She rolled her shoulder in that dismissive shrug again as if being billionaires was just so much dross.

His pupils dilated. He was enjoying himself. Good. "I don't seek the office of the governor for myself, you understand. I have everything I could ever want." Wyatt's gaze dipped to her breasts. She repressed a shudder. "It's time to give back to the good people of Illinois. They deserve more and, having managed my company for so long, I alone have the skills to set things right and steer this great state into the future!"

The fawning jackals broke out in applause. Flashbulbs flashed.

Jeannie snapped for the poor waiter again because Lady Daphne FitzRoy was a bitch—and an alcoholic at that. She exchanged her half-empty glass for a full one and drank deeply. She needed to look sloppy drunk.

She could feel Robert's gaze on her.

She refused to look.

Thirteen

"Come with me."

Robert kept his voice low, using the laughter of the crowd to hide his words. He didn't look at Cybil Wyatt as he spoke. Instead, his gaze was locked on to Jeannie—or, rather, Lady FitzRoy. He couldn't believe people were buying this line of BS, but even Landon seemed smitten with her. Or at least smitten with her breasts.

"…in a hospital, for God's sake," she said, wobbling toward Landon as she said it. How much had she drunk? Aside from the wine at lunch last weekend, he'd never actually seen her drink before.

Everyone laughed at his expense, Landon loudest of all.

"I can keep you safe," he added as Landon's predatory gaze zeroed in on Jeannie. Jeannie had sworn she could handle herself. And he had to admit, she was one hell of a distraction.

His mother's grip on his arm tightened before she removed her hand entirely. "It's not safe," she said, smiling that smile he hated because it was a mask, a lie. "He'll come after you. He'll find me."

Like last time. She didn't say it, but she didn't need to.

Mom looked awful. The way she held her body—didn't anyone else here see the lines of pain around her eyes? The way her shoulders weren't even? Had that bastard broken her ribs again?

Landon Wyatt was going to pay for everything he'd done.

The world went a little red at the edges, narrowing to Landon and Jeannie. She had another champagne flute in her hand and was waving it around. Champagne sloshed everywhere and people stepped back to make sure they didn't get hit. Then she took another long drink and all but dropped the flute. A beleaguered waiter caught it before it hit the ground and then Jeannie had a fresh glass.

Landon slid a taunting glance his way and then slid his arm around Jeannie's waist, pulling her closer so he could whisper in her ear.

Robert's stomach rolled. Hard. Because he was supposed to be protecting the women he cared about. He wasn't a kid anymore, forced to stand by and watch helplessly as Landon hurt women in the name of a teachable moment.

This wasn't happening. Jeannie wasn't a paid escort. And she knew who she was dealing with.

Trust me, she'd said.

Did he have a choice?

She looked at Robert, a mean smile on her lips. But then her glance bounced to his mother and back to him, her eyes widening just a little, and Robert got the distinct feeling she was telling him something.

"He won't find you," Robert told his mother, hiding his mouth behind his glass as he spoke. His plan had been set into motion tonight and he couldn't stop it if he wanted to— and he didn't want to. He just needed to be sure Cybil was nowhere near Landon when the chips began to fall. Robert couldn't bear to think of that bastard blaming Mom when things all fell apart. "He can't win. But I need you to come with me."

For what felt like a century, she didn't answer, didn't look at him. She laughed politely at something rude Jeannie had said—about Robert, probably. He wasn't paying attention.

"When?"

Relief hit him so hard he almost cried. "My car is waiting. Jeannie or I will take you there."

That got her attention. She turned to fully face him, which was a rare mistake. It was never a good idea to give Landon Wyatt your back. "Who?"

"My date."

Color deepened on Mom's cheeks as if she was embarrassed that someone else knew their private shame. But all she said was, "Ah," and turned back to face Landon just as Jeannie pulled away from his grip.

She took another deep drink of her champagne and then held the glass at such an angle that nearly half the contents poured directly onto the floor. "But I'm ignoring our hostess!" she cried in what was truly a terrible British accent.

Robert couldn't *believe* people were buying this act. How was he even looking at the same person who blended behind the bar at Trenton's, ready with the perfect Manhattan and a sympathetic ear? How was this the same woman who'd wrapped a silk tie around his wrists and then wrapped her nearly nude body around his?

She was so much more than just the sum of those moments.

And she was heading straight for him and his mother, pausing only long enough to get another glass of champagne. Landon's friends—men who had power and wealth, although never as much of either as Landon had—sniggered at the sight of this supposed *lady* making a complete ass of herself.

"Do you know," Jeannie began, her words now noticeably slurred, "that I do think this is very good champ—*whoopsie!*"

She stumbled forward, splashing Mom right in the chest and somehow managing to get a good part of the champagne onto Robert's sleeve and face, as well.

He nearly burst out laughing. *Whoopsie.* She'd had this planned from the moment she'd informed him she was coming with him, hadn't she? By God, he'd never known a woman like Jeannie before.

She wobbled dangerously on her heels, her dress nearly falling off her shoulders and exposing her breasts as she stumbled into Mom. "Oh, dear," Jeannie said, a hysterical laugh in her voice that made her accent even more awful. "Oh, I've made a mess of your lovely dress. Oh, what a pity, it was so pretty. Grafton will be *so* displeased. Oh," she said, clutching Mom by the arm and looking properly terrified, "you won't tell him, will you?"

Mom looked around wildly, wine dripping off her chin and running down her chest. Her makeup gave up its hold on her skin as flesh-colored rivulets ran onto the bodice of her dress.

An uneasy hush had fallen over the crowd. People weren't sure if they should laugh or offer assistance or what. Another round of flashbulbs went off, reminding everyone that this series of unfortunate events was on the record.

Landon Wyatt shot Robert a look that promised pure pain. Robert didn't allow himself to shy away. He met Landon's stare head-on and then wiped alcohol from his chin. Really, Jeannie had done an excellent job making as big a mess as humanly possible.

"No, no," Mom said, finding her voice and grabbing Jeannie's hand before she could start smearing the body makeup. "But why don't you and I go to the ladies' room? I bet you'll feel better after we both freshen up." She looked to her husband—for permission. The pause made Robert's teeth grind.

This, he vowed, would be the very last time Cybil Wyatt asked her husband for permission to do anything.

Landon nodded. "Perhaps we should cut the duchess off." He turned back to the crowd. "I suppose the Brits can't hold their liquor."

"I'd like to hold *her*," someone muttered. Robert didn't see who'd spoken but he refused to allow himself to react.

Leaning heavily on Mom, Jeannie allowed herself to be led toward the ladies' room, babbling about how Grafton would be *most* upset...

She'd missed her calling as an actress; that much was clear. Robert felt an odd sort of pride at her performance. But that was immediately followed by an even odder sort of fear as he caught Landon looking after the women. Robert recognized that look. It seemed benign, that level gaze, that slight quirk to the lips. Friendly, almost.

A shiver raced down Robert's back and he had to dig his nails into his palm to keep from letting it out. Because the times he'd seen Landon Wyatt look like that—especially if he made it to a full smile—those were some of the worst moments of Robert's life.

Like a nightmare come to life, Landon's smile widened.

It didn't matter that Jeannie hadn't looked or acted like herself. She was in danger for embarrassing Landon in front of his friends and donors and cameras. Jeannie might as well have painted a big red target on her back, and Robert? He would be in just as much trouble for bringing the notorious Lady FitzRoy to the party in the first place.

That was bad enough. When Landon discovered Jeannie had actually absconded with his wife...

Robert's lungs wouldn't move, wouldn't inflate. It only got worse when Landon turned back to the crowd. His gaze snagged on Robert and the man smirked.

Smirked.

This was Robert's doing, all of it. He'd agreed to let her come, agreed to let her act the part of a noble drunk. It was Robert's job to keep Jeannie safe. A deadening hole opened up in his stomach as he realized what that meant.

He had to stay as far away from her as possible. No more lunch dates, no more evening drinks at Trenton's. It didn't matter if she went back to work or not; Robert couldn't risk her by ever darkening the restaurant's doors again.

Well, that was being a little melodramatic. But as long as Landon Wyatt had power and a means to wield it, he was a threat. Robert had always known that. That was why he was sending his mother halfway around the world. Landon was a threat to Robert, to Mom and now to Jeannie.

Tonight would be it, then.

Robert fought the urge to look at his phone. God willing, in less than two minutes, Reginald would be on his way to the private airfield north of the city, where the plane and flight crew were on standby.

Landon's smile shifted subtly into a more genial look as Robert felt another trickle of champagne drip off his chin. "She got you, too, eh, son?" he said to chuckles, as if he was a sympathetic father.

"I shouldn't have let her drink," Robert replied, because that was a sentiment Landon would approve. "I'm sorry for the mess."

How many seconds had passed? Had it been a minute? Were they in the elevator yet?

Landon stared at him, his eyes flinty, before his whole face changed into one of good humor. "Go get cleaned up— but I expect to see you back here. I'm giving my big speech in a few minutes and the cameras will be rolling."

"I wouldn't miss it," Robert said, managing to paste some sort of smile on his face. It must have been appropriate because people made noises of sympathy.

He hadn't taken three steps before his phone buzzed. Jeannie. *Thank God.*

In car

Go

Waiting for you

Go, dammit

Thirty seconds

Jesus, that woman.
Robert broke into a run.

"Buckle up," the woman in red said, sounding not particularly drunk nor particularly British.

"Who are you?" Cybil asked, impressed that she could speak at all.

This was really happening. She was really in a private car with a complete stranger who had dragged her into an elevator and then shoved her into a car.

And she was going along with it because the alternative to what was potentially a kidnapping was to stay with Landon.

"A friend of your son's," was the reply she got, which was almost comforting. Then the woman in red had her head through the dividing window and was talking to the driver. "Thirty seconds!" the not-lady all but shouted. "Just a few more seconds!"

The driver replied, but Cybil couldn't make out his words over the pounding of her pulse in her ears.

Landon would be so mad if he knew about this. Bobby was putting himself directly into harm's way—the very place Cybil had worked so hard to keep him from—and for what? For her?

"I should get back," she said, fumbling with the seat belt.

"Sorry, Mrs. Wyatt, but that's not happening." The woman in red slid into the seat next to her and put a firm hand on the buckle. "And I apologize for ruining your dress. It was pretty." This strange creature turned her head to the side, appraising Cybil with unnervingly frank eyes.

"He'll come after Bobby," Cybil said, her voice breaking on the end. She scrabbled at the woman's hands, trying to pry them loose of the seat belt. Panic tasted metallic in her mouth. "He'll hurt my son! I have to protect him!"

"He's a grown man," the stranger said, taking hold of Cybil's hands. Her grip was firm but not cruel. "Bobby is capable of protecting himself. And you, if you'll trust him. Just trust him."

The car started to move. "Five more seconds!" the woman yelled at the driver.

"He said to go now!" the driver yelled back.

"What's happening?" Cybil said, hating how the weakness bled into her voice. Hating that this was what she'd been reduced to. Begging a complete stranger for information.

To her surprise, the woman carefully wrapped an arm around Cybil's shoulders. "You're going somewhere safe. Believe me, your husband will never be able to find you."

The car began to roll again just as the passenger door wrenched open and Cybil screamed as the woman in red shielded her because for a second she thought it was Landon there, eyes blazing, chest heaving, and she knew this time, a few broken bones would be child's play. But then it was Bobby, her Bobby, climbing into the car and slamming the door shut behind him. Bobby yelling at the driver to *go, dammit*. Bobby helping the woman into the seat across from Cybil.

Bobby sitting next to her, wrapping his arms around her.

"My son," she said, promptly ruining his tuxedo jacket with her tears and smeared makeup and spilled champagne.

"I've got you, Mom," he said, his voice breaking as he held her—but gently, like he could tell where she was hurting. "You're safe now."

"You're not," she wept because Landon would destroy him. Landon would destroy them all. "*Why*, Bobby? Why would you risk yourself for *me*?"

"He's stronger than you think," the woman said, her voice kind. "Because that's how you raised him to be."

Cybil got herself under control. Years of practice made it practically second nature. "Who are you?" she asked because clearly this was someone her son trusted.

The woman smiled. It looked real and soft, and unfamiliar hope fluttered in Cybil's chest. Had Bobby found someone?

But then the woman spoke and dashed her hopes. "I'm his bartender."

Fourteen

"Are you sure about this?" Mom asked as Robert guided her up the narrow stairs into the plane.

"I'm sure. We'll talk anytime you want and in a few months, I'll fly down and visit you." Robert settled her into her seat. "He won't keep us apart."

Mom was crying softly. "Don't let him hurt you," she said, her voice surprisingly level despite her tears. "I couldn't live with myself if…"

Robert pressed a kiss to her good cheek. "I'm not a little kid anymore, Mom. I promise you, I've got the situation under control. You focus on getting well." He motioned the nurse forward. "Bridget here will be with you the whole time."

Mom nodded, looking panicked. Then she glanced out the window and seemed to calm. Robert followed her gaze and saw Jeannie standing near the limo, wind billowing her skirt. "I hope you know what you're doing," she whispered.

"I do."

Landon Wyatt wouldn't have any idea what'd hit him. The disappearance of his wife was merely the first domino to fall.

Mom turned back to him. She took a deep breath and nodded. "All right. But promise me this, Bobby—if you get the chance at real happiness, grab it. Hold on to it." She gripped his hand with surprising strength. But then, she'd always been so much stronger than she let on. "Be happy, Bobby." She looked at Jeannie again. "Be well and be happy. It's all I've ever wanted for you."

Robert had to swallow a few times before his throat worked right. He'd gotten a little bit of happiness for a short time. It would have to do. "That's what I want for you, too." Mom gave him a scolding look, tinged with a smile, so Robert promised. "I will. I swear."

He kissed her goodbye and checked in with Bridget one last time. Then he was climbing down the stairs and Jeannie was waiting for him. After tonight he wouldn't get the comfort of going to her when he needed her.

How was he supposed to go on without her?

But he didn't have the luxury of loving Jeannie, not until Landon was either behind bars or six feet under and not until Robert could be sure the bastard hadn't left behind instructions that would endanger Jeannie or his mother.

Jeannie slipped her hand in his and a brief moment of hope flared in his chest as the plane door shut and locked. She'd said she'd wait for him, hadn't she? If Robert knew that she'd be there with the perfect Manhattan and that take-no-crap smile—maybe even with a silk tie tangled in her fingers—after this thing with Landon was settled, he'd be content to wait.

But that wasn't fair to her. She had a life—a baby to care for, a job she enjoyed. He was a customer, a benefactor— and a lover, perhaps—but that didn't make her his.

Robert knew what Landon would say. He'd say Jeannie

belonged to Robert. He was a Wyatt and Wyatts took what they wanted. Landon would spout off about how Robert had to demand respect when he meant fear, as if fear was somehow more magical than love or trust.

Yes, that was what Landon Wyatt would do.

Which was exactly why Robert would let Jeannie go.

As the plane began to move, Robert caught a glimpse of his mother's face, tear-streaked and shocked. She lifted a hand and Robert returned the small wave.

Jeannie leaned against him, shoulder to shoulder, almost the same height he was in her heels. They stood together in silence as the plane taxied down the runway and took off.

It was done. Mom was on her way. Everything else was falling into place.

So why couldn't he move?

Because moving would bring him closer to the end of tonight. To the end of his time with Jeannie.

He wasn't sure he was strong enough to do what had to be done.

"Sir?" Kelly came forward. "Do you want the updates?"

Mechanically, Robert nodded. But he turned to Jeannie. "Wait for me?" Because he wasn't strong enough. Not… yet, anyway.

Her fingers tightened around his hand. She was less than a breath away—closer than that when she lifted her other hand and brushed her thumb over his cheek. "Of course."

Then she kissed the spot she'd just stroked, her lips lingering. He could smell champagne on her breath mingling with the orange scent she always wore.

He had to let her go. He *had* to. And if she wouldn't listen—because this was Jeannie, after all—then he'd have to keep her away.

He wrapped his arm around her waist and held her tight, inhaling her scent deeply. Each moment was another memory he tucked away, another glimpse of happiness that he'd hold on to for later.

He'd promised, after all.

"I'll wait in the car," she whispered in his ear.

But he didn't let her go. Not just yet. Another moment, that was all he needed. He couldn't take her home because Landon might show up at any moment, full of rage and hate, and follow them. And Maja was at Jeannie's house, to say nothing of the baby.

"After this," he murmured against her temple, "I'll take you to see the stars."

He felt the tremor of excitement move through her. "From your terrace?" Her body pressed against his, a promise of more than just another moment. She reached up between them and tugged the ends of his bow tie loose and just like that, he went rock-hard for her. "I'd like that. But I couldn't wish for anything more."

He shook his head. "You deserve more than one star. You deserve them all." That would be his parting gift to her. The night sky and all those stars to wish upon.

She pulled the tie from around his neck as she put distance between them. Black silk dangling from her fingertips, her knowing smile in the dim lighting made him want to forget about Landon and revenge and corporate takeovers and everything but Jeannie and him and this wanting that existed between them.

She turned on her heel and, with a come-hither look over her shoulder, strode to the car, where Reginald was waiting to open the door for her. Robert couldn't move as she climbed in, revealing the curve of her leg as she pulled her foot inside. He wasn't even sure he was breathing until the car door closed.

Then Reginald had the nerve to wink. At Robert! Really, this was too much.

But that cheekiness broke the spell Robert was under.

He turned to find Kelly pointedly looking at everything but Robert or the limo and, one presumed, Jeannie.

"Is everything on track?" Robert asked, straightening his cuffs. He felt undressed without his tie. Which was most likely the point.

Well, one of them.

"Yes. The photographer reports that Landon is still at the gallery, although he's delaying the start of his speech and growing more agitated by the second." Kelly held out his phone. "Would you like to see the shots?"

"No." The less space Landon took up in Robert's brain from here on out, the better. "The lawyers have been notified?"

One for the divorce, a few from the District Attorney's office and several for the former employees who'd been subjected to Landon's sexual assaults. In just a few short days they'd found four former maids and six former employees of Wyatt Medical willing to come forward. A few claims were past the statute of limitations, so Robert was funding the civil suits. The others had been turned over to the authorities. The actual number of victims was probably quadruple the ten they'd confirmed, easily.

"Yes. The judge should be approving the emergency search warrant as we speak."

"Excellent. The guards are on standby?" One posted at Jeannie's house, just in case Robert had left a loose thread out there for Landon to pull. The others, including two off-duty police officers—one of whom was extremely grateful that his eldest son had just celebrated his sixth birthday after a successful heart valve repair—were watching his house.

"Yes. The forensic accountant has already found some very large…discrepancies between the Wyatt Medical financials and Landon's campaign fund." Kelly closed his portfolio. "You're sure about this?"

This was completely and methodically destroying his father, piece by piece.

Robert almost smiled. He was a Wyatt, after all, and Wyatts demanded respect. They didn't hesitate or have second thoughts. When someone slighted a Wyatt, they responded by dominating. By destroying, if that was what it took.

It wasn't enough to have Landon publicly humiliated.

He had to be ended. Simple as that.

And Robert was the only person who could do it. Because he was a Wyatt and this was what Landon had made him into. Someone cruel and hard and utterly without mercy.

So he nodded once. Landon Wyatt would get no mercy. Not from his only child.

Kelly let out a breath he apparently had been holding and said, "Then we're doing this."

Kelly was a good kid, not the kind of man who'd been raised to engage in this level of back-channel manipulation. Robert appreciated that his assistant wasn't entirely comfortable with the situation but he also appreciated an employee who did as he was asked.

"I may be...offline for a few hours," Robert told Kelly, fighting the urge to touch his shirt collar, "but keep me informed."

He thought Kelly's cheeks might have darkened but it was hard to tell. "Yes, sir."

Robert nodded again and turned back to the car but then an image of Jeannie notching an eyebrow at him in challenge floated before his mind's eye. He turned back before he could think better of it. "Kelly?"

"Sir?" The young man snapped to attention.

"Thank you. I know this is far outside your normal purview but..." Bordering on criminal, in fact. "But I appreciate everything you've done for me and my mother. So thank you."

There, was that so hard? Jeannie's laugh echoed in his mind.

No, it wasn't. In fact, it was getting easier all the time.

"Oh. Well. Uh, you're welcome?" Kelly sounded just as confused by receiving this compliment as Robert had felt giving it.

"Where to, sir?" Reginald asked and dammit, the man had a twinkle in his eye.

"The beach," Robert said decisively because he was a Wyatt and the time for second-guessing was over. "Take us to see the stars. Please."

Reginald nodded smartly as he opened the door for Robert. It wasn't until the door had closed behind him, leaving him completely alone with Jeannie, that Robert was able to breathe.

Champagne and oranges and Jeannie. The scent surrounded him and he felt his shoulders relax. "Well?" she asked as he settled into his seat. Instantly, she was at his side, curling into him.

Without consciously choosing to do so, his arm went around her shoulder, gathering her tight. He could hold her like this now without hesitation, without flinching. She'd given him that.

"Everything is fine," he said and, at least for the next hour or so, it truly was.

"Good," she replied, her hand sliding under his tux jacket. She undid his vest and then rested her hand on his stomach. That simple touch, muted through the layers of his shirt and undershirt, still pushed his pulse faster. It took so little for her to affect him now.

She pushed herself onto her knees without letting go of him, her breasts brushing against his chest as she shifted. Her scent, warm and inviting, filled his nose. He could get drunk on her, he realized. Maybe he already was. "What are the rules?"

Here in the dark interior of his car, nothing else existed. Just him and her. A woman who had stood by his side through one of the hardest moments of his life and yet still wanted *him*. Not his fortune or his name or any of it. Just him.

It was a hell of a thing.

He wished he could give her so much more. But tonight was all he had. So he said, "Same as last time."

But this time it wasn't because he was worried he would hurt her. He wouldn't. No, this time he needed the restraint to remind himself that she was not his to have and to hold.

Would that she was. But it wasn't safe. Not now. Maybe…

If her lips twisted to the side in disappointment, he couldn't say. "Hold out your hands."

It felt right, letting her do this again. It'd worked the last time. He'd lost himself in her, but he hadn't lost control. Hadn't become the man Landon had demanded he be.

Tonight Robert had come closer to being that man, that *Wyatt*, than he ever had before and it was necessary and important but it was also…unsettling that he had it in him.

He could do bad things, even if for good reasons.

But not to her. Never to her.

He trusted Jeannie, tonight more than ever. He needed her this one last time and then he'd let her go.

Jeannie lifted his arms into the air and then slid onto his lap. Instantly, the warmth of her core rocketed through his body. She wasn't wearing panties, he realized with a jolt.

"Jeannie," he groaned as she pulled his arms down so his knotted wrists were looped around her neck. Because this counted as touching and God help him, he needed it. Needed to feel her over him, around him, under him.

One last time, he repeated silently to himself. That was all this was.

"Hush." She shifted back, her weight perfect on his lap

as her hands moved to his trousers. She undid his belt and zipper in silence.

He opened his mouth to tell her where the condoms were—inside pocket of his jacket—but that was when she reached over and snagged that tiny purse Maja had handed her. When she opened it, a strip of condoms popped out like a jack-in-the-box without the terrifying clown.

"You're prepared," he said, his breath coming faster as she snapped off one and tore it open.

"Luck favors the prepared. Now quiet." She had to grab at his jacket as they took a corner. In that moment he felt the strength of her thighs' grip on his legs. She was so strong. God, he loved it.

Then she grinned at him as she smoothed out his lapel and added, "Or else."

Desire pounded through him at that challenge. She'd already tied him up. How far would she go?

She rolled on the condom and Robert realized he was holding his breath as her fingers stroked over his length, hard with wanting her.

"Or else what?" he heard himself ask through gritted teeth.

Her grip on him tightened. "Or else," she whispered, leaning forward to let her lips brush over his earlobe, trapping his aching erection between them, "I'll touch you. Slowly."

As if to demonstrate, her fisted hand slid up over his shaft, the lubrication of the condom smoothing the way. His breath caught in his throat as he strained against her. It was too much—far, far too much—and yet not enough.

"Yes, like that," she whispered, her voice nothing but breath that caressed over his skin. "And harder." Her grip tightened as her hand moved back down, inch by agonizing inch.

A groan ripped free because she was touching him and

he was letting her and it was something new, and he'd never been so turned on in his entire life.

"Then," she said, shifting so his length was pressed against her sex, trapped in her embrace, "then I'd touch you here, too."

Her hand slipped down, cupping his balls and pressing up ever so gently as her hips moved, dragging his tip over her.

"Jeannie," he moaned, helpless to stop her, helpless for her.

"And then?" She pushed back, his arms still around her neck, his hands in tight fists as he let go of everything but the way her hand squeezed him, tormented him—made him whole again.

She smiled, wickedness brought to life. "Then I'd stop."

She pulled her hand away.

For all that he'd trained himself to control his emotions, control his reactions, Robert couldn't help it—he whimpered.

Her smile was pure victory. "Will you be quiet?"

He nodded. It was all he could do.

"Thank God," she said, raising herself onto her knees and positioning him at her entrance.

Then she sank down on him, taking him in completely until Robert was on the verge of losing control.

"Just be," she said, her breathing faster now. "Just be with me, Robert."

Although it was a risk, he had to let her know. "Always."

She would always be this perfect memory, this utterly wonderful moment in time when he was the man she needed and she was his everything.

One last time.

The car came to a somewhat sudden stop and she scrabbled to grab hold of his jacket to keep from falling right off him. He used his bound hands to pull her back to him, her breasts flush with his chest and in that moment, he wished he hadn't insisted on the clothing because he wanted to see her in her nude glory, feel her body against his.

He didn't just want part of her. He wanted all of her.

One last time. Dammit.

Giggling, she leaned back, but he didn't let her pull away. He kept her against his chest, feeling her nipples harden through the thin fabric of her dress as she rose and fell on him.

He needed to touch her. He'd never needed anything so badly in his life.

Somehow, he got his wrists shifted so he could cup the back of her head and tangle his fingers in her short hair.

"Robert," she sighed softly as he angled her head toward his. "What…"

"Kiss me." He wasn't begging because Wyatts didn't beg, but it wasn't an order, either. "I need you to kiss me while I'm inside you."

He felt the shudder move through her body and then her lips were on his, their tongues touching and retreating and touching again, all while she rode him and he held her, and this was the moment he would never forget. No matter what happened in an hour or tomorrow or next month, no one would ever take this moment from him.

She moved faster and faster, chasing her climax and all he could do was grit it out and hold on until she'd found her release.

When she threw back her head, the lines of her neck taut, he did the only thing he could—he leaned forward and buried his face between her breasts. The diamond pendant hit him in the nose but he didn't care as he kissed her there, thrusting up into her as he let go.

He let go.

How could he ever let her go?

Fifteen

Jeannie could feel the goodbye in the air as Reginald opened the car door after what felt like an unnaturally long pause. Probably giving them time to set their clothing to rights.

Thoughtful man, that Reginald. She hoped Robert gave him a raise.

But he needn't have worried because after the most amazing orgasm of her entire life—which was saying something because the one last week had been pretty damn spectacular—Robert had gently lifted her off him and then buttoned up. In complete silence.

Yep. The goodbye was definitely in the air.

Robert helped her out of the limo and then, with an unbelievable, "Thank you, Reginald," he swept Jeannie right off her feet. Literally.

"Robert!" she shrieked as he tossed her into the air a little, adjusting his hold.

"Your shoes aren't made for sand," he said as if that was all the explanation necessary.

"Honestly," she laughed, but she linked her arms around his neck and let her head rest on his shoulder.

He hummed. He sounded happy. *Please*, she thought, *let him be happy*.

Without another word, he carried her down the beach. She didn't know where they were, but far north of Chicago proper, she guessed. She could see the orange glow of the city to the south but out over the lake, all she could see were…

"Stars," she breathed. Hundreds of them. Millions, maybe.

"Yes," he agreed in that Robert way as if he had personally decreed there would be stars and lo, the universe had made it happen.

He walked on, his pace slow as he ruined his shiny tuxedo shoes in the sand. "Where are we going?"

"Away from the light," he replied, as cryptic as ever.

The night sky stretched out vast and endless before her. The moon was nowhere to be seen, so the only way to differentiate between the water and the sky was the twinkling of light.

"It's beautiful," she sighed. So many stars—if only she had that many wishes.

But she'd already gotten what she'd asked for, hadn't she? More than that. She had a nanny and a maid and a reasonably good grip on how to care for Melissa. She had a lawyer who was working on a settlement from the hospital to make sure Melissa would always be cared for.

And she'd had the most amazing, complicated, messy, perfect man in Chicago at her mercy.

No, she wouldn't wish on another star. If there was one thing she'd learned over the years, it was not to push her luck.

After long, quiet minutes, Robert set her down on her feet. She slid her hand into his and leaned against his shoulder. A breeze flowed off the lake and despite the warm summer temperature, she shivered. It was always cooler by the lake.

"Here," he said gruffly, removing his jacket and draping it over her shoulders.

"Thank you." The superfine wool smelled like him, dark and spicy with just a hint of champagne and orange on top. The smell of them together. He wrapped his arm around her shoulders, holding her tight.

Her knees began to shake. "Robert?" She wanted to ask before she lost her nerve.

"Hmm?"

"Have you ever been in love?"

"No." He didn't even hesitate. The word was out like a gunshot and it made her heart ache for him.

Then he leaned down and pressed his cheek against her hair. "At least…not yet."

Dammit. He was going to make this painful, wasn't he?

"What about you?" he asked when she failed to come up with anything to say.

Oh, how their situations had reversed. "A few times."

"What happened?"

She shrugged. "I was young and foolish. Sometimes…" She had to swallow to get around the rock that had suddenly appeared in her throat. "Sometimes you fall in love with the wrong person at the right time and you don't realize it until times change. And sometimes…"

She blinked against her stinging eyes and focused on the stars. Their light, hopeful and bright against the darkest of times, wavered. Must be the breeze.

"And sometimes," he finished for her, his voice thoughtful, "you fall in love with the right person at the wrong time."

She had to blink some more. Damned wind.

"I don't want this to be the wrong time," she said. *De-*

manded. "This isn't the wrong time. And you're *not* the wrong person."

"No," he finally said.

But she knew him too well, didn't she? She heard the pain and confusion and loss and love in his voice, all blurred together in that one syllable. Two measly letters were all it took to break her heart, apparently.

"Robert, listen," she began, desperate to hold on to him. They'd only just gotten started! There was so much more between them. So much more than a perfect Manhattan and a fake lady. "I'll—"

"No." Another two measly letters. She was really beginning to hate that syllable. He looked down at her, cupping her cheek in his strong hand. "I won't ask it of you."

"Please," she whispered. "We can—"

He just shook his head and then he leaned down and kissed her.

He kissed her goodbye.

"Ask me," she murmured against his ear. "Please, Robert. Just ask."

He stared down at her, his forehead resting against hers. "I have to keep you safe, Jeannie. I won't let any harm come to you or Melissa."

"You won't. I know you won't."

When he didn't reply to that, she snapped. To hell with his rules. She dug her fingers into his hair and dragged her lips across his, biting and sucking and showing him how much more there could be between them, if only he'd trust her.

If only he'd trust himself.

He was breathing hard when he broke the kiss. He pulled her hands away from his head and then swept her back into his arms. The walk back was silent and awful and far, far too short because he'd made up his mind and who was she to try and change it? She was nobody.

She was just his bartender. A pretend lady, a willing accomplice, a sympathetic ear and a shoulder to lean on. Nothing more.

She would not cry. Wind be darned.

Eventually, they made it back to where Reginald and the limo were waiting. This time Robert opened her door for her and handed her inside. But instead of climbing in after her, he shut the door.

"Robert," she almost shouted, feeling frantic. Was he not even going to give her a proper goodbye?

Of course not, because talking was not Dr. Robert Wyatt's strong suit. Instead, he heard the muffled sound of Reginald getting behind the wheel and, even more distant, Robert saying, "Take her home."

"Yes, sir."

The car started and she rolled down the window. "Robert!" she yelled. "I'll wait." The car started to move. "I'll be waiting!" she shouted out the window.

The car turned and the breeze blew so she couldn't be sure but she thought she heard him say, *"Sailboat."*

Damn him.

But then, what had she expected?

"You're back early. How was your evening?" Maja said from the recliner where Melissa was asleep on her chest. The whole place smelled like lemons and every surface shone like the top of the Chrysler Building.

That was because of Robert.

The right man at the wrong time.

"Fine," Jeannie said dully. Because, really, it was the wrong time. He was about to go to war with his father, and Jeannie had to figure out how to be a mother for the rest of her life and she couldn't expect Robert to foot the bill for polished woodwork and overnight nannies forever.

Maja's grandmotherly face wrinkled in concern. "Is everything all right, dear?"

"Fine," Jeannie repeated. She stared down at her sandals and the Valentino dress that had cost God only knew how much, at the heavy diamond pendant that had definitely cost too much.

Robert was the right man and she was hopelessly in love with him.

But Dr. Robert Wyatt, billionaire bachelor and noted surgeon—he was the wrong man. For someone like her. Because she could pretend to fit into his world, but they both knew she didn't belong there.

God, she hated goodbyes.

"Dear?"

Jeannie looked up with a start to see Maja standing in front of her. "I've decided to go back to work. In two weeks. I don't know how long you're going to be able to watch Melissa for me but—" she swallowed "—if you could at least help me line up alternative childcare before you go. Something I could afford."

Because she couldn't afford Maja or Rona or Reginald or any of them.

Maja looked tired in the dim light. "I'm paid for three months, which leaves us quite a bit of time to make plans." She sighed again, disappointment on her face. "I'm sorry things didn't work out with your handsome doctor."

But he'd never been hers, had he? They had been like… this outfit. Like Lady Daphne FitzRoy. An illusion.

"So am I," she said, the tears starting to fall. "So am I."

Sixteen

Robert called for a ride, which was a novel experience. By the time the driver picked him up, Robert had himself under control. He'd done the right thing. Jeannie might be upset now but he was confident that a woman as worldly and intelligent as she was would see how this was for the best by the light of day.

She still had his jacket, but his vest smelled faintly of oranges.

God, he was tired. Tired of dealing with Landon, worrying about his mother, tired of holding himself back, tired of being Robert Wyatt.

Just be with me, Jeannie had said. Of all the things she'd given him, that might've been her greatest gift.

But it didn't matter how tired he was—his night was just beginning.

Kelly texted just as the car hit Lake Shore Drive.

He's at your house.

Status?

Speech was a disaster.
Social media is asking if he was high.
Visibly upset.
Banging on your door.
Hasn't broken anything.

Don't interfere yet.

Yes, sir.

Robert focused on breathing. Slow. Steady. Orange-scented. Everything was going according to plan. Landon had discovered that his wife, son and a random woman who might or might not have been nobility had all disappeared from his grand kickoff campaign gala. As Robert had hoped, Landon had not taken the news well.

Robert was counting on the next part. He didn't have long to wait.

He just put a planter through your front door.
Alarm is blaring.

Wait until he gets in
then have him arrested.

Because that was the fail-safe of his plan. He could fund civil lawsuits and give federal investigators access to financial reports but Landon was a slippery bastard and money talked.

Breaking and entering, however, was harder to disprove. Especially when there were security tapes, off-duty officers as witnesses and a son who refused to drop charges.

The driver turned onto Robert's street. "Here is fine,"

Robert said, fishing a hundred out of his wallet. He didn't know what the tipping protocol was but rare was the person who'd turn down cash.

"Hey—anytime, man! You're going to get a great rating out of this!"

Robert had no idea what the man was talking about but he didn't care. As he got out of the car, he could hear his alarm screaming into the night and, underneath that, sirens in the distance.

"Get your hands off me! Do you know who I am?" Landon Wyatt's screech of rage cut through the noise.

"What's going on here?" Robert said, aiming for concerned innocence. "Father? What are you doing here?"

"Where is she?" Landon screamed, lurching at Robert.

"Easy, buddy," the officer said, hauling Landon back. Robert recognized Officer Hernandez; he'd covered the Hernandezes' outstanding balance for a recent procedure.

Landon's arms were handcuffed behind his back. The sight made Robert almost smile because it was something he could definitely get used to seeing. "Where is who?"

"You know damned well, you useless bastard. Where is *she*?"

Robert made a big show of looking up at his dark house. "No one's home. I just got here." Kelly sidled up the sidewalk and Robert spotted the reporters, cameras flashing and video recording. "My date got sick and I took her home. I don't think we'll be seeing each other anymore," he explained for the audience.

Landon snarled and lunged again. This time the other officer had to use so much force to hold him back that Landon wound up on his knees in the middle of the sidewalk.

"You'll pay for this," he said, his eyes bugging out. "By the time I get done with you, you all will wish you'd never been born!"

The officers made as if to haul him up but Robert waved

them off. Instead, he crouched down in front of Landon, who was struggling to get to his feet. Robert put a hand on the older man's shoulder and forced him back down because that was what a Wyatt would do. Dominate. Control.

Robert demanded respect, but right now, from this man, he'd settle for fear.

The older man's eyes widened with surprise as his muscles tensed under Robert's hands. "What do you think you're doing?"

Robert leaned close. He didn't want anyone to hear this. "You'll never see her again."

"I'll find her," Landon barked with a truly maniacal laugh. No wonder everyone at the gallery had been asking if he was high. Robert's plan was working perfectly. "You can't keep her safe. You never could. She's mine! And after I find her, I'll find that duchess of yours, whoever she was. And I'll make her pay." He licked his lips and tried to surge to his feet again. "I can't wait. Will she scream your name in the end, do you think?"

Robert didn't allow any emotion to cross his face. But he tightened his grip on the old man's shoulder, feeling the muscles clench and grind under his hand and he made *damn* sure Landon stayed down on his knees.

"Do you have any idea how easy it would be to get you out onto a boat and drop you in the middle of the lake?" It was a struggle to keep his voice level, but given the way Landon went rigid with what Robert hoped was fear, he thought he'd done a good job. "But I'm not going to do that because you deserve so much more than a quick, easy death." He tightened his grip on the old man's shoulder and by God, he bowed under the pressure. "No matter how hard you look, you'll never find either of them."

Robert had lived his entire life in fear of this man but in the end, it wasn't that hard to take control. He was a Wyatt and that was what they did.

"Try me," Landon said but the menace had bled out of his voice and instead, he sounded like a man who was starting to realize he'd made a grave tactical error.

Because he had.

"You're going to be divorced, sued, arrested and tried and, if I have anything to say about it, found guilty on charges of sexual assault, embezzlement, campaign finance fraud, breaking and entering, and God only knows what else my people are uncovering as we speak." Robert forced himself to stare into Landon's eyes because Robert was in charge now. It was Landon's turn to cower because he'd come up against a force he couldn't dominate. "And we haven't even rolled Alexander yet. But we will."

"Sir?" Kelly cleared his throat. Robert was running out of time to say his piece. "Sorry to interrupt but I've just received word that Alexander Trudeau has been picked up on charges of money laundering."

It was hard to tell under the yellow light from the streetlamps, but Robert thought Landon had suddenly gone pale. "See?" he said with a smile. Because now he could smile in front of Landon, just to watch the old man squirm. "Not that hard to roll, after all."

"You son of a bitch," Landon said, starting to struggle again. "I'll get you for this."

"Oh, you'll try, but you'll be busy with the lawsuits and trials. And I do think this marks the end of your career in politics, doesn't it? Everything you ever had or wanted, gone." Robert snapped his fingers. "Just like that. And do you know why, *Dad*?"

Landon glared at him but Robert didn't feel the usual panic churning up his stomach.

He smiled again, this time for real. "Because this is what you raised me to do." He let go of the old man's shoulder and, as he broke that singular point of contact, a sense of finality washed over him. "I hope you're happy with what you created."

This wasn't over, not by a long shot. But they were done.

Freed of Robert's grip, Landon surged up. "I'll kill you!" he screamed, flecks of spittle flying off his lips. "I'll kill that bitch and that whore in front of you and then *I'll end you*!"

Robert got ready to throw a punch but then Officer Hernandez and his partner were there. One drew his gun but Robert said, "No need for that, Officer." Landon straightened and smiled in victory, but then Robert added, "If you have to subdue him, use the Taser."

Landon screamed in rage but Robert just smiled. God, it felt good to smile.

It felt good to *win*.

The cops led a struggling, furious Landon to the police car. As they closed the door on what had, just a few hours ago, been the most powerful man in Chicago, Robert straightened his cuffs and stood tall.

Landon Wyatt's era was over and there would be no redemption tour.

There was a lot of talking after that—Robert gave a statement to the cops and confirmed that, yes, he would like to press charges and yes, his father had a temper but no, he'd never made death threats before and yes, perhaps a restraining order would be a good thing.

He obtained security footage and talked with lawyers and judges and began circulating rumors that Cybil Wyatt had been on the verge of leaving Landon but had been convinced to stay for the campaign but after this…

And even when dawn broke over Lake Michigan and the last star blinked out of sight, Robert didn't stop because there was so much to do. He had to contact members of the board of Wyatt Medical and make sure that his mother had landed safely in LA and taken off again and he had to do rounds at the hospital.

He couldn't stop.

Because if he did, he'd think of Jeannie. And if he thought of her, he might not be able to stay away and it wasn't safe yet. Not yet, damn it all.

Sailboat.

Seventeen

"He's not going to come back just because you're back, is he?" Miranda asked as Jeannie grabbed the crate of clean wineglasses. "If he is, I'm not dealing with him."

"He won't," Jeannie replied. "Can you move? This is heavy." Honestly, could Miranda just give her a little space?

It'd be nice if everyone at Trenton's could give her a little space on her first night back. Sure, there'd been a cake and a few baby presents but did anyone actually ask about Melissa? Nope. It was all Robert, all the time. Had he contacted her after he'd left the bar? Did she know anything about the all-out war being waged in the press and in the courts between the elder Wyatt and his son? Or, worst of all, what did she make of that mysterious "duchess" who'd appeared on Robert's arm at the ill-fated campaign kickoff but had disappeared right before everything had gone to hell and didn't she look familiar?

Maybe Robert had left a bigger mark on her than she'd realized because she had apparently perfected his icy glare.

At least she could blame her mood on the baby. Poor Melissa, taking the fall.

But it was fine. Things were always rough after a breakup and this was kind of one.

She was just about to back through the swinging door that separated the kitchen from the bar when it burst open, knocking into her. She had to juggle the crate of glasses but she managed not to drop the danged thing. "What the—"

"He's here!" Julian said in a panic, moving so fast he ran into her again.

Jeannie managed to get the crate of glass onto a countertop because suddenly, her hands had started to shake.

Miranda asked, "Who?" in a terrified whisper, the blood draining from her face.

"Him! Wyatt!"

"Breathe," Jeannie said. What was he doing here? He'd made it clear they were done and he was protecting her or something by staying away and she wasn't to wait for him. Done, done, *done.*

Or not.

"Should we call the police?" Julian asked, hands clutched in front of his chest.

Jeannie rolled her eyes. "For the love of everything holy, no. I'll handle this."

She took a second to compose herself. Which wasn't easy because not only did she have to deal with Miranda and Julian quaking in fear but also the whole kitchen staff had gone quiet, and even the normal sounds of the restaurant and bar were almost nonexistent.

She pushed through the swinging door to find herself squarely in the sights of Dr. Robert Wyatt, in his normal spot. When he saw her, his eyes narrowed and—big surprise—he adjusted his cuffs.

He'd come for her. And to think, there hadn't been a single star in the sky last night. Not even an airplane she could pretend was a star. But she'd hoped against hope that one day Robert might slide into his seat and order his Manhattan and give her that almost invisible smile and tell her everything was perfect again.

That they could be perfect together, because the time was right.

But Jeannie saw more than that. She saw how he was moving as if his leg was bouncing against the rung of the bar stool. And how, when he wasn't adjusting his cuffs, he was tapping his fingers on the bar.

How about that. Not only had Robert put in a surprise appearance, but the man was nervous about it, too. None of that mattered, though, because he'd come for *her*.

Unless something else had gone wrong? That thought led to a sickening drop in her stomach because what if he wasn't here for her? What if he…just needed a sympathetic ear and a drink?

"Well?" asked Julian from behind the door. "Cops?"

"*No*, for Pete's sake. Just leave us—him—alone." She let the door swing back and heard a muffled yelp. That was what Julian got for peeking. She made her way down the bar. Robert's intense gaze never once left hers.

"Robert." She winced. "Dr. Wyatt. The usual?"

"Jeannie."

For as long as she'd known this man—years now—every word he spoke could either make her fall further in love with him or break her heart.

Dear God, please don't let the sound of her name on his lips be another heartbreak. She couldn't take much more.

Then he smiled. That small movement of his lips curving up just at the corners, where no one else would think to look for it. But she saw it. She saw him. Maybe she always had.

Her hands hadn't stopped trembling but she ignored them as she filled a glass with his Manhattan and added the twist.

She had to use both hands to steady it as she placed the drink on the bar.

"Here for your drink?" she managed to get out, proud of the way her voice stayed level. Not a verbal tremble in sight.

"No." He didn't even look at his drink. "I'm here for you."

Her breath caught in her throat. "Me?" she squeaked. Dammit.

"Us," he corrected. Before she could process those two little letters—that one measly syllable—he dropped his gaze to a tablet she hadn't noticed on the bar next to him. "Here's the thing."

"Oh?" Her heart began to pound wildly out of control but she didn't say anything else. He'd get to it in his own sweet time.

He tapped the screen and called up a picture of a…mansion?

"Robert?" If he'd bought her a huge house out of guilt or something, she was going to have to draw the line. She and Melissa did *not* need a mansion.

"I bought it through a shell company, so there aren't any names on the paperwork, just to be sure," he began, tapping more to bring up additional pictures of a gorgeous house with amazing decorating—clean lines, warm colors and not a single shred of tacky wallpaper. "It overlooks the lake and there's a path down to a small private beach." More pictures whizzed by—was that an indoor pool? "It's got a clear view of the night sky—the light pollution doesn't drown out the stars." A victorious smile spread across his face. "I made sure of that."

"Robert," she said, barely able to get the words out. "What is this?"

He straightened in his chair before straightening his cuffs. "My mother sends her thanks for your help. I put my home in her name so that, when she's able to come back, she can enjoy the wallpapered ceilings to the fullest extent."

Oh, God. "Did you…give up your house?"

He nodded once, a quick and efficient movement. But she could tell that his leg was still jiggling and, when he started to straighten his cuffs for the third time in as many minutes, she reached over the bar and took his hands in hers. Behind her, someone gasped. Probably Miranda.

"Robert," she said again, softly. "Tell me what's happened."

A look of need flashed over his face and was gone, replaced by imperial iciness. "I don't want you to wait for me," he said in a gruff voice.

None of this made sense. There was something going on here, something that would tie the houses and his jumping leg and his very straight cuffs together and she was missing it.

"I will," she told him. "As long as it takes, I will."

He shook his head firmly and said, "No, I mean…wait." He took a deep breath and then, miracle of miracles, laced his fingers with hers. "I was supposed to stay away from you because Landon still has a lot of power and if he knew who you were, you'd be in danger and you…" Jeannie's heart kicked into overdrive. "You're very important to me."

"Oh?" He wasn't the only one who could wield single syllables in a conversation, dammit.

He stared down at their hands. "I've never been in love so I don't know for certain that this is that. But I need you. I need to see you every day so I can talk to you and you can make me laugh and touch me and make me feel…right. I don't feel right without you anymore and I tried. *I tried*," he repeated, sounding mad about that.

No, she couldn't imagine that Dr. Robert Wyatt tried and failed at too many things. Her eyes began to burn and this time there was no lake breeze to blame it on.

"But then I realized that by staying away from you to

keep you safe, I was still letting him win because he still dictated what I did and how I did it and you know what?"

"What?" she said breathlessly. Why was there a stupid bar between them? Why wasn't he in her arms for this—this—this declaration of love? Because that was what it was.

He loved her.

Oh, thank God.

"To hell with him. He can't win," Robert said fiercely and she knew this was a man who would lay down his life to protect her. "I won't allow it. If I want to be with you, I'm going to be with you because you are the right person for me, Jeannie Kaufman, and I will *make* it the right time."

Of course he would. He was a Wyatt. "So you bought a mansion?"

"For you. You and me and Melissa and…us." He looked up at her and she saw love and worry and hope in his eyes. Finally, hope. "For our family, whether it grows or not."

She almost fell over. *"Robert."*

"Marry me," he said and damn if it didn't sound like an order. But before she could call him on it, he quickly added, "Wait. No, let me do that again." He lifted her hands to his lips and kissed her knuckles like he really was a duke of the realm and she was the tavern wench who'd won his heart. "You've shown me what love is, Jeannie. And I want to spend the rest of my life sharing it with you. We can get married or not. I'm not your boss and you're not my employee or even my bartender. You're the woman I need and I hope I can be the man you want."

"Oh, Robert," she said, tears flowing.

"You're crying," he said, alarmed.

"I love you, too, you complicated, messy, wonderful man." But then the past few weeks flashed before her eyes—his reaction after the first time they'd made love, the way his father had treated him and his mother, the fact that the legal mess was going to be the headline for weeks and months to come. "And I do want to marry you—on one condition."

"Name it," he said with a devastatingly gorgeous smile. "Anything. I can buy a different house or…"

"I've never wanted you for your money." Something deepened in his eyes. An answering shiver of desire raced down her back. "But I want you to see a counselor to help you work through your…*issues* because marriage isn't a magical cure-all. You have to work on some things yourself."

He didn't even hesitate, bless the man. "Yes. Of course. I'll work on talking and hugging and…" His cheeks darkened and she had to wonder—was he *blushing*? "What else?"

She began to laugh and cry at the same time and that was when Robert let go of her hands and then vaulted over the bar. *Vaulted!* Then he had her crushed to his chest, his mouth on hers and those were definitely gasps because not only was he kissing her, he was also doing so in public. "Anything else, Jeannie?" he said against her lips. "*Anything* for you. If you want to work a bar, I'll buy you one. I'll buy you this one, if you want."

Behind them, she heard a squeak of alarm and rolled her eyes.

"We can make plans later but—will you adopt Melissa?"

He scoffed at that. "Of course."

"Will you just *be* with me, Robert? Through good times and the not-great times?"

His hands flattened against her back. She couldn't get close enough. "There is nowhere else I'd ever want to be if it's not by your side."

"Then the answer is yes because you're the right man, Robert."

He grinned wolfishly and dear Lord, he was just the most handsome man in the world and he was choosing her.

"You're the right woman for me and when it's right, there is no wrong time. Not if I have anything to say about it. After all, I'm a Wyatt." He leaned down but instead of kissing her, he whispered in her ear, "And soon you'll be one, too."

And just like that, she fell more in love with him.

"Perfect," she told him.

Because it was.

Epilogue

"Package for you, Cybil," Bridget said as the physical therapist, Anne, moved Cybil into the last stretch. "It's on your chair. I'll get your water."

"Thank you." Cybil smiled, despite the burning exhaustion that went with a tough PT appointment.

She liked being *just* Cybil. She liked being Bridget's equal. She liked the quiet villa in Kauri Cliffs, at the far north end of New Zealand. She even liked being disconnected from the rest of the world. By and large, she didn't want to know what was happening back home. She had no interest in keeping up-to-date on what her soon-to-be ex-husband was doing. She wasn't available for comment on news stories.

She could focus on herself. It was selfish and something she was still getting used to—but with the help of a psychologist and a physical therapist, she was rediscovering who she'd been before Landon Wyatt and, more important, who she wanted to be after him.

But most of all, she was getting used to talking with her son again. Not every day, because he was still a busy man, but at least every other day. At one in the afternoon her time, Bobby would call at what was eight his time. They talked of her progress and his work. They'd avoided discussions of Landon, but after a while, Bobby had begun to mention Jeannie more and more.

She wished she could've been there for the wedding, but someone named Darna had streamed the whole civil ceremony, all fourteen minutes of it, for Cybil to see.

For the first time in decades, she could breathe again.

"There," Anne said, helping Cybil to stand. She wobbled a little—today had been tough. "Make sure to drink plenty of fluids, okay? I'll see you in two days."

Cybil patted the young woman's shoulder and gratefully sank into her chair, the package in her hands.

She'd received mail from Bobby before, legal notices of her divorce proceedings, usually—her son had hired an absolute shark of a lawyer. But this felt different.

Her hands began to shake and it wasn't just from the physical exertion.

Ah, her divorce papers. It was done. She was no longer legally bound to Landon Wyatt and it appeared half of his earnings from throughout their awful marriage were now hers. She was an independently wealthy woman. No longer would she have to beg for money or wear what Landon bought for her. She could do as she saw fit.

The next thing in the envelope was the front page of the *Chicago Tribune*, with a handwritten note that said, "Any deposition can be handled safely and your income will be protected—R." Landon Wyatt was being charged for criminal sexual assault—several maids and employees had come forward to press charges. Represented, she knew, by a lawyer Bobby had chosen. Oh, but this was new— Wyatt Medical had voted him out as CEO and Landon was

also being investigated by the SEC for insider trading and
campaign fraud? Apparently, Alexander, Landon's assistant, had turned on him. All his friends had abandoned
him and his political aspirations were dead in the water.
His disgrace was complete and if Bobby had anything to
say about it, Landon would spend a good chunk of the rest
of his life in jail.

How fitting. She wanted to savor this moment, this permanent freedom.

But then a cream envelope fluttered out of the package and Cybil's breath caught in her throat. She knew she
was crying as she read the engraved print, but she simply
didn't care.

"Dr. Robert Wyatt and Jeannie Kaufman are pleased to
announce their marriage in a private ceremony on October
12. They are also proud to welcome Melissa Nicole Wyatt
to the family."

The next thing was a slim hardbound book. Oh, he'd
sent her a wedding album! When she opened the cover, a
handwritten note slid out. "I took a chance on happiness,"
the note read in Bobby's scrawled handwriting. "That's because of you."

"Oh, Bobby," she sighed. He'd always been such a
thoughtful boy. Thank God Landon had never succeeded
in destroying that.

She flipped through the album, greedily taking in the
signs of happiness.

The first picture showed Bobby and Jeannie standing
side by side. Bobby was smiling down at his bride. Smiling! Dear God, it did her heart good to see her son looking
at peace—the same peace she was beginning to feel.

Cybil barely recognized Jeannie as the same woman
who had gotten her away from Landon with a well-placed
glass of champagne. In real life, Jeannie smiled wider, had
kinder eyes and looked downright sweet in her tea-length

lace gown in a soft shade of rose pink that was gorgeous on her.

Cybil fondly traced a finger over the picture. Bobby would need someone bold and daring, someone strong enough to withstand his personality—and someone who would understand why he was the way he was but would never pity him. If that was his bartender, then that was the perfect woman for him.

The second picture showed Bobby and his new wife with a small infant. Only a few months old, the little girl was wrapped in a soft blanket, grinning a toothless grin up at Bobby from Jeannie's arms. Bobby's hand cupped the baby's cheek with such tenderness that Cybil's eyes watered again.

A note was paper-clipped to the page. "We'll bring her out soon—R."

"Everything all right?" Bridget said, concern in her voice as she sat the tea tray down. "You're crying!"

"I'm a grandmother," Cybil got out as she showed Bridget the album. "Look at my family!"

"Oh, wow," Bridget said, sounding wistful. "They look so happy!"

Happy. It was a long-cherished dream, one that had gotten Cybil through so many dark times. "You know," Cybil said, dabbing at her tears, "I do believe they are."

* * * * *

COMING SOON!

We really hope you enjoyed reading this book. If you're looking for more romance, be sure to head to the shops when new books are available on

Thursday 7th February